I0846843

The Colonel's Daughter

Prequel to *The Senator's Wife*

The Colonel's Daughter

Prequel to The Senator's Wife

First Print Edition

ISBN: 979-8-9916564-3-6 (paperback)

Published by Doss About Publishing

Edited by Margaret Hulings

Cover design by ThirdEyeMedia / Mahfuz

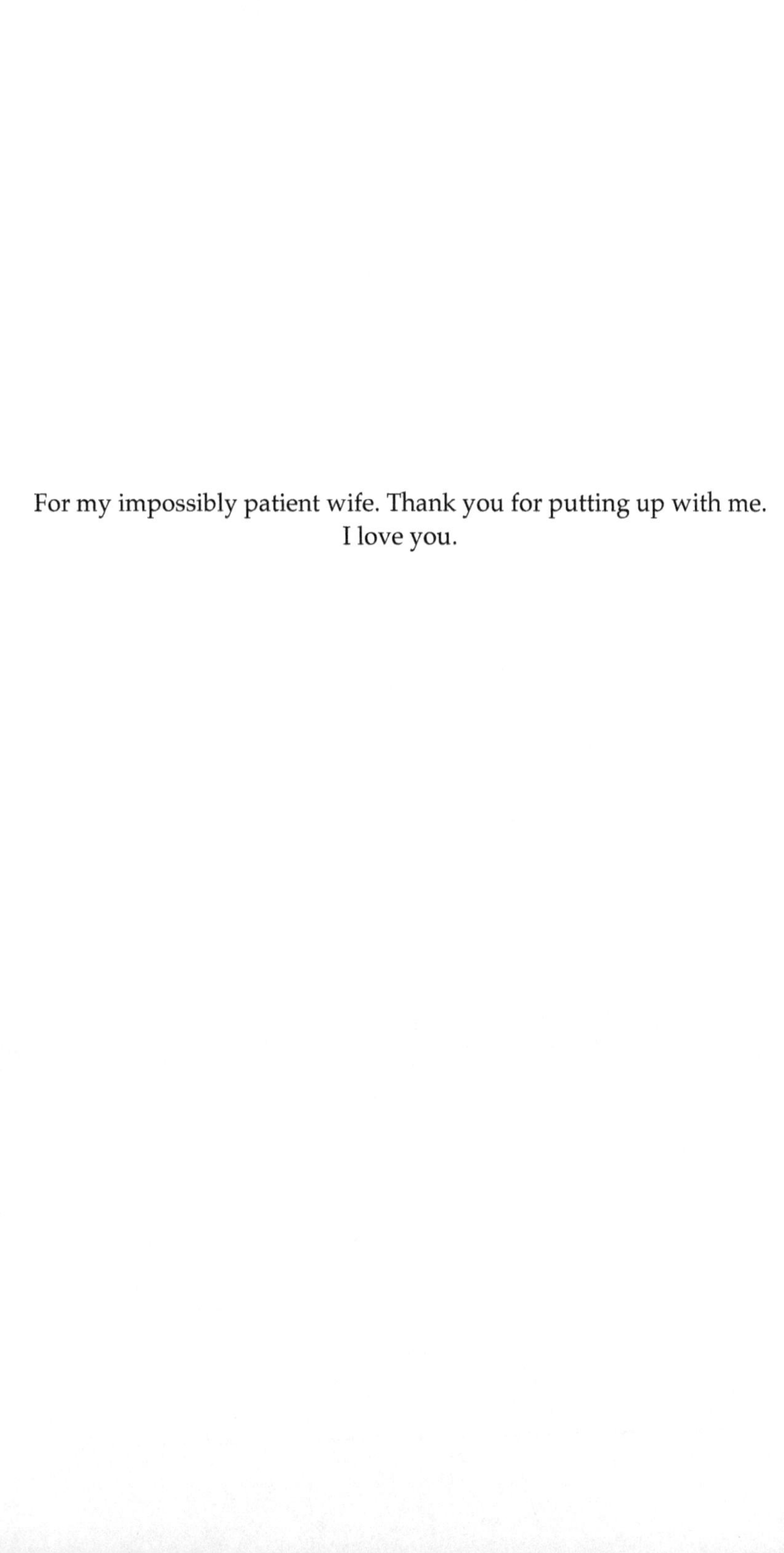

For my impossibly patient wife. Thank you for putting up with me.
I love you.

Author's Note:

Dear Gentle Reader,

Although this is a prequel to *The Senator's Wife*, it is recommended to be read as the fourth book in the series. It will put much of the previous three books into context.

Due to its unique setting, I have included a glossary of Oxbridge terms (along with a few British-isms some readers outside the UK may not be familiar with). It is included at the back of the book.

If you've read my other novels, you already know I tend to write love stories, not romances. As do all of my preceding works, this book contains subjects that some readers may find difficult. For a full list of content warnings, please visit the CW page on my website.

If my other novels weren't your cup of tea, I'm afraid this one won't be either. My apologies.

Most sincerely,

Jen

Journal Excerpt, Nathalie Comtois
Brasenose College, Oxford

I met a girl tonight. She said her name was Catharine,
but she seemed more like a Cate to me.
I think we could be friends.
I guess we'll see.

Chapter One

THE BRIGHT CLANG OF A bell cut through the laughter and chatter beneath the canvas awnings, but the boy in front of Catharine paid it no mind.

"It's *Women's Single Sculls*... who cares?" He brushed off the finish line result and swiped two tall glasses of Pimm's from a passing tray without sparing half a glance at the server. "So, as I was saying—about this weekend?"

Catharine's attention was on the river. Over his shoulder, she watched the boats coast to a stop, finishing less than a length apart. The umpire's flag was raised toward Berkshire Station, signaling the rower from Sweden had beaten Belgium to win the Princess Royal Challenge Cup.

"Are you even listening to me?" Annoyed at her preoccupation, the boy pressed the drink into her hand.

It was unsurprising, his lack of interest in the women's races. For one thing, his own crew had lost to Harvard the day before after putting in a poor showing in the men's eights, which meant—to him—the rest of the competition was irrelevant. And for another, he'd made it clear he didn't believe women belonged on the water. Never mind that Catharine herself rowed stroke seat, or that his older sister was a two-time FISA World Rowing Champion.

The truth was, Edward Arthur Haverfield III cared nothing about anything if it wasn't about himself.

"Yes, I heard you." Catharine tried to disguise her annoyance behind a deep sip of the cocktail. The summer air was muggy, promising afternoon showers, and a breeze toyed with the brim of her straw hat. Around them, spectators were abandoning lawn chairs to wander toward the luncheon tent as the next race got underway.

"And?" he demanded, draining his glass.

They both knew the following evening's formal Regatta reception wasn't the actual question. It was expected she would go with him. Same as it had been expected of her a month earlier to attend the May Ball on his arm. No different than the pressure she'd felt to acquiesce to his request for a date the week after they'd been introduced in Hall at the start of her first term.

All of it was expected. After all, he came from the richest family in the North of England. Her father was the wealthiest businessman south of Birmingham. They both attended Christ Church, arguably the most prestigious college in Oxford.

They were—as everyone was frequent to point out—made for each other.

He was captain of the rugby team.

She was the sole heir to a global shipping enterprise.

They both rowed crew.

It was not unrealistic to assume he would achieve his goal to become prime minister, and—as he'd pointed out the night of the white-tie Christmas Ball, sliding his hand from her knee to her thigh beneath the dinner table—she was simply too pretty not to be a PM's wife.

Little did he realize, if the comment was intended to be a segue further up her skirt, he'd missed the mark. The last thing she aspired to be was a pompous politician's trophy bride.

Still, she'd let him kiss her in front of the Christmas tree in the center of the quad and ignored his sullen glower when she'd insisted on returning to her staircase alone.

But that was six months ago, and now his patience was wearing thin.

"I already told you—I'll go with you to the reception." She took another sip of Pimm's as the first heavy raindrops pelted onto the lawn.

"*Catharine.*"

It needled her the way he could turn her name into an admonishment—no different than her father had always done. But Edward *wasn't* her father. As bold as he was, she wasn't obligated to be at his command.

"Come on, let's look at the art gallery." She discarded her glass on a vacant table. Her hair was getting wet, and she didn't want to continue this conversation.

He didn't budge. "Stop toying with me, Catharine. You know what I—"

On the other side of the lawn, a face in the crowd caught her attention—a face she'd been searching for all morning long.

"Nathalie!" She seized the opportunity of the distraction to pull free of the arm Edward had slipped around her waist, putting a handful of steps between them. The young woman across the enclosure gave her an enthusiastic wave.

Catharine had almost given up on her, but there she was—albeit late, as always—swimming upstream through a sea of boldly fashioned blazers heading for the cover of the marquee. The rain was coming down in earnest now, but Catharine forgot all about her desire to stay dry.

"You invited *her*?" Edward hissed, following her gaze. "*Here*?"

"Of course." Catharine feigned ignorance. "Why wouldn't I?"

She didn't need him to give her an answer. The question wasn't absurd. They were in the Stewards' Enclosure at the Henley Royal Regatta. An exclusive members-only viewing area for the most prestigious rowing event in the world. The patrons surrounding them were all of a certain class. A certain status. The brightly colored guest badge swinging from the young woman's blouse didn't make her one of *them*.

But Catharine didn't care.

Nathalie was her closest friend. Different from anyone she had ever known. Sneaking her name onto the guest list under the guise of her father's membership was a risk she'd been more than willing to take to avoid spending an afternoon with Edward alone.

"She's wearing *trousers*!"

It was a jumpsuit, but Catharine didn't bother to correct him. Nathalie had wound her way around the rapidly unfurling umbrellas and approached them with a smile.

"I'm sorry I'm late." Her melodic Bordeaux accent matched the warmth in her glittering brown eyes. "The trains were absolutely packed." She shot a brief look at Edward, undoubtedly aware of his disapproving stare, but paid him no further mind.

It was something Catharine admired about the French girl. She was unapologetically herself—cowing to no one. In the eight months they had known each other, Catharine had never once seen her put on an air. No part of her fit in with the circle of stuffy, old-money peers Catharine was surrounded by at Oxford. Which was exactly what she loved most about her.

"You're just on time!" Catharine looped her arm through Nathalie's, turning toward the river. "Cambridge's eight just started against Leander! They'll be passing Fawley by now."

"Am I supposed to know what that means?" Nathalie's laugh was rich, her damp skin warm through the sodden cotton of Catharine's sundress.

"No—you just have to cheer for Leander!"

"*Catharine.*"

Catharine cast a quick glance over her shoulder, forcing a smile at Edward. "Don't tell me you're rooting for Cambridge, Edward. That would be positively sacrilegious—"

"I'm not playing this game, Catharine. It's pouring. I refuse to stand here in the rain waiting for those yobs from Cambridge to slog by." He jerked his head toward the tent. "It's almost time for lunch."

"Then how fortunate are we to have a gentleman like you to save us seats at the table?" said Nathalie, offering him a level smile.

He ignored her. "I'm going inside. Are you coming?"

Catharine hesitated. She could feel Nathalie's fingers press her arm. Down the river, the first shouts and whistles came from the general public in the Regatta Enclosure. The eights were coming into view, the steady stroke of the battling crews cutting across the water.

"No." She didn't have to look back to feel his anger boiling over. "I'm going to watch for a while."

She only released her breath when she heard his oxfords tramping furiously away through the puddles.

"You shouldn't tease him, you know," she said quietly, watching Cambridge pull ahead of Leander.

Nathalie leaned against her. "And you shouldn't allow him to treat you the way he does. You are too good for him."

ANOTHER GLASS OF PIMM'S AND three races later, Catharine dragged Nathalie away from the river and into the ladies' lavatory. She was soaked to the skin, her satin gloves sagging off her fingers, but between the alcohol and ineluctable buzz she always got in Nathalie's presence, she didn't notice the chill that had rolled in with the clouds.

"Admit it—you're having fun," she laughed, tugging on one of Nathalie's long mahogany locks of hair. "This time next year, I'll have you rowing with me in the women's doubles!"

"Please," Nathalie offered a mock tsk of disapproval, "if you think anything is going to get me out of bed at four in the morning, you're completely crazy. Never mind that I hate the water."

"Yet here you are," Catharine goaded, flashing her a coy smile.

"Yet here I am." Nathalie mimicked the lilt of Catharine's English accent with unerring accuracy. Her own smile was furtive, matching the subtle arch of her brow. "You can be very persuasive, Cate Brooks."

Feeling a flush of color tinge her cheeks, Catharine busied herself pulling off her sodden gloves. She loved when Nathalie called her *Cate*. Never in her life had anyone called her anything other than Catharine. There was something behind the moniker that made it feel special—something just between them.

And it thrilled her—the casual, unpretentious way Nathalie showed her attention. It wasn't the fawning flattery she received from the boys at university, or the adulatory doting that came from the circle of girls aware of her family status and keen to make her their friend. Nor was it the intentional, possessive ingratiation she'd come to expect from Edward, who she knew only wanted one thing.

Nathalie was simply different.

Despite Catharine having been ferried around the globe by her parents—her existence a simple afterthought to her father's business administrations—and educated by the finest tutors money could buy, the Frenchwoman somehow made her feel provincial. At nineteen, Nathalie was two years older than she was, with a confidence and courage Catharine wasn't certain she would ever achieve. She admired the way Nathalie knew exactly what she wanted. The way she had her future mapped out down to the most minute detail.

She was going to be an actress. When she graduated from Oxford, she would move to Paris and train with Jacques Lecoq. She would master Sophocles and Plautus, Marlowe and Molière, and then forge her way onto the world's grandest stages. She would perform Shakespeare at *The RSC*. Play Roxane in Cyrano at *Palais Garnier*. She would bring audiences to their feet for her portrayal of Nina at *The Bolshoi* in Moscow. And move them to tears as Francesca at *La Scala* in Italy.

Catharine didn't doubt her for a minute. It didn't matter that Nathalie came from modest circumstances. That her mother was employed as a vineyard worker, and her father died in a harvesting accident when she was only eight years old. Nor was it relevant that Nathalie was the first of her family to attend university, or that her tuition was covered by the London financier who owned the vineyard where her father had lost his life. The tenacious French beauty would succeed at whatever she put her mind to—it was just who she was.

And to the fifth-generation Oxford student—and daughter of the esteemed business tycoon, Colonel Benjamin William Brooks—Nathalie Comtois was the most captivating individual she had ever known.

Tossing her gloves onto the basin, Catharine turned her attention to the full-length mirror.

"Oh my God," her thoughts were immediately curtailed by the disheveled image staring back at her. "He's going to kill me." Her hands flew to her hair, unkempt and tangled from the rain, lying loose across her shoulders from beneath her soaked hat. The straw brim drooped, its peach ribbon saturated to a deep coral. Pointlessly, she dabbed at a streak of mascara that had run down her cheek like an inky tear, smearing the makeup further.

"For what?" Nathalie stepped behind her, reaching to tuck a strand of golden hair back behind Catharine's ear. "Staying to watch rowing at a regatta? Isn't that the entire purpose of attending?" Her fingers trailed to one of the cap sleeves on Catharine's dress, smoothing out the cotton material from where it had become folded under in the rain. "It's not like you can control the weather." She smiled over her shoulder, catching Catharine's eye in the reflection. "Though I imagine your set might try."

Nathalie loved to tease her about her highbrow circle, but there was never any real malice in it.

Catharine's focus was torn between her dismay of knowing what Edward would say when he saw her—or even worse, her father—and Nathalie's fingertips still lightly pressed against her skin.

There was something there—she knew it. As sheltered, as naive, as cloistered as she was to the ways of the world outside the gilded cage from which she'd been raised, she wasn't oblivious to the current she'd felt flowing between them. She knew it probably should have bothered her that on more than one occasion, she'd wondered what it would be like to kiss Nathalie. What exactly that would feel like? But it just wasn't a trouble at the forefront of her mind. It wasn't something that ever felt wrong.

Nathalie had been with women. That wasn't a secret. It was something she'd casually slipped into conversation the first night they'd met.

A week into her new life at Oxford, Catharine attended a guest dinner at Brasenose College with a friend. She'd wanted to get to know the other colleges within the university, to explore life beyond her peers at Christ Church. Nathalie, also a fresher, had been seated across from Catharine at the long dining table, and when she discovered the girl from London was fluent in her native language, her interest had been piqued. They chatted about the Maastricht Treaty, the challenges of the French government being in a state of cohabitation, the scandals surrounding Mitterrand. The evening had evolved to talk of movies, opera, theatre.

Catharine learned Nathalie was studying English Language and Literature at Brasenose since the university failed to offer a degree in drama, but was pleased the student-led dramatic society provided plenty of opportunities to hone her craft.

"And what will you do when you graduate?" Catharine had asked.

"*Briller sur scène,*" Nathalie said, staring at her as if it were the most obvious thing in the world.

Shine on stage.

Catharine laughed at the sheer certainty behind the answer.

"Do you doubt me?" Nathalie's dark eyes held a challenge beneath her raised full brows.

"I don't." And she didn't. She could picture the girl on stage with her Renaissance beauty, her heart-shaped lips, and bright, cunning gaze. She had a charisma that was meant for an audience. A magnetism that would resonate.

"Good." Nathalie's expression shifted into a smile. "Because I will. I am going to win the hearts of Paris. New York. Milan. Tokyo. Sydney. Vienna."

"London?" prompted Catharine.

"Most definitely."

"And no doubt a boy in every city to keep you entertained." Catharine didn't even know why she'd said it. She wasn't the gossiping sort. Unlike the other first-year girls who talked nonstop about the boys they'd met and who they had their eye on, Catharine cared little for the uni matchmaking game. At the time, she'd yet to even be on a proper date. But it had just seemed the sort of thing college girls were meant to say.

"*Boys*?" Nathalie laughed—a deep, musical sound that filled the hall. "No thank you. There will be only women for me."

The challenging stare had returned, her gaze unblinking as she held Catharine's eye. She was waiting for her reaction. But Catharine was too well-bred, too well-mannered, too ingrained with the habit of hiding her emotions, to let on her surprise.

"Lucky them," she'd said instead, plastering on a convincing smile as she raised a spoonful of tomato bisque to her lips.

"And what about you?" Nathalie asked, scraping mint sauce off her lamb.

"Oh," Catharine choked on the soup, all of her prized etiquette dissolved into a round of coughing as she was forced to clear her throat. "No—I—I'm not, I mean, I don't…"

"I meant *what are you studying*?" Nathalie's eyes glittered. Whatever the contest had been, Catharine was certain she had lost.

"Sorry." She cleared her throat one final time, dabbing at her lips with a cloth napkin. "I'm reading *Economics and Management*."

"How boring."

Catharine shrugged, unable to find herself affronted. "I'm good with numbers. They're only boring when you're bad at maths."

"Touché." Nathalie speared a roasted potato on her fork. "And what do you want to do with these numbers when you graduate?"

"I'll work for my father."

The potato hovered at Nathalie's lips. "That's what you want to do or what you're told you'll do?"

Catharine pushed around the smoked salmon on her plate. *Touché indeed.* She'd have preferred to go back to choking on the bisque.

"So, Lady Macbeth or Blanche DuBois?" She diverted the conversation, racking her brain to arrive at the two most coveted roles she could think of for women in the history of theatre.

Instead of pressing her, Nathalie accepted the shift in topic, though Catharine could tell she'd recorded her non-answer as another touch on the board in whatever silent bout they were playing.

"Phèdre, actually." Nathalie waited, apparently keen to test Catharine's knowledge of classical French drama.

She was relieved she knew the answer. For whatever reason, she wanted to impress the French girl. To appear more worldly than she was.

"Jean Racine." She nodded. "Based on Euripides' *Hippolytus* and Seneca's *Phaedra.*"

"An Englishwoman with a modicum of culture. I'm impressed." The corners of Nathalie's mouth lifted. "I was made to play Phèdre. What could possibly be better than playing the part of a woman consumed by her passion, exploring forbidden love, guilt, and despair?"

"If Racine had written Hippolyte as Phèdre's stepdaughter instead of her stepson?"

The jest clearly caught Nathalie off guard, and Catharine immediately regretted it. It wasn't like her to be crass. To step that far out of bounds. But then Nathalie laughed again, her smile brilliant, bringing color to her soft, fluid features.

"*Tu me prends de court, Mademoiselle Économie,*" she acknowledged, her expressive eyes glowing.

Catharine flushed, uncertain anyone had ever found her surprising before.

"Tell me," Nathalie continued, popping another potato in her mouth, "what are you doing Friday night?"

"Studying."

"Pfft. You have all weekend to study," said Nathalie, brandishing away the word with a wave of her empty fork. "I'm playing Jill Mason in *Equus*. It's not the lead, but still…" She hiked a shoulder. "Have you seen it?"

Catharine would have lied even if she had. "I haven't."

"I'll leave a ticket for you at the Playhouse."

And so, not yet a full fortnight at university, their friendship had begun. A friendship unlike any Catharine had ever known.

She stared a moment longer at Nathalie's reflection in the mirror of the lavatory before reaching to collect a hand towel. "At the regatta, rowing comes secondary to socializing, let me assure you," she said, dampening the linen to work at the mascara stained down her cheeks.

Nathalie was perceptive enough to recognize her anxieties and refrained from teasing her, knowing she was flustered. She was aware Catharine was terrified to disappoint her father. Edward. Anyone and everyone who kept her on a short leash.

"You look fine, I promise," she said gently, adjusting one of Catharine's pearl earrings. "Flowers only grow more lovely in the rain."

Catharine tried to laugh. "Tell Edward that."

Behind her, Nathalie didn't smile. She *would* tell Edward, Catharine knew, if Catharine would let her. Nathalie would have liked to tell him many things. But for the sake of their friendship, she kept quiet.

"Come on," Nathalie said instead, plucking the towel from Catharine's hand and tossing it in the bin. "We wouldn't want to be late for afternoon tea."

"*Luncheon*," Catharine corrected, ribbing her.

Nathalie rolled her eyes, holding the door for her to pass through. "Same boring thing."

"I'M SORRY, MISS BROOKS." THE steward at the entrance to the luncheon tent elevated his square chin, peering down at Catharine beneath graying brows. "We adhere to a strict dress code policy, as I am certain you are aware. There must have been an oversight at the gate. Trousers are not permitted in the enclosure."

"For women, you mean?" said Nathalie beside her.

From the corner of her eye, Catharine could see her friend's fist balled at her side, her annoyance unmistakable.

"Yes." The steward gave a stoic nod. "For women."

"But not for men—?"

"Mr. Aldon," Catharine intervened, aware of the queue accumulating behind them. The wind had picked up, blowing the rain sideways, the canopy above the entrance to the tent as ineffective as the assemblage of deployed umbrellas. The steward was a friend of her father's. A man her parents had entertained at their estate in Henley on more than one occasion. "Do you think, perhaps, you could make an exception?" She glanced over her shoulder at the other patrons growing increasingly impatient. "We can sit by the—"

"Tradition is of utmost importance to the regatta, Miss Brooks —"

"It's fine, Cate." Nathalie stepped out of the line. "I can get something to eat on the way back to Oxford."

Catharine peered into the tent, where the tables were set for a formal luncheon. Her father would be in there somewhere, no doubt with Edward close at his side.

She would be expected. There was no tolerance for tardiness in her life.

Wavering, she took one last look past Mr. Aldon, and then, in an uncharacteristic act of rebellion, caught Nathalie's arm, pulling her onto the grass.

"I'll go with you—"

"Cate—"

"No," she tugged her away from the tent, "come on, who wants to sit with a bunch of stuffy old fossils anyway!"

Heart galloping at her own recalcitrance, they'd made it around the Fawley Bar and art gallery, almost to the exit, when Catharine heard her name. A shout above the rain clattering against the cover of the grandstand.

"What are you doing?" Edward was dashing across the lawn, his boater hat in one hand and the other shielding his eyes from the increasing downpour.

"Leaving—"

"You can't. Your father's just been seated. He'll—"

"Tell him I felt unwell, will you?"

"No!" He glanced between her and Nathalie, growing cross. "You appear perfectly fine. If you want to slope off with your friend, you'll have to—"

"Edward," she dropped Nathalie's arm, stepping closer to him, "they're going to postpone the races anyway—there's lightning, and look at the current." She gestured toward the river. "I'll be here all day tomorrow, I promise—"

"I'm not going to lie to him for you, Catharine. I—"

"Please! Just tell him I—"

"I refuse to—"

"Listen—" in a rising sense of urgency, she took his hand, "I'll go with you to Caldy."

The proposal stopped him mid-argument, his brow furrowing as he considered the implications of the offer.

An offer she immediately regretted.

But it was too late to back out now. It was the only way she was going to convince him to let her sneak away without a fuss. Without getting her in trouble with the colonel.

"When?"

"Sunday morning. After the reception. I'll drive up with you."

A bright blaze of lightning divided the quickly darkening sky, accompanied by a crack of thunder. Around them, the lawns, previously packed with people, were nearly vacant, the rain driving even the most dedicated spectators under cover.

"You better mean it, Catharine." He laced her fingers in his, drawing her to him. "You know how much I hate getting strung along."

"I'm not stringing you along." She forced herself to keep her hand in his. "You'll tell my father I went home?"

"Just leave him to me." He bent to kiss her, his mouth tasting of champagne. "We wouldn't want our girl catching a chill, now would we?"

Straightening, he smiled a crooked smile—a smile half the girls at Oxford would have killed to receive. A smile Catharine repeatedly told herself she should find appealing.

He was handsome, after all. Strong. Athletic. When he put in the effort, he could even be charming.

But as he walked away, all she felt was relief.

"What's in Caldy?" Nathalie asked once they were walking along the Henley Bridge toward the Buckinghamshire side of the river.

If they'd turned the opposite direction, they would have come to a pair of towering iron gates not far past the cricket grounds, where the mile-long drive through rolling parklands would lead them to Honour Stone—the centuries-old estate and Brooks family manor. But it wasn't a place she wanted to show Nathalie. Most certainly not now, while her father was in Henley. And maybe not ever.

She paused to look out over the water thirty feet beneath them. The river—formerly crowded with brightly colored boats and ferries—was empty, the burgeoning current rushing under the historic stone arches. As she'd anticipated, the races had been delayed due to the unexpected turn in the weather. But it wasn't the rain that had dampened her spirits.

"The Haverfield summer home."

"Ah." Nathalie rested her elbows on the balustrade. The deluge had at last died down to a steady shower, but it hardly mattered. Neither of them could have gotten any wetter had they jumped into the river.

"Edward's family having a garden party?"

"No." Catharine was quiet, watching a swan coast along the shoreline. "His parents are in Rome."

It was Nathalie's turn to linger in silence. She flicked a loose bit of stone off the bridge, where it abruptly disappeared into the water.

"You know you don't have to... You don't owe him anything, Cate."

"I know." Catharine resumed their walk along the narrow footpath. She didn't want to talk about it. "Come on, I'm starving. Let's get lunch at The Argyll."

THIRTY MINUTES LATER, THE GIRLS found themselves on the south side of the bridge, half a mile down the Thames Path. Both The Argyll and The Old Bell had been heaving with locals and visiting rowing spectators, the two sets seeking shelter from the temperamental July weather. Catharine hadn't been keen on the idea of being jostled around by a horde of drunk and rowdy boaties, and so instead, she and Nathalie raided the shelves of Sainsbury's, and sought out the peace of a riverfront bench, where they sat rifling through packs of Hobnobs and Penguin Biscuits.

"What was the name of the Emperor Penguin?" Catharine read the small printed joke on the back of the red wrapper.

"Julius Freezer," said Nathalie, swiping the biscuit from her hand and stuffing the entire chocolate-covered bar into her mouth.

"No fair," Catharine humphed, "you read that one already." She opened another. "How does a penguin build its house?"

Nathalie's answer was muffled by chewing. "Igloos it together!" The asininity of the punchline was made all the more amusing by the suave inflection of her French accent. An accent Catharine knew she could exaggerate or eliminate at whim. Her English was exceptional. If she wanted, she could have passed as a native speaker.

A perception the proud Bordelaise abhorred.

"And lead people to believe I was born on this dreary bore of an island?" she had stated on more than one occasion. *"Non merci."*

Catharine took a modest bite off the end of the chocolate bar, folding down another label to reveal a new pun. "Why can't penguins play football?"

"Because—" Nathalie gulped down the rest of the biscuit "—there's snowball."

"You're impossible!" She flung the unopened package at Nathalie, who laughed, recovering it from a puddle at her feet. It had stopped raining, the clouds parting to reveal a hint of blue sky. Down the river, the ferries and water taxis had resumed carrying patrons from one side of the Thames to the other. Rowers were back in their boats, gliding beneath the Henley Bridge, warming up their muscles. If the weather held, she'd have at least four more hours before she had to beat her father back to the manor.

"Let me guess—packaged biscuits are not a staple of the *haute cuisine* at the Brooks' table?"

Catharine rolled her eyes. "We have biscuits, thank you very much." She took a second small bite of the bar.

"But not these ones," Nathalie said smugly, opening the wrapper. "Or you'd know where penguins keep their money."

Catharine hated that she didn't know the answer.

"In a snow bank."

Groaning, she watched Nathalie indelicately shove another whole biscuit in her mouth.

"Okay, fine. We didn't—we don't—I haven't had these."

Nathalie swallowed, still smiling, an indecent smear of chocolate decorating her cheek. She left it there, Catharine was certain, just to wind her up.

"So, Dover sole in lieu of fish fingers? Beef Wellington in place of Pot Noodle?"

"You can't convince me you ate many Pot Noodles growing up in Bordeaux." It was a weak argument, and Catharine knew it.

"No, I learned about them at uni. But I grew up on my share of *pâtes au beurre.*"

"I'm very aware of the inequalities between us," Catharine snapped, growing defensive at the teasing. Nathalie's prodding rarely bothered her, but at the moment she was more sensitive to it, stemming from her embarrassment following the events of the afternoon.

Edward.

The dress code policy.

Nathalie being refused admission to a luncheon where a hundred crass boys could mask their oafishness beneath striped blazers and polished oxfords, simply due to their family name.

She did not doubt that if Edward's sister, Rebecca, had turned up in a jumpsuit, Mr. Aldon would have looked the other way.

"As am I," said Nathalie, "but not for the reasons you might think." She paused, pulling open a bag of crisps. "I don't care that you grew up eating Lobster Thermidor while my mother dished out yesterday's onion soup. Nor am I offended that your earrings are worth more than the car I sold to pay for my move to Oxford. Or that I stole my hat from our costume rack at the theatre department, and yours was tailor-made. What I do notice, however," she said, looking away from Catharine to scatter the crisps along the shore for the waiting geese, "is that you refer to your father as 'The Colonel,' while I have never considered calling my mother anything other than *maman*. I see someone pressured by expectations to be perfect, whereas I was praised just for passing my *baccalauréat*. A girl who's been told what to study, how to dress— even who she's permitted to see." Nathalie emptied the remainder of the crisps and crumpled the bag before looking up at Catharine. "Someone so controlled, her life's been dictated right down to what spoon to use to stir her breakfast tea."

Catharine stared at the river. A classic wooden skiff floated by, the oarsman pointing out something along the shore to the tourists he was ferrying. The varnish of the hull appeared blurry, and to Catharine's dismay, she realized her eyes were watering.

Dragging the hem of her skirt across her face, she pulled out a bottle of sparkling water from their shopping bag. She felt irrationally angry. Nathalie hadn't said anything untrue. Anything out of context. But Catharine hadn't asked to be analyzed. Scrutinized. Assessed. She hated that Nathalie could see right through her, past the facade she'd been raised to wear. Past her practiced smile, her forced composure, the carefully constructed silence she'd learned to hide behind when it came to situations she didn't know how to face. Her entire life had been scripted long before she ever learned to wield a pen, set down in permanent ink, black and white, with no room for revision.

"Well," she said finally, shoving herself to her feet, frustrated to find her voice was quivering. "Aren't you lucky to have all the answers?"

"Don't be unfair. You know that's not what I'm saying." Nathalie remained seated.

"No?" Catharine wheeled to face her, the heels she wore—an impractical pair dictated by 'tradition'—sinking in the damp gravel of the path. "Because you certainly seem to feel you know my life better than I do. Perhaps *you'd* like to be the one to tell me what I should study? What I should wear? Who I should date?" Unwilling to meet her eyes, she tried to busy her hands undoing the metal cap on the water, but realized too late it required a bottle opener. Angry at no one more than herself, she flung the untouched drink into a bin beside the bench, startling the waterfowl who'd come to eat the floating crisps.

"Cate." Nathalie stood, her tone cautious. As much as they'd ribbed one another over the course of their friendship, they'd never had anything close to a row. It wasn't like Catharine to lose her temper, to let on that she'd been hurt. "You're not happy."

"And you're suddenly the expert?" She tried not to notice Nathalie's flinch.

"No," Nathalie exhaled, "of course not. But I'm not blind, Cate. I can see how miserable you are. And I hate it. Because I *know* you. I know you're funny, and clever, and brilliant—you're meant to be so much more than an extension of your father's hand. You could be anything you wanted if you ever learned to stand up for yourself." In Catharine's silence, she reached to touch her arm. "Listen —don't go to Caldy. Don't let him—"

"Is that what this is about, then?" Catharine's laugh was brittle, an automatic defense to hide the tears that threatened to return. Just the thought of driving up the coast alone with Edward twisted her insides in a knot. She didn't want to think about it—about the agreement she had made. But Nathalie would never understand. "I promised him—"

"Then take it back! I know you don't want him, Cate! He doesn't deserve your promises! He doesn't deserve *you*!"

"And who does?" Catharine snatched her arm away, hugging it to her chest. "Let me guess: *You*?!"

It was entirely uncalled for. Entirely unfair. There was a flirtatious raillery between them—it couldn't be denied—but never once had Nathalie crossed a boundary. If anything, it was Catharine who toed the line. Catharine, who let her imagination run away from her. Catharine, who stood there now, wanting nothing more than to reach up and wipe the chocolate from the corners of Nathalie's lips. She wanted to tell her she was sorry, she didn't mean that—to please forget the whole thing.

Instead, she turned her back to her, returning her gaze to the river. On the other side of the bank were a handful of narrow docks, and beyond that, a dense woodland. What would Nathalie say, she wondered, if she told her the ash and beech trees running along the riverbank were the beginning of the Honour Stone parklands? That the expanse of her father's estate was so vast that even without the cover of the trees, they wouldn't be able to see the Jacobean manor from the shore. What would she think about the chapel, the croquet lawn, the stable block and staff quarters? Or the lake at the bottom of the rolling hills, the acres of orchards and rose gardens? How, then, would she view the disparity between them?

The Haverfields owned half the waterfront property on the Wirral Peninsula. Their holiday home in Geneva wasn't far from her father's château. Edward Arthur Haverfield II often invested in the corporation, and served on the advisory board. Colonel Brooks didn't care if his daughter disappeared for a weekend with a boy like Haverfield's son. If it benefited Brooks Corp, he would drive her there himself.

What he would care about, however, was that all she wanted was to throw herself into the arms of a girl from Bordeaux.

"Cate…"

Catharine's shoulders tensed, her eyes still on the Honour Stone woodland. "If you go now, you can still catch the three o'clock train."

Chapter Two

THE AIR ALONG THE WIRRAL coast smelled of brine and sea lavender —a refreshing change from Edward's overpowering cologne. Even leaning over the low stone wall, allowing the summer breeze to flit through her hair, Catharine felt like she would never get the scent of it off of her.

Lemon verbena and peppermint.

She'd tried to scrub it from her skin the night before after Edward dropped her off at Honour Stone, but still, it had lingered. Same as it had done earlier in the evening, sitting beside him at the Regatta dinner. The way it had grown more pronounced when he pulled to the side of the lane before the towering iron gates of the Brooks' estate, and bent over the console to kiss her mouth, her neck, the tops of her bare shoulders.

The scent had clung to her, no matter how scalding her midnight shower. It was there on her pillow, trapped in her sheets. And it was back again this morning, even more pungent than the night before, when he arrived to pick her up in his flaming red Testarossa—smothering, hovering throughout the entire four-hour drive to Caldy.

She closed her eyes, inhaling the earthy tang of the brine, focusing on the hints of seaweed and algae rising from the mudflats. The tide was out, leaving the rocky foreshore exposed, the beach beneath the cliffside dotted with tide pools.

"So, beach or pool?" Edward hopped onto the low wall, leaning back over the steep drop down the escarpment. His honey-blonde hair fell across his eyes, its color nearly flaxen in the sunlight. Since they'd arrived at his family's holiday home on the Wirral, he'd changed from his polo shirt and chinos into a plain white tee and swim shorts. Catharine had yet to unzip her jacket.

"I didn't bring a swimming costume."

"Well, pool it is, then." He smiled out of the side of his mouth, sitting upright to grab hold of her hips, drawing her to him. "I'm not about to let you put on a show for all the holidaymakers up from London."

Catching his drift, she moved to pull away. "Edward, I'm not—"

"Oh, for fuck's sake, Catharine—lighten up, will you? I'm only having a laugh. Christ. You can be so bloody frigid." He let her go, sliding to his feet. "The way you're carrying on, one would think I dragged you here by force."

The rebuke stung.

He wasn't wrong. She'd agreed to join him voluntarily. And she knew, despite what she tried to convince herself, that she would have come even if she hadn't used the trip as a bargaining chip to get out of the regatta luncheon two days earlier. Her mind had already been made up that morning: she wanted to get it over with. To do whatever it took to get him to stop pestering her.

It wasn't such a big deal, after all. Every girl in her staircase had shagged her way through first year.

"Edward, wait." Reaching for the hem of his shirt, she stayed him. "I'm sorry. I just—it was a long drive."

"You know, petulance is such a poor look on you. You're so much more attractive when you're contrite." He looped a strand of her hair around his finger, drawing her closer. "But don't worry…" A slow, waggish smile flitted across his lips as he leaned to press his mouth against her ear. "I can think of a few ways you can make it up to me."

Before Catharine had time to respond, before the uncomfortable chill that started in her spine had even reached the back of her neck, he was standing upright again.

"But first," he said, giving a playful tug to the zipper of her jacket that was still drawn all the way to her chin, "I saw a crisp rosé waiting for us in the wine chiller. I'll pour us a glass and find you one of Rebecca's bikinis. And let me assure you—" the roguishness of his smile returned as he strolled backward toward the house "—you're going to look a hell of a lot better in it than she does."

BY THE TIME THEY PICKED their way barefoot up the bridle path from the beach, it was pushing on evening. The sun still hung high over the north coast of Wales, visible on the opposite side of the estuary, but the air had grown cold, and Catharine was shivering.

"I warmed up the hot tub," said Edward, returning from the house to drape his Barbour jacket over her shoulders. He set a tumbler of whisky on the garden table, where she sat perched on the edge of a chair beneath the pergola overlooking the water. "Thought a bit of amber comfort might warm you up."

"Thank you." Idly, she rotated the glass between thumb and forefinger.

He was trying to be sweet. He'd put in an effort all afternoon. At lunch, he carted a picnic basket down the steep, single-track trail that led from the garden to the waterfront. There, they drank rosé atop a tide-polished rock, sharing smoked salmon and cream cheese sandwiches. *He made them himself*, he'd boasted, filling her glass a second time as he passed a bowl of cut apples and strawberries.

The beach had been vacant, the equally grand residences to the left and right of the Haverfield summer home empty for the weekend. Catharine might have liked the place—appreciating its rugged coastline and panoramic view—if she hadn't felt his isolated presence so acutely. Aware every time their hands brushed as they picked their way along the tide pools searching for periwinkles, or forcing herself to laugh when he grabbed her waist and swung her over his shoulder, dragging her into the slowly rising water.

She'd reprimanded him as they splashed along the surf, smacking away his hands when he tauntingly threatened to tug loose the ties of the bikini top she'd borrowed from his sister. But when the tide came in, forcing them to the shelter of the cliff base as it reclaimed the foreshore, she'd given in. She let him pull free the strings, taking things a step further than she'd ever dared before—until a pair of dogs came bounding down the beach, barking at the seagulls.

"Bloody curs," he cussed at the interruption, crushing a hermit crab scuttling along the foot of the cliff with his heel. Catharine closed her eyes, unable to look at the flailing creature.

The remainder of the afternoon he'd spent trying to impress her. Swimming deep into the estuary and diving for long spells under its surface, then returning to do handstands on the logs of driftwood stranded along the shore.

Catharine had perched on a boulder in the sun and given him all the appropriate adulation the ego of a young man required—yet her mind had wandered, and she'd found it impossible not to think about how none of his stunts were as enchanting as spontaneously performing Helena's grand soliloquy from *A Midsummer Night's Dream* on the doorstep of Blackwell's Bookshop.

Or slipping into French to quote Hugo, or Colette, or Sartre. Or casually mentioning that Shakespeare invented the name *Miranda*. Or that Proust once spent three years revising the placement of a single comma.

Or holding the answer to the all-important question: what does a penguin sing at a birthday party?

Freeze a Jolly Good Fellow. The answer was clearly obvious.

No, a handstand could not hold a candle to originality. To brilliance wrapped in wittiness.

Taking a deep sip of the whisky, she tried to cover her cough as the honeyed blaze seared down her throat.

Spirits weren't a regular part of her repertoire. Her father was an avowed teetotaller, and her mother never had more than the occasional glass of wine when the colonel was out of town.

Catharine's experience was limited to shandies and Pimm's at her friends' garden parties, and mulled wines and ciders when attending formal dinners in Hall. Rarely had she ever had anything stronger.

But the effects of the rosé had worn off, the sun dipping quickly —too quickly—toward the horizon, and there was something in the way he set his hands on her shoulders that gave rise to an accentuating wave of panic.

Forcing back the rest of the tumbler, the burn doing nothing to alleviate the pounding pulse at her temple, she stood.

"I'd like to sit in the hot tub, I think." She dropped his jacket onto the table and stepped out of the lounge trousers she'd pulled on over the swimsuit, before crossing the lawn to the bubbling spa overlooking the estuary.

The water was hot, a sharp contrast to the chill that had settled along the coast, and between the heat and whisky, she found herself uncomfortably lightheaded.

"So, how are you finding Caldy?" He asked, dropping in beside her, tipping another finger of whisky into the tumbler he'd retrieved from the table. "I know it's not quite Saint-Jean-Cap-Ferrat in springtime, but it has its charms."

Catharine stiffened at the hand he brushed over her knee, accepting his offer of the shared glass. "It's very quiet." Her gaze shifted to the garden walls concealing them from the rest of the world, her mind struggling for anything more intelligent to say as his hand crept to her hip.

"Catharine." He blew out a long sigh, her name a subtle rebuke. "I'm beginning to think the lads aren't wrong, the things they say about you. You really do need to learn to unwind." He smiled—a smile she was beginning to realize she loathed—and toyed with the seersucker waistband of the bikini bottom. "I keep telling them you're not as much of a prude as you come across, but honestly, they might have a point. It's time we found a way to loosen you up, don't you think?"

He took the glass from her, discarding it carelessly on the lawn, and pulled her onto his lap. At once, the smell of lemon verbena became overpowering, suffocating in its nearness, drowning the scent of the sea.

A wave of nausea threatened.

She turned her face away, every fiber in her body reviling against his touch as it suddenly became clear to her that no part of him cared what she wanted. That in no measure would he ever make the slightest effort to see her happy.

His patience was fabricated, his tolerance only skin deep.

He was keen on the way she looked, the way she'd been raised to acquiesce, the way her family's wealth exceeded his own. But value her for who she was? Respect her for her own opinions, her dreams and ambitions? Not once in eight months had he heard a single word she'd said—not once had he ever even asked.

From their first date, he'd been mapping out their future, never with a concern for her consent.

In two years, they would graduate. Then wed in the spring and move to London, where they could start their family as he began his climb through the political ranks in Westminster. She would stay home and tend to the children. He would become Prime Minister.

In his mind, it had never been a question. How could it be, when there was an endless sea of girls eager to throw themselves at his feet? Who was she to refuse?

If it was what he wanted, it was what he would get. Because all his life, no one had ever told Edward Haverfield no.

"Look at me, Catharine." Catching her chin, he turned her face to him, tightening his hold around her waist, his fingers digging into her elbow. "I've warned you already—enough with the games. I've exercised more than my share of patience. Certainly more than anyone else would show you." Without any delicacy, he pressed his mouth to hers.

For a moment, she was still. Early in her childhood, she'd learned how much less challenging life was if she just did as she was directed. She'd given up piano to study financial derivatives and hedging—until she could recite yield curve forecasts in her sleep. She'd closed the pages of *Little Women* and *A Room with a View* to read *Essays in Persuasion* and *The Wealth of Nations*. Her fourteenth birthday had been spent translating Sun Tzu's *The Art of War* into French. Her fifteenth, slogging through *War and Peace* in Russian. Her sixteenth, recapitulating the nuances of depreciation versus amortization, the tensions between Keynesian economics and classical liberalism.

Disobedience came at the cost of beratement, belittlement, living in the throes of constant anxiety for fear of disappointing her father in his impossible demand for perfection—his currency for approval set at an unattainable sum.

Tonight felt no different. There was no way to win. How much easier it would be to say nothing, to just give in and let Edward take what he wanted, what he unquestionably was certain he deserved.

She'd come to Caldy with him, hadn't she, aware they'd be alone? Even if it had never been outright discussed between them, they'd both known what he expected. What position was she in to tell him no?

Yet still she couldn't shake what Nathalie had said down by the river.

You could be anything you wanted if you ever learned to stand up for yourself.

It just wasn't as simple as that.

But had she ever even tried?

A slow, dawning clarity came over her about what would happen if the night played out as planned. What her life would look like in the morning. Three months from now, at the start of term. Two years down the road.

It *wasn't* what she wanted. It never had been.

And for the first time in seventeen years, she refused to do as she was told.

The taste of whisky on his tongue snapped her from her torpor.

"Edward, stop!" She wrenched loose her arms that he had pinned to her sides, and shoved away from him. "I can't." Waist-deep in the water, she stumbled backward. "I'm sorry. I thought I could—but I—I just can't."

He might have looked less stunned if she'd hauled back and struck him. Unmoving from where he was seated, his lips parted, but no sound came out as she staggered up the steps.

"Catharine," he finally managed, her flight across the lawn stirring him to action. She could hear the slosh of water as he leapt from the hot tub. His sodden footsteps as he reached the cobblestone.

She stopped at the table to tug on the linen trousers she'd worn over the swimming costume.

"Calm down. You're being dramatic," he chastised, his tone dripping in condescension. "None of this has to be as hard as you're making it."

She couldn't find her sandals. Her blouse was gone.

"I'm sorry." She turned to face him, feeling the world sway around her. The effects of the whisky had been heightened by her rush of adrenaline. "It's not you, I promise." A tendril of fear had crept its way into her voice—one she quickly tried to silence. The last thing she wanted was for him to realize she was afraid of him.

Unable to find anything else to pull on, she picked up his jacket. "Would you bring me my purse, please?" She knew where it was —with everything else she'd brought with her: upstairs in his bedroom.

"Where do you think you're going?" The patronizing edge to his tone was slipping. She knew all too well what would follow. She'd experienced it her entire life in the way her father's controlled facade dissolved into outrage.

"Never mind, it's fine." Giving him a wide berth, she side-stepped away from him. "I'll get it when I return your jacket."

"You want me to beg you?" he laughed, the sound brimming with anger. "Is that what game you're playing?"

Never taking her eyes off him, she moved cautiously across the lawn, expecting him to lunge at any second.

"No." She couldn't hear her own voice over the pounding in her chest. "It's not a game."

He remained dangerously still, water dripping off the hands he had planted on his hips.

"You think you can just walk away from me? You think there's not a girl I can't have—that you're any better than the rest of them?"

After what felt like an eternity, her feet found purchase on the path that led to the garden gate. Unable to think of anything beyond her need to get to the other side of the wall, she turned and raced along the cobblestone.

"You stupid little bitch!" The insult was hurled across the lawn, echoing through the space between them. She reached the gate and fumbled with the handle. It was dark out, the sun having surrendered its hold on the day, and the mechanism of the latch was unfamiliar.

"You'll come crawling back!"

The bolt was stuck.

"You'll have no choice, you hear me?"

Her hands tore at the cold iron, flakes of black paint lodging beneath her fingernails. At last, the latch gave way just as a piercing crash forced her to shield her face, something cold and wet raining down atop her head.

A glass had been thrown, shattering against the wood above her.

"There's not a fool at Oxford stupid enough to touch you! They all know you belong to me!"

Unsteady and covered in glass, she flung herself through the gate and disappeared into the dark, accompanied by nothing more than the slamming of her erratic heartbeat.

Passing under the third brick-arch bridge, Catharine finally slowed her pace. The dwindling glow of twilight had faded over the last half mile, making the unlit path even more challenging to navigate.

Four bridges, left on Grange Rd.

She'd been given the directions to West Kirby Station by a man with a dog at the start of the bridleway. Her cheeks had crimsoned at the way he'd shone his torch from her bare feet to her unkempt hair, but then he'd been pulled along by the impatient collie, and left with only a word of caution over his upturned collar.

Not safe out here for a lass like you.

Safer than behind garden walls, she thought, before setting off down the unpaved trail.

To her credit, she hadn't cried.

She prided herself on that. Slipping along the muddy path, the linen of her trousers snagging on hawthorn and bramble, she didn't shed a single tear. If anything, despite the absolute helplessness of her situation, she found an unexpected rush of exhilaration building with the burgeoning distance.

She'd left. For once, she'd actually held her ground. She—who was praised for her obedience, conditioned to forever do as was expected—had been the girl to tell Edward Arthur Haverfield III *no.*

There would be consequences. It wasn't as if she didn't know that.

Edward would want his revenge.

And when word got back to her father that she'd compromised his relationship with the Haverfields… well, he was not an understanding man.

But in the moment, as she picked her way through the dark, she found it impossible to care. Her only focus was forward, one foot in front of the other.

By the time she reached the main road, it was late. After ten, she would have guessed, though she had no way to tell. The moon was young, its golden sliver shrouded beneath the clouds, and her watch was in the holdall she'd abandoned back at Edward's.

As was her driving license. Her father's credit card. Her cash.

Her autonomy.

Stopping on a bench in front of the train station, she combed through her hair with her fingers and did her best to scrub the mud off her feet. Her arches were bruised and tender. One of her toes was bleeding from a tree root she'd tripped over, falling to her knees.

An inane, overwrought part of her wanted to laugh. What would the impeccable, forever presentable Colonel Benjamin Brooks say if he knew his daughter had wandered through the streets of Caldy in this state?

But the amusement was fleeting. She'd lost her first tooth after he caught her playing barefoot in the garden—courtesy of his signet ring. It was the first time he'd struck her, one of the few times he'd struck her, until more recently. Now, his temper seemed to grow shorter and shorter every day.

Tucking the memory back where it belonged, she took a deep breath and headed up the steps of West Kirby Station.

If the ticket office was open, she would explain that she'd lost her purse and hope an attendant might accept her contact details, with a promise to pay.

If that failed, she'd wait for the right opportunity and board anyway. Over the last year at Oxford, she'd watched countless students slip into toilets and covertly change carriages to know how to evade the ticket conductor on the train.

Whatever she had to do, one thing was certain: she wasn't spending the night in Caldy. And no matter what happened, she would never again set foot on another Haverfield Estate.

As it turned out, late on a Sunday in a sleepy coastal town, the ticket office was closed and the platforms were empty. The departure board indicated the last train before 6 AM would arrive in fifteen minutes, running through Liverpool Lime Street.

Catharine waited, leaning against a pillar at the edge of the tracks.

"Ya alright, love? Heading over the water?"

Startled by the gravelly voice, Catharine turned to find an old woman in a tattered peacoat hunched over the handle of a suitcase she imagined had never been used for holiday. She took a step back, uncomfortable with the woman's proximity.

"Sorry love," the woman held up a palm, "didn't mean to scare you. Don't get your dander up, just being friendly." She gave Catharine a hard once-over. "Though, if you don't mind me saying, it looks like you've already been put through the mill."

Catharine unclenched her hands. The woman wasn't threatening.

"Oh. I'm fine, thank you." She hesitated. "I'm sorry, but would you happen to know if they check ticket service between here and Liverpool?" She suspected the woman—dressed as she was—didn't live on the peninsula.

"On the Wirral Line? This late on a Sunday?" A high wheeze rattled the woman's noisy expiration. "No, love, you're sound. No one on Merseyrail going to bother you." Her gaze was fixed on Catharine's bare feet. "You sure you're alright?" She eyed the fine linen of the palazzo trousers, now covered in mud, and the over-sized waxed cotton jacket that clearly wasn't her own.

Uncertain what to say, Catharine only nodded.

"Where you off to after Liverpool, then?"

"South."

The woman frowned, the weathered lines on her face deepening. "And you not got someone you can ring?"

Catharine shook her head. She'd walk the two hundred miles to Henley before she called her father.

In the distance, the lights from the arriving train came into view, the ground of the platform rumbling. The woman blew out another high-pitched wheeze before bending over to dig through her suitcase.

"Here, love," she righted herself as the train squealed to a stop. "No ticket on the Wirral Line is one thing—but you're going to need this to get wherever it is you're going." She pressed two crumpled twenty-pound notes into Catharine's hand. "That should see you on your way, I'd think."

"I can't take this." Catharine stared at the money. She couldn't possibly accept it from this woman. It was no doubt all she had. "I —"

"Get going, love—that train don't wait for no one." She chucked her chin at the door opening nearest them on the platform.

"I—" Catharine cast a swift glance at the train. "Tell me how I can reach you! I can pay you back—"

"Don't you bother about it—had a bit a luck today. Take it, love, and hurry."

"Honestly—please, I can pay—"

"You just stay away from them lads, you hear? They's nothing but trouble." She shooed her toward the door.

"But what about you?"

The woman smiled, her cloudy eyes softening. "Always another tomorrow, love. Now get you going."

THREE AND A HALF HOURS and two connections later, Catharine stepped off the train in Oxford.

Her intention had been to go to Henley. With college on break, she'd moved out of her Christ Church accommodations and back to Honour Stone for the summer. She wouldn't return to university until October.

However, over the last two hours, she'd had the late-night carriage to herself and spent the time staring out the window, trying to decide what she'd tell her father.

She knew if she rang Honour Stone from the Henley station in the middle of the night, dressed the way she was, it wasn't Edward he would hold accountable. Her father's concern wouldn't be for her well-being. He would only want to know if she'd jeopardized his business relations with the Haverfields—and in what ways she had embarrassed their family.

It wasn't something she felt she could face in the middle of the night.

So in her rising panic, when the train pulled to a stop at Oxford station, she made a last-minute change of plans and darted out the closing doors.

It was a half-mile walk to Brasenose. Up New Road, past Castle Mound, around to High Street, and on to Radcliffe Square.

The streets were empty. With the majority of students away on the Long Vac, Oxford turned into a different city. There were no late-night pub crawlers staggering back to their rooms. No bleary-eyed freshers returning from eleventh-hour study sessions to cram for the next day's prelims. The lanes and passages were devoid of lovers seeking a midnight tryst. All around her, it was quiet.

Cold, exhausted, and loathing the way the cuffs of Edward's jacket swallowed her hands all the way to her fingertips, she shouldered open the heavy wood door and stepped into the Brasenose Porters' Lodge.

The eyes that flicked up from behind a pair of John Lennon glasses belonged to a face she recognized. Throughout the year, her visits to Brasenose weren't uncommon. Less than a five-minute walk from Christ Church, she was familiar to many of the porters.

"Hi, Mr. Liddell," she crossed her arms, tugging the jacket more tightly around her. From his place behind the old oak counter, she hoped he might not be able to see that she was barefoot. "I know it's late, but—" Before she could recite the story she'd rehearsed on her walk from the train station, the man disappeared back into the novel propped on his desk.

"Be sure to sign in," he gestured toward the register.

Five minutes later, she climbed to the top of a narrow staircase on the north side of the Old Quad and stopped at the first door on the right. It was almost 3 AM.

After the way she'd behaved in Henley, she had no right to be here. But she also had nowhere else to go. And in truth, there was no other person she wanted to see.

Gathering what was left of her courage, she tapped quietly on the door, uncertain if the rooms on either side were occupied.

The knock was met with silence. She tapped again, a slow dread creeping in as the anxiety she'd managed to bottle over the past five hours threatened to bubble over. Her feet were throbbing. Her entire body was numb. Even her thoughts felt slow and disconnected. She hadn't allowed herself to think about what had happened—or what would follow. Her only focus had been to get to this door—a door that wasn't opening.

Raising her fist to try once more, she paused at the muffled sound of footsteps. A breath later, the handle turned, and Catharine winced as a sliver of light flooded into the hallway.

"Cate!" The door swung all the way open. "*Qu'est-ce que tu fais ici ?*"

Chapter Three

As many times as Catharine had visited Nathalie at Brasenose, she'd never been inside her room. Occasionally, they'd met at the door to her staircase, but more often than not, Nathalie would be waiting for her in the quad. From there, they'd walk to Spires Café for a coffee or stroll a casual loop around Radcliffe Square, lamenting their upcoming lectures and tutorials. Even when it was raining. Even when it snowed. Even when the air was so thick it could be cut through with a knife. Nathalie preferred to be outside.

The college lodgings were small, after all. Cramped matchbox-sized spaces with single beds, a chest of drawers, a writing desk, and little more. Catharine's own room at Christ Church was less than the size of her dressing room at Honour Stone—as was it a far cry from the high ceilings and stone fireplace, the private balcony and clawfoot tub inside the suite she kept at her father's residence in Belgravia, just minutes from Buckingham Palace.

But unlike Edward, who griped and cursed over what he felt were substandard accommodations, Catharine would have gladly traded all the opulence, all the comforts, all the cornice and marble and mosaics of travertine for the second-floor box room she had called home during her first year at university.

It was a space that had brought her peace, offered her privacy, given her a sense of freedom she had never known. A place where she could kick her feet up on the edge of her bed and study with her Walkman on, unconcerned she'd get caught listening to

Madonna. Where she could leave her jacket draped over the back of a chair and her essays piled, unalphabetized and uncategorized, waiting to be filed. Where she could have a friend over after Hall and drink chianti from a take-out cup.

She had quietly envied Nathalie when, as an international student of limited income, she was granted 'vacation residence' by Brasenose. An allowance that permitted her to keep her accommodations through summer, until the start of Michaelmas in their second year.

"*Bon, entre,*" was all Nathalie said when Catharine gave no immediate explanation for her middle-of-the-night intrusion.

The Frenchwoman's tone was guarded, her lips disappearing into a thin line as she tossed a pile of laundry from her armchair onto the desk beneath the window, brusquely motioning for Catharine to sit. She made no excuses for the casual disarray of the space—a clutter of mugs with lipstick marks and tea rings on the counter, or the scattering of textbooks strewn across the windowsill. Instead, she simply flicked on the kettle, grabbed a rubbish bin overflowing with papers, and disappeared into the ensuite.

A moment later, a tap cranked on, followed by the sound of running water and a string of French expletives as a clatter of debris hit the floor.

Catharine sat with her hands tightly clasped and waited.

In the yellow light of the lamp glowing on the bedside cabinet— the indentation of Nathalie's body still visible in the crumpled sheets—she tried not to show too much interest in her surroundings. She'd turned up here without invitation and felt suddenly guilty for invading her friend's privacy.

Still, she couldn't help but take a cursory glance around her, taking stock of the room.

Nathalie was untidy but not unclean. There was a pile of classic literature on the floor beside the radiator—*Pride and Prejudice, Jane Eyre, Great Expectations*—the books propped open on broken spines with highlights and annotations peppered throughout the text. An ashtray on the windowsill housed a handful of postcards, the top one signed *Bisous, Maman*. Blu-tacked onto the wall nearest her bed were programmes from the shows Nathalie had taken part in over the last year: *Hamlet. Oedipus Rex. The Way of the World.* Catharine's gaze settled on the advertisement for *As You Like It*.

Starring Henry Taylor and *Nathalie Comtois*, it read across the front.

Nathalie had been furious when she showed the programme to Catharine.

"Rosalind is the unequivocal lead!" She'd tossed the pamphlet onto the bench where Catharine sat waiting for her in Christ Church Meadow. "And still, they gave him top billing! As *Orlando*!"

On a different day, Catharine would have laughed when she saw the X in black marker drawn across Henry Taylor's name. The boy had been a vain, loudmouth, egotistical thorn in Nathalie's side throughout the production, whom she had likened to 'snogging a stale baguette' when forced to kiss him in the fifth act. Tonight, however, Catharine only averted her eyes to her lap when she heard steps approaching from the ensuite.

"Here," said Nathalie tersely, setting the rubbish bin in front of Catharine. "Put your feet in this."

Tentatively doing as she was told, Catharine realized the bucket had been filled with warm, sudsy water. A balming relief to her frozen and aching feet.

With the fluid poise of a dancer, Nathalie settled cross-legged onto the floor, reaching into the water for one of Catharine's bare ankles.

"Nat—!" Catharine tried to pull her foot away, abhorred by the thought of her friend touching the filth she'd accumulated between Caldy and Oxford, but Nathalie paid no heed to her protest. Holding her ankle fast, she pulled a hand towel from beneath the cloudy surface, and swabbed it over the raw skin of her heel.

The gesture was far more gentle than the hard set of her jaw suggested.

"Now," she said, dabbing at her blistered arch, "tell me: what has happened?"

The rush of adrenaline that had carried Catharine through the past few hours had finally depleted, and the tears she'd managed to keep in check threatened to return.

"You were right." She didn't elaborate. "About everything."

Staring at the soapy water turning murky with grime, she knew she owed her so much more of an apology. For the things she'd said at the river. The things she'd implied. For turning up on her doorstep in the middle of the night. But with her eyes swimming the way they were, she was afraid she wouldn't get through an adequate recompense without crying.

In the prolonged silence, Nathalie's hands—always so expressive and dynamic, hands Catharine loved to watch on stage—stiffened, stilling at their task.

"Did he hurt you?"

Catharine hesitated. She thought about the way he'd dragged her against him, his fist tangled in her hair. The bruising he'd left behind on her elbow. Or the heel he'd ground against the defenseless crab on the rock face. The shattered glass in the garden.

The blisters on her feet felt like small penance for her naivety.

No, stupidity.

She shook her head.

Without meeting her eye, Nathalie's gaze swept over her muddied trousers, the soil of Wirral Peninsula caked on her knees, Edward's jacket—oversized, overbearing—hanging off her frame, and then returned to the turbid water.

"Did you…?" She paused. "With him?"

"No." Catharine brushed the back of her hand across her eyes. "I—left. I walked to the train station."

"Barefoot?"

"Yes."

The lean curve of Nathalie's shoulders—her muscles tense beneath her camisole—slackened as she resumed the careful, circular motion of the hand towel. "And you came here?"

"Yes."

"Why?"

"Because…" Her voice trailed off.

Because of a dozen reasons she didn't know how to explain.

Because—at almost eighteen years old—she'd never really had a true friend. Because Nathalie was the first person she'd met at Oxford who didn't treat her the way her family name dictated she be treated. Because, in the ten short months they'd known each other, Nathalie actually liked her for who she was, and not what she had to offer. Because Nathalie was able to look past Catharine Ann Brooks, daughter and heir of the estimable Colonel Benjamin William Brooks, and see only *Cate*.

And more than anything, because every time Edward kissed her, all Catharine had ever been able to think about was how she wished it were Nathalie, instead.

But she couldn't tell her that.

So she went with a truth that was incomplete. One that didn't begin to scratch the surface.

"I had nowhere else to go."

The rigidity returned to Nathalie's shoulders. "How lucky am I? Only one year at Oxford, and I've already climbed my way to Catharine Brooks' last resort—"

"Nat, that's not—"

"It's fine, Cate," Nathalie bristled. "I know what you meant. You made that loud and clear on Friday." With an effortless grace attesting to her years of ballet, Nathalie swept to her feet and dropped a folded towel in her lap. "The shower takes an eternity to heat up, but there's shampoo on the counter. I left a change of clothes on the basin." She snatched up the bin and cursed under her breath when water sloshed over the side. *"Putain !"*

"Nat?" Collecting the towel Nathalie had tossed at her, Catharine leaned forward to mop up the floor. "I can go—if you'd rather?"

For a moment, Nathalie was quiet, but as Catharine climbed to her feet, struggling once more to shove the cuffs of Edward's jacket up her forearms, her expression softened, and she sighed. "Have you eaten?"

Catharine shook her head.

"Well," Nathalie waved her toward the shower, *"pâtes au beurre* it is, then."

ST. MARY'S BELLS HAD RUNG in the 6 AM hour by the time Nathalie dropped a plastic bowl of buttered pasta into Catharine's lap.

"Sorry, I only break out the bone china for anticipated guests," she quipped, settling onto the floor beside her. The asperity of the jest was softened, however, by the unmistakable concern behind her tight smile. "Are you feeling any better?"

Catharine's shower-damp hair dripped onto her knees as she twirled the fork in the center of the linguine. She could smell the tuberose of Nathalie's perfume, the rich, velvet scent a permanent fragrance on the collar of the well-worn t-shirt she had borrowed. She found it comforting, a gentle cleansing of the lemon verbena.

"Yes." She absently stirred the dish. "Thank you."

"Do you want to talk any more about it?"

Catharine didn't know if *it* meant Edward, or *it* referred to the convoluted mess she continued to make of their friendship with feelings she didn't know how to express, but whichever the case, neither did she wish to recapitulate.

Raising a bite of neatly wrapped noodles to her lips, she went to shake her head, and then panicked when butter dripped onto her chin, realizing she didn't have a napkin.

Nathalie laughed, the tension broken by her evident dilemma. "Just wipe it on the sleeve."

"What—?" Unfurling her legs, Catharine began to rise. "No! I can't!"

"Yes, you can!" Nathalie caught her arm.

"I'm not going to wipe butter on your shirt!"

Catharine knew her strength from the past year of rowing superseded Nathalie's lithesome dancer's build, but she put in no real effort to free herself as she was tugged back down, upsetting the bowl of pasta.

"Nathalie—!" she squirmed, laughing, the feeling cathartic after the stress of the evening.

Pinning her to the floor with her knees, Nathalie grabbed a handful of the linguine and held it above her face, taunting her with the dangling noodles. "Come on—it's just a shirt! I want to see the ever-proper Catharine Brooks do something she's never done before."

Between the proximity of their faces and the way Nathalie was straddling her, Catharine imagined there were a lot of things she could be convinced to do that she had never done before.

Nathalie, no doubt, was aware of it, too, though she mercifully kept her smile casual. "Last chance."

"You wouldn't dare," Catharine goaded, knowing she would, and wanting her to. She wanted to know what it felt like to break the rules. To laugh until her sides hurt. To do all the things she wasn't supposed to do.

Nathalie lifted an eyebrow. *"C'est un défi, ça ?"*

Before Catharine could turn her face away, Nathalie dropped the handful of noodles, muffling Catharine's mock protest with buttery hands against her cheeks, her neck, her hair.

Catharine fumbled for the bowl beside her, retaliating in turn, Nathalie's shriek of feigned dismay cut short, the two of them grappling for flailing limbs with slippery hands, their fingers unable to find purchase as they choked with laughter, sprawled across the centuries-old hardwood floor.

"You should know better than to challenge me," Nathalie gasped when they both lay on their backs amidst the ruin of pasta, trying to catch their breath.

Catharine brushed strands of butter-slick hair out of her eyes, turning to look at her, her cheek pressed to the floor. "Who's to say I wasn't up for the challenge?"

Propped on an elbow, Nathalie's smile was slow, her dark eyes turning amber in the light spilling over the windowsill. "I like when you surprise me, Cate Brooks," she said, before inelegantly climbing to her feet, trying not to slip on the greasy hardwood. With a careless indifference, she shook linguine out of the hem of her shirt, and then pulled it over her head, standing silhouetted, bare to the torso, gazing out the window at the quad two floors beneath them.

Catharine was too slow to avert her eyes when she turned back around, and flushed, aware Nathalie had caught her staring.

"I'm going to shower. I can't promise I'll leave you any hot water," Nathalie said, nonchalantly stepping over the mess they'd made, and disappearing into the ensuite.

THE SUN WAS WELL INTO the sky when Catharine woke, the harsh rays of late-morning light shining through the unfamiliar window.

It took her a moment to remember where she was—how she had gotten there. But then the faint scent of starch and butter stirred her memory, and the events of the night returned to her.

She was at Nathalie's, the pair of them squeezed into her narrow bed. They had fallen asleep arguing about who would win a duel: Sartre or Shakespeare.

Her sleep had been deep, but dreamless, both her mind and body too depleted to find discomfort in sharing such intimate space with another. Now, however, as wakefulness settled in, she became acutely aware of the warmth of the body beside her.

Part of her didn't want to move, loath to disturb the fragile tranquility of the morning. But she also knew it had to be closing in on noon, and it was time to face whatever awaited her at Honour Stone.

"Nat," she whispered, rolling onto her side, lifting her head to see over the shared pillow between them. "I have to go. I need to get back to Henley."

Nathalie stretched, making no effort to stifle a yawn, and turned to face her.

"Do you want me to go with you?"

"No." The offer caught Catharine off guard, and she could tell by the look on Nathalie's face that she'd answered too abruptly. But her thoughts had been too focused on trying not to notice the press of Nathalie's shoulder against her breast, or the way her side-swept bangs caught at the corner of her lips, to form a more delicate declination.

"I take it I'm not the sort of company your father would approve of."

"Trust me," Catharine tried to reassure her, "it's not just you. My father is approving of no one."

"He didn't seem too disapproving of sending his seventeen-year-old daughter to spend the weekend alone with a boy in—what did you call it?—his *summer home*?"

"Nat." Catharine sighed. She didn't want to talk about her father. Or Edward. Or anything to do with her life. What she wanted was to reach up and brush Nathalie's wayward hair behind her ears. To go back to arguing about silly hypothetical duels, to food fights.

But none of that would assuage the sore subject between them.

"It's just different." She didn't know a better way to explain her father's mindset. "That was—business."

"Business?" Nathalie huffed. "Business in what, matchmaking?"

Frustrated, Catharine yanked at a loose thread on the pillowcase, unintentionally unraveling its hem. "My father views everything in life as either a liability or an asset. Edward just happened to be the latter."

To her surprise, instead of bristling, Nathalie grew quiet, contemplative.

"And now?" she asked, watching her intently through astute brown eyes that Catharine knew missed nothing. "What will he do when he finds out you've called it off with him?"

Hold her accountable for the loss—that was all Catharine could think. But it wasn't a conversation she wanted to get into.

"I don't know, probably nothing." She tried for a casual shrug. "I don't think he liked Edward all that much anyway. He's never been fond of boys who don't wear socks with their loafers."

"Cate." Nathalie didn't laugh. "I'm serious. I'm worried about you."

Catharine found she had to look away to hide the tightness building in her throat. She wasn't accustomed to someone worrying about her. Someone taking the time to read between her lines.

"Do you know," she said, her eyes still averted to the ceiling, suddenly too aware of how close they were, how easy it would be to lean forward, to close that forbidden gap, "that you're the best friend I've ever had?"

It wasn't all she wanted to say, all she wanted to confess, but it was the most she could bring herself to admit in the moment.

"Pfft." Nathalie scoffed, though from the corner of her eye, Catharine could see her smile. "You're only saying that because none of your other friends have stooped low enough to wash your feet."

Catharine wanted to tell her she didn't have other friends. She had acquaintances. She had peers with whom she was friendly. But no one like Nathalie.

Instead, she went along with her teasing.

"Don't pretend that was from the kindness of your heart." She looked back at her, offering a dramatic eye roll. "I know you were just polishing your method acting in preparation for your audition to play *Mary* in *Jesus Christ Superstar* this spring."

"*Mary*?" Nathalie took the bait, her eyebrows climbing in disbelief. "Oh, please. I'd turn the role down before it was even offered to me! Now, *Jesus*, on the other hand—" her smile grew arch, a smile, Catharine found, that brought a flush to her cheeks "—*that* I might consider. And if I'm not mistaken, I believe he, too, washed his disciples' feet."

"You think I'm your disciple, do you?" asked Catharine coyly. "And exactly which Apostle would I be?"

Nathalie considered. "Thomas, maybe? All that doubt and second-guessing."

Catharine tutted. "I think I'd prefer Peter. He was brave enough to cut off the soldier's ear in Gethsemane."

"Is this where I point out he also denied Jesus three times…"

Catharine could feel the color in her cheeks deepen at the suggestive tone. Desperate to shift the direction of the conversation, she tried to make light. "Better than Judas. At least you know I don't need thirty pieces of silver."

"No?" The wickedness of Nathalie's smile turned smug, and Catharine knew at once she'd forfeited the advantage. "Tell me—with no shoes, no clothes, no cash—how is it you're getting to Henley?"

Chapter Four

CATHARINE DUCKED UNDER THE BOOM to the port side deck and trimmed the jib, allowing the flapping sail to fill with the summer breeze. Behind her, at the stern of the little Wayfarer, she could feel her mother's weight shift as she leaned across the cockpit of the dinghy to test the tension on the line.

"There's too much slack in your kicker, Catharine. You'll hardly win the summer series spilling all the wind from your main."

The critique, though brusque, was not an admonishment. Her mother was rigid, exacting, expectant of her daughter to succeed in all things—but she was not Benjamin Brooks. The high standards she held were not cruel. Beneath the immalleable poise demanded of a woman of her station, she was kind. Even loving.

Following her mother's advice, Catharine hauled on the vang line to adjust the rigging. The minute correction made an instantaneous improvement, and the luffing sail flattened, increasing their speed.

"Well, look at that." Her mother settled back at the helm, her smile growing complacent.

"I never said you were wrong." Catharine suppressed the urge to roll her eyes. Her mother may not have been Benjamin Brooks, but she was still her mother. It would not do to disrespect her.

"But you didn't believe me." Pushing the tiller away, her mother prepared another tack as they approached the shoreline. "Because —" the boom swung across the stern and Catharine released the jib, "—what could an old woman possibly know that her seventeen-year-old daughter doesn't?"

Settling on the starboard side, Catharine cleated the jib sheet before turning back to face her. Her mother was still smiling, wisps of her dark hair fluttering around her ears, her face tanned from a summer on the water.

When it came to sailing, Catharine wasn't sure there was a soul in England who knew more than Emily Brooks. She had practically been raised at the helm. Her father, who died before Catharine was born, had been a Rear Admiral in the Royal Navy. Emily had often joked that the only thing he loved more than his family was any day spent on the sea. It was a passion he had passed on to his daughter, and one, in turn, Emily had handed down to her own.

Which meant: no, when it came to seafaring, Catharine never questioned her mother's supreme authority.

But in this case, Catharine knew the comment had nothing to do with sailing.

"You're hardly an old woman," she said, hoping to divert the impending topic with flattery. She'd known as soon as her mother caught her sneaking through the foyer earlier in the afternoon, attempting to make it undetected to her suite in the west wing, that she wouldn't escape a discussion about Caldy.

Emily had taken one look at her—dressed in Nathalie's clothes, home two days earlier than expected from her holiday with Edward—and informed Catharine they were going sailing. Code for —*we're going to talk about this.*

It wasn't an option.

Her father, it turned out—to Catharine's immense relief—had gone on business to Rotterdam that morning, and would be gone for a week.

"Kind of you to say." Emily's smile shifted, her smugness transforming into understanding. "But I'm a long way off from seventeen. I imagine you think I've forgotten what it feels like to navigate life at your age."

Catharine busied herself trimming a sheet that needed no adjusting. It was true, though her mother was barely forty, Catharine struggled to fathom her as anything other than Mrs. Benjamin Brooks, polished wife of her illustrious husband. It was the only way Catharine had ever known her.

But Emily, she also knew, hadn't always had her identity defined by her role as a wife and mother. She had once graduated with a First Class degree in the Law Tripos from Cambridge. She'd planned for a career as a barrister, with ambitions of being appointed to the Queen's Counsel. Instead, the summer after her graduation, she met the decade-older Benjamin Brooks through a friend of her father. By late winter, they were married. The following autumn, she gave birth to Catharine. She never even sat the Bar Finals Examination.

"Will you tell me what's happened between you and Edward, Catharine?" Her mother eased the mainsheet, slowing the Wayfarer, and leaned back against the transom.

"Am I compelled to answer?"

"No." The compassion in Emily's tone did not change. "You are a young woman now, entitled to your secrets."

For a few hundred yards, Catharine stared over the side of the dinghy, watching the water slap against the hull as they cruised along the shoreline. It had grown late, nearly eight, and dusk would soon be approaching.

"Did you want to marry my father?" Catharine asked suddenly, realizing she had never known the answer.

Her parents, who put on a facade of unity in their social circles, were not a loving couple behind closed doors. Where her mother was warm, and often affectionate to Catharine, she showed the colonel none of the same kind-hearted attention. She was devoted to him. Obedient. Deferred to his will in nearly every situation. But love? If the feeling had ever been there, it was no longer a sentiment expressed within their marriage. And Catharine knew, despite having never seen him lay a hand on her mother, that she was afraid of him.

Had that always been the case? Or had there once been a time when they, too, picnicked on the beach and searched the tide pools for periwinkles? Before the threats. The vitriol. The slammed doors and shattered glasses.

As they neared the Henley Bridge, Catharine thought her mother might not answer. They would bear away here, she knew, setting a new course downwind to return to the private dock belonging to Honour Stone.

Completing the maneuver, Emily motioned for Catharine to take the tiller as she settled onto the thwart, leaning back to trail her hand through the water.

"Yes, I suppose." She didn't look at Catharine. "He was the most handsome man I'd ever met—with an intellect that was incomparable. I was enamored with him." She caught an English oak leaf floating past the hull, twirling the foliage between her thumb and forefinger.

"Do you regret giving up your dream of becoming a barrister?"

Emily dropped the leaf back into the water. "I would regret more not being your mother."

Catharine didn't return her smile. It hurt, knowing—*believing*—how much she loved her, but also knowing, as her mother, all the ways she'd failed to protect her.

It was one thing when she'd stood idly by as Catharine quietly sobbed out her twelve-year-old heartbreak over being forced to give up the piano to allow more time for her studies. Or when she had not told her husband he was being excessive for forcing their nine-year-old to hand-copy the entire text of *Middlemarch* after missing a perfect score on a Year Four reading test. Catharine had also forgiven her for remaining silent when the colonel demanded Catharine attend Christ Church to study economics, even when her mother knew her daughter's heart had been set on an MA in International Relations at St. Andrews.

Nor, even, did Catharine blame her for not stepping in on the more recent occasions where her father's anger had boiled over to the point he had struck her. On those occurrences, Emily Brooks' intervention would only have made things worse. For both of them.

What she found impossible to forgive, however, was her acceptance of the life she lived, knowing its cost, yet failing to do everything in her power to prevent Catharine from following in her same footsteps.

She had known about the trip to Caldy. She had been there when Edward asked her father's permission for Catharine to join him on the holiday. And both she and the colonel had been well aware Edward's parents and sister were in Rome.

"She's a grown woman, Emily," she'd overheard her father tell her mother after Edward left. "She can take care of herself."

Whatever quiet concern her mother had raised was coldly brushed aside.

"I know Haverfield well enough to know if his boy gets her in trouble, they'll do the right thing."

That had been it. Her mother made no further objection.

And she had let her go, knowing—*knowing*—what Catharine was getting herself into. Knowing the kind of boy Edward was. Knowing, in twenty years, Catharine could find herself nothing more than Mrs. Edward Haverfield, having the exact same conversation with her own daughter, history repeating itself. Knowing— same as she once had, before she was Emily Brooks—that Catharine wanted so much more than that.

"I broke it off with Edward."

Again, Emily skimmed her fingers through the water. "I know. He called, looking for you."

Catharine was silent. Ahead of them, the Honour Stone dock came into view, the varnish of her father's classically restored nineteenth-century Edwardian launch boat gleaming in the setting sun. From force of habit, Catharine uncleated the halyard, allowing the line to slide through her fingers as she lowered the mainsail.

"When?"

"Late last night."

The line slipped from Catharine's hands, her shoulders deflating.

So her father already knew.

Her mother was quick to read her mind. "He was asleep, Catharine. I didn't tell him anything."

Relief quickly dissolved into anger. "Didn't you worry where I had gone?"

"No." Emily tugged loose the jib halyard. "I felt certain I already knew."

The boat, slowed by the lowered sails, drifted into the dock.

"And where is that?" Catharine challenged, looping the bow line over a horn cleat, securing them to the jetty.

"The porter at Brasenose confirmed you signed in as a guest shortly after two-thirty."

Catharine fell silent again. She was stunned her mother knew her well enough to know she would go to see Nathalie. And she was even more surprised she'd cared enough to call.

Emily hardly knew the French girl. They'd met only once, when her mother came to watch Catharine compete in Torpids, the Oxford rowing race held every spring. Nathalie, in true Nathalie fashion, had introduced herself at the boathouse.

"You are very beautiful, Mrs. Brooks. I am Nathalie Comtois, a friend of Catharine."

When Emily had gone, Nathalie gave Catharine a pointed once-over. "You look nothing like your mother."

"My *beautiful* mother, you mean? Wow, thanks," Catharine feigned indignation, and Nathalie laughed, catching hold of the towel Catharine snapped at her hip.

"A trait perfected by the next generation," she'd whispered coyly over Catharine's shoulder, before strolling away.

And though it had been their only meeting in person, Catharine knew she'd brought up Nathalie to her mother when she occasionally went home to Henley.

Nathalie was playing Nina Zarechnaya in The Seagull *at The O'Reilly next weekend.*

Nathalie was home to Bordeaux for Easter.

Nathalie had been awarded The Chancellor's English Essay Prize *for her examination of* The Power of Silence in Life and Literature.

Nathalie knew everything there was to know about French art, from Delacroix to Seurat.

A moment of panic struck Catharine as she wondered if her mother had paid more attention than she thought. If she'd guessed at the extent of her daughter's feelings for her newly found college confidante.

But if she had, she didn't let on.

"Do you want me to tell him, Catharine? Before he returns from Rotterdam?"

The offer was a gamble. Was it better to tell him now that his daughter had compromised the business relationship with one of Brooks Corp's most valuable connections, and hope his anger ebbed while he was out of town, or would his fury only fester until he returned to Honour Stone?

It was impossible to foretell which way it would go; her father's temper was anything but predictable.

She decided she would wait.

"I'll tell him when he gets home," she muttered, raising the centerboard and pulling the pin on the tiller. Before she could drag the rudder into the cockpit, her mother stayed her hand, placing gentle fingers over hers.

"You know, if you ever—you can talk to me, Catharine, is all I'm trying to say."

"It's a little late for a heart-to-heart, don't you think?" Catharine yanked her arm away, hauling the rudder over the transom, and dropping it on the sole. She braced herself for a reprimand, a chastisement for her sharp tone. Never had she spoken to her mother like that. But instead, when she glanced up, she found her mother's face fallen.

"I know you may not believe me, but there is nothing I want more than for you to be happy. I want to see you graduate. I want to see you fall in love. I want to see you live a life that's all your own. If Edward isn't a part of that, then I'm proud of you for trusting yourself. I don't want you to make the same mistakes I made."

"Convenient of you to say so—while we're here, without *him*," Catharine snapped, unable to stop herself. Where had her mother's concern been two nights ago? Where had it been all along?

But on the long walk through the woodlands, after forgoing a ride back to the manor, she knew it was unfair to judge her as harshly as she had.

Colonel Brooks wasn't the kind of man you challenged. He wasn't a man you told no. Her mother loved her the best she could, in the only ways she knew how.

But it didn't change the fact that Catharine knew, a week later, when her father returned from The Netherlands, she would have to face him alone.

"8,035,200 SECONDS—HOW MANY MINUTES is that, Catharine?"

The question was simple. It was a straightforward conversion; the relationship between seconds and minutes a fixed ratio: sixty equal to one. A single-step calculation.

Still, her mouth felt dry as her tongue formed the answer, the silence of the inimical room betraying the quiver in her voice. "133,920."

"And hours?"

"2,232."

"Which is how many days?"

"Ninety-three."

"Hm." The sound was dismissive, the basal mathematical exercise rudimentary to a man who could derive exact interest on a compounded investment over decades without ever reaching for a pen. "Now, pray, tell—why might ninety-three days from today be of note?"

Catharine despised knowing her father could see the pounding pulse at her temple. "It will be my birthday."

"Ah, yes. Your birthday. One in particular?"

"My eighteenth."

"Speak up!" The knuckles clamped around his Montblanc pen turned white. "I will not tolerate your mumbling!"

"My eighteenth," she pronounced more clearly, pressing her palm against her thigh, aware of an unwanted tremble in her right hand.

"Just so. Your eighteenth. And what will that make you?"

"An adult."

"An adult." He tapped the cap of his fountain pen against the smooth edge of the Georgian-period partner's desk—a desk, she knew, that had been passed down to the firstborn son of the Brooks family in every generation for over two hundred and fifty years.

One he would leave to his own son—if only a son had been had.

Which ultimately left the burden to her.

"Are you aware of what that entails?"

She dreaded the soft timbre of his tone, the false sense of soothing. It was a deceptive stillness she'd learned to fear.

"Yes, sir."

"You see, I don't think you do." He abandoned the pen into its crystal stand, the harsh clang of metal against glass causing her to wince. "Tell me, what does responsibility mean?"

"The state of being reliable, accountable, or answerable. An obligation."

"Yes. An obligation. One, as a child bearing my name, you are bound to uphold." He stood, the sharp crease of his wool trousers snapping in alignment as he unfolded to his full height. He was tall, lean, his ramrod posture unwavering after twenty-five years of service to the British Army. Two years retired from the armed forces, he remained as fit, as stern, as stoic as he had ever been.

Catharine hated that she looked like him. She would have given anything to have inherited her mother's kind, caramel eyes, her round face with its gentle contours, the deep, rich copper of her hair. Instead, when she saw herself in the reflection of her father's silver cufflinks, it was only his high cheekbones, prominent jaw, gilded hair, and glacier-blue stare she found looking back at her.

"Listen to me carefully, Catharine: you are no longer a child. When I die, this—" he extended an arm to indicate their surroundings "—will all fall to you. The toils of centuries of labor. Of hardship. Of sacrifice. And yet," his cold blue eyes drilled into her, "how do you choose to honor this immense privilege you've been born into?" His tone was changing, his composure slipping, the words *sacrifice, privilege*, hammering through her core. "By being reckless. Selfish." He slammed his palm against the desk. "*Ungrateful.*"

She knew his calculating gaze did not miss the hitch of her breath or involuntary flinch as he stepped away from his Baroque throne chair. To her surprise, however, he did not approach her. His attention had drifted to the wall of dynastic portraits, mounted beneath the mullioned windows of stained glass from the manor's Gothic era. The brilliant prism of early morning light illuminated the painting of a young man—no more than a teenager—with the same piercing blue eyes and golden halo of hair that had been passed down through the Brooks family for generations.

Catharine could feel her father's gaze linger on the portrait.

It was Samuel Brooks, Benjamin's older brother—a boy who had hanged himself on the eve of his eighteenth birthday. Catharine knew, by way of her mother, that Benjamin—four years younger than Samuel—had been the one to find him in their father's library. The same library where they now stood, the same beams in the rafters.

The colonel turned his focus back to Catharine.

"I forget, sometimes," he said, "how young you are. How disappointing you can be." His fingers drummed an impatient tattoo along the edge of the desk, the tendons in his hand taut, belying his falsely returned tranquility. "But I made a mistake, Catharine, and I will own to the error."

She knew him well enough to say nothing. To wait. To find out where his baiting would lead.

Strolling across the room, the leather soles of his polished Oxfords were muted by the ornate knotted silk rug that had once belonged to a Mughal emperor—a gift from Queen Victoria to Benjamin's great-great-grandfather. He came to a stop at the oriel window overlooking the rose garden.

"As you well know, the foundation of Brooks Corp dates back to the seventeenth century. It was built on the back of my father, his father, his father before him—and so on and so forth." He flicked a disregarding hand as he stared into the garden. "It has always belonged to a Brooks—and it forever shall—be the cost what it may."

He turned from the window. "The Haverfields are aware of this. Aware that, no matter who you wed, your husband will have no say in the future of the company. It will pass only to your children —who, in one way or another, will carry on the Brooks legacy." He barked a short laugh, full of derision. "Unsurprisingly, as opportunistic as the Haverfields are, they've been receptive to the arrangement. It was a suitable pairing—advantageous to both families."

Catharine raised her eyes to read his face, to decipher the word *was* and what he meant. But the rising sun had edged over the windowsill, silhouetting his austere frame, and casting his expression in shadow as the lambent light flickered across the walnut floor at her feet.

"Yes, Catharine, *was*—you heard me correctly." His scrutinizing eyes missed nothing. "Because, as I said—I made a mistake."

With a flick of his wrist, he drew back his cuff, exposing his watch, and glanced at the time. The gesture was one of irritation, as if the entire conversation was an inconvenience. As if he were not the one who had arrived in the middle of the night from Rotterdam and ordered her to his library before the crack of dawn.

"I misjudged you." He looked up, the sun shifting behind him so that she was able to see the contempt in his eyes. "I gave you too much credit. I placed too much faith in you being a Brooks, with not enough accord for accepting the inevitable reality that you simply are who you are." Again, he laughed, the cruelty of the sound as jarring as if he had slapped her. "You are no match for

Edward Haverfield. That boy is ambitious. Driven. Calculating. He knows what he wants, and he will get it. If he were my son, I would find him admirable. But alas—I am left only with you." The veins in his hands were showing again, the tendons flexing over whitened knuckles. "A simpleton of a girl who is weak. Vulnerable. Inadequate in every way to uphold this family name. And yet—with you, I must do."

He raised an angry palm to the terrestrial globe by the window, spinning it in its stand. For a moment, Catharine thought he might kick it over, toppling the elegant model in his ascending resentment. But as the globe slowed its rotation, he turned away, grasping at a measure of control.

"I cannot permit you to marry Edward Haverfield, because no matter what safeguards I detail in your premarital arrangement, you will never contend with him intellectually. He will think circles around you, Catharine—and in doing so, assume control of the Brooks legacy. I will not allow it. I will not have my life's devotion commandeered through ambition untempered by loyalty."

Catharine stared over his shoulder at the rising sun, no longer able to hold his eye. Why it still hurt, knowing how little he valued her, knowing all the ways he found her disappointing, she would never understand. All her life, he'd made it clear he found her wanting—forever deficient, insufficient, and failing to meet standards she would never attain. She knew she wasn't inferior to Edward—that her intellect surpassed his on every level. She knew, also, that her father was equally aware, and this was just his way of berating her, punishing her, for going against his will.

Yet still, it stung, more deeply than she would ever let on.

"Do you understand me?"

"Yes."

"Excuse me?"

The violent flash of his gaze sent a tendril of ice down her spine.

"Yes, sir," she repeated, more firmly. "I understand."

Without acknowledgment, he brushed past her, back to his desk.

"We, all of us, have made sacrifices for this family, Catharine," he said, resettling into his chair. "It is our duty. It is our debt. A time will come when you will be expected to pay yours. You *will* marry into a suitable match—one that upholds the legacy entrusted to your care. Do I make myself clear?"

"Yes, sir."

"I will handle the Haverfields." He began to pull a ledger from his top drawer, an indication she had been dismissed, but paused with the book in his hand.

"Catharine?"

Her temporary relief at the dismissal was short-lived as she forced herself to turn back around. "Sir?"

"Have you found yourself compromised?"

An unwanted rush of heat touched her cheeks, a recollection of the way he had so carelessly waved off her trip to Caldy the previous week.

If his boy gets her in trouble, he'll do the right thing.

"No, sir."

"Are you lying to me?" His gaze was hooded, his face very still.

"No, sir." She tried to school her expression to match the impassivity of his own. "I would not lie to you."

"Let's hope that's true." He dropped the ledger onto his desk. "I imagine I do not need to outline the consequences should you be found wanton—is that correct?"

"No, sir." Regardless of her innocence, Catharine found her breathing turn shallow, and cold sweat beaded across the nape of her neck. Innocence didn't matter. "You are correct," she added quickly, for fear she would be misunderstood.

"Very good." He flipped open the ledger and took up his pen. "After breakfast, I will have your assistance in reviewing port efficiency data from this past quarter in Rotterdam. There are discrepancies amongst the records." He flicked the nib of his Montblanc toward the door. "You may go."

Chapter Five

For the second time in as many weeks, Catharine climbed the staircase to Nathalie's first-floor room and knocked on the Frenchwoman's door, uninvited. This time, however, she'd turned up at a reasonable hour—it wasn't quite dusk—fully clothed (including shoes) and come bearing gifts.

"Bonne fête nationale !" she greeted, holding out the bag of French delicacies she'd snuck past her father's household manager. Despite Mrs. Ainsley's keen eye, Catharine was certain the woman wouldn't notice the missing wares from the manor's excessively stocked culinary pantry.

It was the fourteenth of July—Bastille Day. A day, Catharine knew, Nathalie lamented not being home in Bordeaux.

"I thought you might be homesick. I brought a few things to celebrate, if you want?"

Nathalie took a cursory glance through the sack—a quiche Lorraine, baguettes, French wine and cheeses—and then, delighted, pulled Catharine through the door.

"You should have left a message you were coming—I could have been at rehearsal!"

Catharine dropped the bag onto Nathalie's cluttered writing desk. "They don't start until next weekend."

"What if I had been at the library?"

"Not on a Saturday night."

"You think you know me so well?" Nathalie gave a subtle lift of an eyebrow. "I could have been out with friends."

"But you weren't."

"But I could have been."

Catharine shrugged. "I took a gamble."

It made something in her chest tingle—the way Nathalie smiled at her. Suddenly, raiding her father's pantry and carting an armful of groceries onto an Oxford-bound train, after massaging a mistruth to her mother about her whereabouts—all while risking, as Nathalie pointed out, that she might not even have been home—felt entirely worth it.

It was the first time she'd seen her friend since returning to Henley. In the week that had passed, their only communication had come three days earlier, the same day her father had excoriated her in his library. Catharine had sent Nathalie a letter, relaying the things he had said, his cruel accusations, and the ironic outcome of his forbidding her relationship with Edward.

If he thinks he is punishing me, he's got it very backwards, she had written, trying to disguise the hurt she felt about the way he had berated her. At the time, she'd been uncertain how long her father would be at Honour Stone, and had closed the letter asking Nathalie not to call or write. She didn't want to risk him intercepting any form of correspondence. But when he'd abruptly departed for Liverpool early this morning, Catharine convinced herself it was a forgivable falsehood to tell her mother she wanted to meet with one of last year's tutorial partners to go over some thoughts on market structures and oligopoly.

That it was likely her mother had not fallen for the excuse didn't really matter.

"If your study session runs too late, you should stay over at Nathalie's," she'd called from the sunroom. Catharine had been in too much of a hurry with her stolen goods to peek in the doorway and see if she was making light. She knew her mother was thrilled she'd made a friend—someone outside the stuffy circles of London

—but she didn't want to put her in a position to lie to her father, if he asked where she'd gone.

"I can't believe he really told you Edward Haverfield would think circles around you," Nathalie said ten minutes later, as they were utilizing the windowsill to lay out a spread of decadent cheeses: *Époisses de Bourgogne, Mimolette, Chabichou du Poitou, Ossau-Iraty*.

Catharine was quiet as she pulled out a bag of grapes and figs, the latter having fared poorly during the jostling walk from the train station.

"You know that's not true, Cate, don't you?" Nathalie said, as Catharine turned toward the small ensuite, wanting to get a towel to wipe the fig juice from her fingers. "I'm sorry for saying it, but your father is a prick. He only says those things to make you doubt yourself. It's the best way he can control you. You need to ignore him."

"Of course," said Catharine, disappearing through the door to the basin. She ran hot water over her sticky palms, wishing she could find a way to let it go that easily. Every moment of her life felt like it had been lived in an effort to please him. And no matter what she did, he never missed an opportunity to let her know how she had failed.

"And really," Nathalie went on, "who does he think he is—dictating who you will marry? It's the twentieth century, for God's sake, not the Dark Ages. He hardly gets to barter you off for land and a couple of milk cows!"

Catharine dried her hands and stared at her reflection in the mirror. There was no point explaining that her father would un-doubtedly be willing to auction her off for much less, if the terms were in his favor.

When she returned from the ensuite, Nathalie was holding a *saucisson sec*. "Do you know, when I was twelve, my aunt made me promise I'd sleep with at least five men before I got married? She felt it was only sensible to try on a few pairs of shoes before walk-ing down the aisle."

Catharine laughed, picking up a baguette. "She didn't seriously tell you that?"

"She did! She was adamant. Unfortunately, she died when I was fifteen, so I won't have the satisfaction of telling her I won't be sleeping with *any* men, let alone *five* of them."

"Ever, you don't think?" Catharine didn't look up from her meticulous process of tearing the baguette into even pieces. Aside from the conversation the night they'd met, when Nathalie casually acknowledged her interest in women, it wasn't something they talked about—despite their own undeniable coquettish raillery.

"*Catharine.*"

So seldom did Nathalie call her anything other than Cate, the sound of the rebuke forced her attention from her task. "What? I mean, you never know—"

"I *know*, trust me." She gave a lewd shake of the sausage. "I'm not about to trade Paris in springtime for a weekend in the suburbs."

"What?"

Nathalie laughed. "Think of it this way—sex with men after being with women would be like having a taste of champagne and then getting stuck with tap water."

The blush that swept up Catharine's neck felt as though it might rival the garnet hue of the wine Nathalie was examining.

"You seriously have a bottle of *Château Haut-Brion* tossed in with the figs and macarons?"

Relieved at the turn in conversation, Catharine returned to tearing apart the bread.

"It was the closest label I could find produced near Saint-Michel." She had sorted through the wine cellar Mrs. Ainsley kept stocked for guests, choosing the bottle solely for its geographical origin. With her father's devotion to teetotaling, she was by no means a wine connoisseur.

Nathalie was still staring at the label. "This is a—a *really* expensive bottle, Cate. Like it could cover all of next year's living expenses and then some." Her head jerked up, only just realizing what Catharine said. "Wait, you remember where I live?"

The flush was definitely deepening.

Catharine tried to brush off the question. "Of course. You bring up Bordeaux practically twenty times a day."

"Bordeaux, maybe—but, I mean, my district? Saint-Michel?"

"You, um—" Catharine's fingers worked furiously at the baguette. She'd have rather continued the conversation about the number of men Nathalie wouldn't sleep with. "You mentioned it at the Freshers' Fair."

"That was the first week we met."

Catharine said nothing.

"How did you know *Château Haut-Brion* was so close to Saint-Michel?"

"I read once that its seventeenth-century trade route ran along the Garonne River, which means it would have shipped out of the Port of Bordeaux. The port is only a few kilometers from the heart of Saint-Michel."

"Read once?" Nathalie laughed. "And your father says Edward Haverfield can think circles around *you*? Psh." She blew out a disapproving grunt. "Give me that. You're turning it into croutons!" She snatched the intact half of the loaf from Catharine's hands. "Grab my corkscrew—it's in one of those drawers," she gestured to the desk overflowing with scripts and books with Post-it Notes. "We can eat and watch movies in the JCR."

During term, a Saturday night in the Brasenose junior common room would have seen at least a dozen students strewn about, arguing whether to watch *Blind Date* or *Gladiators*, while finally settling on *Noel's House Party*. No different than they did a quarter-mile away at the Christ Church JCR.

Tonight, however, the lounge was empty. The handful of students remaining in residence had gone off to local pubs or stuck to their rooms, leaving Catharine and Nathalie the place to themselves.

"We have options," said Catharine, reviewing the drawer of VHS tapes in the cabinet beneath the TV. "*Lawrence of Arabia, The Third Man, Goldfinger…*"

"Bor-ring," Nathalie drawled out the word, pulling the plates they'd snuck from the gyp room out of her backpack, followed by a pair of plastic cups. "Find something tragic. Or romantic!"

Catharine moved on to the second drawer. "So not *The Wicker Man*?"

"Only if you have a twisted sense of romance." Nathalie popped the cork on the *Haut-Brion*. "Do you know how wrong it is to be drinking this out of cheap tumblers?" she asked, pouring them both a glass.

"What do they say—'it's the company, not the crockery, that counts'?"

"Who says that?"

Catharine laughed. "I don't know, I made it up."

"Cate Brooks, the great stiff-upper-lip English romantic philosopher!" Nathalie whizzed a grape at the back of her head. "Find us something French—after all, it is *le 14 juillet !*"

"I'll have you know I can be very romantic," Catharine blustered, knowing that was entirely untrue. There wasn't a romantic bone in her body. It was something Edward had harped on about every chance he got.

You know, Catharine—if romance were a flame, you'd be the proverbial wet blanket. Or: I've seen statues in my father's garden who exhibit more warmth than you.

She was surprised, then, when Nathalie made no jest at her expense.

"I don't doubt it for a minute," she said, continuing to pull provisions for their picnic out of her pack. Catharine could see her unhurried motions in the curvature of the TV screen, paralleling the nonchalance of her tone. "I can't say I've ever had anyone else show up at my door with fruit and wine and cheese and the willingness to dine on mismatched plates when they could be home eating caviar in their grand ballroom."

"Great Hall," Catharine corrected, attempting to match her friend's same insouciance. She didn't dare dispute that the gesture had no romantic intentions. The ever-present flush of her cheeks would counter the argument, only making her look more culpable in the end.

Because what else was there to call it, when she'd spent half a day deliberating over which color blouse might soften the frigid hue of her glacial blue eyes? Or risked a thorough unbraiding from Mrs. Ainsley for absconding with her finest imported French cheeses? Or fabricated a fictitious tutorial partner in a lie she'd once never dreamt of uttering to her mother?

What other label was there to assign it when she found herself disappointed at Nathalie's suggestion to leave the privacy of her tiny room, and her returned relief at finding them alone again in the JCR?

How could she pretend she didn't notice the way the wine stained the corners of Nathalie's lips, or her fascination with the dexterous movement of her practiced fingers as she sliced thin wedges of the soft cheese without ever allowing it to lose its shape? Or of wondering what it would be like to spend the French holiday home with Nathalie in her mother's modest *échoppe borde-laise* in Bordeaux?

No, there was no sound defense, and so Catharine sought only to deflect in a different direction.

"Honour Stone doesn't have a grand ballroom. And for the record, I hate caviar." She returned to scanning the titles of the movies. "There's always *Monty Python and the Holy Grail*?"

"'*Fetchez la vache*' wasn't the French masterpiece I had in mind." Nathalie came up behind her, presenting one of the plastic cups around her waist. "*Pour toi, mademoiselle*—in a bespoke chalice worthy of the vineyard."

"*Parfait !*" Catharine took the wine, acutely aware of her nearness, of the warmth of her body pressed against her back as she peered into the open drawer of videos—the faint aroma of the *Haut-Brion* on her breath.

Once again, Catharine could feel the dynamic shift between them, a sensation she'd come to know well.

The first time she'd experienced it was just weeks into their friendship. Nathalie had dragged her to a bop at Brasenose, and then, tipsy on boxed wine and laughter, walked her to her staircase in Blue Boar. Side-by-side, they'd strolled down the cobblestone walkway of St. Mary's Passage, their fingers brushing and hips bumping, neither taking any measure to draw apart. At the iron gates of the porters' lodge, they'd kissed cheeks goodbye. *Well, goodnight* had been their shared murmur, both lingering in the shadow of Tom Tower. And then they'd parted, nothing more said between them—but still, something had been there.

Or again in winter, when Nathalie pulled Catharine from her studies into the unexpected snowfall settling in Radcliffe Square. The way they'd laughed until their voices were hoarse and noses were running, their attempts to build a snowman futile with only a dusting of snow. The way Catharine could feel Nathalie watching her—the way she herself had taken sidelong glances beneath eyelashes flaked with frost.

The fleeting butterflies over shared coffees and the way Catharine made no effort to avoid Nathalie's lipstick mark on the takeaway cups. Or the time Edward had thrown Catharine into the Isis, claiming *initiation rites*, but it had been Nathalie who draped her jacket over her shoulders on the shivering walk back to Tom Quad.

"Here," said Nathalie now, breaking their contact as she reached to pluck a tape from the bottom drawer. It was the famous Chinese classic, *The Love Eterne*. "This looks perfect!"

"You don't speak Mandarin."

"So," Nathalie shrugged, shaking the VHS from its battered sleeve and slipping it into the VCR, "you can translate."

Catharine knew the film well. She'd watched the Huangmei opera at least a dozen times, using its lyrical dialogue to perfect her Mandarin tones.

"It's very sad. And melodramatic."

Nathalie grabbed the remote. "I can think of nothing better." Annoyed as the video started at the ending credits, she hit rewind and strolled to the coffee table, where she'd laid out their fare. "You're going to need to drink faster if we're going to get through two bottles," she motioned at Catharine's untouched tumbler, pulling the second bottle—a *Château Margaux*—from her pack.

Taking the cue, Catharine drained her glass as she selected from the array of cheeses, and poured another before turning back to the TV. Reset at the beginning, the familiar music began to play, and Nathalie waved her toward the light switch.

"Turn them off, will you? Movies are meant to be watched in the dark."

Catharine did as she was told, and upon returning, found Nathalie curled onto the sofa, and was left with the option of joining her or selecting one of the two armchairs.

In an unmistakable invitation, Nathalie kicked off her shoes and drew her knees to her chest, making more room.

Catharine chose the sofa.

"Okay, so give me a brief synopsis." Nathalie tipped her chin toward the grainy intro of the 1960s classic.

Catharine smeared a wedge of *Chabichou du Poitou* onto her baguette. "Zhu—the girl there," she indicated the actress on the screen, "disguises herself as a man in order to attend college. She befriends a boy, Liang, and secretly falls in love with him during the three years they are at school. The entire time, Liang doesn't realize Zhu is a girl."

"So, *Mulan*?" said Nathalie, leaning forward to refill their wine with the last of the *Haut-Brion*.

"Well, yes, in a way—but Mulan's themes focus on duty more so than romance."

"*As You Like It*, then?"

"In that they both feature hidden identity, maybe, but less happily-ever-after and more star-crossed-lovers-destined-for-a-tragic ending."

"*Twelfth Night* meets *Romeo and Juliet*?"

"Do you want me to tell you the story or would you prefer to just keep guessing?" Catharine scolded, tossing a grape at Nathalie, which she deftly caught in her mouth.

"Fine," Nathalie threw herself against the armrest and kicked her feet into Catharine's lap, nearly upsetting her plate. *"Speak on, but be not over-tedious!"*

"Zhu's family—"

"Wait—" Nathalie interrupted, "—do you know what play that was from?"

"Henry VI."

"Are you sure?"

"Part 1, Act 3, Scene 3—Duke of Burgundy to La Pucelle. Now, if you interrupt me again, you're going to have to translate on your own."

Nathalie's smile was slow, sly—enough to make Catharine swallow. "No, I won't. You adore me. You'd give in."

"Zhu's family," Catharine enunciated dramatically, grateful for the darkness that hid the rapid pulse she was certain would otherwise be visible at her throat, "calls her home, and it isn't until Liang comes to visit that he discovers her true identity."

"And let me guess, they profess their undying love?"

Catharine threw another grape, which again, Nathalie caught between her teeth.

"I'm right, aren't I?" she said, chewing.

"Only Liang arrives too late. Zhu's father has already promised her to marry the cruel son of a powerful and wealthy family." She paused. On the screen, it was still the first act, Zhu, dressed as a man, meeting the kind-hearted Liang for the first time.

"What is she singing right now?" asked Nathalie, her attention on the TV.

Catharine translated. "In this fleeting life, a true friend is hard to find."

For a moment, Nathalie was quiet, sipping her wine, before turning back to Catharine. "Go on."

"Liang is devastated. He tells Zhu: *If we cannot be together in life, then let us unite in death.*"

"So, like I said—*Romeo and Juliet!*"

Catharine pinched Nathalie's foot. "You're ruining the story."

"I'm complementing it!"

Discarding her plate on the table, Catharine picked up the bottle of *Château Margaux* and twisted the corkscrew into the top.

"Are you trying to get me drunk, Cate Brooks?" Nathalie asked coyly, holding out her glass for filling.

"If that's what it takes to keep you quiet."

Without spilling a drop of the red blend, Nathalie caught Catharine's arm with her free hand and tugged her down beside her on the sofa, their faces just inches apart. She rested her glass on Catharine's hip. "Go on. What happens next?"

"Liang goes home and dies."

"What! How?"

"Of a broken heart."

"And what happens to Zhu?"

"On the day of her wedding, she goes to visit Liang's tomb. She cries a vow of eternal devotion: '*If our love cannot be fulfilled in this world, I will follow you into the next.*' In response, there is a violent supernatural event sent from the heavens. The tomb splits open, and Zhu hurls herself into the void to be rejoined with Liang."

"Well," contemplated Nathalie, "who could blame her? I'd do the same."

"I'd expect nothing less from you."

"What's that supposed to mean?"

"It means if you look in the dictionary under the word *melodramatic*, it's your headshot next to the definition."

Nathalie tutted. "Are you saying you'd just go off and marry whatever bastard your father assigned to you, even with a broken heart?"

"I don't know what I'd do."

"I thought you were supposed to be romantic! Your *English* is showing through." Nathalie's chestnut eyes glinted the reflection of the TV in the dark.

"There's nothing romantic about throwing yourself in a grave."

"Tell that to Aida and Radamès."

Catharine rolled her eyes.

"I want to hear the story of Zhu and Liang again," Nathalie said, reaching over Catharine to set her wine on the table, before settling back beside her. "But this time, tell it to me in Mandarin."

"We could just watch the movie." Despite the suggestion, Catharine made no effort to turn her face to the screen.

"I'd rather hear you tell it." Nathalie slipped a hand between them, bringing her thumb to rest on Catharine's lower lip. "I like to listen to your voice."

Catharine stopped breathing.

On the TV behind her, Zhu was reflecting her inner struggle for her growing love for Liang. With her focus on the warmth of Nathalie's touch, Catharine was finding it hard to understand the song.

How I wish to reveal the truth, yet fear the bond we share will break, was all her mind could translate.

She could lean forward and kiss her. She knew she could. She knew it was what Nathalie wanted. More than that, she knew it was what *she* wanted. This wasn't fleeting. This wasn't two drunk university students on a Saturday night finding themselves swayed by solitude, by sweeping romantic cinema, by darkness, by curiosity, by the thrill of doing something daring simply because they could.

This was real. Genuine. A pull not rooted in circumstance but in the undeniable gravity between them.

Which was exactly what forced Catharine to bolt upright, tipping over the wine glass she'd left sitting on the armrest. "God, I'm sorry."

It wasn't the spill on the carpet she was apologizing for.

She flung her feet to the ground and grabbed the kitchen roll they'd swiped from the gyp room, kneeling to mop up the mess. "I don't know what's wrong with me."

Nathalie, sitting up, set a hand on her shoulder, but Catharine shrugged it off.

"Cate—"

"I can't." She didn't clarify what she couldn't. They both knew.

"If you're worried about your father—"

"It's not that," Catharine lied. She would never be able to explain the fire they were playing with—the consequences if he ever found out. She couldn't risk it. Not only for herself but for Nathalie as well. "I just—" she pressed the paper hand towels against the stain "—this isn't me."

It wasn't entirely a lie. This *wasn't* her. This risk-taker. This impulsive Ulysses. This girl who lied to her mother, who found her disciplined thoughts wandering, daydreaming of Nathalie. She *wasn't* a romantic. A dreamer. A stargazer who fantasized about a future she knew would never be.

"I'm sorry." She stood, staring at the soiled towel in her hand. "I wish it were."

"I don't believe you." Nathalie's voice was quiet beneath the cheerful singing on the screen.

"You should." Catharine forced herself to meet Nathalie's eye, unblinking. "I don't want to lose your friendship—but I need you to believe me."

Nathalie, finally, was the first to look away. "Of course." She picked up the remote, and Catharine tried not to notice that her hand was shaking. "Put in Monty Python, will you?" She swiped her forearm across her eyes, but by the time she looked back, she was smiling. Albeit a little too brightly. "Watching King Arthur tuck tail and run from flying French cows feels a little more fitting for a day celebrating *Liberté, Égalité, Fraternité,* anyway."

Chapter Six

THE DAY BEFORE THE START of her second year at Oxford, and exactly one week from her eighteenth birthday, Catharine shouldered through the heavy-planked door of the Christ Church Boat Club.

It was dawn. Rowers were already scattered amongst the weights and mats and ergs, grumbling about the early autumn chill and dreaded first day back at training.

She kept her attention forward, away from the gym, where she knew Edward would be surrounded by his jackals.

The previous year, she had loved arriving at the boathouse. In the winter, there had been nothing more peaceful than the dark, brisk walk through Christ Church Meadow to get to the Isis. To feel the first spray of water on her cheeks and listen to the coxswain's rhythmic cries break the silence of morning. It had been as blissful as sunrise sails in Henley and was the solace that got her through the high-pressure academic year and adjusting to college life.

Today, however, she just wanted the morning to be over.

With her hands stuffed in the pockets of her Levis, and the collar of her knit jumper pulled up to her chin, she stepped into the boat bay.

She was looking for Anouk van der Meer, a third-year student from The Netherlands, who also happened to be the Christ Church women's rowing captain.

Catharine liked Anouk. She was straightforward, unbiased, and unquestionably talented on the water. She was also a compassionate advocate for her crews and had been instrumental in Catharine's fast-tracked advancement from novice to senior rower.

This year, Catharine knew, Anouk had plans to push her to compete for a position in the First Eight. It was something she'd looked forward to all summer.

Until yesterday.

Rounding the first wall of racks, Catharine found Anouk checking the pitch on the rowlocks of a shell being readied for the landing stage.

"Brooks!" The woman smiled when she saw her. "I can't believe I can no longer greet you as my favorite stroke fresher—you're practically a seasoned veteran now." She held the pitch gauge up to the next gate. "You ready to show Coach Chowdhury what you've got?"

"I—" Catharine wedged her hands deeper into her pockets. "I actually need to talk to you."

The hesitation in her tone caught Anouk's attention, drawing her blue eyes from her task.

"Is everything all right?"

Catharine glanced over her shoulder, cognizant of the rough and rowdy voices coming from the weight room.

"Here," Anouk stepped further down the racks, drawing them into the privacy of the stacked shells, "tell me, what is this about?"

For once, Catharine hated the kindness in her subtle Dutch lilt and the unmistakable concern in her receptive gaze. She would rather the woman had been cold and unsympathetic.

"I have to step down from the crew."

Whatever Anouk expected her to say, it wasn't that. "Catharine —what's going on?"

"I'm sorry." Catharine had prepared this speech. "I'm truly grateful for everything you've done for me and for the opportunity to row with such an elite club. But my course load is heavier this year, and I regret that I won't have time for anything outside my studies." She knew she sounded robotic.

"But we spoke just last week. You didn't mention this?"

How could she tell her she hadn't known at the time? That her father hadn't yet come home seething with rage, confronting her with a rumor he'd carried from London.

"Haverfield's boy is claiming he severed your relationship after discovering you'd fucked half the men in the boat club!"

Catharine's head had snapped up as much at her father's use of the expletive as it did at the accusation. Never once in her life had she heard him utter an obscenity. He considered it beneath him.

"He's lying!"

"You think that matters?" The colonel exploded, upending the Boulle French clock sitting above the mantel. The marquetry inlay splintered on impact, sending shards of brass and tortoiseshell skittering across the floor. "Your word against his—who do you imagine they will believe, Catharine? You put yourself in this position, and now half of London is talking about how my daughter is the whore of the Christ Church boathouse!" He crushed a gilt bronze mount beneath his oxford. "You're going to quit rowing."

"No!" Forgetting herself, she reached for his elbow. "Please! I swear, I haven't—" No sooner had her fingers touched the tweed of his blazer did she find him spinning, his hand arching up to strike her.

It had been a glancing blow, but enough to send her stumbling into the fireplace.

Now, she could feel Anouk's perceptive gaze drawn to the small bruise on her temple where she had collided with the mantel. Abruptly, she tugged down her woolly hat to better conceal the mark.

"Is he the cause of this?" Anouk demanded.

Not far off, raucous laughter filled the bay, and Catharine shrank deeper into the collar of her jumper.

Who *he* was needn't be defined. Anouk knew Edward well— they were both in the same year, reading *Classics*.

"No!" Catharine hastily brushed the accusation aside, unprepared to answer any questions about Edward. "I just—it's nothing to do with him. As I said, I have my studies, and—"

"Catharine! If he did this to you—" she flicked a finger in the direction of her face "—you have to tell me!" Grabbing her arm, she lowered her voice. "He's done this before and gotten away with it. Our first year, there was an incident just before Christmas. One of our coursemates claimed he…" A rack away, a crew lumbered in to find their boat, the cox issuing the order for *hands on*. Anouk leaned closer, her words no more than a hissed whisper. "Our senior tutor didn't believe her. He never even took it to the dean! When we returned from break, she'd dropped out of the college." She pressed strong fingers into her wrist. "If he's done the same to you, you have to say something! They would be forced to listen! He could be sent down!"

For a moment, all Catharine could do was stare. One year ahead of her, Anouk had come up with Edward. There had never been a question that the Dutchwoman didn't like him, even if it wasn't explicitly said. When she'd found out she and Edward were dating, she'd been unusually curt to Catharine for several weeks.

Their bow seat, Becky, told Catharine to brush it off, whispering with a wink that Anouk just wasn't fond of men. But the rowing captain never seemed to have an issue with any of the other boys the girls on her crew were seeing.

"I—I don't know anything about that," Catharine said. She thought about the way Edward had grabbed her in the hot tub— the glass he'd shattered above her head. What might have happened if her father weren't who he was—if *Brooks* weren't her family name?

Would he have taken no for an answer?

She wasn't sure.

But what Anouk was asking—she was wrong. Edward may have been the root of the cause, but he wasn't the end result. And Catharine didn't want her questions, or even worse, her pity.

Behind them, another crew entered the bay. It was Edward's, she knew, even before glancing between the racks and finding his hostile gaze. They hadn't spoken since the night she left Caldy. At one point, he had rung the house asking for her, and her father had taken the call. After that, he hadn't called again.

But she'd known, coming here, it would be impossible to avoid him.

One of his mates whispered something, and a snigger of laughter rippled from cox to bow seat.

Catharine could feel her cheeks color. She turned away, but without enough conviction to look Anouk in the eye.

"I'm just not cut out to row, alright?"

"That's not true. I know there's more to this, Catharine—"

"Stop acting like you know me. We're not even friends!" Catharine yanked her arm from her hold, immediately regretting the cruelty of the statement, but stepping away all the same. "Look —just tell Coach Chowdhury I had to quit, okay?"

Whatever Anouk called after her was lost as she hurried out the double doors, aware only of Edward and his crew laughing, carrying their boat to the landing stage.

THE FOLLOWING THURSDAY, CATHARINE STEPPED out of the last lecture of her day onto the bustling pavement of High Street. She hadn't quite made it to the end of the first week of Michaelmas, but already she felt like she was struggling to keep her head above water.

It wasn't the stress of her heavily loaded schedule. Without rowing to occupy her early mornings and evenings, she found her timetable more than manageable. The subject matter was simple: Econometrics, macroeconomics, microeconomics. Finance and accounting. Organization Theory and Industrial Relations. Very little of it challenged her. She had been well-versed for years in analytical and quantitative disciplines.

It wasn't even her dismay surrounding her father's demand that she give up rowing, or her guilt over the infelicitous way she'd handled her resignation from the boat club. Nor, surprisingly, was it the looming knowledge she'd have to share lecture space with Edward when their papers overlapped the following week. Even the dread of that wasn't enough to set her so off balance.

Rather, it was Nathalie—and her own inability to get her off her mind.

Catharine had seen her only once since the start of the term, just hours after resigning from the boathouse. That Sunday, she'd left the rowing captain and walked aimlessly along the river and parks, browsing the Botanical Gardens, until she found herself wandering through the heart of town.

She should have been back at Christ Church, settling into her new staircase, where her status as a scholar had secured her one of the most coveted rooms in the Meadow Building. Instead, she'd found herself tracing wide circles around Radcliffe Square.

It had been three months since Bastille Day. There had been a handful of letters between her and Nathalie, and two short phone calls, but nothing more. Catharine had been dragged off with her father to Zürich and Geneva, Bangkok, Hong Kong, and Singapore, to aid the colonel on business matters. There had been no time to visit Oxford, and even if there had—Catharine wasn't sure she would have gone.

Their friendship was strained between them. A situation, Catharine knew, of her own creation, after the night in the JCR.

Hoping to make amends, she'd left a note at the Brasenose Porters' Lodge two days earlier, on her first morning back in Oxford. In it, she'd highlighted the location of her new accommodation and asked if they could meet for coffee. She wanted things back the way they were—where they could catch up, compare schedules, complain about their workload—just as they'd done the previous year.

But Nathalie hadn't responded.

On her third revolution of Radcliffe Square, she stopped once more in front of the entry to Brasenose, determined to leave another note. Perhaps Nathalie hadn't received the first one.

But before she'd worked up the courage to approach the entrance of the college, the door pushed open, and Nathalie's unmistakable figure emerged onto the cobblestone.

Catharine's first instinct was to call out, but she immediately fell silent when she realized Nathalie was not alone. Another shape stumbled out behind her, grabbing for her elbow as they fell into step side-by-side, their laughter carrying across the crisp autumn air.

The young woman was familiar to Catharine, despite not being a student at the university. Her name was Maddie—or Millie—something like that. A townie who lived over in Botley.

Catharine remembered her short blonde hair and lanky figure from the Oxford Theatre Guild's spring production of *The Secret Garden*. She also distinctly recalled Nathalie griping about how she found the older girl's laughter annoying—a fact that could have fooled anyone, given the way they now strolled down the street linked arm-in-arm in the opposite direction.

Stunned, and struck by an unfamiliar tightness in her chest, Catharine trailed them onto Turl Street before she even realized what she was doing. When they disappeared into the entrance of the Covered Market, she scolded herself, knowing she should turn around. It was getting late. She needed to return to her own college, to prepare for the following morning's start of term. But instead, she ducked into the market, swimming upstream through the afternoon crowd, and squeezed between strolling tourists and hordes of students until Nathalie and Maddie were once again in sight.

From three shops away, she watched as they slowed in front of the florist, Millie pausing to smell a bouquet of bell-shaped flowers sprouting from a vase. Crown Imperial, Catharine registered, making note that—in addition to her obnoxious laugh—Marjorie wasn't terribly bright. The burnt orange blossoms were beautiful, but the tall-stemmed perennials were known for their pungent skunk-like musk, often used in gardens to repel rodents and deer.

It gave her a twinge of satisfaction to watch Minnie crinkle her nose.

The pair moved on, bypassing the bookstore—something Catharine had never known Nathalie to do—and turning into the vintage shop selling second-hand accessories and clothing. They tried on hats, and jumpers that didn't match, playing dress up with gaudy costume jewelry and fake leather riding boots.

Caught up in analyzing the way Molly capitalized on every opportunity to put her hands on Nathalie—adjusting an earring, tucking in a scarf—Catharine failed to notice Nathalie's gaze shift through the window, and didn't realize she'd been spotted until a hand was waved in her direction, drawing Catharine's attention to her friend's slow, amused smile.

"Cate!" Nathalie poked her head out the door, pulling off a necklace of fake pearls. "I'm surprised to see you here!"

Her accent was laid on thick, a habit she was prone to when putting on a show.

Who she was performing for—her or Mamie—was yet to be determined.

There was no use in pretending she hadn't heard her or attempting to vanish into an adjacent stall. Resigned to her predicament, she stepped from beneath the awning of the pie shop and crossed the path with a pasted-on smile.

"Hey."

Mabel, ditching the cloche hat she'd been wearing, bounded over the threshold to Nathalie's side, greeting Catharine too brightly.

"Oh, we met last year, I think." She held out her hand. "Maggie Chapman."

Maggie. Yes, Catharine remembered that now. Like the ballad, *Maggie Mae*—the nineteenth-century folk song about the working girl from Liverpool who seduced seamen and stole what wasn't hers to take.

Gather 'round you sailors, and a tale to you I'll tell...

"Hello. I'm Catharine." She curtly shook her hand.

It's all about a damsel fair and her treacherous ways.

"Ça va ?" She glanced at Nathalie.

"As good as the last day of holiday will allow." Refusing Catharine's bait to slip the conversation into French—an option she rarely declined—Nathalie rehung the pearls on the shopfront mannequin. "We're on our way to tech rehearsal. Maggie is playing Helena."

"You're going to come see the play, I hope? We're doing *A Midsummer Night's Dream*," piped Maggie, slipping her arm through Nathalie's, the way Catharine had done a thousand times before. "We open Tuesday night at the Playhouse."

"Yes, I know," said Catharine. "Nathalie is playing Hermia."

"And a wicked job of it she does," said Maggie, bumping her shoulder into Nathalie, blissfully unaware of the coldness in Catharine's tone. "She steals the show! You should hear her—the way she delivers *'o me, you juggler! You canker-blossom! You thief of love! What, have you—"*

"I *have* heard her." Catharine cut her off. "I helped her prepare for the audition."

The final week before summer, the two of them had stayed up half the night in the Old Quad, drunk on cider and poking fun at each other, Catharine jumbling every line she read. The following morning, she'd taken her Quantitative Methods final with a raging headache and blurry eyes, without a single regret.

"Are you an actress, too, then?"

"No," Nathalie was quick to answer, her smile small. "Cate is far too refined for that. This life's just not for her."

This isn't me. Catharine recognized the echo of the subtle dig.

"Pity!" Oblivious, Maggie continued to smile. "You're so pretty! You'd look good on stage. And we performers have all the fun."

She stole the hearts of sailor lads with her cunning ways and guile…

The song continued to play through Catharine's head.

"Cate's more of a fiscal-policy-and-garden-parties, investment-strategy-and-afternoon-tea-in-the-great-hall kind of girl."

"I like the arts very much," Catharine defended, "they're just not something I participate in."

"Well, that's fair—not everyone can be an artist. Who then would be the patron?" Maggie laughed, certain she'd been very clever. She waved a hand adorned with black nail polish in the direction of a pasty shop further down the row. "We're just going for a sausage roll. They've got the best ones in town. Do you want to join us?"

"No." Catharine tried not to stare at the casual way Maggie pressed her hip into Nathalie's. "Thank you. I have a welcome dinner I have to attend. But enjoy your—" she turned, catching Nathalie's eye "—rehearsal."

"Are you going to come to the show?" Nathalie asked, the simple inquiry nucleus to a hundred unspoken questions.

"I don't know." Catharine's gaze flickered down to the painted black fingernails toying with the dark tips of the Frenchwoman's shoulder-length hair. "It's a busy week. I have to check my schedule. Nice to meet you, *Millie*."

On her walk back to the Meadow Building, Catharine tugged loose her scarf and unzipped her jacket, hoping the chill would drown out the lyrics to the God awful folk song.

She gave a lonely sailor a wink and a smile, and soon he forgot his troubles for a while.

But the tune was still there as she sat through tutorials and took notes at lectures, outlined her essays and flipped through page after page of *The Economics of Industry*, sipping black coffee at midnight in the library.

And there it remained, cycling through her thoughts almost a week later, as she stood on the corner of High Street and Saint Aldate's, deciding whether to turn left to Christ Church or right toward the Oxford Playhouse.

The curtain for Nathalie's show was in less than half an hour. She had already skipped Tuesday and Wednesday, telling herself she didn't have the time. But tonight, there was no excuse. Her reading was done, and her essays were written. Her first obligation Friday morning was an 11 AM *Behavioral Economics* lecture.

She shifted the tote on her shoulder, staring at her leather loafers. In chinos and a polo neck, she wasn't dressed for the theatre.

But she knew, if she went back to her room to change, she wouldn't go at all.

Smoothing the lapels of her peacoat, she caught her reflection in the corner art gallery window. In truth, she looked perfectly acceptable. It wasn't like the show was at the Palladium. It was just an amateur Shakespeare production at the local playhouse.

She stepped off the curb in the direction of the theatre. No matter how much she hated Maggie—and she had to admit, she *did* hate Maggie (her justification irrelevant)—she couldn't bring herself not to attend. Her delay had dragged on long enough. It was a production she knew Nathalie was proud of—one she had been eager to share.

And they were friends, after all. If Catharine's feelings were hurt, they were injured of her own volition. Maggie was merely an innocent bystander, caught up in the repercussions of Catharine's inability to be herself.

Still, it didn't stop her from humming all the way down Cornmarket Street.

That dirty, thievin', no good, Maggie Mae.

Chapter Seven

*"*W*HAT, WILL YOU TEAR IMPATIENT* answers from my gentle tongue? Fie, fie, you counterfeit, you puppet, you!"*

Maggie portrayed Helena with all the usual exaggeration demanded of the role, her escalating anger humorous as the scene swelled into rhapsodic absurdity. The audience laughed, fresh from the interval, those familiar with *A Midsummer Night's Dream* clinging to their seats, eager for Hermia's dramatic reprisal.

Because, three acts into the play, it had become apparent—Nathalie *would* deliver.

Hermia was a role the Frenchwoman was born to play. Headstrong, fiercely independent, with an unwillingness to bend to societal expectations. Her real-life tendency to speak her mind lent an authenticity to the character that couldn't be simulated.

"Puppet?" answered Nathalie, her outraged Hermia staggering forward with flawless comedic timing. The dialogue between the women was quick, witty, a staple of Shakespeare's brilliant blend of humor and emotion.

In the present scene, both Lysander and Demetrius were under the influence of a magical love potion, their affections comically fixated on Helena—Hermia's best friend. The unexpected turn of events had left Hermia, once confident in Lysander's love, feeling betrayed and furious, convinced her closest friend had conspired to steal her lover.

"Because I am so dwarfish and so low? How low am I, thou painted maypole? Speak!" Hermia continued, drawing nearer to Helena, her blistering indignation radiating with tension. *"How low am I? I am not yet so low but that my nails can reach unto thine eyes!"* Nathalie lunged forward on the iconic line, her delivery impeccable. Scratching, clawing, there was a skirmish onstage, the two women grappling with such passionate intensity, even Catharine could not deny they played well off one another.

"Good Hermia," cried Helena, their bodies twisting together with practiced blocking as Maggie pinned Nathalie to the stage beneath her, *"do not be so bitter with me. I evermore did love you."*

The line, so often shouted with dramatic flare, was instead delivered with quiet fervor. It was an interpretation of the dialogue Catharine had never seen before, and from her seat in the 5th row, she watched, astonished, as Helena leaned down and tenderly kissed Hermia.

There, on stage, on the *mouth*—in front of a nearly sold-out crowd—Maggie was kissing Nathalie. Or, it was hard to tell— maybe vice versa.

The audience fell silent.

Oxford was known for its progressive climate. The town was a hub of academia, after all, and its diversity was prone to foster inclusivity and open-mindedness. Yet still, its roots were grounded in tradition. Men didn't kiss men. Women didn't kiss women. Even as the decade edged nearer to the twenty-first century.

Lips still hovered together, Hermia's transfixion with the gesture waned, and suddenly Nathalie was letting out a blood-curdling shriek, shoving Maggie off her.

Maggie, as Helena, continued with the script, pleading with Hermia to remember the value of their friendship, but Catharine could no longer focus on the play. All she could think about was how Maggie's lips had lingered against Nathalie's—the comfortable way they'd lain there.

Apparently, the extra effort they'd put into after-hours 'rehearsal' had paid off in their favor.

This director is huge on innovation, Nathalie had written in one of her letters. *He's given rein to explore scene interpretation, encouraging the cast to challenge the status quo!*

Well.

Catharine sat in her seat, unblinking.

Clearly.

"You see how simple and how fond I am!" On stage, Helena was beseeching Hermia to forgive her.

That dirty, thievin', no good Maggie Mae seemed to be playing in the background.

WHEN THE FINAL CURTAIN FELL, Catharine found herself selfishly relieved the cast wasn't granted a standing ovation. She'd been certain when Nathalie stepped to the apron to take her bow, the house would be on their feet. Her performance was deserving. If Catharine had stood, she knew others would follow.

But instead, she remained seated, her attention firmly directed to her programme. Despite her proximity to the stage and the bright house lights that had come up in the auditorium, she convinced herself that so long as she didn't draw attention, her presence would go undetected. She could escape without Nathalie ever knowing she was there. But when she risked a glance up during the final bow, she found Nathalie staring directly at her.

Catharine couldn't bring herself to smile. And unlike every other performance she'd attended, Nathalie didn't wave. They just held each other's gaze until Catharine finally looked away, gathering her coat and purse, and turning for the door. By the time she reached the foyer, the performers had disappeared into the wings.

"Catharine!" a resonant voice called as she passed the bar. "I didn't take you for the theatre type."

Through the crowd of patrons, she found Timothy Harris, a stipendiary lecturer in Game Theory who had instructed her through several tutorials the previous year.

"Oh, hi," she stopped, caught off guard. "How are you, Mr. Harris?"

"Better now that that's over," he laughed, jerking his head toward the stage. He was young, mid-twenties, a graduate student pursuing his DPhil in Economics. Catharine had found his tutorials rudimentary and, despite his amiable nature, was glad when his name had not appeared on her second-year academic schedule.

Swirling the wine in his glass, he offered a furtive grin. "Please tell me I'm not the only one who felt this play was five acts too long?"

Catharine forced her lips into what she hoped was a polite, yet oppositional smile. She may have been at odds with Nathalie, but she wasn't about to dismiss credit where it was due. All five acts had been exceptional.

"I thought it was very well done."

"Ever the diplomat," he winked, tipping back the rest of his wine before signaling for another. "You just never struck me as someone easily impressed by dramatics." He paused as the boy working the counter appeared with a bottle. "Care for a glass?" Catharine didn't have time to shake her head before he indicated for the bartender to pour a second. "I take it you know someone in the cast?"

"I—" Catharine left the glass on the bar top. "Yes."

"I figured. You're too analytical to be here for pleasure." Again, he beamed in a way that was no doubt meant to be charming.

He was handsome; she wouldn't deny him that. Half the girls in her year went out of their way to seek his attention. Aside from his distinction as the youngest lecturer at Christ Church, he'd also been part of the Oxford University rowing crew that won the inaugural Temple Challenge Cup in Henley three years earlier. Word around the boathouse was, two weeks after the regatta, he'd torn his rotator cuff in a drunken punting accident, and been forced to give up elite competition.

"Are you here with someone?"

Catharine's gaze trailed over his shoulder to the door. She really wanted to be halfway to the Meadow Building by the time the cast started trickling down from the dressing rooms.

"No, I'm—I was just here to support a friend."

"I take it it's true, then—about you and Haverfield?" He leaned back against the bar, the cheap cut of his blazer too snug across his chest.

"I'm sorry?" Catharine's attention snapped back to him.

"Boathouse whispers, you know." Very suddenly, she didn't care for the suggestive nature of his simper. "That you two called it quits."

"We—yes."

"Don't look so alarmed," he leaned closer, conspiratorially, "I'm not one to believe rumors. I never pegged you for that kind of girl. But even if you were," again he smirked, straightening, "who am I to judge? You're still too good for Haverfield. The lad's a cad. It might not seem like it, but him cutting you loose has done you a favor." Nonchalantly, he slid the untouched glass of wine in her direction. "Now come on, have a drink with me. We can talk about the future of your academic trajectory. I know you've said you're not interested in pursuing a DPhil, but you should reconsider. Not many girls have a mind like yours when it comes to numbers. Shame for it to go to waste."

She clenched her fist around the strap of her purse, her fingernails digging into her palm. It was hardly possible to keep pace with the string of insults he was accumulating behind his patronizing smile.

"After graduation, I'll attend INSEAD." There was no point trying to explain why an MBA from the world's leading business school would better serve her ambitions than the Doctor of Philosophy he was presently chasing. Timothy Harris would never leave Oxford. Twenty years from now, he'd be lucky if he were appointed to the title of professor. With his limitations, it was unlikely he'd ever hold a statutory chair.

And she—well, she'd be leading Brooks Corp.

He laughed. "If you're going to shoot for the moon, why not Harvard?"

"HBS is US-centric. INSEAD's emphasis lies in international markets and multicultural collaboration—it's the program that suits me best in the long run."

"I applaud your ambition. Remind me—what's the percentage of women in their program this year? Fifteen percent, was it?"

"Eight."

"Ah. Eight." He took a long sip of his wine before smiling again. "As I said, I respect your confidence. I love to see my students finding their footing in self-assurance."

Catharine was no longer willing to shrug off his condescension. "Confidence comes naturally when it's backed by qualifications. I imagine INSEAD values substance over statistics."

Behind his wine glass, Timothy's smile turned amused. "You know, when you say things like that, you make it very easy to forget how young you are." He set the glass back on the bar, leaning closer. "This plonk is insufferable. Why don't we find something better over at The Jericho?"

Catharine maintained her neutral expression, determined not to let him see how uncomfortable he made her. "Thank you, but I can't."

"What, it's not like you could damage your reputation," he gibed, leaning his elbow on the bar. "But if you're skittish, we could skip the formalities—you could come straight to mine for a nightcap?"

The crowd in the foyer was thinning, the theatre-goers spilling onto the street to continue their Thursday evening. Pinned in the way she was, he was effectively blocking her exit.

"I appreciate the offer, but I don't think it's appropriate, considering your position as my lecturer."

"So proper." His smile didn't waver. "Come on, Catharine—drop the charade."

"If you'll excuse me—"

He didn't move. "Honestly, stop chatting bollocks. We both know you're not a cocktease—"

"I mean it, Mr. Harris—!"

Across the lobby, several loitering patrons turned at the sound of her raised voice. Conscious of their stares, Timothy casually stepped aside.

"I was trying to do you a favor," he hissed, swiping up her untouched wine. "A pity fuck, was all it was. Because let's be real—no one wants the boat club's hand-me-downs."

Quivering with rage, Catharine spun away from the lobby and into the auditorium. The house lights were still up, the stalls empty, without an usher in sight. Before she even knew what she was doing, she found herself pushing through the restricted access door and into the stairwell that led to the dressing rooms.

On the third floor, Catharine found the door she was looking for.

An engraved sign read "Dressing Room Seven A."

Beneath it, two temporary cards were slipped into a laminate holder: *Ms. Nathalie Comtois / Ms. Maggie Chapman.*

Catharine rested her forehead beneath the spyhole on the door, trying to catch her breath. She was shaking from so much more than just her run up the stairs. From more, even, than Timothy Harris and his whispered insults and unwanted advances.

Because, in truth, Timothy was irrelevant. He was just another prick who used his authority to get what he wanted once his charm had failed him. Catharine had dealt with self-entitled boys and imperious men like him her entire life. They just seemed to come with the world she belonged to. And she was not so naive as to think there would be any shortage of them in the future.

What she did care about, however, was that the one person she wanted to see—the one person whose opinion of her *did* matter—was less than ten feet away, and she wasn't even sure if they still had a friendship.

She stepped back, drying her palms on her trousers and trying to pull herself together. Through the gap at the bottom of the door, she could hear muffled voices. Maggie's, in particular—incessant and grating. If the woman ever paused to take a breath, the moment was so brief, Catharine found the action indecipherable.

She closed her eyes. She either had to turn around and head back to the lobby, or drum up the courage to knock. She couldn't stand in the hallway forever.

Counting to seven, she forced her trembling fingers into a fist and rapped against the hardwood. The room momentarily silenced. Catharine considered fleeing down the stairs, but before she could convince her feet to move, the door swung open.

"Oh, Cate!"

It was Maggie.

Catharine suppressed the urge to tell her—to *her*—it was *Catharine*. There was only one person who called her *Cate*.

"Hi," she managed instead, trying to peer over her shoulder into the room.

The woman was taller than she was—something Catharine wasn't accustomed to—and at least five years older. Catharine read in the programme that Maggie had attended the Oxford School of Drama. A surprising revelation, given her obvious inclination toward *Method* acting.

"Is Nathalie…?" Catharine motioned through the doorway.

"Oh. Yes. Of course." Maggie stepped aside to reveal the Frenchwoman sitting at her dressing table, stripping stage makeup from her cheeks with a face flannel.

"Hello, Catharine." Nathalie didn't look over or pause in her administrations, her tone as flat as the blunt eyeliner pencil lying on the floor. "Did you enjoy the show?"

Anger that had ebbed during her deliberation in the hall abruptly resurfaced.

"No," she said, her voice clipped. "Not particularly."

"*Bof,*" Nathalie shrugged, continuing to strip thick mascara from her eyelashes. "*Quel dommage.*"

Her deliberate indifference and refusal to cast so much as a glance in her direction was the tipping point in Catharine's attempt at civil conversation.

"Excuse me," she turned to Maggie, who was still lumbering around the doorway, playing spectator to a scene only meant for two. "Would you give us a moment?"

Maggie's large, doe-like eyes widened. "You want me to leave?"

"Yes." Catharine managed not to blench at her own impudence. She was too angry to care how she was received.

"I'm—" The woman looked around the dressing room. "I'm not quite finished."

"Ten minutes." Catharine grabbed Nathalie's jacket off the back of her chair and held it out to Maggie. "There's no heat in the green room."

For a moment, Maggie stood stunned, looking to Nathalie for direction, but Nathalie's attention remained fixed on her eyelashes.

"Alright," she finally conceded, snatching the coat from Catharine's fingers. "But only ten minutes."

When she had gone, Nathalie dropped her makeup cloth with a sigh and slowly swiveled in her chair.

"You've got a lot of nerve, Catharine."

"Stop calling me that."

"It's your name, isn't it?" She tipped her head to the side, and it was all Catharine could do not to slap the insolence off her face.

She settled for swiping a can of hairspray off the counter. "Stop!"

Again, Nathalie made a show of releasing an exasperated sigh and stood to retrieve the hairspray. "What is it you want, Cate?"

Her uncharacteristic rationality did nothing to calm Catharine's ire, instead acting as a catalyst to heighten her frustration.

What did she want? She'd asked herself that same question a thousand times over. She'd asked it while riding the train home to Henley after *le 14 juillet*. She'd asked it on the plane to Singapore, sitting beside her father. She'd asked it countless nights, lying in bed staring at the centuries-old ceiling of her room in Honour Stone—wondering if any other girl had ever stared at those same beams, trying to answer the impossible. Or was she the only child of a Brooks who'd been born with something wrong with her?

But the question wasn't impossible. She *knew* what she wanted. It had just taken the risk of losing the person she loved for her to accept it.

She turned to Nathalie. "I want you to kiss me."

Nathalie's eyes flashed up, her laugh on the edge of venomous. "Why? Because you watched me kiss Maggie?"

"No." Catharine didn't allow herself to recoil. "I want you to kiss me because I've wanted you to kiss me since you first called me *Mademoiselle Économie* the night we met in Hall. I want you to kiss me because, this morning, instead of studying Nash equilibria, all I could think about was how you put chocolate shavings on your toast. Because I can spend hours walking through Christ Church Meadow, trying to classify the color of your eyes." She faltered, but still managed to hold her gaze. "Because I can't seem to go fifteen minutes without you crossing my mind. And I know you've felt it, too."

Releasing a shaky breath, she silently begged Nathalie to say something. Anything. But she just stood there, holding the can of hairspray.

"I realize," Catharine continued her impromptu monologue, not knowing what else to do, "that I'm the one who's—that I'm the reason we're—where we are. And it's because it terrifies me. And it's also because I don't know if I can ever give you what you want." She swallowed, resisting the urge to fuss with the buttons on her coat. "I'm not—I can't be the person who meets you at the stage door with flowers. I can't—I *won't*," she corrected, aware of the distinct difference between the two, "be someone who can hold your hand at the market. Or kiss you on Magdalen Bridge. And I don't know if it will be enough—if *I* am enough." Finally, her emotions getting the better of her, she was forced to draw the cuff of her coat across her eyes, looking away. "And I hate her." She stared at Maggie's empty seat. "I hate her—and she's done nothing wrong."

For a long beat, Nathalie was silent. Catharine didn't dare look at her, afraid of what rejection she might find. She didn't know what her expectations were before coming here. Nor did she know what she expected now. She only knew she'd had to tell Nathalie. She couldn't bear another night keeping it to herself.

"Did you ever consider," Nathalie finally said, still unmoving, "allowing me to be the judge of what is and isn't enough? Of giving me the chance to decide?" She set the hairspray on the counter, taking a long moment before she turned back around. "Because maybe having part of Cate Brooks is better than having none of Cate Brooks at all."

Catharine didn't dare allow the flicker of hope lodged in her chest to kindle. "Is it too late now?" Her gaze never lifted from Maggie's vacant chair.

"We're—she and I—it's just fun. It doesn't mean anything."

"Does she know that?" asked Catharine carefully.

"She knows my heart is set elsewhere."

"If you and I…" Catharine finally forced herself to look at Nathalie. "If we… I want it to mean something."

To Catharine's surprise, Nathalie laughed. "For someone as brilliant as you are, Catharine Ann Brooks—you really can be quite thick. How do you think it could not mean something—this thing between us?"

An anvil—a boulder—a mountain—felt as if it had been hoisted off her back. The idea that maybe she hadn't messed things up beyond repair brought a lightness to her she wasn't certain she'd ever known. It was a feeling she'd glimpsed laughing on a floor with *pâtes au beurre* tangled in her hair. And again, lying face-to-face on a sofa in the JCR—*Haut-Brion* on their breath.

And somehow, despite her best efforts of self-sabotage, she was being given another chance.

Somewhere down the hallway, a door slammed. Heavy footsteps sounded on the stairs. It was Maggie, Catharine had no doubt—and by the arpeggio of laughter, it appeared she was not alone.

Nathalie glanced toward the door. "Everyone is going to The Lamb and Flag. I—I should really go."

"Yes."

"You could come?"

Catharine released a slow exhale. The laughter was getting closer. "I can't." She couldn't tolerate the thought of being around so many people. "Not tonight. But—I'll see you tomorrow?"

Nathalie nodded, thinking. "I don't get out of lecture until four and have to come straight to the theatre. Come to the show?"

"You want to make me jealous—watching you kiss her again?" Catharine only half laughed.

"I think you're already jealous." Nathalie's smile broadened. "And I like it." Her expression shifted, just as quickly, to one of sincerity. "But I won't be kissing her tonight. Or off that stage again. From here forward, it's just the show, Cate—between her and me. I promise."

Behind them, the door handle turned.

"You'll come?" Nathalie pressed.

"Yes." Catharine glanced over her shoulder to find Maggie and a trio of tipsy stage crew funneling into the room. "I'll wait for you at the stage door."

Walking back to Christ Church, Catharine wasn't certain her feet ever touched the ground. She'd forgotten all about Timothy Harris and rowing and thievin' Maggie Mae. She may not have gotten the kiss she wanted, but she'd gotten so much more.

Chapter Eight

THE NIGHT WAS TOO BRISK for the satin champagne dress Catharine slid over her hips, but she didn't care. She'd hated every skirt and cardigan hanging in her wardrobe. Every jumper was too conventional. No trousers fit quite right.

Refolding the cable-knit top that had once been her go-to on nights out with Edward—the one he'd complained hung too loose, was too conservative, falling to mid-thigh—she stuffed it back in her top drawer.

The slip dress was perfect. Snug, but not too revealing. She liked the way the narrow straps and straight hemline complemented her neck and shoulders, the cool undertones of the fabric bringing out the flaxen of her hair. It didn't matter that it was something she typically would have reserved for a more befitting occasion—there was no rule that said a Friday evening performance in Oxford couldn't be treated like a night out to the West End.

Tugging a cashmere wrap off a coat hanger, she slung it around her shoulders and grabbed her purse.

It was a quarter after five. She didn't need to leave for the playhouse for another two hours. The walk was less than ten minutes, even in heels. The time should have been spent reviewing price elasticity in preparation for Monday's tutorial. Instead, she checked her image one last time in the mirror and dashed out the door.

"Hiya, Catharine!" Matthew Briggs, a second-year physicist, was jogging up the stairs. He waved a folded paper in her direction. "It looks like Mr. Hardy's been at it without his glasses again. I found this in my pidge." He held out the note. Catharine could see her name scripted in the wide, shaky letters she'd grown accustomed to from the elderly porter. It wasn't the first time Mr. Hardy had misread Briggs for Brooks. She doubted it would be the last.

"Oh, thanks, Matthew." Her heart did a little acrobatic flip. She was sure it would be from Nathalie—maybe an acknowledgment of their previous night's conversation, or a few words to say she was looking forward to seeing her again. Nathalie had probably stopped by on her way to the theatre and handed the note off to Mr. Hardy to drop in her pigeonhole. She'd done that before.

Matthew smiled behind his large wireframe glasses. "Secret admirer?"

Catharine abruptly tucked the note, unopened, into her purse, making Matthew laugh.

"Well, that answers that," he grinned. There was nothing about the slight, curly-haired Yorkshire native that was unlikeable. They had come up as freshers together, and by good fortune, Catharine had found him sharing her staircase both years. He was unequivocally intelligent, with a penchant for principia, but his heart was set on entering the archaeological field. The past summer, he'd spent the break at the *Center for Advanced Spatial Technologies* in Arkansas, helping to develop digital mapping software. Catharine had enjoyed teasing him that he'd returned to Oxford with a US twang.

Matthew paused at the top of the stairs. "You look stunning tonight, I should mention," he said, tugging his woolly hat off his head. "Whoever he is is a lucky lad." With a wave, he disappeared down the hall.

Mr. Moore was on shift when Catharine passed through the plodge.

"Off to the Randolph, Catharine?" The porter looked up from his paperwork, brushing back his salt-and-pepper hair.

Catharine had forgotten all about the Christ Church Boat Club pre-season dinner, held the first Friday of term.

"Oh, the Playhouse, actually." She paused at her pigeonhole. There was a notice about a change in lecture venue the following week and, on top of it, an origami raven.

Catharine smiled, forgetting all about the unopened note in her purse. She knew the raven was from Nathalie.

The elegant black birds were Catharine's favorite animal.

"They're like the philosophers of the sky," she'd told Nathalie the summer before, the two of them lying on their backs on the bank of the Isis, watching a gathering of the birds in Meadow Park.

Exceptionally intelligent, with the ability to survive in the harshest of environments—from Arctic tundras to the unforgiving elements of the desert—Catharine had grown fascinated with the resourceful creatures after reading about them in Norse Mythology. As a child, she had dreamt of Huginn and Muninn, the ravens who circled the earth gathering knowledge for Odin, the All-Father. Later, her appreciation for the clever corvids had deepened as she grew to respect their uncanny capacity for empathy and their tendency to form long-term partnerships, mating for life.

"Aren't a flock of them called a *murder*?" Nathalie had asked skeptically, tossing crust from her bread to a waiting swan.

"*Crows* are a murder. Ravens are an *unkindness*."

"I'm not sure that's any better."

Catharine laughed. "Well, they're also known as a *conspiracy* or *treachery*. So take your pick."

"This is only getting worse," Nathalie tugged on one of Catharine's long tendrils of hair. "I love that your favorite animal is literally the omen of death. I would have pegged you as a lover of something gallant—like an eagle. Or wise, like an owl."

"Eagles have been known to flee from birds a tenth of their size. And contrary to popular belief, owls are nowhere near as intelligent as they're made out to be. Ravens, on the other hand, are bold, cunning, and resilient. Besides," she teased, turning to smile at Nathalie through the curtain of meadow grass, "someone has to appreciate the things that are dark, enigmatic, and misunderstood." Without waiting for a response, she'd jumped up, dragging Nathalie to her feet, and pulled her along to Folly Bridge to rent a punt.

Now, on her way out of Tom Gate, she unfolded one of the delicate Origami wings. Nathalie's cramped handwriting was scrawled across the bird's breast.

Maybe they're not misunderstood. Maybe they're just waiting for others of their kind to see them clearly.

Catharine bit her bottom lip, running her finger across the dried ink. Not one thing Edward had ever said made her feel like this.

"O, HELL! TO CHOOSE LOVE by another's eyes!"

In the same seat, in the same row, Catharine watched the same show through a different lens. She found herself captivated by Hermia's fervent devotion to Lysander. No longer did she view Helena as a rival, but instead laughed at the comedic chaos, even finding pity for her lamentation of unrequited love. This time, when Maggie kissed Nathalie, she found her jealousy tamped down by the reassurance it was just another scripted scene— nothing more. Her focus shifted to the brilliance of Nathalie's performance, mesmerized by the crescendo of her voice, the dexterity of her hands, the subtle flicker of her expressive eyes.

When the play was over, Catharine was grateful to see three of Nathalie's Brasenose peers jump to their feet in the front row, leading the sold-out Friday night crowd to an enthusiastic ovation. She stood with the rest of the audience in the stalls, watching the curtain call through the staggered arrangement of heads between her and the stage, and found her pulse jump a beat when Nathalie caught her eye.

For the second night in a row, she couldn't bring herself to smile —but for very different reasons than the evening prior.

It had been one thing to tell Nathalie what she wanted. To admit her year of frustrations, confusion, and unintended injury to their friendship. To confess the feelings she'd been trying to hide.

It was another, now, to act on it.

But it wasn't a question of *if*. Catharine knew her own mind. And she wasn't about to allow her medley of fears to drag her back to where they had started. Not tonight.

Funneling with the rest of the patrons out of the foyer onto the pavement, she slipped around the building and to the stage door. A small crowd had already gathered—mostly other students— waiting for their friends in the cast to come down from the dressing rooms.

Catharine fidgeted with her cashmere wrap beneath her coat and shuffled her programme from hand to hand. One by one, the performers trickled out into the brisk October evening, greeting their entourage with waves and laughter. The man who played *Oberon* swept two small children into his arms, kissing the woman wrangling them on the lips. A cheer went up as a petite, wiry young man appeared on the threshold, pausing to make a dramatic bow. It was the actor who played *Puck*, Catharine realized, hardly recognizing him without his silver body paint and horns.

Shouts of *Bravo* and *You're a legend, Robbie* greeted him as a hail of flowers was tossed his way by a cat-calling group of his peers. He gathered the long-stem roses, tucking one in his teeth, and posed for a photo. It was his stage debut, Catharine had read in the programme. He was a chemistry student at Merton College and had auditioned for the role on a dare. His fellow chemists appeared more than eager to cheer him on, while enjoying ribbing him for the snugness of his costume.

"You looked dead lush in all that Lycra!" said one of the girls, kissing him on the cheek.

"I think it was the loincloth of leaves that did it for me!" A boy— a whole head taller—swatted him on the bum with a flower.

The group departed, sweeping Robbie away with them, chattering about a pub offering two-for-one bevvies.

A few minutes later, Nathalie emerged, framed by the young men who played Demetrius and Lysander.

She was laughing. Dressed all in black—palazzo trousers, polo neck jumper, and wool beret—her eyes swept the surrounding faces until she found Catharine's.

"*Coucou*," she lipped the affectionate greeting, her dark eyes reflecting the dim light of the lamppost. This time, Catharine returned her smile, feeling a fluttering of nerves humming with the allegro rhythm of her heartbeat. She wasn't the only one whose eyes were drawn to the captivating French beauty. A dozen or so well-wishers and local theatre aficionados waved her over, offering cut flowers and chocolates, praising her performance.

"You're going to be a star," a middle-aged man in teal corduroy trousers pressed her fingers between his hands.

Tell her something she doesn't already know, thought Catharine, as Nathalie politely extracted herself from the remaining guests and came to greet her, a few feet off from the others.

"*Hé là, toi !*" Without hesitation, she leaned forward and kissed Catharine's cheeks. "You came."

"You knew I would."

The corners of Nathalie's lips twitched. "I did." Her hand lingered on Catharine's forearm. "Did you get my note?"

"Oh, was that from you?"

"Aren't you very funny?"

"Some people think so."

Nathalie's thumb found the delicate skin of her wrist beneath her cuff. "Not too many, I hope."

Catharine was sure Nathalie could feel her pulse quicken, but before she could answer, a singsong voice interrupted them from behind. "Nathalie!" It was Maggie, who tonight—still frosty from their interaction in the dressing room—did not smile at Catharine. "We're going to *The Jolly Farmers*. Are you coming?" She had an arm linked through the elbow of the boy who played Lysander.

For a moment, Catharine panicked that Nathalie might agree. And worse, that she'd ask her to join them.

The Jolly Farmers was a pub near the City Centre, whispered about for its queer clientele. It wasn't a place Catharine could go. Not without raising questions.

"Not tonight, thanks." Nathalie didn't even glance over her shoulder, her focus never leaving Catharine. "Do you want to go to *Turf Tavern*? They'll still be serving dinner."

The thirteenth-century tavern was a favorite hangout of theirs, just a few minutes walk from Brasenose College. Despite being nestled down a narrow passageway in a secluded courtyard, it would be teeming on a Friday night. But that didn't matter. Catharine simply wanted to be with Nathalie—just the two of them. Together.

"Yes."

With less than an *adieu* to anyone else, Nathalie slipped her arm through Catharine's and pulled her onto Beaumont Street.

"Isn't the boat club dinner tonight?" Nathalie asked as they approached the corner in front of The Randolph. The doors to the handsome Victorian Gothic hotel were wide open, flooding warm foyer light onto the pavement. Laughter filtered through the pointed entry arch from the ground-floor dining room.

Catharine didn't glance inside. "Yes."

"But you're not there?"

"No." They continued past the Martyrs' Memorial, where a handful of students sprawled across the steps, smoking. "I'm—not rowing anymore."

Nathalie stopped short in front of St. Mary Magdalen's Churchyard. "What do you mean?"

Catharine wanted to lie to her, to tell her she had chosen to place her full focus on her academics, and rowing took up too much time.

But she didn't.

"My father didn't want me around the boys at the boathouse anymore."

"So he made you quit rowing? Cate! You loved—"

"Please," she squeezed Nathalie's arm, "just—it doesn't matter. I'm happy tonight, alright? I wouldn't want to be anywhere else." And she meant it. She would have traded all the formal dinners at The Randolph to be strolling down Broad Street with Nathalie, exactly as they were right now.

Surprisingly, Nathalie relented, trailing her fingers along the top of the wrought iron fence containing the two hundred-year-old graveyard.

"Okay."

Catharine knew her well enough to know the conversation would be revisited, but for now, Nathalie let it go.

"You were remarkable tonight," she said after a short silence as they crossed beneath the shadow of the Sheldonian.

"But not last night?"

Out of the corner of her eye, she could see Nathalie was smiling.

She shrugged. "There were a few wobbles to sort."

"On my part or yours?"

"God, you're so arrogant," Catharine laughed, bumping her with her hip. "Just take the bloody compliment, will you?"

"Cate Brooks said I was remarkable," Nathalie announced to the empty passage of Bath Place as they turned onto the narrow brick alley. "I'll file that away forever."

"It'll be the last time I say it if you carry on about it any longer."

"No, it won't." Nathalie stopped her in the dark passage before they reached the tavern. "Shall we wager?"

Whatever brazen retort Catharine intended to deliver dissolved as every fiber in her body registered just how close they were standing. She was acutely aware of Nathalie's hand—slipped down her arm, entwining their fingers. All she had to do was lean forward—to accept the invitation to kiss her.

But just a hundred feet away, laughter and chatter from the courtyard beer gardens wafted around the corner. It wasn't so late that the passage would stay empty for long.

"I guess you'll have to put your money where your mouth is to find out, won't you?" she managed, slowly pulling her composure back together. Releasing Nathalie's hand, she flashed a coy smile over her shoulder and turned toward the tavern—only to stumble as her heel caught the uneven edge of a brick on the walkway.

Behind her, Nathalie laughed. *"Défi relevé !"*

Challenge accepted.

TWO PINTS OF *OLD PECULIER* later—with the crust of a shared toastie growing cold between them—Catharine listened, amused, as Nathalie regaled her with a story of how a boy in her new staircase, discovering she was French, tried to ask her out for a drink.

"He stood in the middle of the landing, his hands on his hips, and very boldly demanded: *voulez-vous prendre un* ver *avec moi ?"*

Catharine laughed. *Ver* was *worm*. *Verre* was *glass*. To an English ear, the words sounded nearly identical, but in the nuances of the French language, he had, in effect, asked if she'd like to take a worm with him.

"You're being a bit harsh, don't you think? I'm sure you knew what he meant."

"Of course I knew what he meant! But I wasn't going to let it go. His accent was terrible!"

"You tell me my accent is terrible!"

"That's only because I want to tease you." Nathalie flicked a crumb of the toastie from her napkin, where it got caught in Catharine's hair. "Your French is perfect, and you know that."

Catharine busied herself trying to pick the bread off her shoulder in an attempt to disguise the blush deepening on her cheeks—not so much from the compliment, but from the furtive brush of Nathalie's foot against her calf beneath the table.

"So, what are we doing for your birthday tomorrow?"

Catharine abandoned the crumb. "How did you know it was my birthday?"

It wasn't something she told anyone. Birthdays had never been a form of enjoyment in her family. They were merely a climacteric event her father used to evaluate the development of her education every three hundred and sixty-five days.

"When we met last year, you said you'd turned seventeen three days earlier. That dinner was on a Sunday, which put your birthday on the previous Thursday. Given the leap year, it would now fall on a Saturday—which happens to be tomorrow."

"And you accuse *me* of paying too much attention to detail." Catharine returned the nudge of her foot.

"I reserve my limited focus only for the things that matter."

Inside the pub, a bell was rung, signifying last orders. Abruptly, Nathalie grabbed the remainder of Catharine's pint and tipped it back before jumping to her feet. "Let's go."

"Where?"

"Somewhere else."

Without further question, Catharine followed her along the maze of narrow passages and into the broader alley. But instead of turning right, under the Bridge of Sighs, back toward Brasenose, she caught Catharine's hand and pulled her through the New College Cloister and onto Queen's Lane.

"So, about tomorrow?" Nathalie resumed the conversation.

As late as it was, and winding their way in the opposite direction of the city centre, the pedestrian path was quiet. Confident in the cover of darkness, Catharine left her hand in Nathalie's warm grasp.

"You have a matinee and evening performance," she reminded.

"I have the morning. I have an hour in between shows. I have the whole night after."

Catharine laughed. "Since when, in the *History of Nathalie Comtois*, have you ever gotten up early before a Saturday matinee?"

Unfazed, Nathalie shrugged. "Never."

"I rest my case."

"Or," Nathalie drew out the word, chastising, "perhaps I just needed something—or *someone*—compelling enough to tempt me from my slumber?"

"Now you're just waxing poetic," Catharine deflected, pressing her lips together to hide her smile.

"And you're avoiding the question."

Turning onto High Street, the dipped beams of a passing bus robbed them of their sanctum of darkness, the headlights illuminating them from head to toe. Self-conscious, and hating herself for it, Catharine dropped Nathalie's hand. "We could get a coffee—before you head to the theatre?"

"The pinnacle celebration—if you were turning eighty, not eighteen!"

"Not everything has to be momentous," Catharine swatted at her, secretly delighted in the playful struggle Nathalie went through to recapture her hand.

"What would be your perfect day?"

Surrounded again in solitude, Catharine leaned against her shoulder, the comfort of Nathalie's hip warm through her dress. It was brisk, but not too cold—the soft blanket of fallen leaves dampening their footsteps. To the right were the treelined gates of the Botanic Garden—the oldest in Great Britain—and opposite—the magnificent Magdalen Tower, the tallest building in Oxford.

This, she thought, wishing she could preserve the moment forever, pressed between glass.

"I could come watch your show again?" she suggested instead.

"Well, that's a given." Nathalie's disappointment in the banality of the answer was evident. "I'd be hurt if you didn't." She prodded her side. "You may want to sit in a different seat, however, or people are going to suspect you're a groupie."

"Who am I to argue?" Catharine said pertly. "You know I've got my sights set on the boy who plays the donkey."

"Then won't you be sad to discover he only has eyes for the boy who plays Demetrius."

Ahead of them, another set of headlights bounced across Magdalen Bridge.

Nathalie stopped. "Come with me," she whispered, raising a sprinkling of gooseflesh as she pressed her lips to Catharine's ear.

Following her off the pavement, they slipped through an open gap in the wall, where a sign advertised *Boats for Hire*.

Catharine knew the ramp to the water well. It led to the Magdalen Bridge Boathouse.

"You know the boathouse is closed?" she said, stating the obvious.

They were all alone, hidden behind ivy-draped walls, with the slow-moving water of the River Cherwell at their feet.

"Is it?" Nathalie feigned surprise before blithely bypassing the brightly painted building that rented punts and sold souvenirs to tourists on holiday.

With no choice but to follow, Catharine carefully picked her way along the slick cobblestone—a task made infinitely more difficult in heels designed for marble and travertine.

"What are we doing?" she called, steadying herself against the damp stone wall as she reached the landing.

A dozen steps ahead of her, Nathalie paused at the iron gate extending over the water—a barrier intended to discourage trespassers from climbing onto the dock after sunset—and then, with no further hesitation, grabbed the furthest bar and swung herself to the other side, landing deftly on her feet.

"Nat!" Catharine hissed, reaching through the gate to grab the hem of her jumper. "Are you daft? We're going to get in trouble!"

"No one's here." She glanced at her watch. "Besides, for the next thirty-three minutes, you'd still be charged in Youth Court. A slap on the wrist for trespassing."

"You're not funny."

"Says who?" Nathalie casually draped her arms through the iron bars separating them and caught hold of Catharine's elbows. Slowly, her expression shifted, the teasing gone as she gently pulled her forward. "Cate." The word was just a breath. "Come here."

For a moment, they stared at one another through the bars, the rusting gate between them. In the dim light of the street lamps shining down from the bridge, Catharine could see the fluttering pulse at Nathalie's temple, where her beret had slipped back on her forehead. She could hear her stilted breath over the gentle ripple of water beneath the dock—a marked contrast to the roar of blood rushing between her ears.

Trailing a hand up her arm, Nathalie found skin beneath the collar of her coat, her knuckles tracing her jawline. Catharine found herself unable to breathe, and closed her eyes as fingers tangled into the hair at the nape of her neck, drawing her closer. She became only vaguely conscious of the cold iron pressed against her cheek, and far more aware of the brush of lips against her own—soft, warm, brief.

Edward had been her first kiss. Their second date—a rugby match between Christ Church and Queen's College—he'd called her dim for not knowing what a *try* was, and when she'd looked away, embarrassed, he'd roughly spun her back to face him, and kissed her hard in front of his friends. "Don't be sore," he'd scolded when she didn't laugh.

Standing on the punt platform beneath Magdalen Bridge, she would have traded anything to rewind the past twelve months and begin again—like this. To give Nathalie her first kiss.

The soft caress of Nathalie's palm slipped to her cheek, and Catharine opened her eyes.

"*C'est encore ce que tu veux ?*"

Was it still what she wanted?

"Yes." Uncertain she'd managed any sound, she nodded.

Nathalie smiled, her thumb brushing across her lips. "You said you couldn't kiss me on Magdalen Bridge—" her eyes flicked to the towering semi-circular Georgian arches stretching up behind them "—it seemed like a fair compromise—beneath it."

Catharine laughed, feeling some of her tension dissipating, and was surprised to find her fingers gripped around the flaking iron bars. "So you didn't drag me here to steal a punt?" She lifted a hand to toy with a tendril of Nathalie's silky, dark hair.

"Not on the first date. There'll be time for that later."

Catharine looped the strand around one of her fingers. She knew she could step out of her heels, knot the hem of her dress above her knees, and climb around the gate the way Nathalie had earlier. She could join her on the other side, removing the barrier between them. It was what she wanted—it was what every thread of her being was begging her to do. But there was another part of her, a patient part of her, that wasn't ready to let go of this suspended feeling, wanting to linger in it forever—caught somewhere between a place of longing and anticipation.

A part that demanded, on this perfect night, in this Elysian moment, she just be happy with this.

To satisfy the one without disregarding the other, she settled for wrapping her arms around Nathalie's neck and drawing their faces together—finding her mouth again, this time with more urgency, more fervor. Learning, for the first time, the sweetness of her taste, the caress of her tongue between parted lips, the overwhelming desire for one another.

When they finally stepped apart, breathless, the smell of rust on their skin and clothes, it was Nathalie who laughed, looking as shaken as Catharine felt.

"You don't kiss like an English girl."

"Maybe you've been kissing the wrong ones, then."

The Frenchwoman's eyes brightened at the barbed retort as she swung back around the extension of the gate protruding over the water.

"Not for lack of trying."

"*Touché*," Catharine conceded, slipping her arm around Nathalie's waist as they slowly ascended the ramp to High Street.

On the return walk to Christ Church, they skipped the city streets, instead opting to skirt along the hedged walls of the Botanic Garden, where they could pick up Deadman's Walk that ran behind Merton College.

The footpath was narrow, unlit, and in the small hours of the morning, entirely deserted.

"Let's go to Soho—after my show."

They'd stopped for the second time in a hundred yards to steal a kiss beneath the bough of an elm tree.

Catharine hooked her thumbs through the belt loops on Nathalie's trousers, relishing her newfound license to simply touch her. "You won't get out until after ten."

"There's a late train that leaves at eleven."

"It's two hours into the city—"

"An hour and forty minutes," Nathalie corrected.

Catharine laughed. "And what exactly is in Soho?" For all of her time in London, the closest she'd ever come to Soho was to visit The British Museum. Her father dismissed the district as a Bohemian mecca, known only for its edgy vibe and gritty reputation—code to indicate a socioeconomic divide and ties to prostitution.

"Strangers who would never think twice if they saw me kiss you on a street corner. People—" Nathalie chose her words carefully "—more like us."

Catharine wasn't so sheltered as not to realize there were places where people like Nathalie—people like *her*, she forced the notion into objectivity—lived and worked and congregated. Brighton. Amsterdam. Berlin. Barcelona. Paris. But her perception of such avenues was limited to men in drag and women in suits, performing on stages lit with neon and glitter. Not everyday life. Not regular people. Not two perfectly normal students from Oxford.

"Nobody would know us?"

"Do you know anyone in Soho?"

"No."

"Then I imagine you're safe." Nathalie resumed walking, Catharine's hand in hers.

"Have you been there before?"

"Yes."

"Other *English* girls?" Catharine needled.

"Wouldn't you like to know?"

"Ha," Catharine scoffed. "Not really."

By the time they reached Christ Church, it was after 1 AM. The Meadow Building entrance was locked, forcing them to take St Aldate's to reach the porters' lodge at Tom Gate.

"So—what time for coffee?"

"You're not really going to get up and have coffee with me before your show?" Reluctantly, Catharine widened the distance between them as they passed the police station. "You'd have to be up by eight."

"Then I'll meet you at Spires Café at seven-thirty."

"You don't have to. I'll still come to the show. I'll go with you to Soho."

"I want to."

Not as badly, Catharine thought, as she wanted to reach out to touch her—to kiss her one final time for the night. But the porters' lodge was less than fifty yards away. There was a cluster of shadows strolling down the street. The sound of laughter trickled down Aldate.

"Okay."

"I'll bring you *un gâteau au yaourt.*"

"Yogurt cake?" Catharine raised a brow, skeptical.

"It's what my *maman* makes for my birthdays. Don't knock it 'til you've tried it—"

"*Miss Brooks.*"

Nathalie was cut off.

The voice was jarringly out of place. Low, staccato, commanding. A voice Catharine had known since she was a child —a voice belonging to her father's valet, Dougal Fraser.

She spun, startled, toward the figure approaching them on the street.

"Mr. Fraser?" A shard of ice felt like it had been wedged between her shoulder blades.

"A message was left for you this afternoon. Your father requests your presence at Honour Stone."

Catharine thought about the unopened note in her purse—the one that had been delivered to Matthew Briggs. The one she'd forgotten all about on her way to the playhouse.

"I—" she glanced at Nathalie, her throat constricting. "I can come in the morning."

"Unfortunately, Miss Brooks, the colonel instructed me to retrieve you tonight."

"Cate—"

"I'm sorry." Catharine shrank from the hand Nathalie reached toward her. "I'll see you Monday, alright?" Unable to look her in the eye, she followed obediently behind her father's valet.

Chapter Nine

The American engineer, whom Catharine had immediately appraised as little more than a glorified salesman in cowboy boots, relentlessly droned on. His pitch was simple: he wanted Colonel Brooks to shift the Brooks Corp manufacturing plant away from LORAN-C receivers, a system he insisted was nearing obsolescence, and invest in the newly emerging GPS technology.

The excessive spiel was pointless; as soon as Catharine saw that Mr. Kobayashi was attending the meeting, she knew her father already planned to move forward with the innovative redirection in production. The Japanese businessman—one of Brooks Corp's most prominent partners in the Asian tech market—would not have flown all the way from Nagoya simply to listen to a sales presentation.

Whose time the colonel was wasting—hers or the American's—Catharine hadn't decided.

More than likely, it was the former.

"I'm telling you, Brooks—this is your chance to get in on the ground floor of something colossal!"

Catharine bit the inside of her cheek to try to keep from yawning.

She hadn't slept in over thirty hours. Not since she'd woken at six the previous morning.

The night before, after leaving Nathalie at Tom Gate, Mr. Fraser drove her straight to Honour Stone. She'd stepped through the archway of the main entrance shortly after 2 AM and been escorted directly to her father's library.

The colonel was at his desk flipping through the Chinese business publication, *Economic Daily*.

"You were expected eight hours ago."

Catharine knew better than to try to explain.

"I'm sorry."

He glanced up, taking in her rust-stained dress and disheveled hair, and flung the paper into his bin. His mood had not been generous enough to offer her the opportunity to change.

"Sit down. We need to go over the R&D and market forecast reports for the navigation department before morning."

A task he had dragged on until sunrise, before ordering her to shower and dress for an 8 AM meeting at the *Brooks Marine Technology Division* manufacturing headquarters in Reading.

"GPS," the American continued, slapping his palm on the briefcase-sized receiver he'd demonstrated earlier, "is the way of the future!"

Colonel Brooks inspected his meticulously maintained nails. "It is a significant risk—changing platforms."

"Significant risk, significant reward, Brooks. As a man of industry, you know as well as I do—fortune favors the bold!"

Absently, Catharine wondered how long her father would allow the man to get away with calling him *Brooks*.

"In my experience, Mr. Shaw, fortune favors the well-informed." He deliberately checked his watch. "Catharine?" The colonel's eyes flicked to her. "Your input?"

She knew he wasn't actually interested in her opinion. His mind had been made up before Gregory Shaw's plane ever left the ground in Houston. He was only testing her, challenging her knowledge.

"Mr. Shaw," Catharine had to clear her throat from the hours of silence, "you mentioned GPS receivers offer global coverage. But with selective availability in place, won't accuracy still be degraded for civilian use? How does the minimal improvement in precision justify the exorbitant cost for Brooks Corp to transition from the already reliable capabilities of terrestrial navigation systems?"

"Oh, darlin'," the salesman drawled, fiddling with the American flag pinned on his lapel, "selective availability isn't something you need to worry your pretty little head over. I'm sure your old man here can see the bigger picture. The Global Positioning System may be in its infancy, but make no mistake—it's leading the charge into a new era!"

Catharine resisted the urge to look to her father for guidance. "While I appreciate that it may be the vanguard of tomorrow, Mr. Shaw, at present, LORAN-C provides a proven, cost-effective, reliable ground-based operation with pinpoint accuracy within 0.25 nautical miles near critical shipping lanes. GPS, as I understand, is hindered by your government's mandates to prevent civilian access to high-precision data, limiting its current utility for applications requiring exact navigation."

To Catharine's discomfiture, the American laughed, slapping his thigh with a heavy hand and looking toward the colonel.

"Well, damn, Brooks—you must be about ready to lock her up in Fort Knox—Tower of London, I suppose, in your case. Beauty, brains, the whole package! I bet you keep a loaded shotgun handy with all the boys trying to win her over."

The sharp tang of iron coated her tongue, and Catharine realized she'd bitten her cheek hard enough to draw blood. She needed her father to say something, *anything*, to defend her.

Instead, it was Mr. Kobayashi—a quiet, observant man Catharine had known since she was a child—who stepped forward.

"I believe you will find, Mr. Shaw, that Miss Brooks' understanding of the global shipping industry is both comprehensive and remarkably insightful. Her keen mind and vision for the future are exactly what this industry needs to embrace innovation. I do not recommend you devalue her considerations."

Catharine could tell from Mr. Shaw's expression that he had not realized the reserved Japanese investor spoke English. Up until that point, he had conversed with Colonel Brooks only in his native language.

"I meant no offense to Miss Brooks, Mr. Kobayashi," the man backpedaled, offering an awkward bow Catharine could only assume was meant to be an eshaku. "I'm merely impressed. My own daughter's probably home right now watching *Beverly Hills, 90210*, and this lovely young lady is here giving a masterclass on the logistics of navigational formulation." He blew a low whistle through his smirk. "I imagine there's not much you don't know, Miss Brooks?"

What Soho was like on a Saturday night.

Catharine did not answer.

"I believe our business has concluded," said the colonel, growing impatient. He exchanged a glance with Mr. Kobayashi before turning his attention back to the salesman. "Brooks Corp is interested in partnering with *GeoStar*—"

"You're making a mighty fine decision, Brooks—"

"—under certain conditions."

The Texan quieted, not so oblivious to miss the implication that the coming terms would not be to his liking.

"The first," continued the colonel, "and most pressing—Brooks Corp can only commit to a substantial equity investment if we acquire a controlling interest in *GeoStar*—"

"I'm sorry?" Gregory Shaw blinked. "Mr. Brooks, as discussed— the offer is ten percent. It is the highest percentage I'm authorized to—"

"Then I am afraid we have all wasted our time here today."

Catharine watched her father calmly begin to pack up his notes in a performance she had witnessed on an endless number of occasions. She didn't need the scene to play out to know exactly how it would end.

"I could likely negotiate twenty-five."

"I'm sorry, Mr. Shaw." The colonel snapped his leather attaché closed. "Mr. Kobayashi and I have other matters to attend. Safe travels on your return to Houston."

"Wait!" The man's voice cracked as he scrambled to block the door. "Just—let me make a few phone calls!"

"Fifteen minutes." Colonel Brooks flicked a long finger toward the phone hanging on the wall before turning to Mr. Kobayashi. "Tea?"

"Please."

The pair filed out of the conference room door. There was no invitation for Catharine to join them.

Not wanting to be left alone with the Texan, Catharine slipped into the hall leading toward the production floor.

She found Mr. Mills, the plant foreman, standing over the massive assembly of a low-frequency transmission antenna, measuring the diameter of a conductive rod with a micrometer.

"Hello, Miss Brooks." He smiled when he saw her. "Geoff was hoping you'd come today. I think he's in the workshop."

Catharine watched his practiced hands take the measurement, wipe the rod clean, and then take the measurement again—an act born of years spent mastering the art of precision. She wondered if he had any idea that, just two hundred feet away, her father was preparing to turn his life on end. Would the shift toward digital technologies leave space for a dedicated craftsman like Mr. Mills, whose family had worked for Brooks Corp for generations?

She watched for a few more moments over his shoulder before bending to retrieve a fallen pen at his feet, and returned it to his clipboard.

"I hope one day I will be able to approach my responsibilities with even half the skill and grace you bring to yours, Mr. Mills."

He laughed, the pronounced wrinkles at the corners of his eyes deepening. "Rest assured, Miss Brooks—as an old man who's had the pleasure to watch you grow from an ankle-high tot into an impressive young woman—a lack of skill and grace will never be your shortcomings."

Leaving him to his work, Catharine wound her way through the rows of assembly lines and workstations, where technicians in lab coats soldered components onto circuit boards and adjusted oscilloscopes to measure and analyze signal waveforms.

She found Mr. Mills' son, Geoff, at the rear of the workshop, lying on his back beneath a hoist supporting the motor of a conveyor belt.

"Oh, bollocks!" He cursed, burning his fingers on the cigarette he'd tried to hide in his palm, causing him to bash his head against the bottom of the motor. "I thought you were your father!"

Catharine dropped to sit on the empty mechanic's creeper beside him. "Just what every girl wants to hear. Thanks."

He sat up, rubbing his forehead, and took a drag off the cigarette. "It's your shadow. It's got that ramrod Brooks authority." He offered her the fag.

Catharine took it and promptly put it out on the concrete.

"Hey—!"

"It's *your* father that's going to give you a good hiding if he finds you smoking around the capacitors."

Geoff rolled his eyes.

He'd been a fixture in her life since before she could walk. Like his father and uncle, his mother was also employed by the Brooks family, working as a housekeeper at Honour Stone. Just six months younger than she was, Catharine couldn't remember a time when he hadn't been around.

She saw a lot less of him now, however, since he'd been hired on at the factory.

"I made you something." He rocked onto his knees, digging through the deep pockets of his canvas work trousers.

"Why?"

"Well, it's obvious, I should think. As of today, you're finally old enough to get married without your old man's blessing—I figured I might as well try my luck." His grin was lopsided, his chestnut eyes shining.

Catharine knew he was teasing. It was a long-standing joke—the way he fancied her. He'd never made it a secret. At just seven years old, he'd stood in the rose garden and boldly—albeit in a whisper, so Mrs. Ainsley wouldn't hear—declared his undying devotion. To prove his sincerity, he'd then braved sneaking into the Honour Stone kitchen to pilfer freshly baked scones from the chef, which they'd eaten behind cover of the cherub water fountain.

Not much had changed in the past ten years. Catharine still knew he had a fondness for her, and Geoff still knew he didn't stand a chance. But that never stopped him from giving her a hard time about it.

He dropped a brown-paper-wrapped parcel in her lap.

Tugging loose the hemp tie string, she unfolded the paper. "You're asking me to marry you with a—" she paused, turning the object over, making certain she knew what it was "—letter opener?"

"That's not just any letter opener!" He snatched it from her grasp. "I made it myself! Forged the steel. Carved the handle—see, it's an oar." He flipped it deftly in his hand, holding it up to show the finely detailed carving of what indeed was a rowing blade.

Catharine pressed her lips together, unexpectedly touched by the gesture, hoping he'd never find out she didn't row anymore.

"It's really lovely, Geoff."

"I know it's a bit naff—"

"Don't be silly. I love it—I mean it." She leaned over, kissing his cheek, and laughed to see him color.

"I bet it's not the *cutting-edge* proposal you imagined," he grinned.

She groaned at the pun, but her attention was diverted to the overhead speakers, where her name was being called through the PA system.

"Bugger," Geoff shoved to his feet to offer her a hand. "You better go. But hey—if you're down from uni for Bonfire Night, there's going to be a do over on Remenham Hill."

"I'll let you know." She grabbed the letter opener and slid it into her purse. "Thanks again, Geoff."

"You embarrassed yourself today." The colonel drummed his fingers on his knee, his jaw set at a dangerous angle. "I expected more of you than that."

Catharine stared out the window of the Rolls-Royce as it wound through the Brooks estate parklands. With the glow of Honour Stone approaching, she'd hoped to make it to the privacy of his library before her father belittled her for all the ways she'd disappointed him; for every wrong breath she'd taken.

She closed her eyes. What did it matter? It was nothing Mr. Fraser hadn't heard before. After years of driving for the Brooks family, he had been privy to it all.

"*Pinpoint* accuracy within a quarter mile? What foolery is that? There's nothing *pinpoint* about it. You should have been focused on profitability, technical reliability, long-term viability. If you were thinking strategically, you'd be asking how we can corner the GPS market instead of blustering over feet and meters."

The rumble of tires over cobblestone indicated they'd pulled onto the broad circular courtyard of Honour Stone. Reluctantly, Catharine opened her eyes. It was shortly after eight o'clock. In Oxford, the curtain at the playhouse would have just risen. On stage, Hermia would be boldly defying her father, Theseus, declaring she would rather live and die a virgin than marry Demetrius, whom she does not love.

So will I grow, so live, so die, my lord,
Ere I will yield my virgin patent up
Unto his lordship, whose unwishèd yoke
My soul consents not to give sovereignty.

Theseus would then give Hermia three choices:

> Marry the man he has chosen for her.
> Face execution for denying her father's will.
> Vow chastity and live as a nun.

Catharine felt certain she knew which option Nathalie would choose. She was too stubborn to submit to patriarchal demands—and too passionate to live the austere life in a convent.

Herself, on the other hand…

She waited obediently to see if there was more the colonel had to say, but as soon as Mr. Fraser opened his door, her father gathered his attaché and left her beneath the porte-cochère.

HALF AN HOUR LATER, SEATED in the formal dining hall, Emily Brooks sought to lighten the mood as the three members of the Brooks family dined in an uncomfortable silence.

"Catharine—" her tone was a half-pitch too bright, "—tomorrow, why don't we go sailing?"

Catharine pushed her fish around her plate. She knew the seared Dover sole à la Meunière, with its quenelle of wild mushroom duxelles and slow-cooked fondant potatoes, was her mother's subtle attempt to celebrate. The meal was one of Catharine's favorites.

But tonight, she had no appetite.

"I really should get back to Oxford. There is reading I need to do before Monday." All day she'd clung to the hope that if she could get out of Henley by morning, she and Nathalie could spend the day together, even if it wasn't in Soho.

At the head of the table, her father set down his fork.

"Mr. Fraser tells me last night you were at the theatre—that after the performance, you went out drinking with a friend. Was I misinformed?"

The earthy aroma of the duxelles became abruptly off-putting.

"No." She didn't raise her eyes from her plate.

"So, you made that choice, knowing entirely well your obligations remained unmet?"

"No. I mean, I…"

"Did you not just tell your mother you had unfinished reading to attend?"

"Benjamin." Emily's voice was quiet—a decoy attempting to draw his attention from his intended target. "It's quite all right, I —"

He ignored her, his focus drilled onto Catharine. "Well?"

"I meant only to review again."

"Then you can do so tomorrow evening. In the morning, you will accompany your mother sailing."

A KNOCK AT HER DOOR jolted Catharine awake. Panicked she'd overslept, she bolted upright in bed.

The gilded face of her clock read ten-thirty. Taking a quick glance out the window, she was surprised to find it was still dark. It meant it wasn't morning—she'd been asleep less than an hour.

"Come in."

She knew it wouldn't be her father. After his initial knock, he didn't wait for permission to enter.

"I'm sorry to wake you."

Catharine tugged on the Victorian brass lamp on her bedside table. She blinked up at her mother, who came to stand at the foot of her bed. "Is everything all right?"

"Your father has left to meet Mr. Kobayashi—he'll be traveling with him to Nagoya. I just," she paused, her fingers nervously working at the tie of her dressing gown, "I wanted you to know, if you'd rather head to Oxford, I don't mind. I know how busy things are at the start of term."

Catharine drew her knees to her chin. As much as she wanted to accept her mother's offer, she also didn't want to risk placing her in the trajectory of her father's wrath. "It's all right, Mum. I think it's better if I stay here."

"I won't tell him, Catharine."

"He'll ask." She hugged her legs to her chest. "And I don't want you to have to lie for me."

"May I?" Emily sighed, motioning to the side of the bed where she waited for Catharine's blessing before taking a seat. "Why don't you call your friend Nathalie? Ask her to join us?"

Catharine's head snapped up, searching her mother's face for any indication there was more to the query than she was letting on. There wasn't, she decided. It was just an innocent attempt to bridge the growing chasm in their relationship.

"I don't think sailing is much her thing."

"How about lunch, then? We could go to the Red Lion—or Villa Marina?"

"I'm sorry," Catharine turned onto her side, pulling the covers up to her shoulders, "it's really late."

Emily placed a tentative hand on her hip. "Please don't close me out, Catharine. I'm not your enemy."

She didn't care what her mother said—she may not have been her enemy, but she certainly wasn't her friend.

"I'm curious, Mum: what did you do for your eighteenth birthday?"

Aware of where the question was leading, Emily's shoulders sank. "I went sailing—with my dad."

Catharine stared at the cream and gold damask pattern of her duvet. "Today, I learned the difference between negotiation and coercion—and that when one company is significantly larger than another, what is presented as an agreement is often merely the smaller entity conceding under disproportionate influence in an effort to retain a fraction of their market share."

For a long moment, the only sound in the room was the swing of the pendulum from the antique Tompion clock perched on her mantel.

At last, Emily stood. "I'm sorry, Catharine. I..." Her voice drifted off, and Catharine said nothing. In the threshold, she paused. "Please call your friend. We can pick her up at the station first thing in the morning." Closing the door, her footsteps retreated down the hall, and Catharine was left alone.

The old manor shifted and creaked, settling in around her. In the glow of her bedside lamp, particles of ash filtered up from her hearth and danced across the room. Ash from today, ash from five hundred years ago—she would never know.

Turning off her light, she closed her burning eyes, trying to abate the reverberating blow of the bass drum resounding in her head. She was exhausted. The lack of sleep from the past two days settled over her like a slow-moving wave she couldn't outrun. There was nothing she wanted more than to sink beneath her covers, permitting the darkness to sweep her into the promise of oblivion. But the carousel of static cycling through her thoughts wouldn't turn off.

In truth, she *did* want to call Nathalie. She needed to apologize for the previous night, and ask how her show had gone. She wanted to tell her she was thinking about her—that all day, she'd just wanted to hear her voice.

Her father would be halfway to London by now. There was no risk of him listening in on the call.

Restless, she flipped onto her back, reaching for the braided silk tassel of her lamp and tugging it on.

It wasn't quite eleven. Nathalie's show would have been over for less than an hour, and without any need to catch the late-night train, it was likely she would still be out with Maggie and the rest of her friends.

And who could blame her? It wasn't her fault Catharine had ruined their plans.

Wrestling down the bitter pill of jealousy threatening to overcome her, Catharine snatched the old-fashioned rotary phone off her bedside table and plopped it down on her pillow. She knew Nathalie's new staircase number by heart. The night before, at Turf Tavern, Nathalie had playfully utilized the burnt end of a matchstick to write it on her palm.

Call once—allow it to ring no more than seven times—if no one answered, go to bed.

That was the deal she made with herself.

Tucking her finger into the circular dial, she rotated it clockwise, listening to the electrical pulses as she waited for the call to connect.

As it was, a boy answered on the second ring.

Catharine stumbled over Nathalie's name.

"The French girl?" he questioned, stifling a yawn. "No clue—I'm not her keeper."

"Do you think you could knock?" asked Catharine. The plonker was probably the same boy who had invited Nathalie out for a worm.

A few minutes later, she was surprised when Nathalie's voice came across the line.

"I—didn't think you'd be in," she admitted, at a loss for what to say.

"I came straight home after curtain, hoping you might call."

Catharine cradled the receiver between her neck and shoulder, unable to stifle the sigh of relief as her head sank deeper into her pillow.

"I'm really sorry I missed your show."

Twenty-five miles away, Nathalie seemed to understand she was sorry for so much more.

"There will always be another." She paused. "I wish we'd been able to spend your birthday together."

Once again, Catharine considered her mother's offer to ask Nathalie to come to Henley. She wasn't certain it was a good idea. But she also wasn't certain she could wait until Monday to see her.

"I—I know it's not exactly Soho, but—is there any chance you'd be willing to come down here tomorrow? I have to go sailing. But, my mother—she said, if you wanted, we could pick you up at the station. That you could join us. I mean, obviously, only if you—"

"Do *you* want me to come, Cate?"

"Yes." Catharine didn't hesitate. Despite her reservations about allowing Nathalie anywhere near her life outside of Oxford, she wanted nothing more than to be close to her. "Please."

"Do you know how much I'd have to like you if I came?" It was impossible to miss the smile in Nathalie's voice.

"Well, I know how much you hate the water, so..." Catharine hugged the phone. "But I can promise you, the objective of sailing is to remain above the surface."

"Just so you know, that's not comforting. I hadn't even consid-ered the alternative." Nathalie deliberated. "I assume you'd want to leave at some God-awful time in the morning?"

"Whenever you get here—but," Catharine wavered, "by eight would be ideal."

"You are something else, Cate Brooks," Nathalie tutted.

Somewhere in the background, a woman's voice badgered Nathalie to get off the phone. She wanted to call her boyfriend.

Nathalie cursed at her in French before returning her attention to Catharine. "I'll be there at eight. *Rêve de moi.*"

Dream of me.

Catharine didn't have a chance to tell her she would before the phone went dead.

For a while after, she lay staring at her ceiling, counting the hours until morning.

It wasn't wise, she knew, inviting Nathalie to come. Even if her father was six thousand miles away, with the shift in dynamic between them, Henley was no longer safe.

But this was also her life. This was the world she belonged to. And she didn't know how to keep her two separate lives from colliding.

What she was certain of, however, was that she wanted to find a way for Nathalie to exist in them both.

Chapter Ten

"WHY, THANK YOU, NATHALIE. LOVELY to see a young woman raised to show such consideration for their elders." Emily cast a faux-indignant glare at Catharine, who had jumped off the boat and onto the dock without pausing to offer her arm.

Catharine huffed her disregard, kneeling to snug up the stern line. Not once in all the years they'd been sailing together had she ever witnessed her mother accept help stepping from a vessel of any kind.

"You know what you ought to do with her, Mrs. Brooks?" chimed Nathalie, gallantly assisting Emily to alight. "Send her with me to Bordeaux for Easter. My mother will have her whipped into shape for you in no time."

"A tempting offer," said Emily, her attention diverted to securing the bow.

Through the fluttering canvas of the uncleated sail, Nathalie caught Catharine's eye, her smile turning coy. "A good old-fashioned French education might be exactly what she needs."

Catharine felt her cheeks crimson and prayed the brisk wind could be blamed.

She hadn't been able to look at Nathalie all morning. Not since the Frenchwoman stepped off the seven-forty train, greeted her mother with a *You look stunning, Mrs. Brooks* smile, then whispered *But nowhere near as stunning as your daughter* as she chastely kissed Catharine's cheeks hello. Or when Catharine had been forced to reach around her—aware all too well of the warmth of their bodies pressed together—as she taught her how to raise the main. Or when they'd sat side-by-side in the cramped cockpit of the sailing dinghy, and out of sight, Nathalie had trailed a slow fingertip up her calf.

"Catharine—!" Her mother's admonishment dragged her from her reverie, "—you've tied that cleat hitch upside down."

She had, she realized, quickly refastening the knot she'd been able to tie with her eyes closed since she was four years old.

After Catharine raised the centerboard and bagged the sails, she stepped off the short gangway to join her mother and Nathalie on the Thames Path.

"Well." Emily tugged the zipper of her deck jacket up to her chin. "What do you girls say to lunch?"

It was after one. Catharine had been counting down the minutes until they could get ashore, bid a quick adieu, and head up to Oxford.

"I'm sorry, Mum—"

"We'd love to, Mrs. Brooks."

The pair spoke over each other.

Catharine tried to cast a pointed look in Nathalie's direction, but she was blithely ignored.

"Wonderful! I was thinking the Compleat Angler?"

"Mum! That's all the way in Marlow—"

"Honestly, Catharine—it's a fifteen-minute drive. Don't make such a fuss."

Catharine understood why her mum wanted to go to Marlow. Henley was a small town. Anywhere local they dined along the waterfront, they were bound to run into someone they knew. Marlow—similarly quaint, and equally charming—was just far enough away to offer a modicum of separation from the Henley gossip wheel.

It was the same reason Emily had chosen to drive today herself. Even if Catharine wasn't expressly forbidden to have a friend down from university, lessening the chance of it getting back to the colonel simply made things easier on them both.

"Fine," she conceded, knowing her mother was trying to find whatever way she could to fit into her life.

Twenty minutes later, with seared scallops and oysters on the half shell ordered, and a crisp bottle of Chablis sweating on the waterfront table, Catharine stood, excusing herself to the cloakroom to wash away the river spray.

She pretended not to hear Nathalie's trailing footsteps until the door clicked shut, enclosing them inside the empty ladies' facility.

"I can't believe you agreed to lunch!" Catharine spun to face her.

"Are you in a rush to get somewhere?" Nathalie casually leaned against the black granite counter, her smirk reflected in the brass fixtures of the basin.

A ridiculous, nonsensical, entirely inappropriate thrill climbed Catharine's spine.

They were in a barside lavatory, inside one of the most opulent hotels in Buckinghamshire. Her mum was browsing the *menu de saison* a hundred feet away. At any second, another guest could walk in from the busy Sunday brunch.

And still, foolish as she knew it was, Catharine grabbed Nathalie's hand and tugged her into the nearest cubicle.

It was the first time they'd been alone since the walk from Magdalen Bridge. She had worried her tendency toward shyness might make her awkward, after what had passed between them. That she wouldn't know what to say, or how to proceed.

After all, it hadn't been like this with Edward. She'd spent the entirety of their relationship trying to avoid him, to distance herself from his hands, his mouth, forever uncomfortable the moment they found themselves alone.

This wasn't that at all. Whatever concerns had weighed on her since parting Friday night had vanished by the time her fingers were buried in Nathalie's rich mahogany hair.

"You're going to get us in trouble," Nathalie admonished, even as she reached behind her and fumbled to lock the door.

She tasted like autumn—windblown and river-stained, her lips chapped from hours on the water, the blossoms of her cheeks still erubescent from the morning chill that clung to the air.

If Nathalie was surprised by the fervency with which Catharine found her mouth with hers, she didn't let on. Instead, the intensity of her response was returned with equal measure, her arms wrapped around Catharine's neck as they stumbled against the partition wall.

"I'm sorry about yesterday," Catharine finally whispered, her forehead resting against Nathalie's as she paused to catch her breath.

"It's fine, Cate. It's not your fault."

It wasn't her fault, but it also wasn't fine. She knew—at eighteen years old—her life should be her.own. How could she explain to Nathalie—with her unshackled independence and effortless autonomy—that this fledgling relationship between them was the first decision she'd ever made that truly felt like *hers*.

Somewhere behind them, the low droning music from the bar momentarily grew louder as the door to the lavatory swung open, and footsteps sounded on the tile.

Catharine stiffened, acutely aware of their two pairs of feet visible beneath the narrow gap at the bottom of the cubicle.

"Look what you got us into," Nathalie breathed, her smile growing arch. Instead of drawing away, she leaned closer, brushing her lips to the tender skin behind her ear, her enjoyment evident at Catharine's rising consternation.

Catharine inhaled sharply.

"Shhh." Nathalie's lips trailed to her jaw.

Catharine tried to focus on the sound of the door latching in the cubicle beside them, to remind herself of the consequences if they were caught as they were. But then the vortex of her thoughts terminated entirely as Nathalie slipped a hand beneath the hem of her polo, cool fingers tracing a slow ascent, starting at the base of her ribs. In concert, her other hand moved to Catharine's chin, tilting her head back to kiss the exposed skin of her throat.

The universe swayed around her, threatening to unravel her where she stood.

In truth, the actions were modest. She'd gone further with Edward. But for whatever reason, this, with Nathalie, felt like uncharted territory, rearranging the map of her world.

She needed her to stop—her legs were unsteady, threatening to buckle at the knees—but at the same time, she was also ready to beg her not to stop at all.

The toilet flushed, and the staccato click of heels moved toward the basin as Nathalie's hand continued its upward climb. Her lips trailed along her jawline, her body pressing her more firmly against the wall, every passing second rendering it increasingly difficult not to make a sound.

It was dizzying, igniting, each beat of her heart rewriting everything she thought she understood about desire.

And then the music swelled and faded with the woman's departure, and Nathalie abruptly stepped away and let herself out of the cubicle door.

Thrown entirely off balance, Catharine had to grab the coat hook to steady herself.

"You're looking a little flushed," said Nathalie innocently, when Catharine finally reappeared. "Should I tell your mum to go ahead and order for you?"

Finding a fragment of composure, Catharine stepped to the basin to splash water on her face. "You are insufferable."

"Could have fooled me." Nathalie's smile was dangerously slow as she caught her eye in the mirror. "Serves you right, though. Starting something you can't finish."

"You're the one who followed me in here!"

"To wash my hands—"

"Oh, please." Catharine dried her face with a finger towel.

"While you're clinging to your pedestal of righteousness," said Nathalie, stepping away from the counter, "you should know— you have lipstick on your collar." She kissed her cheek and disappeared out the door.

Late that afternoon, after turning down her mother's offer to drive them to Oxford, Catharine watched out the train window as the rolling countryside left Henley in the distance. An increasing sense of relief settled over her with every passing mile.

"Are you ever going to let me see your home?" asked Nathalie, seated beside her.

She knew Nathalie was disappointed. When her mother suggested they drive by the estate for Catharine to pick up anything she might need over the next few weeks, she had vehemently declined. She didn't want Nathalie anywhere near Honour Stone.

"Trust me, it's not a home," said Catharine, turning away from the window.

Under cover of the jacket laid across her lap, Nathalie reached to squeeze her hand, and then let the topic go.

It was one of the things Catharine appreciated most about her—she knew when to push, and loved to tease—but she also knew when a conversation was closed.

They talked about the upcoming weeks. Nathalie had been invited to audition for *Sleeping Beauty*, the Christmas pantomime—where tradition called for a woman in breeches to play the part of Prince Charming.

Catharine wanted to be thrilled for her. If she got the role, it would be her first paid production.

But she also knew the show was at The Theatre Chipping Norton, which was over an hour bus ride from Oxford. It would mean six nights a week, for the next two months, she would hardly see her.

"I'd be off all evening on Mondays," Nathalie consoled, recognizing her despondence.

"It's the only day I have a late evening tutorial."

"Okay, well—I've proven today I can get up early." Still holding her hand beneath the jacket, Nathalie stroked her thumb across her palm. "And I think I could find ways to convince you to stay up late."

Catharine laughed. "Is that part of your curriculum for my 'good old-fashioned French education'?" She could feel the heat rise up her collar at just the hint of the suggestion.

"Fundamental studies." Nathalie wagged her eyebrows, offering her crooked smile. "I think, in time, if given the opportunity, you'll find I am a *very* good instructor."

Catharine was certain the innuendo should have further deepened her flush, but instead, it had the opposite effect. Two things in the jesting remark stood out to her:

In time meant Nathalie was not in a rush.

And *if given the opportunity* implied the choice was entirely up to her.

Neither consideration was something she was often afforded—not at Honour Stone, not at Oxford, and certainly not how her relationship had ever felt with Edward. Having control over the *when* and *where* made her feel safe—made her feel secure.

Despite the handful of other passengers—none of whom paid them any mind—she leaned into Nathalie.

"Well, I'll have you know I was made a Scholar and am consistently amongst the top in my year," she whispered, settling her head against her shoulder. "So I think you'll find I'm a very good student."

Out of sight of the ticket inspector coming down the aisle, Nathalie kissed the top of her head. "Then I look forward to the challenge of setting the bar as the best tutor you've ever had."

Chapter Eleven

THE FIRST FRIDAY OF NOVEMBER, Catharine jogged down the Christ Church Meadow Walk and into the ankle-deep grass that ran along the college wall.

She was late. Her afternoon lecture had run half an hour over, and she was worried Nathalie might have given up on her.

Ducking beneath the heavy bough of a weeping willow, she brushed aside the golden leaves and found what she'd come to think of as *their secret bench*—empty. Her heart sank. It was the first time since returning from Henley that both of them had the evening free.

The previous two weeks had passed in stolen moments. A sunset stroll among the fruit trees of Christ Church Orchard, brushing fingertips, stealing a kiss that tasted of the pear they had shared. Early mornings at Spires Café, where Catharine took pleasure in ordering Nathalie's coffee exactly the way she knew she liked it. Afternoons in the Rad Cam, feigning interest in eighteenth-century texts as they played a game of footsie beneath heavy oak tables. Or the late-Saturday night rendezvous the weekend before, where they'd sipped whisky neat at The Bear Inn before wandering, tipsy and high off each other, onto the dark footpaths of Aston's Eyot—taking solace in the privacy of the woodland, getting lost in long, lingering kisses, with no prying eyes save those of the badgers and birds and deer.

The willow had become their hideaway, a sanctuary of green and gold, where they could meet in the spare moments between studies and whisper words unfit for college halls.

Disappointed to find herself alone, Catharine dropped her leather book bag onto the bench and flopped down. Her shoes were wet from traipsing through the damp grass, and her cardigan clung to her skin from the exertion of the run.

She'd wanted to surprise Nathalie. All week, she'd deliberated over how they should spend their Friday evening. It was Guy Fawkes Day—Bonfire Night—and both the town and colleges were buzzing with festivity, the students eager for the weekend.

Catharine had wanted to book a table at *Le Manoir aux Quat'-Saisons*, knowing Nathalie would appreciate the French cuisine. But it had been too late to make a reservation, and there was no way she was going to call her mum to pull any strings. So instead, she'd decided on dinner at *Gees*. She felt Nathalie would love the airy ambiance of the greenhouse-turned-restaurant. After, they could make the short walk to the Phoenix Picturehouse and catch up on the latest niche cinema.

A proper date, so to speak.

"Sorry I'm late!" The branches facing Christ Church Meadow parted, and suddenly Nathalie was standing in the shelter of their tree.

"I thought you'd come and gone already!" Catharine leapt to her feet. "I just got here." She paused, taking in Nathalie's sagging shoulders and fallen expression. "What's wrong?"

"I didn't get the role." Nathalie slumped onto the bench. "They cast some girl from Glasgow. Her accent's so thick, the audience is going to need a translator." She plopped her chin into her hands.

Catharine knew Nathalie had been on tenterhooks, waiting for the casting of the pantomime to be announced. She'd felt the audition had gone well. They'd called her back twice.

"I'm really sorry." Catharine set a hand on her back. Beneath the low-hanging boughs of the willow, the sounds of a kickabout could be heard across the path—a grounding reminder of the fragility of their seclusion. She slid closer to her anyway. "It's their loss."

"It's *my* loss," Nathalie snapped. "The gig paid £300 a week!" Frustrated, she shrugged away from Catharine's consoling touch. "I realize that's not something you can understand."

Catharine was quiet. It wasn't infrequent that Nathalie poked at the imbalance between them, but seldom were her remarks barbed.

"I'm sorry." Nathalie stood, her anger waning. "I know it's not your fault. I'm just—disappointed."

"For what it's worth—" Catharine decided on an alternate route to try and lure her from her melancholy, "—*Sleeping Beauty* wasn't originally about finding true love's kiss. It was a gruesome Italian folk tale about a nobleman's daughter, Talia, who pricks her finger on a flax fiber and falls into a deep sleep. A king stumbles across the unconscious girl and assaults her. Talia wakes after giving birth to twins with absolutely no memory of what happened. The king's jealous wife discovers his infidelity and orders the babies to be cooked and served to her husband in an act of cannibalistic revenge. The cook refuses, so the queen tries to burn Talia alive, but the king discovers her heinous plot, and burns his wife at the stake instead. Then he marries Talia, as if nothing ever happened, and that's the *happily ever after*." Catharine shrugged. "So really, you dodged a role in a so-called romantic fairy tale with more murder, male dominance, and revenge than *Titus Andronicus*, if you ask me."

Nathalie stared at her. "Sometimes I don't know whether to laugh at the things you say, or flick you upside the head."

"I could think of a third option—if you'd rather?"

"Oh?"

As Catharine had hoped, the teasing abraded the remainder of her foul mood.

Nathalie's eyes scanned the curtain of willow leaves, assessing their privacy, before turning back to Catharine. The subtle tilt of her head was daring her to kiss her, but Catharine didn't take the bait. A game of footsie under the study table, or a bit of midnight snogging in the overgrown scrub of the Eyot, was one thing. Testing the waters fifty feet away from a dozen lads playing football, was another.

"Tu es une trouillarde !" Nathalie razzed her for being chicken-hearted.

"Be nice to me." Catharine traced a suggestive finger along the collar of Nathalie's blazer before catching her hand and pulling her to her feet. "I'm taking you on a date."

"A date?" Nathalie picked up Catharine's leather bag and held the bough of the weeping willow aside for her to step from the safety of their bower. "Where?"

"Aren't you suddenly gallant?" She reached for her satchel, but Nathalie slung it over her shoulder.

"I am *always* gallant, thank you very much."

She was. Catharine couldn't deny her that.

"Mind out!"

Before Catharine could process the shouted warning, a ball glanced off her shoulder.

"Crétins !" Nathalie spun in the direction it had come from, cussing at a trio of boys jogging across the grass.

One of them, Catharine realized, was Edward.

"My fault!" He lifted a hand in recognition, his snide smirk saying he was anything but sorry. "Didn't see you there."

It was total rubbish, Catharine knew. He'd been an absolute bastard the previous week when they'd shared an overlapping lecture. He'd deliberately sat behind her, whispering uncouth comments to one of his mates:

Not even a decent shag.

Barely worthy of a knee-trembler.

Like rutting a plank.

Catharine had stared at the chalkboard behind the podium, trying to focus on the Professor of Moral Philosophy pontificating about *Aristotle's Nicomachean Ethics*, all the while listening to them snigger and feeling her ears turn pink.

As soon as the lecture had concluded, she bolted for the door, refusing to give him so much as a backward glance.

"Tu es un salaud !" Nathalie took an angry step toward him, but Catharine caught her arm.

"Just forget him—let's go."

Nathalie didn't budge.

"Something wrong, froggie?" Edward scooped up the ball, bouncing it on his knee.

"What a shame," she spit, her dark eyes unblinking, "all that money, and not a hint of class to show for it."

"What did you just say?" He took a threatening stride forward.

"You are as simple-minded as you look if you think you scare me."

Edward turned away, as if to leave, then suddenly drew back his foot and hammered the ball directly into the side of her face.

"What the fuck, Haverfield?" One of his mates grabbed his arm, yanking him around. "They're bloody girls!"

"Not that one," he sneered, glaring at Nathalie, who—stunned—had doubled over, holding a palm to her cheek. "She's nothing more than a leech—clinging to coattails. Stick to your own class, scrubber!"

Furious, Catharine spun to face him. "You are a pathetic, insecure little boy masquerading as a man—so desperate for attention, you don't even realize you make a clown of yourself."

"Let's go, mate!" A second boy stepped between them, shoving Edward. "I'm not going to watch you lamp on a woman!"

"You better mind the company you're keeping, Catharine!" Edward threatened as his friends hauled him back to the game.

When they had gone, Catharine gingerly tried to lift away the hand Nathalie still had pressed to her face.

"Nat?" Through her splayed fingers, she could see the angry red mark rapidly spreading across her cheek. "Are you all right?"

"I'm fine!" Curtly, Nathalie brushed her away. "It doesn't actually hurt. He just..." Her fingers were trembling.

"Do you want to make a complaint?"

Nathalie's laugh was brittle. "Against Edward Haverfield? How well do you think that would go for me?"

Catharine knew the answer. After all, Christ Church was one of the last colleges in Oxford to relinquish its tradition of male exclusivity. Little more than a decade had passed since the doors had been pried open to allow women the opportunity to earn their degrees. The university system may have claimed to value gender equality, but it was still very much a patriarchal society.

She thought about what Anouk had said—about the girl who'd made a complaint against him and never returned after the Christmas break.

"Come on." Nathalie started down the path. "That prick doesn't get to ruin our evening." Wiping away grit with her sleeve, she checked behind her to make sure Catharine was following. "You promised me a date."

She had.

And now, suddenly—*You better mind the company you're keeping*—the festive atmosphere of Oxford didn't feel quite as safe.

Across the grass, a pair of boys were trying to belt each other with sparklers. Another was jogging toward them—shirtless—despite the fact that it was nearly freezing.

"I thought we might…" She hesitated, a different plan coming to mind.

She considered the consequences. There was an essay on *Romer's Endogenous Growth Model* due Monday morning. Her intention had been to complete the paper after they'd returned from watching the movie.

Oi, pass the bloody ball! A shout went up from where the kickabout had resumed.

Catharine decided the essay could wait.

"Have you ever properly celebrated Bonfire Night?"

"You mean applauding the failed rebellion to overthrow the English government? No. In my country, we prefer to celebrate when the revolutionaries actually succeed."

"The *Gunpowder Plot* was hardly a rebellion—more like a thwarted act of terrorism. But that's beside the point. It's an excuse now to light bonfires, drink mulled cider, and—"

"Burn Catholic effigies? How very *English*."

"Fine," Catharine huffed, "if you find our English traditions so intolerable, I have reading I need to attend—"

Stepping into the shadow of the Christ Church College walls, Nathalie pinched her on her bum. Catharine yelped with laughter, before casting a quick glance toward the football match to make certain Edward hadn't been watching.

"What did you have in mind to commemorate the failure of ol' Mr. Fawkes's futile coup?"

Catharine paused. "I thought we might go to Henley?"

"You want to go home?" Nathalie's surprise was unmistakable.

"Not exactly." Catharine resumed the walk, pulling Nathalie along. "Come on, I'll tell you on the train."

"So that's the heart of the great Brooks Empire?" Nathalie asked, leaning over the footbridge railing. A few miles away, the *Brooks Marine Technology Division* cast a dim glow over the horizon. Catharine had reluctantly pointed out the industrial estate as they waited for Geoff to pick them up at *Reading West Station*.

"It's… part of it." Catharine didn't elaborate. The last thing she wanted to explain was that the factory was little more than her father's vanity project—a whim to dabble in manufacturing. She checked her watch. "He should be here any minute. The plant closed at six."

Geoff had been surprised when she called him at work from a phone box in Oxford Station. She'd asked if the offer was still open to join him at the party on Remenham Hill, and if it was, could she bring a friend.

He'd been delighted.

Beside her, Nathalie flicked paint off the railing. "Is he handsome?"

"Who?" Catharine turned her attention away from the manufacturing plant.

"Your foreman's son."

"My *father's* foreman's son—and Geoff? I don't know. I've known him all my life."

"You still know if he's handsome."

Catharine thought about the scar on his chin he'd received during his attempt to rescue her scarf from the mere. His rogue front tooth that refused to fall into alignment with the others. The callouses on his hands from working long hours on an assembly line. The way he always took the roadside of the pavement when they walked to town, shielding her from the splatter of the lorries.

"Yes, I guess so."

"Should I be jealous?" Nathalie was teasing, her hand inching closer to where Catharine's was resting.

"Do you want to be?"

"Perhaps." Nathalie stretched her pinky to graze hers. "A little jealousy makes everything more thrilling."

The touch, no more than fingertips, sent Catharine's pulse racing. To come undone so easily was madness—madness, yet endlessly exhilarating.

"Then yes—I find him devastatingly handsome."

Nathalie slid her hand closer, entwining their fingers palm to palm. "I suppose I shall have to work twice as hard to sweep you off your feet, then."

The platforms beneath them were quiet, with only a few local commuters waiting for connecting trains. But still, even a few people were a few too many. Gently, Catharine withdrew her hand.

"Our chariot awaits." She motioned toward Geoff's lime green Austin Metro pulling into the car park.

IT SHOULDN'T HAVE BEEN SURPRISING that the two of them—Geoff and Nathalie—hit it off right away. They found an immediate common ground in taking the piss out of Catharine. Geoff, jesting that he regretted being unable to find her a more qualified chauffeur, and

Nathalie, teasing that Catharine had already debased herself by riding coach on the train—surely her standards couldn't fall any lower.

Catharine ignored them both and climbed unceremoniously through the front door and into the cramped backseat, where the upholstery carried the faint scent of diesel.

They drove the half-hour to Henley through the same rolling hills and woodlands she had watched unfold through the window of her father's Rolls-Royce on her birthday just two weeks earlier. This time, however, it was Geoff behind the wheel, instead of Mr. Fraser, and the entire drive was filled with laughter. A sharp contrast to the previous tongue-lashing Catharine had received for all the ways she'd failed her father.

"I never really thought you'd come," Geoff said into his rearview mirror as they pulled across the Henley Bridge and continued onto White Hill. "It's just a bunch of local lads and their birds. We've got a fire stacked out behind the old Hayward place. I, uh—" he checked the mirror again, catching her eye, "may have procured a few pallets for fuel from the plant."

"Well, then, I guess it's good you invited me and not my father," said Catharine. Staring at the back of his head, she could see his ears rise with his smile.

"We've also got a bunch of rockets and aerial shells Kev filched from the cash-and-carry he worked at over the summer."

"You're going to give her an aneurysm knowing she's in the presence of stolen goods," said Nathalie, unclipping her belt in the front seat to twist around and face her. She held Catharine's eye as the little Metro sped along the winding road, its tires slipping on loose gravel, daring her to chastise her. "You know, just hanging around miscreants can turn you into one. You better mind the company you're keeping, *Catharine*." She mocked Edward's earlier advice.

"You sound like the bloody Colonel." Geoff crammed the gear into second and veered onto a dirt road leading through the farm-land.

At the end of the drive, just beyond a dense beech and yew woodland, was a wide clearing overlooking the hamlet of Aston. A handful of cars and pile of push bikes littered the verge.

Geoff rattled to a stop behind a rusted Lada Riva. "Alright! We made it before they lit the pyre." He threw open his door and tipped his seat forward, offering a hand to help her climb from the car. "Shall we crack on, then?"

Nathalie slid between them, slipping her arm through Catharine's. "Cate's promised to prove me wrong that English parties are more than soggy sandwiches and warm beer." She eyed the slender shadows that could be seen loafing about the straw bales circling the unlit fire. "I'm not feeling optimistic."

Geoff laughed. "*Cate*? I've never heard anyone call you that."

"Case in point," Nathalie hummed, starting across the field, pulling Catharine along with her. "You English are so loathsomely formal."

Circled around the newly lit fire, no one asked Catharine her name, but they all seemed to know her.

It was impossible to miss the whispers of *Oh look, Miss Posh* and *There's that Brooks girl* make their way from stranger to stranger.

One boy, already up in his cups, confronted Geoff. "You really invited Lady Muck to our piss-up?" he challenged.

"Shut your face, Travis." Geoff shot a look over his shoulder, clearly embarrassed to find Catharine had heard him.

"Ain't that rich—Geoff's trying to work his way up from stable lad to lord of the manor. Hoping to give the boss's daughter a different kind of ride, are ya?"

The taunt earned the ruddy-faced boy a hard hook to his pimpled jaw despite outweighing Geoff by at least three stone.

Away from the fray, Catharine slipped further from the dancing flame and into the shadows, still holding an untouched cup of cider.

"This was a bad idea," she whispered to Nathalie. "We shouldn't have come here."

"Just…" Nathalie gestured for her to relax. "Let me deal with them, all right?" Tipping back the rest of her drink, she tossed the cup into a growing pile of rubbish. "This is my sort of crowd."

Before Catharine could stop her, she sauntered—casually, confidently—toward the group of boys, interrupting their roughhousing.

"Please tell me one of you lot has a light?" Producing a crumpled packet of Gauloises from inside her coat, she shook out one of the unfiltered cigarettes and twirled it between her fingers.

Catharine stared at the practiced gesture. Despite having occasionally caught the scent of smoke on her, she'd never actually seen her with a fag before.

"And if I did?" A boy pulled a BIC from his pocket, sparking the wheel. "What would I get for it?"

"The satisfaction of pretending not to be a knuckle-dragger." Nathalie coolly leaned over the flame, taking a deep, unhurried drag.

"What is that, some dodgy homemade roll-up?" Travis, distracted from his altercation with Geoff, spat on the ground, still rubbing his chin.

Nathalie blew a long exhale. "They're French."

"No wonder they smell like shite."

There were a few sniggers around the fire.

Unperturbed, she shook out another. "You think you're man enough to handle one?"

"Some weak Parisian perfume stick? I'd sooner huff a dog's arse."

"Just as I thought. All mouth, no trousers." Nathalie slipped it back into the packet.

"Fuck it—give me that!" He snatched the deck from her hand and flipped open his clipper. Lighting one of the fags, he immediately coughed on the first inhale. A couple of his mates jeered him.

"Tell you what—" Nathalie flicked ash into the bonfire "—since you're so tough, how about you and me: deepest drag, longest hold. See who outlasts the other."

"And if I win, you going to polish my knob?"

"Are you going to provide tweezers and a microscope?"

His cheeks blazed as a ripple of laughter spread through the group, all heads turned in their direction.

"Whatever. Don't think I'll go easy on you just because you're a thick bint."

Travis tucked the fag between his lips and took a deep pull. Nathalie did the same. Not five seconds in, he choked, sputtering to catch his breath. Her eyes alight, Nathalie released a slow, controlled stream of smoke through her nose before flinging the stump into the base of the bonfire.

"Fackin' legend!"

"French girl goes harder than you, Travo!"

"She's fucking done you, mate!"

Leaving the fuming boy to his friends, Nathalie glided back into the darkness, returning to Catharine's side.

"Well." She took the plastic cup of cider from her hand, downing it in a single swallow. "I won. Do I get a reward?"

"The right to don the title as my knight in shining armor?" Catharine stifled the desire to reach out and touch her.

"You know he who wins the joust is typically given a token of his lady's favor."

"And just what sort of token might you be looking for?"

Before Nathalie could respond, Geoff's sinewy frame ducked into the shadows. "I'm sorry about them." He shook out his swelling knuckles. "Trav's a muppet, but the rest of the lot's alright, I swear."

"Every village needs its idiot." Nathalie held up the empty cup. "Is your chivalry only good for throwing punches, or does it cover drink refills, too?"

"I've got a bottle of Tesco's finest single malt waiting in my boot."

"Well then," Nathalie said, tapping one of her fuchsia-painted nails against the cup, "it's your shout."

When he had gone, she turned back to Catharine. "As I was saying—"

"I really need to kiss you." Catharine cut her short.

Caught off guard, Nathalie laughed. "As supportive as I am of that sentiment—and as readily as I would accept it as my due token—I'm not sure this is the right crowd."

Catharine took an assessment of their surroundings. Behind them, a pair of boys were being goaded into seeing who could hold a lit cigarette to the back of their hand the longest. A girl, drunk and shedding clothing rapidly, flung a bundle of Chinese crackers into the blaze, setting off a string of explosions that brought a chorus of expletives and cheers. A hundred feet away, Geoff was strolling toward them, carrying his bottle of scotch.

And at the far end of the clearing, a copse of trees stood silhouetted against the moon.

She gave a subtle nod in their direction.

"Who said anything about a crowd?" Starting for the thicket, Catharine trailed a fingertip across Nathalie's hip as she brushed past.

"Cate," Nathalie hissed, "where am I supposed to tell him you went?"

Catharine didn't look back. "If you want a token of my favor, you'll figure it out."

TEN MINUTES LATER, BEHIND THE dense branches of a hawthorn, Catharine kissed Nathalie hard—the scent of cigarettes and cheap scotch a sharp contrast to the overripe berries and musty smell of bark.

"You taste like smoke," she murmured, her cold fingers finding their way into Nathalie's back pockets, drawing their bodies closer together.

"You taste like I'd like to get out of here."

Catharine laughed at her slight slur. "You're drunk."

"Yeah, because you left me there, and I had to down three shots with him before he got sidetracked lighting a bottle rocket."

As if on cue, a high-pitched whistle screamed through the air. Across the field, a scattering of sparklers burst into flames, the smoke from the bonfire temporarily lit in scarlet and evergreen.

"I don't want to go back to Oxford tonight."

The admission brought Nathalie's hands—fumbling with a button on her jacket—to a momentary halt.

"Where do you want to go?"

Honour Stone was less than two miles away. A five-minute car ride. A forty-minute walk. Her father would be in Liverpool, as he always was the first weekend of the month—like clockwork. Her mum was probably in London, though she couldn't be sure.

It didn't matter. She didn't want to take her there.

"I know an inn in Aston—not far from here."

Overhead, a gleam of light arched into the sky before erupting into a spiral of sparks, twirling to the frozen earth of the clearing. A second and third streak followed, the explosions vibrating the roots of the hawthorn.

"It's too close. It's not a good idea."

Nathalie's concern, Catharine knew, was for her. She knew how terrified she was of even the slightest rumor getting back to her father.

"That's why you're going to be the one to check in. We'll pay in cash. You can say you're traveling with your sister, here from Bordeaux."

"I see you've given this some consideration." Nathalie's smile was brazen, her hands resuming their slow progression as she worked to untuck her blouse. "And when they tell me they only have one bed?"

"You can put on a show of being scandalized, and then sigh in resignation—*merci, madam, it'll have to do, our budget won't accommo- date two rooms.*" She tried to hide her stilted breath as Nathalie's fingers finally found their way beneath all her layers. "You're an actress," she managed, her voice strained as icy palms slid to the small of her back. "This should come easy for you."

Another flash of fragmented light blazed across the sky, exploding into a cascade of color. Catharine closed her eyes, drawing Nathalie's mouth back to hers, forgetting about the shouts and mayhem no more than a football field in the distance.

"Catharine?"

A branch broke, the rustle of dead leaves unmistakably close. Catharine's eyes flew open.

A few feet away, Geoff stood staring at them. His mouth was agape, his wide eyes illuminated by the volley of mortars crisscrossing the sky.

Catharine's entire body felt like it was buckling.

"I—um—" He cast his gaze to the ground. "I saw, uh—I needed to—find—you…"

"Geoff, look—" Nathalie stepped forward, putting herself between him and Catharine.

He waved her off. "It—it doesn't matter, we have to go. *Now*. Kev—" he looked over his shoulder toward the bonfire "—he saw coppers crossing the bridge. They'll—um, they'll come shut us down." He seemed to regain some of his composure, the urgency of the situation driving away his discomfiture.

"Geoff." Catharine's mouth was dry. "I—"

"Honestly, Catharine, we don't have time." He looked to Nathalie. "Please, just get her to my car."

Chapter Twelve

By the time they reached Geoff's Metro, the pile of push bikes was gone, tire tracks leading off in every direction. Half a dozen boys had crammed into the rusty Lada Riva. In the driver's seat, a girl swung her bra out the window.

"Old Bill's gonna get ya!" she cackled wildly before speeding down the rutted dirt drive toward the main road.

Catharine tried to focus on the immediate objective—get in the car, clear out before the police arrived. But she couldn't shake the horrifying realization: Geoff had seen her kissing Nathalie.

The knowledge was entirely paralyzing.

Her hand slipped on the door handle, and Nathalie cussed at her from inside the car, where she'd already climbed through the driver's side and into the backseat.

"Cate, get in the damn car!"

Geoff turned over the engine.

If he told his father… or worse, *her* father…

"Come on, then!" Reaching across the console, he shoved the passenger door open. "Get in the bloody car, Catharine!" The door smacked her in the shin, snapping her back to attention.

She stumbled into the seat.

Without another word, Geoff ground the gear into first and spun a hard U-turn around the deserted fire. They followed in a cloud of dust behind the Lada Riva.

"Bloody Kev pushed it too far with those mortars—they had to hear them all the way up in Wycombe!" Up ahead, the taillights on the Riva disappeared as the car fishtailed onto the tarmac. Geoff floored the accelerator, trying to keep up. "I bet that wanker Dean grassed us up. He didn't get invited since he and Gemma split."

Catharine stared into the blackness out the passenger window. She didn't care who had snitched on their illegal firework show. She cared that Geoff had the power to destroy her life completely.

She wanted to glance into the backseat at Nathalie, but didn't dare.

"Oh, shit!"

The exclamation returned her focus to the road just in time to see a cyclist flooded by the full beams. Geoff swerved hard, missing the boy, and skidded onto the soft verge.

For a moment, everything was dark, with only the sound of the whining engine cutting through the night. Then the headlights flickered back on, revealing the tall grass and angled gully where the car was wedged nose-first.

"Are you all right?"

Catharine ignored Geoff and turned to the backseat. "Nat?"

"I'm fine!"

The engine revved, and gravel scattered beneath the spinning tires. "We're stuck!" Geoff jammed the accelerator. The car went nowhere.

Further up the road, headlights were winding in their direction. Both the cyclist and Lada Riva were long gone.

"Geoff," Catharine ordered, jolting into action, "get out of the car and give me the keys."

"What—"

"You've been drinking—"

"Catharine—"

"Just fucking do it!"

Stunned by her outburst—no more than she was herself, as it was the first time in her life the word had ever crossed her lips—Geoff did as he was bade.

By the time the police car rolled to a stop, Catharine was sitting in the driver's seat, and Geoff was pacing through the meadow foxtail.

"Everyone all right in there?" The officer strolled across the street, shining his torch into Catharine's window. Before Geoff could say anything, she opened the door.

"Yes, sir."

"Need I ask where you lot are coming from?"

There was no point in lying—he obviously knew. Still, given the rhetorical question, Catharine decided not to offer any information that wasn't explicitly demanded.

"No, sir."

He flashed the beam into the backseat and then to Geoff, standing by the bonnet.

"Everyone mind stepping out for a moment?"

When they were assembled on the side of the road, the officer took a quick inventory of the car—noting the handful of spirit bottles in the boot—and sauntered back to question them.

"Had a few drinks tonight, have we?"

"No, sir."

The officer chuckled. "Heard that a time or two."

"*They* have," Catharine clarified. "I've not."

He tipped the torch in Geoff's face. "I know you—you run with that Kevin Griggs and his lot."

"He's a mate. What of it?" Geoff said, defensive.

Catharine reached through the dark to find his hand, giving it a warning squeeze.

"Been up at the Haywards, have you?"

"It's Bonfire Night," said Geoff, "we were just having a bit of fun, that's all."

"Pretty sure half of London saw your show tonight. Bloody fine display." The officer raised an eyebrow. "So, whose old man gets the lucky call to come pick you up? Gonna take a recovery vehicle to drag that out in the morning." He flicked his torch toward the stranded car.

"We can walk—" Geoff started to argue, but the officer waved him off.

"Lot of reckless motorists out tonight." He shot a pointed look at Catharine. "Parents come get you, or it's down to the station— your choice."

"Geoff, give him your dad's number!" Catharine pressed, unwilling to risk a call to Honour Stone.

By the time Mr. Mills arrived, Catharine was certain she was going to be sick. She'd sat, shivering on the bonnet, unable to seek comfort from Nathalie, and agitated by the nonstop cracking of Geoff's knuckles.

The officer had a quick word with the elder Mills, gave Geoff a stern warning to have his bucket of rust gone by morning, and went on his way.

"Your mother's going to give you a proper kicking," Mr. Mills snapped at Geoff, before turning to Catharine. "Miss Brooks, if my son has in any way behaved inappropriately—"

"This is all my fault, Mr. Mills. I pressured him to bring us here." She cast a quick look at Geoff. "He didn't even want to come."

"Hmph." Her father's foreman let out a skeptical grunt. "Right. Well, in we go." He gestured toward his sedan. "I'll get you girls back to Honour Stone."

"If you wouldn't mind, Mr. Mills," Catharine rushed, "could you just drop us at the Henley Station? We'll be heading up to Oxford."

"Not tonight, you won't. Last train was off at eleven." He slammed his door as Catharine and Nathalie climbed into the backseat, and Geoff sulked into the front.

"There's an inn—"

"My wife wouldn't hear of it. You'll stay with us tonight, Miss Brooks—and I'll see you to the train in the morning." He left no room for argument.

AN HOUR LATER, AFTER A silent car ride and an even more uncomfortable tea in the Mills' kitchen, Geoff was relegated to the lounge sofa as Mrs. Mills fitted her son's bed with fresh linen.

"Is there anything else I can get you, Miss Brooks?"

It mortified Catharine, the woman's subservience in her own home.

"You've been wonderfully kind, Mrs. Mills." She hesitated. "Is there a chance you might not mention this to my mum in the morning?"

"Meant to be at your studies, are you?" The housekeeper she'd known since childhood pressed a gentle hand to her shoulder. "Don't let my boy turn your head. He's a good lad—" her eyes settled on a framed photo on Geoff's desk, where he wore his football kit, "—but I don't think the colonel..." She trailed off.

"We're just friends, I assure you, Mrs. Mills."

"Very good, then." With a soft sigh, the woman bid her and Nathalie goodnight.

"Well, *Miss Brooks*!" Nathalie dropped dramatically onto the single bed, the coil springs groaning beneath her.

"Don't you even start with that!"

"Would you like me to turn down your bed, Miss Brooks? Perhaps I could lay out your clothes and polish your shoes before morning?"

Catharine wanted to laugh, but with the anxiety of the police encounter behind them, her concern returned to their run-in with Geoff in the woodland.

"I have to talk to him."

Nathalie's teasing faded. "He would have said something already if he was going to."

"I just—if his mates find out, or worse, anyone at the factory—"

"Have a little faith in him, Cate." Nathalie reached for her hand, gently pulling her to sit beside her. "It's obvious he adores you."

"That doesn't mean—"

"Give him a chance to be a friend. I promise, not every boy is Edward Haverfield."

Shoulders slumped, Catharine tipped her head back to stare at the ceiling. "I'm sorry about tonight. About all of this. It's not at all what I envisioned."

"You mean fleeing the scene of a crime, crashing a car, being detained by the police, and spending a romantic evening in the home of a family who works for your family wasn't part of your master plan to seduce me?"

Catharine couldn't help but smile. "It was only that last bit that derailed me. Prior to that, it was quite exhilarating. Well, other than…" Her mood plummeted with the reminder.

"It's going to be okay, Cate." Nathalie scooted to the wall to make room for her. "Things could always be worse. We could be sleeping in a cell together."

Catharine wasn't certain that was worse than sleeping in her father's foreman's son's bedroom—after he'd discovered her kissing a girl in the woods, leaving no room for doubt that there was more between them than just friendship.

"If by next weekend my father hasn't booked me a one-way ticket to some dreary Swiss institution for 'troubled ladies,' or locked me behind the solid stone walls of an Irish convent, will you let me make this one up to you?" she asked, wishing it felt more like teasing.

"I don't think so." Nathalie's lips flickered into a smile. "You had your opportunity. Now it's *my* turn to choose the entertainment and venue. *Compris ?*"

Catharine slipped under the duvet, grateful for Nathalie's arms draped around her. "*C'est bon.*"

It would all be okay, she tried to reassure herself.

But as soon as she felt Nathalie's body slacken, and heard Mr. and Mrs. Mills retire, she tiptoed through the dark house to the lounge.

"Could we talk?" she whispered across the unfamiliar threshold. She knew, from Geoff's uneven breathing, that he wasn't sleeping.

"You don't have to tell me anything, Catharine."

She padded across the worn carpet to sit on the edge of the sofa. So much of her wanted to excuse herself. To dismiss whatever he thought he saw.

It's not what you think. It wasn't like that.

But it is. And it was.

And she wasn't willing to deny it. Aside from Nathalie, he was her closest friend. She owed him more than rubbish.

"I—I need to."

But how? She could hardly explain it to herself, let alone to anyone else.

How did she tell him Nathalie made her feel different than any boy she'd ever known? That she was the first person who made her feel like there was more to life than just what she'd been taught?

It was impossible to describe.

So instead, she chose to plead her case with the only truth of which she was certain.

"She makes me happy."

Geoff was quiet for a long time. "Then that's all that matters."

"You're not going to…?" She didn't dare ask.

"I won't tell anyone, Catharine."

It was the reassurance she'd come to seek, but still, her heart felt hollow.

"Do you hate me?"

To her surprise, he actually laughed. "Hate you?" He sat up, the shadow of his face unreadable. "You should know by now, there's nothing you could do that would make me hate you. I've loved you my whole life. If anything," he huffed, a smile evident, "I'm a little relieved. She's sound. I really like her." He leaned forward, just his eyes catching the reflection of the streetlamp shining through the window. "And to be honest, I can stomach the idea of her a lot better than I can those posh cads you hang around with."

The entire weight of the evening seemed to shed from her shoulders. That he didn't call her deranged, or sick, or twisted—that he reached out to squeeze her hand, and wasn't disgusted. Just knowing someone else could know her secret, and not find her any different than he had just hours earlier. That? That was everything she needed.

"Thank you."

"But Catharine?" He caught her arm as she started to rise. "Promise you'll be careful?"

The worry in his tone sent the sliver of an icicle creeping up her neck.

"I am. We are." She forced a smile, bending to kiss his forehead. "Tonight notwithstanding."

"Just so you know," he whispered as she reached the hall, "that mattress is past its prime and these walls are paper-thin."

"As if I'd ever!"

He laughed at her indignation. "Let a guy dream, will you?"

Chapter Thirteen

The sign above the open gate read *Weekend Hours: Dawn—Dusk.* Catharine cast the steadily eloping sun a dubious glance before returning her attention to where Nathalie was stashing their bikes behind a hedge of blackthorn and hazel.

"It's going to be dark in an hour."

"Is it?" Nathalie played coy, reappearing to pick up her backpack.

"It also says a permit is required to enter."

"Does it?"

"Nat!" Catharine jogged to catch up as Nathalie set off down the trail. "Are you going to get us sent down?"

"Me, maybe." Nathalie shrugged. "You? Unlikely. Worst case, your father will just have to fund another library or lecture hall or quad."

"You know, trespassing through a restricted research preserve wasn't quite the *walk* I had in mind—!"

"Relax. I have a permit, okay?"

Catharine fell into step beside her as the entrance gate to Wytham Woods disappeared behind the oak and beech and sycamores. "You do?" She was surprised.

"I like to walk here sometimes. Is that a crime?"

"I just never took you for the—" she paused, choosing her words wisely "—outdoorsy type."

"Give me a little credit," Nathalie tsked. "I may not be Sir Francis Drake on the water, but I do enjoy what nature has to offer on land." She continued her brisk pace into the heart of the woodlands, turning off the hard-packed track onto a narrower path shaded entirely by the thick canopy of trees. "Are you afraid of the dark?"

"I—don't think so?" Catharine hadn't considered it. She was accustomed to the looming shadows of Honour Stone over long, grey winters, and Cimmerian walks to the boathouse when she used to row before dawn.

"Even if I told you about the girl who wandered into the woods and never came out again? They say her ghost still whispers through the leaves after sunset."

"I grew up in an eight-hundred-year-old manor—ghosts are hardly a novelty."

"Well," huffed Nathalie with exaggerated defeat, "there goes my best excuse to lure you closer to me."

"As if you need an excuse," chided Catharine, catching her hand. "All you need do is ask."

"Oh?" Nathalie paused as the path wound higher along the northern boundary.

They felt very alone, suddenly, enveloped amongst the dense walls of foliage climbing toward the darkening sky. Judging by the overgrowth crossing the trail, they were in an area that didn't get much foot traffic—at least not with winter approaching.

Nathalie smiled, the waning remnants of light catching the chestnut of her eyes, mirroring the rich autumnal hues of bracken fronds littering the forest floor. "Is that all?"

The question was layered, laden with implication.

Since returning from Remenham Hill, a nearly palpable electricity had been coursing between them—one left unsatisfied by the fleeting moments they managed to steal throughout the week. Catharine had found it impossible to keep her mind on her studies; her thoughts revolving around when they would next see each other—and when those few minutes were over, when they would come again?

The elusive seconds, the clandestine kisses, the cursory exploration of hands over coats and jumpers were no longer enough. She wanted hours—days—nights—whatever they could afford—together. Uninterrupted. Alone.

Every morning, she watched boys slip from staircases that weren't their own and girls skitter across quads back to their rooms, and no one paid them any mind. Lovers could walk freely amongst the meadows and riverbank, hand-in-hand, without ever raising a brow.

For her—for them—there was no such freedom.

She'd been unenthusiastic when Nathalie proposed a hike to begin their Friday evening. It wasn't the *entertainment* and *venue* she'd had in mind. But after the catastrophe of Bonfire Night, she didn't dare suggest otherwise.

Now, however, deep into the seclusion of the forest, a hike wasn't turning out to be such a bad idea after all.

She leaned against the smooth bark of a hornbeam trunk, her suggestive gaze veiled by lowered lashes. "That's all."

"And will your answer be yes?"

"You think I'd be out here if it wasn't?"

"All right."

To her disappointment, Nathalie didn't step forward to kiss her but rather turned up the path, leaving Catharine to follow. They passed through a brief clearing and then wound up a gentle slope before Nathalie paused at an almost indiscernible opening in the emerald curtain barricading either side of the trail. It was a game track, the route of rabbits with foxes hard on their heels, and nothing Catharine felt was suitable for a stroll.

Still, when Nathalie ducked beneath the ivy and disappeared into the bramble, Catharine pursued her.

As the last rays of light faded, and Catharine had finally had enough of squeezing her way through honeysuckle and dog rose, she opened her mouth to protest going any further, when the trail came to a sudden stop by an unexpected obstacle.

At first, she assumed they'd come to a stone wall before realizing it was actually the ivy-covered facade of a structure slowly being reclaimed by nature. Through the settling dusk, she could just discern the outline of a small chapel, with its crumbling steeple and front-facing arched window.

Moving deftly, Nathalie swept aside the mantle of ivy and tugged on an iron ring until a rotting door creaked open.

"After you."

It was only Nathalie's obvious familiarity with the mysterious ruins that sent Catharine into the pitch black opening. She expected to be met with cobwebs and the fetid smell of mildew. Instead, the fragrance of cinnamon mingled with the not unpleasant scent of aged wood and candle wax.

"What is this place?" Her whisper was lost in the darkness as the door clicked closed behind her. For a harrowing moment, she panicked, uncertain Nathalie had followed, but then a hand was set on her hip as the scratch of a match head was dragged across a hard surface.

"Not quite the Ritz."

The flickering silhouette of flame leapt across the mossed walls, casting the single room into vibrant shadow. There were six pews, three rows side by side, facing a decaying communion table. On one wall sat the remnants of an organ. The roof remained surprisingly intact, with only the south-facing window open to the elements, where a tree branch had grown through the tracery.

Nathalie moved about the space, lighting the slumbering wicks of untouched candles.

Between one row of pews, Catharine noticed the floor had been swept clean, and a pile of wool blankets was stacked on the bench that looked suspiciously familiar to those she'd seen on Nathalie's bed in Brasenose. A bottle of wine, two plastic cups, bag of dried apricots, and package of Penguin biscuits lay beside them.

"How did you do all this?" she asked as Nathalie returned down the center aisle.

"Magic." Nathalie flicked the burnt match into a tarnished brass bowl. "Do you want a glass of wine?"

She didn't, but said yes anyway—anything to quiet the nerves that had crept up without warning.

As Nathalie poured the wine, Catharine stood in the space between the pews, uncertain what to do. She had a thousand questions, none of which mattered in the moment, and in her newfound apprehension, was afraid she'd say the wrong thing. So instead, said nothing at all.

Glancing up from corking the wine, Nathalie must have recognized her tension, because she left the glasses where they were and stepped to join her.

"If it makes you feel any better, I'm a little nervous, too."

"I'm not sure that's reassuring." She managed a laugh. "One of us has to know what they're doing."

"Oh, I know what I'm doing." Nathalie's smile was unhurried, waggish, certain—embodying everything Catharine loved about her: her confidence, her playfulness, her certitude. "That's one thing you don't have to worry over." She reached for the sash of her coat. "May I?"

It was an inquiry seeking an invitation—not an expectation.

"Yes," said Catharine, trying to find a deep breath to disguise the rapid fluttering of her pulse.

She stood unmoving as Nathalie slipped free the knot, easing the coat from her shoulders and dropping it onto the pew. Slowly, deliberately, her careful hands moved on—unwrapping her scarf, drawing her jumper over her head, pausing only when she came to the top button of her blouse.

A shiver rippled across the nape of Catharine's neck that had nothing to do with the cold.

Nathalie looked up, catching her eye—a question. Catharine could only nod. She wanted this. More than anything she'd ever known.

Holding her gaze, Nathalie unclasped the first delicate pearl, then leaned to press a kiss at the exposed hollow of her throat. Her breath was warm, the gentleness of the touch steadying. Catharine tipped her head back, Nathalie's mouth trailing from her neck to her shoulder to her collarbone. She found it impossible to suppress a shudder, drawing a stifled gasp as lips grazed the swell of her breast. With an almost painful slowness, Nathalie continued her path along the bare skin revealed with every freed clasp.

The blouse fell, discarded at their feet.

Catharine released a slow exhale, attempting to ground herself.

She watched steady fingers work loose her trousers, sliding them to her ankles before Nathalie knelt, unlacing her shoes and slipping them off, one by one. Nathalie murmured an apology for the chill of the stone floor, but Catharine could think only of the hands gliding up her legs, the drawn-out kisses pressed to her calves, her thighs, the crest of her hip.

It was dizzying—the prolonged seduction of it, the sensuality— and she had to steady herself against the back of the pew when Nathalie hooked her thumb in the last remaining layer of silk, slipping off the final barrier between them.

"You're trembling." Without rising, Nathalie reached for a blanket and draped it over the pew, gently guiding her to sit.

Despite the dim light, she could feel the sweep of Nathalie's eyes through the mantle of darkness—the wanting she could see there no doubt a reflection of her own. She couldn't catch her breath.

Whatever cord tethering her to reality was unraveling.

In the shelter of this world that contained just the two of them, shrouded by four stone walls, she could hear the crackle of burning wicks, smell the subtle scent of honey from melting beeswax, feel Nathalie's hands drift to the sensitive skin of her thighs, easing her legs apart. Her own fingers, she realized, were tangled in Nathalie's hair, with no recollection of how they'd come to be there.

Desperate to anchor herself, to cling to the quickly unspooling thread of her equilibrium, she turned her focus to the warped book of hymns lying abandoned on the floor. The pages were swollen and yellowed with age, the psalm—*I Surrender All*—marked with a tattered tassel.

Catharine had to look away, afraid she might laugh, and look away again when her gaze landed on the rusted crucifix above the communion table.

Still on her knees, Nathalie's breath grew more intimate, and all thoughts of the hymnal and cross faded.

She dug her toes against the stone, her hands curling into fists around the collar of Nathalie's jacket.

The tether was fraying.

Shadows danced along the walls where the draught crept in through long-forgotten spaces. Outside, the wind howled, whipping through the trees, rattling the crumbling tiles of the rooftop.

And then Nathalie's mouth found her.

The tether snapped.

The hymnal, the wind, the cross, the trees all vanished, replaced with nothing more than an ethereal sense of suspension. Catharine struggled to cling to the chapel, to the battered stone beneath her heels, to the ghosts who'd come before them—anything to ground her in the moment—but the effort was senseless. Her grasp on self-restraint spiraled, her existence surrendering to the overpowering demands of her body.

LYING ON THEIR BED OF blankets in the cloister of the pews, Catharine stared into the rafters. The aroma of beeswax had returned, circulated by the howling breeze creeping in through the darkness—but this time, the fragrance was infused with the ambered scent of Nathalie's skin, and the song of the wind harmonizing with the percussion of her heartbeat.

She understood, now, the full meaning of desire.

Of want.

Of need.

Of urgency and the reverent ache of anticipation.

It wasn't a demand, something only to be taken, but a sensation shared in equal measure. Given freely—with hands, with lips, with unadulterated devotion.

Above them, the centuries-old crucifix loomed over the hollowed chancel, its decaying silhouette casting a solemn shadow. She turned to look at Nathalie, resting her cheek against her breast.

"Have you ever wondered if this is wrong?"

Nathalie stroked an idle hand through her hair, unmoving from their makeshift sanctuary. "Does it feel wrong?"

"No," said Catharine simply. "If anything, it's the first time in my life something's felt exactly as it should."

From their pillow of discarded clothing, Nathalie flashed her lopsided smile. "Well, then I suppose my work here is finished: *veni, vidi, vici.*"

Catharine rolled her eyes. "*Please.* You came, you saw, you conquered nothing."

"On the contrary. I think I could make a solid case for all three. Beginning with—"

"Oh shut up, will you?" Catharine cut off her cheeky repartee, flushing at just the thought of where it was headed. "I'm serious!" To hide her blush, she rolled to face the ceiling. "Why do you think it scares people so much—this?"

She didn't define *this*. There was no question what she meant. The past hours had been spent entangled in one another's arms, demystifying the secrets of their bodies. Fingers exploring taboo lines and unspeakable curves, mouths mapping forbidden places, their shared need coaxing shivers from the other. Every staggered breath, every involuntary sigh had been more intense, more intoxicating than she ever fathomed possible.

Lazily, contentedly, Nathalie considered the question. "Ignorance?" she suggested. "Projection and repression?" She gestured at the cross. "Hatred fueled by religion? I could go on, if this is your idea of pillow talk, but to be honest, at the moment, there are a few other things I'd rather philosophize."

She sat up, the blanket dropping around her waist, and laughed when a lifetime of living by the rules of propriety forced Catharine to avert her eyes from her bare chest.

Casually stretching her arms above her head, Nathalie put on a deliberate exhibition.

"You can look, you know? I'm pretty sure I read somewhere that once you've had my nipples in your mouth, we're past the expectations of modesty."

The devilry of her smirk did nothing to fan Catharine's flaming cheeks as she tried to pull the blanket over her head.

"Oh no you don't!" Still grinning, Nathalie grappled for the cover. "I want to see you! No way I'm letting you off that easy."

In a short-lived game of tug-o-war, with Catharine offering no real resistance, she finally gave in, relinquishing her control of the blanket. Triumphant, Nathalie errantly tugged it to her hips, gazing down at her freely, but the provocation of her smile faded, her expression growing solemn. "God." She sat fully upright. "You don't even know, do you? How beautiful you are."

Catharine stared up at her, struggling not to self-efface. Nathalie may not have been the first person to tell her she was beautiful, but she was the first person to make her believe it meant something.

Lost in reflection, Nathalie trailed a knuckle down her cheek. But then, with the subtle flicker of her lips, the seriousness was cast away. "As proof, you've stolen my train of thought—o, siren! o Aphrodite! What was I even saying?"

"I believe you were philosophizing."

"Ah, yes. My list of things I'd rather deliberate than listen to you agonize over an antiquated code of morality. First question—" She gathered the hair that had fallen over Catharine's shoulders and fanned it above her head, taking away her last modicum of modesty. "How am I to be expected to walk past you on the High Monday morning and pretend I'm not picturing you exactly as you are right now?"

Without warning, and without waiting for a response, she swung her leg over Catharine's hip, straddling her. "Question two

—" deliberately shifting, she settled more closely against her, and smiled at Catharine's sharp inhalation. "Is it wrong I'm already plotting how to convince you to skip your Tuesday afternoon tutorial so that we might pursue more pleasurable endeavors?"

Catharine didn't tell her she would need no convincing—not with the way her body had already made up its mind.

"And three—" leaning forward, the steady roll of her hips becoming nearly intolerable, she kissed the hollow groove just above Catharine's collarbone. "The sudden, inexplicable need to know the scientific name for this perfect, irresistible indentation."

Catharine's mind wouldn't allow itself to shut off.

"Supraclavicular fossa."

Amused, Nathalie sat up. "You're too smart for your own good." Nonchalantly, she slid a hand between them, unmistakably enjoying the way it made Catharine arch. "I don't know how you know the things you know."

Clinging to composure, Catharine tried to shrug. "I was a lonely child. I read a lot."

Though Nathalie's expression softened, she didn't still the lazy torment of the pressure she'd built between them. "Maybe I could find a few ways to help you not feel so lonely?"

Catharine's body demanded she give in—to cast aside the playful repartee between them. But another side of her, a prideful side, was unrelenting.

"Oh?" She desperately sought to smother her physical response. "And what might those be?"

Nathalie, more than willing to accept the challenge, smiled. "Well—I think tonight I've demonstrated a fairly brief but foundational tutorial on the subject matter. You've mastered the fundamentals, but I should warn you—the advanced coursework takes time… commitment."

Catharine pasted on an air of indifference. "Am I to suppose, then—given that neither of our accommodations are conducive to this particular sort of field research—that you're expecting me to invest in a pair of walking boots?" Her eyes swept the span of the chapel, already dreading the return to civilization. A thought that brought her back to one of her earlier questions.

"How did you find this place, anyway?"

"Happenstance." Nathalie hiked a noncommittal shoulder, which promised there was a far more elaborate backstory.

"Meaning?"

"You won't appreciate the answer."

"You can hardly say something like that and not tell me." Catharine caught Nathalie's wrist, stilling her.

"It's not important."

"It is to me."

"Fine." Nathalie's lips disappeared into a thin line. "I used to meet someone here."

"Who?"

She hesitated longer than Catharine would have liked her to. "A tutor."

"*What!*"

"See?" Nathalie rolled off of her. "I told you you wouldn't like it."

Catharine sat up, all thoughts of modesty abandoned. "You had an affair with a *tutor*?!"

"The word *affair* is pushing it."

"Nat!"

"More like a fling."

"Semantics!" Catharine brushed the deflection off. "Who was it?"

"No way am I telling you that."

Catharine couldn't help but laugh. "Oh, you'll tell me." With her newly discovered power of negotiation—both to withhold and to offer—they both knew she had the upper hand. "Was she from your facul—?" She stopped mid-sentence. "It *was* a *she*, right?"

Nathalie made a face. "*Évidemment !*"

Catharine wasn't certain why it was such a relief, but it was. "And she was in your faculty?"

"Yes."

"Do you still have tutorials with her?"

"Sometimes. Yes."

Catharine flopped back beside her. "It's the one who tutors you in *Romantic Literature*, isn't it?"

Surprised, Nathalie turned to her. "What made you guess that?"

"I remember how enchanted you were by her interpretation of Wordsworth's conception of the *sublime* in nature. You raved about how she felt literature should not just be studied, but *lived*." She rolled her eyes. "Am I right?"

Nathalie's silence was enough of an answer.

"Let me guess—she seduced you with poetry—maybe something from Tintern Abbey—*Nature never did betray The heart that loved her*. Or perhaps she preferred Lord Byron? *There is a pleasure in the pathless woods, There is a rapture on the lonely shore*. She suggested an excursion to Wytham on the pretense of a field study— the perfect opportunity to *connect* with nature—and somehow, remarkably, you both ended up in a secluded fairytale chapel? Am I on the right path?"

"Well," Nathalie was impressed, "something like that. But to be fair to her, I was a very willing participant."

For the first time, Catharine felt a creeping hint of disappointment. "So, is this where you have all of your trysts?"

"Cate," said Nathalie carefully, recognizing the shift in tone, "it's not like that at all. Nothing with her was romantic. I'm far from the first student she's been with. We met a few times—there was never anything real between us."

"And it's over?"

"Don't insult me. You know me better than that."

Catharine averted her eyes to the dwindling wick of a candle, knowing she was right. She *did* know her better than that.

Nathalie continued. "In the dressing room—when you said you wanted this to mean something—I told you there was no way it couldn't. I meant that, Cate."

Repentant, and a little alarmed at her own sudden insecurity, Catharine found her hand and laced their fingers together. "I'm sorry. I just… I've never had anything like this." She tried to defuse her embarrassment with a laugh. "And I know for you, it's not exactly the first time you've swept someone off their feet."

"It is, however, the first time I've made three trips through the woods, hauling in half the city, with only the *hope* of sweeping someone off their feet."

"You made *three* trips?" Catharine looked around, taking another inventory. Candles. Blankets. Wine. Broom. Biscuits. She'd assumed some of it had been left over from… whenever. "When did you even have time?"

"This morning. I skipped my lecture on *Rehabilitating the Fallen Woman* in Victorian literature."

"Nat!"

"Let me assure you—it was worth it. As it turns out," she pushed herself onto an elbow to lean over Catharine, her free hand trailing a path from her knee to her thigh, "Wordsworth was right—nature *is* sublime."

Chapter Fourteen

ON THE FIRST SATURDAY OF December, a week before Christmas break, Catharine climbed the stairs to the Burton Taylor Studio. A poster in the lobby of the black box theatre displayed a festive graphic: *Magdalen Players* presents *The Long Christmas Dinner*. The drama group had asked Nathalie to play the role of Genevieve in Thornton Wilder's one-act show.

The last-minute invitation had sent Nathalie into a wave of panic. She'd launched into a week of evening rehearsals, each one followed by a long night with Catharine, who—forfeiting sleep and studies—dutifully poured coffee and helped her memorize her lines.

All for a single Saturday evening performance—one that Catharine couldn't even attend.

The venue door was open, and the house lights were on, which meant the dress rehearsal was over. Catharine paused a few feet before the threshold, attuned to the sounds coming from inside. Several actors laughed over a mix-up on blocking, while backstage crew shouted advisements on where to stick spike tape, and how to adjust the PAR cans.

Through the din, she finally heard the voice she'd been listening for.

"Not that I would ever forget a line, but should I theoretically do so, I'm counting on you to carry on and make me look brilliant." The velvet hum of Nathalie's French lilt carried into the hall.

A man's laugh responded.

Catharine slipped through the door.

The auditorium was tiny—just fifty seats—and the stage even smaller. As she skirted along the side wall, a few curious pairs of eyes turned her direction, taking in her dress and heels—noticeably out of place amongst the theatre blacks and grease paint—but none questioned her. She was relieved, for once, not to know anyone else in the cast.

Following the sound of Nathalie's voice, she found her tucked behind one of the canvas curtains strung from the overhead grid.

"Cate!" Caught off guard by her unexpected presence, Nathalie paused with a spliff midway to her mouth. "I thought you were—I didn't—" Sheepishly, she handed off the smoke to a boy in a pink bowtie standing at her side. "I figured you'd be halfway to London by now." Despite her obvious fluster at having been caught red-handed with a joint, her expression brightened. "Unless…?"

"No. I'm sorry." Catharine grimaced, realizing she'd inadvertently given her hope she'd be able to attend the performance. "I'm on my way to meet my driver, actually. I just…"

Her voice trailed off, aware they were not alone.

Nathalie, on the other hand, appeared to have no such reservations.

"Just couldn't leave without seeing me?" She tilted her head, her smile artful.

In the full wash of the stage lighting, surrounded by strangers, Catharine attempted to tamp down her rising anxiety in response to the cavalier flirtation. What she once would have laughed at, returning the teasing tit-for-tat, she now found too dangerous. Too revealing. The evolution of their relationship from friends to lovers had instilled in her a guardedness she hadn't previously known. Aware of their every touch, their every glance, worried that anyone who looked their way might read the subtext radiating between them.

It scared her.

She noticed now when their hands brushed in public, or if they stood too close. She balked when, out of habit, Nathalie linked their arms.

"You look very guilty," Nathalie had ribbed the day before on their walk back from Wytham. It was the second time they'd been to the woods since that first night at the chapel. The second time, in as many weeks, that Catharine had snuck out early from a lecture or skipped a tutorial.

And while the privacy of the woodland had given her what she wanted, the return to civilization was met with a different perspective. Before they'd even reached the city centre, she found herself veering to the edge of the pavement, distancing the space between them. An abrupt departure from the intimacy they'd just shared in the isolation of the forest.

Catharine had apologized, and Nathalie only laughed, brushing off her contrition, but Catharine knew it had bothered her more than she let on.

Now, standing as they were on the stage of the black box theatre, Nathalie again was perceptive to her quiet discomfort.

"I need to check the fit of my costumes. Walk with me?" she asked.

Catharine followed her into the hall.

"Just so you know, that wasn't mine," said Nathalie, holding her thumb to her forefinger as they descended the staircase toward the dressing rooms. "Archie brought it. I was just—"

"Do you really think I don't know you smoke cannabis?" Catharine shot her a pointed glance as she stepped through the door Nathalie held open.

"We like to call it weed in this century, *Grandma*," Nathalie badgered, closing them into the wardrobe. The lights were off, the workspace quiet. "Wait—you knew?"

Emboldened by their solitude, Catharine caught Nathalie's hand, pulling her between two racks of costumes. "Don't be daft— I can taste it on you."

"Pull me any closer, and your father's going to think it's you that's been hitting the hash," Nathalie warned, ignoring her own advice and stepping into her arms.

It had been two weeks since that first night in the abandoned chapel—two weeks of the best scattered hours of Catharine's life.

Despite drowning in problem sets and research-intensive essays, despite Nathalie's chaotic rehearsal schedule and her predictably late start on the thousand pages of *Bleak House* she was meant to finish by end of term, despite the lack of privacy, the apprehension, the constant need for discretion—the moments they were together made it all worthwhile.

"Do you really have to go tonight?" Nathalie brushed her thumb across Catharine's lips, careful not to smudge the makeup she'd applied more heavily than usual.

"You know I'd stay here if I could."

"But alas—" Nathalie heaved a dramatic sigh "—how could the Chinese Trade Minister and Russian Deputy Governor of Foreign Economic Relations possibly get on without you?"

"I think it's actually the Chairman of Saudi Energy Investments that my father wants me there for."

"But of course." Nathalie slid her hands to her hips. "How could I possibly compete with him?"

"Rest assured, it's my father's wrath that is your only competition."

Nathalie's mouth tightened. "One fight I'll never win." Disentangling herself from Catharine's embrace, she tried to mask her disappointment by sorting through the hanging costumes. "I imagine you won't be back before tomorrow night?"

Catharine hesitated to answer. She knew her father would expect her to stay in London tonight. After the *Global Transport Council* met over dinner at *The Connaught*, he would invite his closest allies back to his residence in Belgrave Square. There, behind closed doors, they would broker strategic alliances, swiftly casting aside the negotiations with their adversaries that had been canvased just hours earlier over cocktails.

To the chagrin of his guests—all men, all titans of power on a global scale—he would insist that Catharine sit in on the deliberations.

These are the forces you'll one day be up against, Catharine. It is best they learn to respect you while I am still around.

It would have been a justifiable perspective—if only he respected her himself.

The following morning, she was obligated to luncheon with her mother in Henley to discuss the upcoming Christmas holiday. She would be lucky if she made it back to Oxford in time for formal hall.

"Even if it's late, I'll still come see you." She touched Nathalie's elbow, hoping she would turn, but her attention remained on the rack of clothes.

"You know it's our last weekend before break."

It had been an unspoken source of tension between them—the six weeks between the end of Michaelmas and the beginning of Hilary term. Catharine would leave for Honour Stone, where it was the Brooks family tradition to spend Christmas, before the manor was left in the care of the staff for the remainder of the winter. From there, she and her mother would go to London, or Geneva, or Saint-Jean-Cap-Ferrat—wherever Colonel Brooks' whims took them.

Nathalie, on the other hand, was once again stuck in Oxford. She preferred Bordeaux in the spring, she said, though Catharine suspected it had far more to do with her financial constraints than any particular fondness for the weather. She'd applied for a seasonal position at a local café, which Catharine knew would help cover the expense of going home over Easter.

But what it didn't resolve was the growing melancholia settling between them—the inescapable reality that, come next Friday, they would be forced to spend the next six weeks apart.

A circumstance the previous year that had come as a mere disappointment—the bittersweet parting between friends. But one that now, as lovers, felt like a life sentence, no matter how temporary the separation.

"Why don't you come with me—for Christmas?" The words were out of Catharine's mouth before she could stop them.

It had been a thought flitting around the back of her mind for the past week. Not as something truly attainable, but a frangible fantasy that helped assuage the coming heartache.

Nathalie's hand paused on the sweeping red velvet of a cocktail dress, one she would wear on stage that evening—a glaring contrast to the argent gown Catharine had donned to please her father's friends.

"You don't mean that."

No matter how foolish the offer had been, Catharine refused to rescind it. "I do."

The dryness of Nathalie's laugh was nearly caustic. "As if you'd ever let me that far behind your walls."

"Nat." Catharine set her hands on Nathalie's shoulders, feeling the muscles tense beneath her touch.

It had been irresponsible—impractical, impulsive—asking her to Honour Stone. A brash moment of desperation, stifling her rationale. Something so very unlike her. But she also knew, with the offer on the table, there was no possible way to back out of it now.

She had stumbled into a Gordian knot she didn't know how to solve.

So instead, she doubled down.

"I'm serious. Come with me."

She could feel from the quiver in Nathalie's held breath that she wanted to say yes.

"You know I can't afford a holiday."

"Please—" Catharine kissed the nape of her neck "—don't insult me. Just say you'll come. I can't bear the thought of going these six weeks without you."

"And what of your parents?"

The stone that had settled in the bottom of her stomach churned. "I'll speak with them tonight."

"Do you really mean it?" Nathalie turned to face her, searching her gaze. "Aren't you afraid that your father…?" She didn't finish the sentence. They both knew what was at stake.

"I want you to say yes. I want to share Christmas with you."

A slow-dawning, brilliant smile washed the last remaining bitterness from Nathalie's face, and for the moment, Catharine forgot about all the reasons this was a terrible mistake.

"Well," Nathalie feigned a moment of deep consideration, "I guess I can clear my schedule." She paused. "Be forewarned—I didn't get you anything for Christmas."

"That's all right." Catharine assumed her same air of insouciance. "I can think of something you can give me."

Nathalie's eyes danced. "You are licentious, Cate Brooks. You have the world fooled with your facade of innocence." She leaned to kiss only the very corner of her mouth. "You'd better go, or your chauffeur's going to leave you here. I wouldn't want the Chairman of Saudi Energy Investments to be kept waiting on my behalf."

"I'll miss you, you know?" Catharine paused at the door.

Nathalie pulled the red cocktail dress off its hanger, holding it up in front of her. "*But, darling,*" she slipped into the American accent she'd adopted for the role of Genevieve, quoting from the play: "*the time will pass so fast that you'll hardly know I'm gone. I'll be back in the blink of an eye.*"

"*Twinkling* of an eye," Catharine corrected, blowing her a kiss before disappearing into the hall.

Chapter Fifteen

"The taste of home is very considerate, Mrs. Brooks." Mr. Kobayashi sampled the hitsumabushi and gave an approving nod. "Please extend my appreciation to your kitchen."

Catharine didn't hear her mother's response. Her focus was on her father's hands, analyzing the way he held his fork, judging his temper by how he set his teacup down. His mood had been difficult to gauge since they'd left London earlier that morning. He seemed distracted—a state which made him even more unapproachable than usual.

But she was running out of time. She knew if she was going to broach the subject of inviting Nathalie for Christmas, she had to do it soon. Once the meal was finished, she would return to Oxford, and her father would depart for a shipping conference in the Mediterranean.

Yet no opportunity had arisen. She hadn't anticipated Mr. Kobayashi joining them for luncheon at Honour Stone. And though she felt his presence might work in her favor, she knew her father wouldn't take kindly to being questioned in front of a colleague.

"Will you be home in Nagoya for Shōgatsu, Mr. Kobayashi?" her mother inquired, filling the lull in conversation with practiced politesse. Catharine flicked a surreptitious glance at her father to see how he would react to her mother's poor Western pronunciation, but the colonel remained preoccupied, absently adjusting his cufflinks.

The soft-spoken man nodded. "It is my intent. My mother is very adamant that all of her children be home for the New Year. If we are not, she can be quite unforgiving." He offered a small smile. "And you, Mrs. Brooks?" Raising a pickled plum to his mouth, he paused. "How will you spend the holidays?"

"Oh, much the same as ever, I imagine. Honour Stone does demand its traditions." Her laugh was stale.

"Speaking of tradition," said Catharine abruptly, seizing the opportunity presented by the turn in conversation. In her rush to set down her fork, she inadvertently upset a Mandel potato, sending the delicate spud rolling onto the table. Horrified, she hastily returned the buttery tuber to her plate before casting a quick look at her mother and finally settling her attention on the colonel. "There is something, sir, that I have been meaning to ask of you concerning Christmas."

Her father's cold blue eyes turned up from fiddling with his cufflinks.

"I have a peer—a… friend—" she stumbled over the word "—studying here from Bordeaux. She is unable to return home for the holiday. I was thinking…" She forced herself to take a breath. "I would like to invite her to join us." She swallowed. "So that she does not have to spend Christmas alone?" She hated the upward inflection that slipped into her voice, turning the statement into a question.

The colonel's gaze remained unblinking beneath his broad, distinguished brow. "What reason does she not return to Bordeaux?"

The inquiry was not curiosity—he wanted to know her family status.

"Her—" Catharine chose her words prudently, "—*circumstances* do not allow for it this year."

Brushing aside the request, her father leaned back in his chair. "Perhaps she should consider part-time employment so that she does not find herself in the same situation next year."

"Please," risking his temper, Catharine persisted. "She is a very good student—she won the Chancellor's English Essay Prize last summer. We often study together."

Unimpressed, he picked up his teacup. "I am disinclined to open our doors to a stranger."

"I have already asked her," Catharine blurted, uncertain how else to plead her case. "It would look poorly on me to rescind the offer now."

Her gaze flicked to Mr. Kobayashi, desperate for an advocate. She knew the businessman's influence held extensive sway over her father—his opinion one of the few Benjamin Brooks truly valued. The mild-mannered gentleman had often spoken strategically on her behalf, and over the years, she'd come to think of him as an ally.

To her surprise, however, it was her mother who intervened.

"*Benjamin.*" Her tone was clipped, almost challenging. It was a way Catharine had only heard her speak to him once before, many years earlier, when they had argued about whether it was appropriate for a girl to learn the art of sailing. Emily had been unrelenting, and as a result, Catharine had spent every weekend afterward on the water with her mother. "I have met Catharine's friend. Nathalie is a lovely, respectful young woman. It would benefit Catharine to serve as her host, offering an opportunity to gain a broader perspective on customs and conventions."

Catharine watched her father's knuckles grow white around the porcelain handle. For a moment, she thought he might fly into a rage, but a veiled glance toward Mr. Kobayashi forced him to maintain his composure. He would not have a scene in front of a guest.

"Well, if you have already extended an invitation—*without* my permission—there is naught to be done but honor it." He returned the cup to his saucer, unsipped. "So be it."

"Thank you," Catharine whispered, the words directed at the colonel, but meant for her mother.

A hush fell over the room, the four of them resuming the meal in silence.

After a few minutes, when Emily had slowly re-engaged Mr. Kobayashi in conversation—discussing the traditions of the Japanese New Year—Benjamin set his cutlery down with a resounding clink, and looked directly at Catharine.

"Last night—am I to understand you were speaking with Emilio Herrera?" He paid no mind that he had interrupted his wife and Mr. Kobayashi.

"I—" Caught off guard, Catharine hesitated. Emilio was the son of one of her father's industry affiliates, the Barcelona shipping magnate, Álvaro Herrera. Both Álvaro and Emilio had joined Colonel Brooks and his circle in Belgrave Square after the council dinner had concluded. "Yes?" She searched his face, trying to decipher his angle. "Emilio asked me about my studies."

"I'm told he was inappropriate in his behavior?"

"Inappropriate?" Catharine couldn't disguise her surprise. Emilio was flirtatious; he always had been. Just like his father, he was often more physical in his expression, but never in a way she found threatening or out of place for his culture. "No, I don't believe so."

"He did not touch you?"

You are more beautiful every time I see you, Miss Brooks, he had greeted her, kissing both cheeks. They stood on the balcony, talking about Oxford. About London. About the incomparable beauty of the lights in Madrid at Christmas. He told her how the previous weekend, he had skied in the Sierra Nevada in the morning and swum in Granada the same afternoon. When he left, he raised her hand to his lips. *Brillas con luz propia, Catharine*—you shine with your own light.

And that had been it.

"He—greeted me. He was polite."

"You command no respect for yourself, Catharine. To permit a man to make an advance on you in the home of your father—what message do you think that sends?"

Catharine felt a flush creep up her neck. She knew exactly what he was doing. Her inquiry about Nathalie in front of Mr. Kobayashi had placed him at a disadvantage, making him look unreasonable if he said no. Now, he intended to retaliate by humiliating her in turn.

"I do not believe he meant any disrespect—"

"Then you are as daft as you are naive. The Herreras' egos are greater than their worth. You cannot afford to be soft, Catharine. If you do not teach men like this their place, they will take yours." He shoved aside his plate. "In response to the impertinence shown by his son, we will strike Herrera where he is most vulnerable."

"I thought you considered Álvaro Herrera an ally in the industry?" She looked to Mr. Kobayashi to confirm. The Herreras had never been their enemy. All night, she'd listened to her father negotiate with the Spaniards, portraying a favorable relationship between the two empires.

"Loyalty lasts only so long as it is reciprocated—or until it becomes an inconvenience." The colonel stood, snapping his cuffs. "I happen to know the Herreras have been surviving on leveraged assets. His banker is in my debt. A single call, and those loans become due."

"Ben—" Mr Kobayashi joined him on his feet "—I think, perhaps, this situation has been overinflated—"

"Was it not you, *Naoki*," the colonel exaggerated the loose informality of his given name, "that told me you felt Emilio Herrera had crossed a line?"

"I told you I thought he might have been smitten with Catharine. I did *not* intend to imply—"

"I will handle the situation with my daughter as I see fit. You see," he looked to Catharine, "every action has a consequence. If a man's authority is undermined in his own home, he has no choice but to respond—especially when his hand is forced."

Chapter Sixteen

The frost-covered earth fractured beneath their boots, each step carrying them closer to Honour Stone.

Catharine found her pace slowing as they neared the edge of the woodland. She wasn't ready to disappear into the folds of the manor. She wanted to linger—to hide amongst the paperbark maples and silver birch trees, until the sun set. Until the glow of the moon dampened the illumination of the cascade of mullioned windows.

But her mother was expecting them.

She'd declined the offer to be picked up in Oxford, preferring to take the train instead. If she could have, she would have delayed even longer, staying an extra night in the tranquility of the Meadow Building, where the other students in her staircase had already vacated for Christmas. She and Nathalie could have spent the luxury of an uninterrupted night together, sleeping in the comfort of a real bed, without the need to traipse miles through the woods or sneak away before sunrise. But the risk was too great—and Honour Stone was calling.

So in a last-ditch effort to prolong the inevitable, when they'd arrived at the train station, she'd chosen not to ring her mother, and instead led Nathalie across the bridge and into the Brooks estate woodlands, where they could walk the final mile on foot. Anything to cling to the last remaining moments of freedom.

"My father won't return from Ibiza for another week or two," she said, ducking beneath the dripping bough of a European ash. It was something she'd told Nathalie at least a dozen times already, but she was nervous and couldn't stop herself from saying it again. "My mum is more lenient. She doesn't require formal breakfast and won't mind if we sleep in."

"Formal breakfast?" Nathalie laughed but fell silent when Catharine didn't return her smile. "You're serious?"

"Dinner is at half past seven. Until the colonel returns, we'll probably be permitted to eat in the Yellow Room." In front of them, the gray light of the overcast afternoon turned brighter, signifying the clearing ahead. Her throat felt dry. "As our guest, of course, you won't be expected—"

"Cate." Nathalie took her hand. "You're shaking."

She was, she realized—her entire body coiled like a spring. It took everything in her willpower not to pull her hand away when Nathalie raised it to her lips. They were too close. Too close to prying eyes that monitored every detail of her life.

"Relax." Nathalie kissed her palm, the gentle gesture sending a different kind of shiver to the small of her back. "You're worrying too much. It'll be fine. Just treat me like any other friend who's stayed over—the only difference being, I imagine none of them have wondered if you lock the door to your bedroom at night?" Her breath was warm where she slid the cuff of her jacket up, baring the soft skin of her wrist.

"That's not a good precedent to follow," said Catharine, addressing the first part of the suggestion while trying to pretend the second half wasn't the only thing on her mind. As if she hadn't spent the past five days thinking of every possible way they could be together without risk of getting caught. "I've never entertained a friend before."

The admission brought Nathalie to a halt. "You've never had a friend stay the night at your house?"

The word *house* was the precise reason Catharine was so anxious. No matter how well Nathalie thought she knew her,

Catharine was certain she wasn't prepared for Honour Stone... for her father... for the behind-the-curtain examination of her life.

"No."

"My friends practically lived at my house over the summer. Maman could only get rid of them when she threatened to put them to work in the vineyard. Then we'd all just move on to the next house, and the next, until the cycle started over."

It sounded like a wonderful way to spend the holidays. Catharine didn't tell her she'd never really had anyone close enough to invite—even if it had been allowed.

Walking on, she left her hand in Nathalie's until they neared the edge of the treeline, where she gently but deliberately disentangled their fingers, putting space between them as they stepped into the clearing and climbed the final crest of the hill.

At the top, it came as no surprise when Nathalie stopped short.

Catharine could hardly bring herself to look out over the horizon.

Below, deep into the valley, across the acres of dormant pasture and dew-laden parkland, loomed the grandiose façade of Honour Stone.

Catharine had long grown immune to the enormity of the manor, failing to appreciate the magnificence of its centuries of evolving architecture. She felt nothing for its Gothic turrets and arches, or the red-brick chimneys added during its Tudor era. She saw no splendor in the ornate detail of Georgian iron balconies or Elizabethan openwork parapets. To her, it was little more than a glorified prison, pieced together from limestone and timber.

Nathalie, however—for all of her blasé manner—could not conceal her astonishment.

For a long time, she stared, saying nothing, until she finally laughed. "Is that a *church*?" She motioned toward a steeply pitched, medieval stone structure standing erect against the eastern lawns.

It was *St. Josephine's Chapel*, constructed in the thirteenth century —the oldest building on the estate.

Despite her father not being a religious man, the place of worship was still opened every Sunday. Two services were held, attended by the staff and residents of the neighboring hamlet. As a child, Catharine had enjoyed sneaking through the towering arched doorway on hot summer afternoons. She would hide, slumped against the cool flint walls, and read *The Chronicles of Narnia*, wishing that she, too, could find a magical wardrobe that would allow her to escape to another world.

She hadn't been inside its walls in years.

"It's a chapel."

Nathalie gave a *same-difference* shrug. "You could have mentioned you had your own chapel—it would have saved a lot of trudging through the woods."

"Don't get any ideas—there's like a dozen generations of Brooks interred in a vault beneath those floors. I'm not risking the wrath of my ancestors over—" she couldn't hide her smile "—improper use of consecrated ground."

Nathalie's deep brown eyes glowed amber in the fading sunlight, and all Catharine could think about was how much she wanted to kiss her—and all the reasons she couldn't.

"It certainly didn't stop you in Wytham."

"In Wytham, I wasn't worried about my great-great-grandfather acting as a voyeur through his tomb."

"You're being selfish," said Nathalie. "Dead a hundred years, the old man would probably appreciate the show."

Catharine made a face. "Come on." She tugged on her arm, starting down the hill. If they stood there any longer, she knew she'd be the one dragging Nathalie back to the cover of the trees. "You're going to make us late for dinner."

"Well, we certainly wouldn't want that."

"You'll soon understand," said Catharine, only half kidding.

They were silent as they crossed the rolling lawns into the courtyard, where the circular drive bordered an ostentatious water fountain, the intricate limestone statue of a female warrior standing ramrod straight beside a lion, clutching her trident and shield.

"Britannia—how original." Nathalie rolled her eyes.

"I assume you would have preferred *Marianne,*" countered Catharine, alluding to Nathalie's obsession with the allegorical woman symbolizing the French Republic.

"Heroic, defiant, bare-breasted—leading our people to liberty? What's not to love?"

"I imagine you find one of those attributes to outweigh the others." Catharine paused at the bottom of the entry stairs. It was the first time in her life she could ever remember laughing on her way into the manor.

"Speaking of such attributes—you never answered my question."

Her foot on the first step, Catharine considered playing ignorant —or ignoring her altogether. She hadn't forgotten—even with the nerves of introducing Nathalie to Honour Stone, of knowing she would meet her father, of all the things that could go wrong—it wasn't as if her thoughts were anywhere else.

Finally, aware she was playing with fire, but unable to bring herself to care, she whispered, "Maybe it's locked—maybe it's not. You'll just have to find out."

And then the double doors swung open above them, and without looking back at Nathalie, she forced her feet up the stairs.

It didn't cease to amaze Catharine—for a hell that swallowed its inhabitants whole—how easily Nathalie defied the imposing demands of Honour Stone.

At dinner, she rested her elbow on the table while pouring wine into her water glass, and then proceeded to spread butter with her fish knife directly onto her roll. When she noticed Catharine's alarm, she laughed and simply said, "I've already committed some unforgivable social faux pas, haven't I?" with no hint of shame.

To Catharine's even greater disbelief, her mother waved off the sins of etiquette with her own tut of dismissal.

"I've never understood half these so-called *rules* imparted on us at the table. You're perfectly fine, my dear."

In a show of solidarity, instead of tearing her bread apart, she took a bite straight from her brioche.

Throughout the dinner, Nathalie made Emily laugh, regaling them with stories of growing up helping her mother in the vineyard. By the end of her dramatic narrative about the time she'd slipped stomping grapes at the harvest festival as a child (emerging from the vat covered in purple stains, which had earned her the nickname *Petite Prune)*, Catharine found her guarded reservations waning.

Nathalie couldn't feel the pressure of the manor. She wasn't burdened by the weight of all the generations. In her blissful ignorance, she brought out a side of Emily Brooks that Catharine almost forgot existed. A playful, clever, bantering woman who, in another life, might have donned the silks of a QC barrister rather than the chains of a wife bound by longstanding Brooks tradition.

When at last they'd retired from the dining hall to the Yellow Room, Catharine could tell her mother was wholly smitten. More so, even, than she'd been after their day sailing in Henley.

And what reason was there not to be? Nathalie was charming. Warm. Witty. A levity surrounded her that became infectious.

Would her mother be as welcoming, however, if she knew where Catharine's mind drifted while watching Nathalie lick a dusting of sugar from her lemon posset off her fingers? If she knew how unbearable the last five days had been, the chaos of the end of term keeping them apart? If she knew the ways Catharine's heart somersaulted at just the idea of Nathalie in her bedroom?

It wasn't really a question.

The sobriety of the thought snapped Catharine's attention away from the stain of wine along the Frenchwoman's full lower lip and back to the conversation.

"I'm sorry?" Her mother had asked her something.

"I was saying you should play a piece for us, Catharine." Settled in her favorite chair, Emily motioned toward the Pleyel upright tucked away in the corner.

There was a time, in her childhood, when Catharine had loved to play for her mother. *Chopin, Mendelssohn, Debussy*—whatever mood suited the evening. Back when her father had been gone for months on end, serving in the military. Now, those days felt like a lifetime ago, and the joy of such pastimes had faded.

"I'd rather not."

"It's a shame. You were so very talented—and you loved it so."

The wine—a rare indulgence while her father was not in residence—must have gone to her mother's head.

"I didn't know you were a pianist," said Nathalie.

Unsettled by the turn in discussion, Catharine hardly noticed that Nathalie had thrown convention to the wind, slipping out of her shoes to sit cross-legged on the settee.

"I'm—not. I don't play anymore." She couldn't stand the thought of running her fingers over the ivory keys she'd once revered. Not after so long an absence.

"Well, if it's something you loved," Nathalie challenged, "maybe you should take it up again?"

"Another time, perhaps."

"The only way to get rid of temptation is to yield to it." The Oscar Wilde quote was one of Nathalie's favorites. "Unless, of course, you have more pressing matters to attend?"

The audacity of the innuendo forced Catharine to cover her flush with a sip of merlot. She worried her mother would be able to feel the current coursing between them—to sense the palpable struggle of being so close, yet unable to touch. But when she glanced at her mum, her focus was turned to topping off her wine.

"It's late. I wouldn't want to start something I wasn't able to finish." Catharine offered a demure smile. "And as the wise Dalai Lama once said, *'sleep is the best meditation.'"*

Unaware of the veiled spar ensuing, Emily looked to Catharine. "Are you early to bed then?"

"It's been a long day." Catharine rose from the sofa.

She expected Nathalie to follow suit, but instead was met with only a rebellious smile.

"Since your daughter is apparently at risk of turning into a pumpkin—and refuses to entertain us—perhaps you'd care for a game of *Piquet*, Mrs. Brooks? I play an excellent hand."

"I haven't played *Piquet* in years." Emily was delighted. "Shall I send Mrs. Ainsley for another bottle of wine?"

Defiant, Nathalie held Catharine's gaze. "*Une excellente idée, merci bien !*"

Out of her mother's line of sight, Catharine arched a brow. "Well, goodnight, then."

"Goodnight, darling," said Emily, the term of endearment further proof she was bordering on drunk.

"Sweet *meditations*," Nathalie taunted, shuffling a deck of cards. "Perhaps tomorrow you'll indulge us with a tune." She waved the Queen of Spades in the direction of the piano.

"*Tu peux toujours rêver,*" Catharine silently lipped—*you can always dream*—before retreating into the hall, leaving Nathalie to her game.

It was after midnight when Catharine heard steps in the hall. The door to the *Garden Room*—the adjacent guest suite Mrs. Ainsley had prepared for Nathalie earlier in the afternoon—opened and closed, and then there was nothing.

Catharine lay awake, staring at the canopy above her bed, listening to the groans of the manor as it settled for the evening. She tuned her ear for the soft pad of footsteps, the creak of a hinge, a whisper in the dark, but the only sound that greeted her was the winter winds rattling the windowpanes.

The household was at rest—and still, she heard nothing from Nathalie.

For hours, she listened to the dull chime of the grandfather clock, its echoes drifting through the long gallery, until at last, she slipped into a shallow, restless sleep.

She woke late the following morning and was still groggy when she stumbled into the breakfast room. Her mother and Nathalie were already at the table, working through what didn't appear to be their first kettle of tea.

"Well, good morning, sunshine," said Nathalie, adding a heaping spoon of honey to her porridge. "Sleep well?"

"Wonderfully *uninterrupted*," Catharine responded, unable to hide the terseness in her tone. "Good morning, Mum." She deliberately took the furthest seat away from Nathalie and looked to her mother. "Did you enjoy your game of *Piquet*?"

"Three rounds and two bottles of wine later," Emily laughed, cutting through a roasted tomato. "I can't recall having that much fun since university. Though I'm afraid to say, I recover more slowly these days." Her smile brought out the flush in her cheeks and the shadows beneath her caramel eyes. "I must admit, I may have enjoyed the evening even more, however, if I hadn't lost every hand."

"Don't feel bad, Mum—" Catharine leaned back to allow Mrs. Ainsley to place a bowl of fruit and yogurt in front of her, "—Ms. Comtois enjoys donning a mask of innocence, but she's a master strategist at heart."

"Bit tetchy this morning, are we?" Raising a spoonful of porridge, Nathalie paused. "Disappointed you missed out on a good time? Just think, you could have stayed—played the piano—shared another bottle of wine. Who knows, maybe I even could have shown you a trick or two?" She swallowed the bite, dabbing a drop of cream from the corner of her mouth with her tongue. "I'm quite good at knowing what to hold and how to play my hand."

The persimmon Catharine was chewing went down the wrong way. She choked, reaching blindly for her water.

"Are you all right, dear?" Mrs. Ainsley, on her way for a fresh kettle, paused with a hand on her shoulder.

"Fine," Catharine gasped, "sorry—thank you." She dried her eyes with her napkin, unable to look at Nathalie.

After breakfast, Emily suggested a walk through the gardens. A light snowfall had settled overnight, turning the parklands white.

"I know what you're up to," Catharine scolded when she and Nathalie had wandered ahead of her mother, who stopped to speak to one of the groundsmen. They'd passed through the walled rose garden and into the dormant orchard, where the barren trees stood like sentries, row after row after row.

"Oh?" Nathalie bent to collect the dried blossom from a quince branch, twirling the coral-pink petals between her fingers. "And that is?"

"You're punishing me for being unwilling to play the piano."

"Punishing? Such a harsh word. More like *encouraging* you to reclaim something you love."

"I haven't played in years—"

"All the more reason you should take it up again—to do something for yourself!"

Further down the row, Emily appeared through the garden gate, heading in their direction.

"Play something for me this evening," said Nathalie, stepping around the knotted trunk of a mulberry tree, "and I just might make it worth your while."

"You're assuming I'll leave my door unlocked."

Nathalie poked her head around the trunk. "Oh, please. Don't fool yourself. You want to kiss me so badly, you haven't taken your eyes off my mouth all morning."

Guilty as charged, Catharine turned her gaze away to where her mother was passing through the first row of pear trees. "I'm not playing the piano for you."

"We'll see." Nathalie reached forward, tucking the dry blossom behind Catharine's ear, before ducking back onto the path to greet Emily with a smile.

As usual, Nathalie was right—though she didn't win, perhaps, as quickly as she had anticipated.

For three more days, stubborn as ever, Catharine strung out the losing battle. They walked the parklands, joined her mother at lunch at the yacht club, and aimlessly window-shopped through town. To Catharine's initial hesitation—uncertain of the lapse in propriety—yet eventual delight, Nathalie convinced Mrs. Ainsley to let them bake gingerbread biscuits with her in the Honour Stone kitchen. In all the years she'd known the prim and proper house manager, Catharine had never witnessed the woman laugh so freely or jest so much as she did that evening, covered in flour and learning the French words for dough and rolling pin.

One afternoon, Geoff came to pick up Mrs. Mills, and while waiting for his mother, Nathalie dragged the three of them through the eastern woodland and along the old hedgerows, gathering bay laurel and pine, holly and ivy. They sat on the garden veranda and wove festive wreaths from the aromatic branches, and Geoff teased that maybe Catharine wouldn't be so uptight if Nathalie had found some mistletoe to tuck into the decorations.

The days ticked by in coded wordplay and covert touches, the occasional long glance beneath lowered lashes. At night, tea was served in the Yellow Room, and like clockwork, Nathalie would suggest how much more festive the evening would be with music, and Catharine would decline, leaving her mother and Nathalie to their cards and wine. Unable to help herself, she would listen for Nathalie's footsteps in the hall, and hold her breath until she heard the door click closed in the *Garden Room*. And then she would drift to sleep alone.

Until the fourth evening, in the middle of a losing hand of *Trois*, Catharine got up and flipped the fallboard on the old Pleyel upright. Disallowing herself to think too long, she slipped onto the bench and touched the middle C, listening to the note resonate. To her surprise, the piano was in tune. The wood was polished, and the keys dusted; evidence that a technician had been employed to keep the instrument meticulously maintained.

She swallowed, her heart hammering an uneven meter as her left hand picked out the broken chord of D ♭ major. The keys felt foreign beneath her stiff fingers, yet somehow they still seemed to know what to do.

Forcing herself to continue, her right hand tentatively answered, unfolding the delicate, arpeggiated prelude of *Clair de lune*. Several bars in, she could already feel her shoulders begin to relax, her wrists loosen. Instinct took over, and despite the years, the ethereal melody—with its slow, expressive phrasing—carried her away.

She closed her eyes, moving through the dreamy arpeggios, the blurred harmonies, finding the music safe. Familiar. A serenity settling over her she'd almost forgotten. Her feet drifted over the pedals, fingertips floating across the keys. The tender crescendos, the breath-like diminuendos, swept her back to childhood—to a place she'd always gone to escape.

But then she stumbled.

Eyes flying open, she dropped her gaze to the keys, desperate to try and keep pace with the fast, ascending passages that had once come to her so easily. Her breath caught over every missed note, her rigid fingers faltering. The independence of her hands grew uncertain, interrupting the balance and fluidity. Chords grew harsh, tones staccato where they should have been legato, shattering the beauty of the piece.

It was flawed. Unpolished. Imperfect.

Everything she didn't know how to allow herself to be.

Humiliated by her incompetence and afraid she was going to cry, she took a staggering step off the bench and snapped the wooden fallboard closed.

"Catharine, that was really—"

She cut her mother off. "I can't. I'm sorry…"

"Cate." Nathalie had come to stand behind her, and though she didn't touch her, Catharine felt the need to move away, too aware of the charged energy flowing between them.

"I'm sorry," she said again—to whom, she wasn't sure—and then, without looking back, abandoned her manners and fled out the door.

She'd only been in her room a few minutes before a quiet knock broke the silence, a soft voice in the hall.

"Cate?"

She didn't answer.

After a beat, the door creaked open, but Catharine didn't turn from the low-set window seat overlooking the darkened garden.

All week, she'd waited for Nathalie to follow her, to find her in her room, to seize whatever stolen hours the ancient walls would afford.

Now, however, the relief in her arrival was met with an alloy of resentment.

She hadn't wanted to touch the upright. She hadn't wanted to remember how it felt, her fingers flying across those eighty-eight keys. To be reminded of what it was like to have something that was hers, and hers only.

Sailing was her mother's, even if Catharine did enjoy it. And despite the satisfaction she'd found in rowing, there had never been any question the sport belonged to her father. Same with tennis. Equestrian. Archery. But music? It had been her sanctuary.

She knew Nathalie had good intentions. She'd only wanted her to play because she thought it would bring her joy. Instead, all it had done was remind Catharine how little of her life was her own. The things she loved were always taken from her, no matter how careful she was to hold them close.

"May I come in?"

Her chest tightened at the hesitancy in the whisper, at the cautious steps that paused halfway across the polished parquet floor. The carefulness of the approach told her Nathalie had not come to prod her. She was not there to tease her or offer a lecture.

Without looking up, Catharine could feel Nathalie's eyes sweep the spacious suite, surveying the room, taking in the florid hand-painted wallpaper and marble-faced fireplace, the ornate canopy bed and antique vanity with its gilded mirror.

For once, she didn't razz her for the ostentatiousness, the humiliating grandeur. Whatever her thoughts, she kept them to herself.

After a long pause, she crossed to join Catharine at the window, reaching a tentative hand to stroke her cheek.

"Did you know *Clair de lune* was named after a poem?"

"Paul Verlaine. Debussy chose the title from his collection, *Fêtes galantes*," Catharine muttered, uncertain why it mattered.

Above her, in the reflection of the glass, she could see the corners of Nathalie's Cupid's bow lips turn up into a smile. "*Ma petite encyclopédie.*" She trailed her fingers through Catharine's long, loose tendrils of hair.

Stubborn, Catharine turned away, drawing her knees up to her chest.

Nathalie only stepped closer, undeterred. "You already know, then, how rich Verlaine's verse, how romantic his atmosphere—the story of masked lovers dancing in the moonlight. In the poem, he describes them as graceful, elegant, dreamy… But the image is a mirage, the happiness only skin-deep. It is the moon that sees beyond the illusion and feels what lies beneath. The quiet sorrow in their laughter, the fragility of their joy. '*Tout en chantant sur le mode mineur.*'"

All while singing in the minor key. The line from the poem was not one Catharine understood as a child.

But she understood it now.

"The metaphor, of course," continued Nathalie, "is that the moment is ephemeral—no different than the glow of moonlight." She set her hand on Catharine's shoulder. "That's the thing about beauty, *ma chérie*—the secret Debussy and Verlaine chose to recognize. It doesn't have to be perfect."

Once again, Catharine felt tears threaten—the same ones that had emerged, unbidden, when she'd stumbled over the polyrhythms in the middle measures of *Clair de lune*. She understood what Nathalie was getting at. To the artist, the dreamer, the romanticist, the world was built on poetry. Life imitating art.

The Japanese had a word for it—*Wabi-sabi*. The philosophy that beauty is found in the transient, the weathered, the worn.

But that was not the world Catharine was born into. Her existence had no place for imperfection, no room for the charm of fallibility and flaws.

And it wasn't something she wished to address.

"I'd rather not talk about it."

"You don't have to." Nathalie brushed her fingers across her temple. "But if you ever want to—"

"I don't." She caught Nathalie's hand, trying to soften the curtness of her tone. She didn't want to talk about Debussy or French poetry or the confines of her failings. Not about music or moonlight or mirage.

She didn't want to talk about anything at all.

Instead, she reached for the cord dangling from the antique brass lamp beside the window, tugging the room into shadow.

"Cate." The single word was a warning, the outline of Nathalie's profile glancing toward the sliver of light shining beneath the door. It wasn't late. The house remained awake, her mother undoubtedly still in the Yellow Room where Catharine's abandoned cup of tea hadn't yet had time to grow cold.

She unfolded her legs, twisting on the low cushion to look up at Nathalie. "I don't care."

And in the moment, she didn't. There was an intoxicating sense of freedom in the recklessness of her actions—a thrill of defiance in knowing the Brooks estate stretched out below them in acres of blackness, their shadowed silhouettes framed by the open damask curtains. She wanted to lose herself in that comfort only Nathalie could offer. To wash away the bitterness of the night with the growing familiarity of her touch, her taste, her smell.

Without allowing time for a response, Catharine slipped her hands beneath the hem of Nathalie's fine-knit top, working loose the buttons on her trousers, drawing her close.

It was still novel to her, this power she was slowly discovering, this quiet current of control that lay beneath the gentlest brush of fingertips. In her limited experience of intimacy—their few meetings at the chapel, a single whispered afternoon within the thin-walled confines of Nathalie's Brasenose room—Catharine was still learning the ways she could make Nathalie shiver; the things she could do to make her breath still, or her eyes close, or her lips part with an involuntary gasp. And even then, it was Nathalie who set the tempo, Catharine content to follow her guidance.

But tonight, when Nathalie reached for her, Catharine purposefully held her aloft. After the stress of the evening, the failure she had felt, she didn't want to be conducted, to have her actions orchestrated by somebody else. She wanted freedom to determine the pace. To feel, for once, like she was the one in charge of the choices that she made.

Leaning forward, she pressed her lips to the pale skin just below Nathalie's hemline, the iridescent sliver glowing silver in the moonlight.

She could feel Nathalie tense.

Emboldened by the week of pent-up frustrations, she slid Nathalie's trousers to the floor, once again brushing away the hands that sought to touch her. It went against Nathalie's grain, she knew, to keep still—to do nothing—and the knowledge of it turned her actions even more leisurely, taking enjoyment from her impatience.

Languidly, tauntingly, she stretched out the time, making a slow, deliberate exploration. Unhurried hands exposed bare skin, soft breath fanning the path of her provocative trace of fingertips. Lips —daring, calculated—mapped a trail that made Nathalie's breath grow ragged, then shallow. Then cease altogether.

Behind them, a susurration of raindrops murmured against the window. The moon had shifted, the house growing quiet. At some point—she hadn't noticed when—the light had been doused in the hall.

Catharine smiled against her, aware of the quiver in Nathalie's limbs, the way her fingers curled into fists, the dusky rose of her painted nails digging into her palms. Catharine sat back, the sudden absence of her mouth drawing a breath of protest from Nathalie.

"*Ne t'arrête pas.*" The plea was little more than a whisper.

There was an exquisite sense of satisfaction in making her wait, in the discovery of what it meant to want and be wanted—to have the power to create this kind of longing. It was unlike anything she'd ever known. A feeling she wished she could trap in amber, preserving it forever.

Music is the space between the notes, Debussy had once said. A sentiment that all at once made sense.

Despite Nathalie's protestation, Catharine took a long moment to look at her, to commit to memory the feel of her hips beneath her palms, to etch in stone the outline of her curves, to imprint the way she felt in this exact instant.

Then at last she gave in, yielding to Nathalie's anticipation—her need—until Nathalie had to brace herself against the window.

And in the shadows, time unraveled, the minutes measured only by hitched breath and trembling sighs, the streak of raindrops blending with fogged breath on clouded glass, the escalating storm smothering Nathalie's gasps until she shuddered and collapsed against her.

THE MOON HAD NEARLY SET by the time Catharine's eyes grew heavy. Soon, the glow of the sun would crest the hills leading into the eastern woodland, its harsh winter light cascading through the barren limbs of beech and sycamore.

She would rather the darkness had gone on forever.

"I should go back to my room," Nathalie whispered, her voice little more than a ghost beside her. At some point, they'd moved to her bed, burrowed in the wealth of silk and down.

Catharine was grateful she didn't have to ask her—that Nathalie understood well enough to offer.

Still, she regretted the necessity.

"I'm sorry." She rolled onto her side. Nathalie's hair still carried the faint scent of jasmine from her supermarket shampoo. A smell Catharine had grown to love.

"It's okay—I imagine I'll find a few ways you can make amends," Nathalie teased, and Catharine felt her neck flush even as a rush of heat resurfaced through her slackened limbs. She tried to save face, combating Nathalie's smug smile by adopting a haughty air.

"You're assuming I've left an open invitation."

"Please," Nathalie scoffed. "We both know this isn't a game you'll ever win." Under the covers, she pinched Catharine's thigh before threatening to slide her hand south, eliciting a smothered laugh that turned into a long, lingering kiss.

Finally, reluctantly, as the luminescent shimmer of daybreak touched the handprint-smudged windowpane, Nathalie extracted herself from Catharine's arms and pulled on her discarded clothing. Catharine watched her leave, already aware of the chilled absence where her head had lain beside her on the pillow.

But despite the inevitable glumness of the early morning departure, the afternoon rolled into the start of the most blissful consecutive days of Catharine's life.

They passed the daylight hours wandering the Honour Stone parklands, shivering from the cold, stealing kisses until their lips turned blue behind the ivy-covered walls of the gardens. Teeth chattering, they were oblivious to the rambling rose and boxwood that snagged at their coats and trousers. They ice skated on the northern dew pond, Catharine gracefully gliding in circles while Nathalie barrelled around the perimeter, her every pass veering closer until she caught Catharine's arm, dragging her to the frozen surface in a tumble of woolly hats and mittens. One morning, in the kitchen, Nathalie persuaded Mrs. Ainsley to allow her to cook French crêpes for breakfast. A surprise which delighted Emily, who —if she noticed—said nothing about the dusting of icing sugar coating her daughter's neck and shoulders.

In the middle of the week, Emily informed Catharine she was going shopping in London. She planned to stay at their residence in the city and invited the girls to join her. Catharine apologetically declined. She and Nathalie had far too much reading to do and couldn't neglect their studies.

Her mother didn't need to know that no books were ever opened in her absence. Instead, the unsupervised days lured

Catharine from her prudence, the pair of them capitalizing on the unchaperoned evenings to retire early after dinner, leaving Nathalie hardly enough time to slink back across the hall before breakfast.

The staff never appeared to notice.

On the Sunday before Christmas, under Nathalie's incorrigible persuasion, Catharine finally relented, and they had sex in the chapel. It was easy to forget—while in the throng of grappling hands and wandering lips—the long-dead line of Brooks' corpses underfoot, and the unblinking stare of St. Michael the Archangel scowling down at them. Afterward, however, she glanced up at the oil portrait of The Virgin Mary and Baby Jesus to offer her contrition.

"Don't look as if we've just done something so scandalous," Nathalie tutted as they pulled on their clothes in the prismatic hue of the towering stained glass window. "It's the final day of Advent —The Sunday of Love."

Catharine doubted that was the intent behind *O Come, O Come, Emmanuel*, but laughed anyway when Nathalie snapped her bra at her. When they slipped outside, she was surprised to find a feathering of snow had fallen, and slunk deeper into the collar of her coat when Nathalie casually called a greeting to the nearby groundskeeper covering the topiary.

The nights passed in tangled sheets on her four-poster bed, and stolen wine drunk straight from the bottle; *La Vie en Rose* cycling on repeat on her record player.

When Emily returned, instead of allowing the mood to dampen, Nathalie coaxed Catharine to invite her mother sailing, followed by an afternoon in Marlow, the three of them enjoying the festive lights and sipping hot chocolate on the foggy riverbank.

That night, Catharine—unprompted—tinkered on the piano, permitting herself to make mistakes as she plucked out *Carol of the Bells* and *God Rest Ye Merry, Gentlemen* from memory. Her mother and Nathalie busied themselves wrapping gifts and drinking sherry, going out of their way to pay her no attention. When she went to bed, wrapped in Nathalie's arms, she was certain she'd never been happier.

The next morning, Colonel Brooks called. He would arrive in Honour Stone by the following evening.

And everything changed.

Already dreading her father's return, Catharine insisted Nathalie wait until after midnight to come to her suite. They lay in bed, somber, saying nothing, the magic of the previous week already fading.

"I need you to promise me something," she finally said, the silence grating.

Beside her, Nathalie entwined their fingers. "Relax, Cate, you don't have to worry. I'll be on my best behavior."

"No—it's… it's not that." She hated that Nathalie even had to feel that way—that that was her concern. She should have been able to be exactly who she was. Someone braver than Catharine could ever fathom.

Staring at the portrait of one of her great-great-ancestors mounted on the wall, she chewed her bottom lip. "If I'm—if I seem *different* tomorrow," she said for lack of a better word, "will you promise to forgive me?"

"Hey." Nathalie squeezed her hand. "You should know by now —I love you every way you are, Cate Brooks. I wish you could see that."

For a long time, Catharine didn't blink, afraid if she did, an uninvited tear might slip free. Instead, she kept her attention fixed on the cathedral-high cheekbones of the unhappy woman in the painting, wondering if every Brooks before her had lain in bed as miserable as she.

By the time she was able to breathe again, certain her eyes would remain dry, she turned to Nathalie, but found her fast asleep, lost to her dreams.

Catharine's gaze drifted back to the portrait, to the woman's hard blue eyes that matched her own—and even in their likeness, she felt incredibly alone.

Chapter Seventeen

"And what, Miss Comtois," said Colonel Brooks, "do you intend to do with your degree in English after you graduate from Brasenose?"

The way he said *Brasenose* was an insult all of its own.

Catharine crossed and uncrossed her ankles beneath the table, struggling to sit still. The meaty scent of Guinea fowl galantine was making her nauseous.

It was the first time her father had addressed Nathalie directly, aside from the curt greeting he'd offered upon his arrival the previous evening. The question, of course, was rhetorical. He'd inquired about Nathalie's background prior to leaving for Ibiza. And he was not the kind of man to forget a single detail.

Across the table, divided by the extravagant span of a Christmas feast—golden roasted turkey, cabbage braised with red wine and apple, Boulangère potatoes, cauliflower cheese—Nathalie pushed a honey-glazed Brussels sprout around her plate before abandoning it beside the cranberry sauce infused with candied ginger.

Unlike when she first met Catharine, where she'd confidently touted her dreams, the Frenchwoman now looked uncertain. Her uncharacteristic lack of confidence made the growing knot tighten beneath Catharine's ribs. She knew the hesitancy was not from a change of heart in the faith of her own talent, but rather out of a desire not to misstep in her answer, to protect Catharine in her own home.

"I hope to make my living in the theatre."

Catharine sank a little lower in her seat. For once, arrogance would have served her better. At least then it would have given her father something to respect.

"Hope?" A disapproving tsk slipped through the colonel's drawn lips. "'*Hope is the worst of evils, for it prolongs the torments of man.*'"

Nathalie's expression remained placid, though some of her pluck had returned. "Yes, but Nietzsche also said, '*One must still have chaos in oneself to be able to give birth to a dancing star.*' I am not concerned with the struggle that lies ahead."

If the colonel was impressed by her rebuttal, he did not show it. "And is your benefactor equally unconcerned with how you use the education he's provided?"

Before Catharine could forget herself and jump to Nathalie's defense, Emily broke her silence from the opposing end of the table, peacekeeping in that passive way to which Catharine had grown accustomed.

Change the subject. Redirect.

"I was very sorry to hear about your father, Nathalie."

Nathalie gave a flippant wave of her hand, though Catharine could tell from the stiffness in her expressive fingers that the colonel's comment had left her seething. Tuition paid for a man's life was hardly a fair exchange. Her so-called *benefactor* didn't even cover her battels.

"It was a long time ago."

"I cannot imagine the hardship for your mother—raising a child on her own."

A gravy-covered bite of Yorkshire pudding was stuck in Catharine's throat. How could her mother even begin to pretend to relate to Nathalie's family? Her upbringing? She wanted to kick her shin under the table. Anything to shut her up.

"She got the job done." Nathalie's smile was strained.

At the head of the table, Benjamin flicked an invisible speck of lint from the grosgrain silk of his lapel. His interest in the subject had waned. It was just like him to capsize a conversation, cast out his cruelty, and then tack to the next topic without a care for who he'd pulled under in his wake.

"I'm sure you've read, Catharine—the Finance Minister in Singapore is threatening a half-percent hike on import tariffs."

The abrupt about-face caught Catharine unprepared. She couldn't think quickly enough to avoid revealing that she hadn't opened a trade journal since the start of the Christmas holiday.

"I was unaware, sir." The scarlet hue of the cranberry sauce was seeping into her untouched potatoes.

"I see." His cold blue gaze flicked over the top of the silver candelabra stationed between them. "Shall I then also assume you are unaware of the implications this would have on freight rates for ships coming through Pasir Panjang?"

For a terminal that handled nearly 100 billion in goods annually, the tax increase would be significant. The cost would be passed along to the importer of record, impacting the consumer market for product. In turn, demand for cargo would decline, leading to a decrease in shipments. An effect that would ultimately force transportation companies to lower their freight rates in order to attract business.

"They will decline, sir."

He scoffed. "Remarkable insight. If this is Christ Church's masterstroke of intellect, I fear for future generations."

Her cheeks flushed under his criticism. She was damned if she did, damned if she didn't. If she explained her reasoning, he would mock her (*how terribly exhausting it must be, Catharine, to be the smartest person in the room*); if she mitigated her answer, he accused her of being dim. It was the way it had always been. But today, with Nathalie privy to his performance, she found the routine more humiliating than usual.

His cufflink clinked against the glass of mineral water he set down. "And with this astonishing deduction, how, may I ask— were *WorldCargo* at your command—would you respond?"

The question was a setup. There was only one acceptable answer—the one he wanted her to feed him. *WorldCargo* was the largest of the subsidiary companies operating under Brooks Corp. It was the face of their shipping empire. With its longstanding relationship with the Port of Singapore—the second busiest container port in the world—the company held a significant deal of clout with the Singaporean trade ministry. The most effective approach would be to leverage that relationship. But it would also lead to an outcome Catharine did not desire.

In a feeble attempt to avoid the inevitable, she chose a less favorable option. "I would lean on my diplomatic channels, creating international pressure in order to urge the MTI to reconsider. If that failed, I would coordinate a market response strategy to demonstrate the economic instability generated by the tariff."

Through the flickering flame of the candelabra, the colonel fixed her with his cerulean stare. "You would lunge straight to an international trade war and stock manipulation?"

No, it was the last thing she would do. She was sensible. Level-headed. Far more so than her father. Her first response would be to send an emissary from Brooks Corp to gauge the situation. It would keep distance between her and the problem, allowing room for negotiation. But she knew her father would not accept that as an answer. He preferred to handle these sorts of predicaments himself—in person.

But based on the growing glower behind his glare, she knew better than to push her position. Instead, she relented and gave him what he wanted. "I would fly to Singapore and set up a meeting with the Ministry of Trade and Industry."

"I knew you'd eventually scrape together a shred of sense in that empty head of yours." He flicked two long, dexterous fingers at her. "We leave day after tomorrow."

Even knowing it was coming, her heart sank. There were still four weeks left before the resumption of university. She'd planned to spend them with Nathalie. Here. Or in London. Or even in

Geneva, or Zürich, or Barcelona, if he insisted on dragging them from Henley.

But a business trip to Singapore? It was the one place she knew her father would never permit Nathalie to accompany them.

"Please," she started, willing to beg if she had to. Willing to risk his anger. "I can't—"

"*Catharine.*" Her mother cut her off.

She glanced at her, feeling a well of rising fury. For once, she needed her on her side—needed her support. Yet here she was, playing the role of the dutiful wife, preparing to manage her.

"I *can't*," she started again, this time directed at Emily. "I—"

"*Catharine,*" her mother's tone was stern, "please give your father and me a moment."

Surprised at the dismissal, she couldn't stop herself from looking toward her father. When he was home, she was unaccustomed to leaving the table without his permission. No matter what her mother said.

"*Now,*" Emily interrupted, too quickly for Colonel Brooks to contradict.

Reading the room, Nathalie was already on her feet, and Catharine was quick to join her.

"Don't go too far, Catharine." Her father's voice fell like a gavel before she reached the threshold. "I will be going over our itinerary with you when I have finished with your mother."

CATHARINE'S PALMS WERE SLICK WITH sweat by the time she closed the door.

"Cate." Nathalie's whispered tone was apologetic. "I—"

She hushed her. Nathalie had nothing to be sorry for. It wasn't her fault her father was a bastard.

"Nat, will you..." She could hear the muffled sound of her father's voice through the gap at the bottom of the door. "Will you give me a minute?" She looked away, embarrassed to ask her to go but even more ashamed to have her stay. She didn't want Nathalie to hear what he might say about her. To have her subjected any further to his vitriol. But she also didn't dare leave the hallway. Not because her father had demanded that she stick around, but because she was concerned to leave her mother alone. She didn't know what was going to happen.

If he lost his temper, if he truly became outraged…

"No, for once, you listen to *me*!" Her mother's voice was uncommonly barbed. It scared Catharine—how he might respond. What he might do.

She turned to Nathalie. "I'll meet you in your room—"

"Cate—"

On the other side of the wall, her father was shouting. She caught the words: *plebeian, insidious, parasitizing*. Knowing Nathalie could hear him too, each syllable slipped beneath her skin, eviscerating.

"*Please*, Nat!"

Yielding to her desperation, Nathalie retreated down the hall, pausing before she rounded the corner. "Cate." Her voice was unfairly gentle, as if she wasn't the one who the colonel was disparaging. It broke Catharine's heart. "It's all right if you need me to go back to Oxford."

Catharine stared at a nick in the 18th-century wood flooring. By the time she forced herself to look up, Nathalie was gone.

Restraining the urge to go after her, she reluctantly dragged her leaden feet closer to the door, where she could hear her parents' conversation more clearly.

"She's just a child, Benjamin!"

"She is a grown woman, and you will bloody well begin to treat her as one!"

"Then for God's sake, you must do the same!"

It was the first time Catharine had ever heard her mother yell. A fleeting sense of awe filled her, startled by the vehemence behind it, the unwavering conviction. It was the voice of a woman—the *passion* of a woman—Catharine did not know. A woman who would have excelled in a courtroom. A woman who could have held her own. But by the time Emily spoke again, her composure had been regained, and Catharine recognized the familiar tone of reason. The carefully chosen sound of negotiation.

But even subdued as she was, her mother did not back down.

"You expect her to carry the weight of adulthood without granting her the freedom it entails. You demand maturity, yet allow her no space to make her own decisions. How is she ever supposed to become her own person if she is glued to your coattails?"

"I am not interested in her freedom—"

"But you are invested in her future, and you know as well as I, the two go hand in hand! It is impossible for you to always be there to guide her. If you wish her to be successful, you must allow her room to grow. Let her make friends. Let her travel on her own. Give her a chance to find out who she is—"

"She is a *Brooks!*"

"And she *knows* that! Since the day she was born, you've never let her forget it!"

Her father's pitch turned dangerous. "What is that supposed to mean?"

"It doesn't matter." Her mother released an audible sigh, but to Catharine's surprise, she didn't retreat. "Listen, Benjamin—please. I ask very little from you, but I am asking you this: give her these two years until she graduates. Allow her to enjoy them. Allow her to befriend who she wants to befriend. To build connections. To explore the world on her own. Grant her the right to make mistakes, and when she does, to learn from them. These formative years—they aren't something she can ever have back. When her time at university is over—when her education is finished—she will dedicate her life to Brooks Corp. She's never given you reason to doubt it. But until then—I am begging you, as her mother— please give her this opportunity. Allow her the simple joy of being a young woman. We owe her that."

There was a long silence on the other side of the door as Catharine waited for her father to explode. The blood rushing between her ears harmonized with the wind rustling against the clerestory windows set high along the vaulted ceiling. She braced herself and waited for a glass to break. A plate to shatter. Perhaps a violent blow muted by the tapestry hanging on the wall, where even still his signet ring would leave a mark.

But instead, there was nothing.

Somewhere above them, water rushed through the old pipes crisscrossing the manor. She wondered absently if Geoff would come to pick up Mrs. Mills. What Christmas must be like at their small home in the village? What she would give to trade places with him—to go to sleep tonight to the drip, drip, drip of a rusted faucet. The hiss and clang of a cast-iron radiator. Maybe even the hum from the glow of lights on a sparsely decorated Christmas tree.

Inside the dining room, heavy footsteps crossed the floor. The door handle turned, and Colonel Brooks' form towered in the threshold.

Catharine flattened herself against the wall, terrified to be caught eavesdropping, but her father paid her no attention. Instead, he turned back to address Emily.

"So be it." The tick along his jaw betrayed his forced equanimity. "But I will say this only once, so hear me very clearly: after she graduates, I will entertain no further protest from you—under *any* capacity." He slammed the door and walked away, sparing no glance for Catharine.

When his footsteps had faded, she slunk down the wall to the floor, trying to recall how to breathe. She realized she was shaking, and was no longer certain if it was from fear or relief.

Chapter Eighteen

AN UNWELCOME VOICE CALLED OUT to Catharine as she stepped onto Blue Boar Street en route to The Bear Inn. For a moment, she considered slipping into the horde of tourists spilling off an open-top bus and disappearing with them through the double doors of the Museum of Oxford. Lost among the artifacts and exhibits, she could pretend she'd never heard her name.

Unfortunately, a lifetime of decorum and politesse forced her to turn around.

"Hello, Edward." Politesse or not, no amount of good breeding could bring her to smile.

"Catharine." He leaned against the limestone wall, an ironic smirk flitting across his mouth. "It's been a while."

Not long enough.

She glanced over her shoulder toward the freedom of the vacant street.

"In a hurry?"

She wasn't, really. It was the final day of Noughth Week before the start of Hilary Term. She'd just come from sitting Collections in Macroeconomics and finished well ahead of her peers. There was over an hour to spare until she was due to meet Nathalie at the pub.

But none of that was his business.

"I am."

Her urgency didn't phase him.

"You're looking good, you know? Something's changed about you." He gave her an appraising glance from head to toe. "You look different."

She felt different. And even if the confirmation came from his unwanted observation, it was oddly affirming that someone else had noticed.

The last three weeks had transformed her. Ever since Christmas, the night her mother confronted her father, she'd felt reshaped—as if she were inhabiting someone else's life.

She hadn't believed it at first. Though she'd never known her father to be outright dishonest, she hadn't trusted him to keep his word. But two days later, he left for Singapore—alone. And after that, everything had changed.

Slowly, tentatively—like an animal testing the open door of a trap, wary of what might be waiting on the other side—she began to discover a freedom she'd never imagined attainable. The walls she'd erected upon his arrival cautiously eroded. Her happiness of the weeks before returned. In his absence, she welcomed Nathalie back to her bed, ever mindful of their surroundings—her mother and the staff—but without the looming threat of the guillotine hanging over her head.

The day before New Year's Eve, she grew bolder and approached her mother to ask permission to spend the holiday in Edinburgh. They hadn't spoken about the arrangement her mother had made with the colonel—like most things in her life, the subject was taboo—but Catharine knew Emily was aware she'd overheard.

Even still, she expected resistance. Expected her mother to agree only if she came along to chaperone. Catharine had traveled the world extensively, but never been granted the liberty to go even so short a distance as London alone.

To her surprise, however, her mother agreed without hesitation, asking only if she had enough cash, if she knew where they'd be staying, reminding her to pack warmly—it could get cold in Scotland. When she dropped them at the train station the following morning, she hugged Nathalie and passed Catharine her credit card. She told them to have fun, but to be safe—*boys*, she reminded, *were more bother than they were worth.*

Catharine searched her face, trying to decipher if the message was coded, or if it was just the kind of thing a mother said when sending two teenage girls off on their own. Staring out the window as the train barreled north, she still didn't know.

By the time they reached Edinburgh, it was almost dusk. The city was alive and boisterous, the streets packed with holidaymakers. Whiskey, tonic wine, and cider overflowed onto the pavement, plastic cups and bottles passed amongst wandering friends and raucous strangers, with little discernment between the two. It was wild, chaotic, and unlike anything Catharine had encountered before.

She was glad when Nathalie grabbed her hand, taking the lead to shoulder their way across Waverley Bridge to where her mother had called and arranged an impossible last-minute reservation at The Balmoral. They dropped their bags on the first of two double beds—*kind of your mum to give us options*, Nathalie quirked an eyebrow—before bolting back to the lift and through the luxury lobby, where they flew past the porter and into the fray of Hogmanay celebrations.

It was invigorating—the newness of the experience, sharing it with Nathalie. They worked their way to the Scott Monument and wandered through Princes Street Garden, where a boy on stilts shouldered a boombox blaring *I'm Gonna Be* as the crowd belted the chorus of the song. Somewhere, in the shuffling across the grass, Nathalie procured a bottle of Famous Grouse, and Catharine shoved aside her revulsion of the secondhand liquor, following Nathalie's example and taking a deep swallow of the grainy whiskey. She pulled a face as Nathalie laughed, unaccustomed to the astringent blend, and sipped again, the cheap alcohol helping to numb her surfeited senses.

They wandered the city centre for hours. Darkness fell, and the mayhem around them grew more unruly. Sparklers lit the overrun streets, and bangers echoed through dark closes. As it neared midnight, fireworks shot into the sky, bursting above the castle. Finding themselves at the foot of the drawbridge in the shadow of the statues of Robert the Bruce and William Wallace, Catharine got caught up in the moment and brushed her lips to Nathalie's, before blushing when she realized they were being watched by a gawking group of pimple-faced boys. Ever the showman, Nathalie blew them a pantomimed kiss, then pulled Catharine into the electric flow of the crowd. The energy surrounding the night had become a living, breathing thing all of its own. By the time they neared the end of the Royal Mile, they were breathless, despite having traveled mainly downhill. The horde of merrymakers thinned as they veered onto New Street, and thinned even more when they turned again, crossing beneath Regent Bridge. Just off the pavement, in between murals of graffiti, Catharine tugged Nathalie through an open archway with a dimly lit sign titled *Jacob's Ladder*. She didn't know where it led, and really didn't care. All she knew, in the tipsy haze of her addled thoughts, was that she wanted to be alone—to be somewhere where she could kiss Nathalie the way she needed to kiss her, and to be kissed in return.

Up what felt like a thousand stairs, they found themselves sandwiched between two stone walls overlooking the railway tracks below. The dramatic silhouette of Edinburgh stretched across the distance, the sky alight with color to bring in the New Year. Somewhere, in the back of her mind, Catharine registered the bells of St. Giles' Cathedral pealing across the rooftops, and above them, the drunken harmony of *Auld Lang Syne* drifting down from Calton Hill. But she was too lost in Nathalie—in the taste of cheap whiskey on her tongue and the salt on her lips from the chips they'd shared, the smell of smoke in her hair and winter clinging to her clothes—to fully appreciate the turning of the year.

By the time they stumbled back to the hotel, their teeth were chattering, the wool of their gloves and scarves damp with dew. But what did it matter when all they cared about was being wrapped up in each other?

In the morning, when Catharine woke, her body spent with pleasure and the warmth of Nathalie beside her—their first time witnessing the totality of the sunrise together—she considered pleading her case that they should just spend the remainder of the trip locked away in the hotel room. They could stay in bed, never get dressed, survive solely on sex and room service.

But by the time she came out of the shower, Nathalie was up and dressed, ready for the next adventure.

"Have you heard of the Loony Dook?" she asked, flipping through a tourism pamphlet.

A few hours later, Catharine found herself in South Queensferry, standing at the edge of the white-capped waters of the Firth of Forth as several hundred crazy participants prepared to plunge into the freezing estuary.

Loony stood for *Lunatic. Dook* meant a dip.

An apparent Scottish Hogmanay tradition.

"These people are insane." Catharine burrowed deeper into her Barbour jacket, trying to find respite from the relentless Northeasterly.

"Let's do it."

Catharine was certain she'd heard her incorrectly. "I'm sorry?"

But as a bagpipe began to play, the exuberant crowd percolating with anticipation, Nathalie shrugged off her coat and draped it over the railing.

"Nat—!"

"T'as les chocottes ?"

Was she scared? No! However, was she stupid? Absolutely not!

But then a horn sounded, and a cheer rang out, and Nathalie was sprinting toward the shoreline.

Men in tutus, women stuffed into inner tubes in the shape of rubber duckies, grandmothers in mermaid costumes, and teenagers with their faces painted blue and white representing the Saltire, all raced for the icy water.

Catharine could have waited from the safety of the dry land. A winter swim in a glacial inlet was not how she planned to ring in the New Year. The entire ordeal was madness. Uncouth, uncultured chaos.

All around her, people were whooping and laughing.

Did she dare… ?

Her fingers dug into the chill of the railing.

Her father would kill her.

But her father wasn't here.

The cold blast of wind whipping up from the firth knocked something loose in her, and before she could overthink it, she was shucking off her shoes and flinging her jacket to the ground to sprint after Nathalie.

And that was how the last two weeks of their whirlwind Christmas break kicked off in January.

They left Edinburgh and traveled to Glasgow. Stirling. Dundee. Inverness. They took the train east and explored Banff, Fraserburgh, Peterhead. Nathalie read about a castle, *Dunnottar*, perched on a dramatic headland in Stonehaven just south of Aberdeen. It had been used as the backdrop for Mel Gibson's *Hamlet*—Glenn Close playing *Gertrude*.

"Cinema royalty!" Nathalie beamed.

They spent two full days wandering the wind-lashed ruins and exploring the grounds, and Catharine fell in love with the passion Nathalie had for the whole world.

By the time they returned to Henley, just a few days before they were due back for the start of Hilary in Oxford, Catharine felt like a different person. She was lighter, happier, more buoyant than she'd ever believed possible.

So yes, whatever Edward saw in her—whatever cosmic shift he felt—she *was* different. She was no longer herself.

"Hm," she gave a noncommittal shrug, once again glancing down Blue Boar Street, anxious to be on her way. "Same old me."

Edward ran a preening hand through his moussed hair. "So, have you sorted your fancy dress for the bop tonight?"

Catharine had forgotten about the start-of-term party hosted by the JCR. The theme was *Vicars and Tarts*. Dozens of her peers crammed into the vaulted undercroft beneath the belly of the hall, the men in cassocks and stoles, while the women donned fishnets, corsets and stilettos. Downing snakebite or cheap vodka, the entire event merely an excuse to get drunk and behave badly.

Even if she hadn't had other plans, it was the last thing she would have attended.

"Sorry, I don't think I'll make it." She tried to step around him.

"If it's because you're embarrassed to show up alone, I'm not one to hold a grudge, Catharine. I'd still be willing to take you. We can put last year behind us—what do you say? Let bygones be bygones?" He leaned closer. "I've got the dog collar. You can come as my tart. Just think—I'll absolve you of your sins." He winked. "No promises I won't add a few more to them, however."

Catharine's entire body recoiled against his nearness, the lewdness he projected. He made it so easy to recall all the reasons she detested him.

"I'll pass, thank you." How she had ever considered suffering through a life of his attentions, she couldn't begin to imagine now. That she had ever allowed him to touch her. Kiss her. To call her his. It was unfathomable. She took a step away. "If you don't mind?" When he didn't immediately remove the arm he had resting against the limestone wall, blocking her escape, she shouldered roughly through him, heedless of her manners.

"God," he barked a bitter laugh, stepping aside with weaponized gallantry, exaggerated by a lift of his chin. "You've grown truly insufferable, Catharine. The stink of all that lowbrow company you've been keeping is rubbing off on you, I see."

She had the wildest desire to turn, to flip him the Vs, but forced herself to forgo the vulgar gesture. Instead, she paused, glancing briefly over her shoulder, and gave him a deliberate once-over.

"Better the scent of it than the unmistakable stench of mediocrity dressed up in a dinner jacket." Leaving no space for rebuttal, she spun and continued down the cobblestone street to where the best part of her life awaited her.

Chapter Nineteen

The audience took a collective breath, waiting. On the stage, Maggie Chapman held a gilded porcelain teacup to her lips, preparing to drink the poisoned tea.

Catharine sat in the third row, hating to admit Maggie—*that dirty, thievin', no good, Maggie Mae*—played the iconic role of *Claire* brilliantly.

Then again, she'd been gifted brilliance to work with. Nathalie's translation of the Jean Genet script—*Les Bonnes*—had been nothing short of revelatory.

When Nathalie first told Catharine the Oxford Theatre Guild had asked her to come up with a fresh translation of the 1940s French drama, Catharine had struggled not to roll her eyes. The English rendition of Genet's play—*The Maids*—had been done so often, she didn't imagine there was much room for exploration, no matter what dramatic license Nathalie had been granted.

But watching the show tonight, Catharine had to concede that she'd been proven wrong.

Nathalie had turned the old, tired, hackneyed mid-twentieth-century classic into something sensual. Erotic. Something edgy and revitalized.

Standing in the single spotlight, Maggie wrenched the offending vessel away from her lips and flung the teacup to the ground. *"No!"* she cried as the porcelain shattered at her feet, shards splintering across the boards. "I will *not* do it!" She waited a beat, claiming the suspense from the deviated ending, knowing those familiar with the play anticipated the character's death, the same old tragic, antiquated finale. She turned her wide eyes up over the audience, lifting her angular chin—defiant, proud. "I will kneel to you no longer, Madame! Madame does not own me now!"

The stage went abruptly dark as the curtain fell. The audience was silent.

And then, slowly, the lights came up—first the soft hue of an amber fresnel, then the brighter back light of a PAR can, and lastly, the bold illumination of filter-free Shakespeares—until the stage was awash with color, and the trio of actresses who made up the cast clasped hands and took a downstage bow.

The Old Fire Station was a quaint venue, not quite so small as the Burton Taylor around the corner, but intimate all the same. The rows of patrons may not have leapt from their cushioned folding chairs—a fringe theatre audience could be notoriously hard to please—but the ovation was still enthusiastic, loud in the compact space.

It was deserved. The re-imagination of Genet's work was worthy of admiration. Catharine couldn't help but feel her own pride swell at Nathalie's success—even if she had not been supportive of the project when it first arose.

At Maggie's bidding, the crew emerged from the wings to join the cast in their curtain call. Nathalie, who not only had transformed the text into its contemporary English adaptation, but had also taken on the role of assistant director, joined them.

Catharine had never fathomed that Nathalie would enjoy a backstage role, and had said as much, unapologetically. Nathalie was flamboyant, naturally dramatic. She loved an audience. Catharine assumed she would be miserable behind the scenes, away from the limelight. But standing there on stage with the rest of the crew, she looked happy, dressed all in black, a clipboard in one hand, her other adjusting the headset dangling around her ears. She searched the first few rows of the theatre and smiled when she caught Catharine's eye.

Catharine felt guilty then, for all the ways she'd begrudged Nathalie for participating in the show.

But it wasn't really the show that had anything to do with it. It had just been the timing of it all.

Six weeks earlier, only a few days before Easter break, Nathalie had arrived late to their standing coffee date at *Spires*. Abruptly, and a little out of breath, she told Catharine she'd had a note in her pidge from Benedict Clarke—a director she admired who frequently worked with the Oxford Theatre Guild. She explained how he'd invited her to translate and adapt the script for their upcoming spring production.

How would she have time, Catharine asked, to get all that done before their trip to Bordeaux? They'd been planning the excursion to Nathalie's hometown for weeks. Catharine was looking forward to meeting Mrs. Comtois. To seeing where Nathalie lived.

Behind the safety of her cappuccino, Nathalie muttered an acknowledgment that if she took the job, she wouldn't be able to go.

"You're going to decline then—right?"

Foam was clinging to Nathalie's upper lip. Any other morning, Catharine would have bitten back a smile, thinking how—if they were alone—she'd kiss it off her. But when Nathalie's gaze dropped to the scratched surface of the tabletop, she realized, in a moment, she wouldn't be thinking about kissing her at all.

"Nat?" She pushed her tea away. "Are you really considering accepting the offer?"

Nathalie fiddled with the spoon on her saucer. "It's a paid gig."

The mention of money irked Catharine, and before she had time to think, to temper her words, she spoke thoughtlessly. "What do you need the money for?" She felt guilty even as the question trickled off her tongue, but when she tried to recover, she only dug the hole deeper. "I'll pay for Bordeaux—you already know that! I'll pay for whatever we—"

"Did you ever consider that's not what *I* want?" Nathalie interrupted, her gaze snapping up from the dissolving foam atop her espresso. Above them, the hanging lamp caught the dangerous flash in her umber eyes. Catharine knew she had misstepped. She knew she had put pressure on a nerve that always lay skin deep, pervasive, yet one they'd managed to dance around, leaving it invisible to the naked eye.

In her silence, Nathalie continued. "I don't mean this as cruelly as it's going to sound, Cate—but you live in your own insular world. And I need you to know, it's not something I fault you for. I don't think it would be possible, being who you are, to expect you to understand. It's simply the truth, even if you can't see that."

Catharine dovetailed her fingers around her cup, unable to meet her eye. Crushed with disappointment, she presented the only stupid argument that came to mind. "But it's—it's not even a role. You won't even be on stage."

Kinder, probably more gently than she deserved, Nathalie reached across the table and touched her fingers to Catharine's arm. "It's going to look good on my CV, Cate. And I'm excited about it. Be happy for me." She sat back up, resuming her cappuccino.

What could Catharine say? This was Nathalie's future. Her career. A stepping stone in the path to her dreams.

So just like that, it was decided. Nathalie would stay in Oxford over the Easter vac, and Catharine would go alone to Henley.

In the end, it hadn't turned out as badly as Catharine anticipated. Her father had been away in Chūbu throughout the entirety of the five-week break, and her mother had spent the weekends in London. Which left Catharine free to take the train every Friday afternoon up to Oxford. There, she would stay in the studio flat Nathalie had sublet from a grad student who'd gone home for Easter. It was a tiny place above a video shop off Cowley Road— smaller, even, than either of their student accommodations. But it had enough space in the kitchenette for a kettle and a microwave, the water in the shower came out hot, if only in a trickle, and more important than anything, it was a private place that they could share, making believe—behind those whitewashed walls—that their relationship was almost normal.

It hadn't been the southwest of France in springtime, but those long weekend days lounging on the musty two-seater sofa, listening to Nathalie transform Genet into a searing, modern-day provocateur, were nearly perfect.

Nearly—only because every Sunday night, Catharine felt pressured to catch the late train back to Henley. It was one thing to travel with Nathalie—she could explain that away as wanderlust, the joy of seeing the country with a friend. It was another, however, to spend every waking moment of the break back with her in Oxford. Her father may have lengthened her leash, and her mother may have championed her independence—but if suspicion ever arose as to the true nature of their relationship, Catharine was aware that her life as she currently knew it would implode.

So, while Nathalie spent the weekdays laying spikes, discussing blocking, and laughing with her cast of friends, Catharine was stuck back in her Lilliputian existence, counting the hours until she would see her again.

Still, the time apart could have been worse.

She could have been with her father in Japan.

Now, however, break was over, and her university life had resumed. It was the Friday night before the start of Trinity, and she should have just been happy knowing, once again, not a day would go by where they wouldn't see each other.

Only, it wasn't as simple as that.

During term, their time together was limited. They were caught inside the Oxford fishbowl, where everyone's nose was in the business of everybody else. It wouldn't do to be seen slinking from one another's colleges in the small hours of the morning, or making late-night visits between their rooms.

After returning from Christmas, in the first weeks of Hilary, they'd established a pattern. Get together for coffee at *Spires*. Chat books and lectures while sneaking the brush of a foot or touch of a hand beneath the table. Talk in innuendos—quoting Shakespeare,

Speak low, if you speak love, or Virginia Woolf, *Love had a thousand shapes*, or Oscar Wilde, *I can resist everything except temptation*. Then their days would be lost to reading, tutorials, and the everyday stress of trying to keep their academic lives above water.

At night, they would meet after Hall in one of their quads, or sometimes down by the river. If they were lucky, they would find a couple moments of solitude to share a kiss or the brief entwining of hands. A few times, despite the dead of winter, they'd made the trek to Wytham, desperate for the isolation of the chapel. Desperate for each other. But overall, the only unbridled, unrestricted time they got to spend together came over the two weekend trips they'd taken away from university.

The first, a two-hour train ride to Stratford-upon-Avon, where they stayed in a B&B on the outskirts of town. It was the ideal hideaway—just two students up from uni to experience the birthplace of Shakespeare.

The following weekend, on Nathalie's twentieth birthday, they'd hired a car to drive out to the Cotswolds. Catharine pulled away from the hire company, grinding the gears at every stop, and promptly crammed it in neutral in the nearest car park, insisting Nathalie take over. She retreated into the high neck collar of her jumper, reddening as Nathalie poked fun at her basic lack of driving skills—*the downfall*, Nathalie razzed, *of life being chauffeured* —but secretly, loving every second of the teasing. Her entire world had come to exist on the joy of Nathalie's affection—on seeking her attention.

Late that afternoon, they checked in at an old coaching inn tucked quietly in the heart of Stow-on-the-Wold, a historic town in the highest region of the Cotswolds. Catharine had looked forward to roaming the cobbled tures and windswept beauty of the rolling hills, but by the time they'd reached the quaint stone-built inn with its low beams and mismatched furniture, she'd forgotten all about browsing antiquarian bookshops and exploring the medieval market. Her only focus shifted to taking advantage of every moment alone with Nathalie. They left the room only once, stocking up on scones and biscuits, and by the time they checked out on Sunday afternoon to drive back to Oxford, Catharine realized they'd never even glimpsed the market square.

"The perfect birthday," Nathalie had flashed her a smile when Catharine made the observation.

But those four stolen days in an eight-week term simply weren't enough. Not after knowing what it was like to wake by Nathalie's side every morning during those last weeks of Christmas, to drift asleep in the arms of someone you loved. Nathalie had turned her existence into a pinwheel of color, exchanging a life of beige and gray for a world now viewed in vibrant hues of scarlet, and orange, and emerald.

She ached in her absence.

Which was exactly why Catharine had been so disappointed when Nathalie canceled the trip to Bordeaux.

But—she reminded herself, watching as the cast and crew took their final bow—that was neither here nor there. There was one more term, two miserable months, and then they would be free for the summer. No last-minute shows (Nathalie had promised!), no boring lectures, no forced business trips with her father.

They would go to Europe, perhaps. Rent a cabin by the lake in Finland. Or maybe down to the golden beaches of Portugal, where they could drink *vinho verde* in a tiny seaside café—somewhere nobody knew them.

Her thoughts continued cycling through the endless possibilities of summer destinations as she filed behind the row of patrons exiting the auditorium. There was an opening night party down the street at The Piper's Pub, a favorite hangout of the theatre crowd, where they served cheap ale and cider. Nathalie had invited Catharine, but not without a word of caution. The place was dingy. There would be drugs. The chips were cold, and the doors to the toilet cubicles rarely had a functioning lock on them.

Catharine was still wavering on whether or not to attend when she spotted Nathalie in the lobby. With no costume and no need to strip her face of heavy stage makeup, she and the rest of the crew had beaten the majority of the audience to the foyer. She raised her hand, preparing to flag her down, but stopped when another woman stepped in the path between them and set a hand on Nathalie's shoulder.

"Miss Comtois."

Nathalie turned at the touch, her face lighting up when she identified the speaker. "You came!" She sounded delighted.

"How could I not? You know, when it comes to French literature, Jean Genet is one of my favorites."

From half a dozen feet away, Catharine could distinguish the subtle lyrical lilt of the woman's Irish accent. Dublin, she suspected. Professional class. Educated.

"I hope you don't think I butchered it?" Nathalie stepped to the side, away from the audience members lingering to chat with one another about the performance.

Catharine moved a little closer, her presence guarded by a colorful poster on an easel advertising the show.

"Butchered?" The woman laughed, one hand now resting at Nathalie's elbow while the other swept a lock of ember-bright hair behind her ear. "Hardly. If anything, I found it brutally elegant. Genet stripped to the bone and left to bleed. Your translation of Solange's monologue—the way you portrayed her hatred toward Madame—obsessive, lustful! That line: *I'll strangle her—with hands full of love.*" She blew out a soft, appreciative whistle. "It was everything I would expect from you. You did not let me down."

A man interrupted just then—tall, lanky, his black hair combed forward to disguise a receding hairline. "Nathalie!" He approached the pair with an air of authority that made him unconcerned with his intrusion. "A *coup de maître*, my dear!" He said, murdering the French acclaim. "I could not be more proud." Finally, he seemed to register his interruption. "Ah, forgive me." He held out his hand to the woman. "Benedict Clarke—director."

"Dr. Fiona Loughlin. Reader in English Literature and Fellow at Brasenose."

Catharine wasn't sure what was said next. All she heard was *English* and *Brasenose*.

Nathalie's mysterious tutor in Romantic Literature, no doubt.

She took a step further behind the foyer board, trying to compose herself.

When Nathalie had admitted to an affair with a tutor, Catharine hadn't expected... well, she hadn't known what she expected—but not *her*. Not *that*. She supposed she'd envisioned someone younger—a junior research fellow, or even a college lecturer still working toward her DPhil. Someone nearer their age than not. A contemporary, not too distant from a peer.

She had never anticipated this sophisticated woman—this *Reader in English*—respected, distinguished, revered. She had to be near her mum's age, late thirties at the very least.

Forcing herself to focus, she took a deep, grounding breath. It didn't matter who the woman was. Whatever she'd had with Nathalie, it was over. Finished. *I'm far from the first student she's been with*, Nathalie had said of their trysts in the woods. *We met a few times—there was never anything real between us.*

And Catharine believed her. It didn't matter if this Irish beauty with her locks of bracken-red hair could romance her students with Wordsworth. If she showed up at their plays in her stiletto heels with sly innuendos disguised as words of praise.

Nathalie was *hers*—and she Nathalie's. No silver-tongued tutor in her tight pencil skirt could change that.

She peeked around the notice board. Fiona's back was to her, her attention detachedly on Benedict. It was clear she was more interested in resuming her chat with Nathalie, but the director was holding her captive, speaking with animated gestures. To her disappointment, Catharine could no longer hear what he was saying. The foyer was crowded now, a chorus of voices rising to an indistinct din.

"Oh, Cate!"

The jarring sound of her name off lips she didn't relish jolted her from her hiding place. Of course it would be Maggie, oblivious as ever, to out her in her eavesdropping. She turned, stepping quickly away from the notice board and into the fray of the foyer.

"Hello, Maggie."

"Hiya!" The woman was absurdly friendly. "You must be waiting for Nathalie?" She scanned the crowd, her gaze landing where the Frenchwoman stood, only a few steps ahead of them. "Oh, she's just there with Benedict!"

Well done, Miss Marple. Aware Nathalie had looked their direction, Catharine summoned a smile. "Ah. So she is."

She thought Nathalie might be embarrassed finding herself surrounded by her present company. Two former flings and her current lover made for an awkward quadrangle, but if she was caught off guard, her masterful acting skills disguised any such discomfort.

"Coucou, Cate." She stretched out a hand, inviting her to join them.

In an attempt to direct attention elsewhere, Catharine offered Benedict an acknowledging smile, hoping he would resume monopoly of the conversation—but she couldn't keep her eyes off the tutor, and realized too late that her undisguised interest had forced an introduction.

Nathalie remained unperturbed. "Dr. Loughlin," she motioned to the woman entrenched at her side, "this is my friend, Cate. Cate—Dr. Loughlin, one of my tutors in English. And of course, our brilliant director, Benedict Clarke."

Benedict's indifference to Catharine was equal to her own, the two of them clearly more fascinated by the presence of the Irishwoman—though, Catharine was certain, for entirely different reasons. The director didn't bother with a hello, his gaze never diverting from the doctor's impressive—it couldn't be denied—cleavage.

"So, what did you think of the show?" Nathalie prompted, ever one to seek validation. Somewhere, buried deep in the glint of her eyes, Catharine could detect the hint of flirtation, but outwardly, the question came across as banal, no better than a meaningless how-do-you-do.

She found herself regretting the respect Nathalie was showing for the caution Catharine necessitated over their public interactions. Nathalie was only following her rules, but in a temporary moment of asininity, Catharine wanted more than anything for her to break them. She despised her own inability to be bold, confident, risk-taking. Someone more like Fiona Loughlin—who, she realized, had now turned to regard her, awaiting her answer.

Catharine considered the woman's earlier effusive adulation—*Genet stripped to the bone*—and tried to conjure something equally provocative, but under pressure of the viridescent gaze, floundered for a response with any real meaning.

"It was great." Three trivial words—pathetic in every way.

At once, Fiona appeared to grow bored, clearly determining the mundanity of the answer to reflect the entirety of her value as a worthy interlocutor. She turned away, and at once, Benedict seized on the opportunity to reengage her.

"We're off for a celebratory pint, Professor Loughlin. Care to join us?"

"*Dr.* Loughlin," she corrected. "The university hasn't yet seen fit to bestow the honors of *professor*."

"My apologies!" He brought a dramatic hand to his heart in feigned distress. "You'll have to forgive my ignorance—my red brick education didn't include a course in decoding Oxbridge." He winked in a way that Catharine was sure some women found charming. "Let me try again—I'd love to buy you a pint, *Dr.* Loughlin. Join us?"

"I'm afraid in this case it would not be terribly professional."

Rich of her to concern herself with professionalism now, Catharine thought, remaining silent. Drinks with students were taboo, but sleeping with them was entirely permissible? Still, she was grateful the woman was planning to move along.

"It's not an Oxford production," Benedict countered, unwilling to give in. "No affiliation whatsoever with the university. In fact, I think Nathalie here is the only student working on the show."

Fiona gave a subtle lift of her brow, her eyes sweeping to Nathalie. "Unsurprising—Miss Comtois is brilliant," she said through a closed-lip smile. She looked back at Benedict. "Very well then, Mr. Clarke—I imagine one drink can't hurt."

Catharine deflated. Fiona had never been on the cusp of declining—she had simply needed to massage the conversation into making her presence acceptable.

"Shall we, then?" Fiona asked no one in particular, though she once again set a hand on Nathalie's arm.

"Cate?" Nathalie shot her an apologetic glance. "You're coming, yes?"

It was the last thing Catharine wanted. And she knew Nathalie had to know that. But she also didn't want to be left behind.

Ironically, it was Maggie who hooked her arm, sweeping her toward the door. "Come on now," she prattled on in her friendly manner. "It's Friday night! They offer two-for-one drinks to the prettiest girls—which means you're bound to score one-for-four!"

Hopefully she meant *four-for-one*, Catharine considered, giving her the benefit of the doubt as she was whisked across the floor.

NATHALIE'S DESCRIPTION OF THE PUB hadn't been an exaggeration. The squat-beamed interior was cramped and sordid. Rugby jerseys were pinned to the ceiling, cobwebs clinging to their sleeves. In the beer garden, joints drifted from hand to hand, and under the shadow of a burnt-out light, Catharine observed a boy she thought might be the costume assistant covertly popping a pale pink pill, before growing overtly chatty. She passed on the chips, and although she *had* been offered three-for-one drinks—which was *almost* a consolation—the ciders were all cheap mass-market brands, no better than apple juice with a splash of vodka.

The only thing she'd yet to confirm was the condition of the locks on the toilets. Another round of three-for-one, and she imagined she'd find out shortly.

The first half hour was spent crammed into a corner table beside Maggie, listening to Benedict fawn over Dr. Loughlin. How fascinating was it that she'd grown up in Ireland? How clever she must be to have received her DPhil from Somerville—the same college Margaret Thatcher had attended. What a feat it was to have earned the title of *Reader* before she turned forty (though given his earlier blunder in addressing her as professor, Catharine doubted the director even knew what this warranted).

Catharine listened to these facts about the esteemed doctor's life with only half an ear, her true attention tuned to Nathalie. She noticed every time Fiona laughed, she set a hand on Nathalie's arm, or bumped her with her shoulder. It amazed Catharine that the woman—this distinguished Fellow—was so unconcerned with how her behavior might be perceived. Especially knowing there was implementation behind her actions. She didn't even have the excuse of being drunk. Unlike Catharine, who'd downed two pints before they got to the table, she was still nursing her first cider.

It was almost as if she was daring the world to notice, ready to challenge anyone who might care to reprimand her.

When Benedict's round came up and he disappeared to the bar, Maggie seized the opportunity to leap headfirst into the conversation. She snatched a nickel-plated knife off the table and clinked it to her empty glass, announcing she had *exciting* news.

She'd been accepted to attend the *Williamstown Theatre Festival*, and was leaving in June. Puffing up like a preening peacock, she asked if Nathalie would care to join her.

"In the States?" Clearly taken by surprise, Nathalie laughed, and Catharine was relieved that it was obvious she would not give the suggestion any consideration.

"It's not so absurd!" Maggie defended, still trying to sell the offer. "It's only eight weeks long and right in the middle of your holiday."

At this, Fiona scoffed, her disdain evident. "We do *not* call it a holiday at Oxford. It is a *vacation*—derived from the Latin word *vacātiō*, which originates from the verb *vacāre*, meaning 'to be empty, free, or unoccupied.' Students *vacate* the university to continue their studies elsewhere. They are *not* flouncing about on holiday!"

"And there you go again with your Oxbridge terminology," Benedict grinned, appearing with five pints he sloshed awkwardly onto the table. "Be kind to us layfolk, *Dr.* Loughlin. Remember, we're but mere simpletons—unworthy of you Sanctified Spires Set."

Catharine couldn't tell if he thought his teasing would sweep her off her feet, or if he'd given up all hope of wining and dining her. For his sake, she hoped it was the latter—because there was no question Fiona Loughlin found him entirely unappealing.

"It can't be that hard to understand basic language." Fiona downed the remainder of her first cider and reached for the one Benedict had just set in front of her. Noticing a faint lipstick mark on the glass, she made no apologies for switching it with Maggie's, before continuing. "Moving on: what *are* your plans over summer, Nathalie? Please tell me you're not really considering summer stock in Ohio?"

"Massachusetts—" Maggie corrected.

Fiona waved her off. "Wherever. All of that summer circuit piffle is rubbish. You belong at *The Almeida*. Perhaps the *Donmar*. Or, if you're keen on returning home, I could pull some strings at the *Festival d'Avignon*. I know the artistic director there." She tapped a taupe nail on the rim of her glass, contemplative. "I will say, however—as talented as you are on stage, have you considered that you might be missing your true calling? After tonight, it's evident you would make an exceptional playwright. Or even an astute director."

"She wouldn't be able to stray that far from the limelight." Catharine was shocked to hear the words slip from her own mouth, given that she'd hardly uttered a word since they left the theatre. But her patience had worn thin, taking her sense of decorum along with it. She gave Nathalie a pointed glare. "She loves the attention too much."

It wasn't really fair, she knew, to be mad at her. The adulation Fiona heaped on her hadn't been solicited. But that said—she'd also made no effort to dissuade it. And Catharine's assessment wasn't wrong. Nathalie *loved* the spotlight. Whether it came from the standing ovation of an adoring crowd, or the affections of a tutor she'd once been fucking—it was like a drug to her, and she craved it.

A silence fell across the table, which Catharine filled by taking another sip of the sickly sweet cider, aware she'd already had too many. She knew everyone was staring at her—this girl who didn't belong there. A third—fourth?—fifth?—wheel, no more able to blend in than corduroy at a cocktail party.

"What great artist doesn't?"

Of course, it was Fiona to come to Nathalie's defense. Catharine looked up to find the cutting jade eyes were fixed on her for the first time since their brief introduction in the foyer. Up until now, it was as if she hadn't existed.

"My point exactly." She held her gaze, reminding herself that since she'd turned twelve, her father had stood her toe-to-toe against industry titans, banking magnates, economic attachés. There was nothing special about this woman.

Well, other than the fact that she'd slept with Nathalie.

Catharine offered a tight-lipped smile. "I don't fault her for it. I'm inclined to believe a proclivity for lionization is endemic to her kind of ambition."

There. She'd redeemed herself from falling short in the theatre. *It was great.* Those three inadequate words would forever haunt her.

To her disappointment, instead of appearing impressed, Fiona just looked amused. "Forgive me, Cate, is it? I don't think you mentioned—what subject are you reading?"

"Cate's E&M at Christ Church," Nathalie cut in, clearly trying to get ahead of whatever feud was building. Beneath the table, she stretched to bump Catharine's ankle, trying to soften her mood. "She's singularly brilliant. A genius, really. Already a Scholar, on track for a First."

"How impressive." Fiona's tone wasn't entirely condescending—it was worse than that. Catharine had the distinct sensation she was being laughed at. Like she was humoring a yawnsome child.

"Tell me, how does a savant economist fall in with a crowd like this?" She gestured vaguely at the bohemian sprawl of their surroundings. "You don't strike me as the artistic sort."

Again, Nathalie intercepted the question. "Cate could tell you facts about everything from Sophocles to Shakespeare, Kan'ami to Kalidasa. She can quote Marlowe, Molière, Miller."

Fiona arched an auburn brow at Nathalie, her smile sly, before shooting a patronizing glance at Catharine. "All that, and you're going to waste it on a life of ledgers and bottom lines?" Leaning back in her chair, she sighed. "Let me guess, Daddy helped you secure a graduate post at Price Waterhouse? Somewhere you can wither away tallying figures in a gleaming glass tower?" A disapproving tsk passed through her pursed lips. "How infinitely boring."

Outraged, a dozen cutting remarks flew to the tip of Catharine's tongue, waiting there, keen to defend herself. Who did this smug, self-aggrandizing woman think she was, pretending to know anything about her? *Dr. Look-At-Me-I-Made-Reader-Before-I-Was-Forty-But-Have-To-Fuck-My-Students-Because-No-One-Else-Will-Have-Me. Ms. The-Cut-of-This-Blouse-Says-I-Think-I'm-Hot-But-the-Bartender-Only-Gave-Me-Two-for-One-Ciders.*

Was her mind-blowing tutor's salary going to land her on *The Sunday Times Rich List*? No? Not even *if* she made professor?

Well, then she could just take a seat on her practical armchair, in her terraced house, and ten years from now, when she was sipping her Tetley tea, she would read about Catharine Brooks, the first woman to lead a ten-figure corporation before she was thirty.

But Catharine wasn't quite so drunk as not to realize whatever words she flung in anger couldn't be unsaid. This woman, however biased, however unprincipled, was still a Fellow at Oxford, still her superior.

So instead, ignoring Nathalie's rebuttal that Catharine's future was far grander than liabilities and ledgers, she stood—grateful to find she was steadier on her feet than her clouded thoughts had threatened—and left the table without excusing herself, making her way to the bar.

"Cate." She was in the middle of winding through the sea of bodies when Nathalie's hand fell on her shoulder.

Catharine ignored her, making eye contact with the bartender while plastering on a flirtatious smile.

"Same again?" He sauntered over, ignoring the half dozen patrons in the queue ahead of her.

She nodded, and a brief pour later, he set down another cider. "This one's on me."

And *that*, Fiona Loughlin, was what the 'infinitely boring' life of Cate Brooks got you. Drinks on the house! So what if it was just flat, oversweetened swill in a sticky pint glass.

She thanked the bartender and tried to bypass Nathalie, who caught her arm.

"You're upset."

"Am I?"

"Cate, just—*stop*." Nathalie tugged her to a halt, their private conversation veiled beneath the commotion of the Friday night crowd. "Listen to me—Fiona and I—it's over between us. I already told you that."

"Does she know that?"

"Catharine." The word was loaded with pent-up frustration, Nathalie's own anger at the turn of the night. She tipped her head toward the garden door. "What you're seeing—that's just her. It's who she is. It's nothing to do with you. She's just very—" she waved an exasperated hand "—unrestrained."

Instead of soothing Catharine, the word hit a nerve the unapologetic Irishwoman had unwittingly exposed. But not for the obvious reasons.

Yes, the woman was poised. Cultured. Polished. Effortlessly cosmopolitan. Unquestionably smart. She was attractive, there was no denying it. That she'd caught Nathalie's attention was no surprise. She'd turn any number of heads.

But Catharine was not so insecure as to be unaware that she herself possessed all those same attributes. That the boys found her beautiful. That she was better read than many of her tutors. More well-traveled than any of her peers.

The one thing she did not possess, however—the one area someone like Dr. Fiona Loughlin would always hold the edge— was in her inability to exist without artifice. To live, as Nathalie had put it, *unrestrained*. Not in Oxford. Not in Honour Stone. Not anywhere.

She looked away from Nathalie, wishing she'd asked for a water, and took a sip of the cider instead. "I'm sorry. It's fine. I just…" She hiked a dismissive shoulder, an entire life of shortcomings hanging on that *just*.

"Nathalie!" Across the room, a young Black man in a fuchsia-striped blazer waved an enthusiastic greeting.

Catharine extracted her arm from Nathalie's hold. "Go—please —mingle. I'm going to get a water. I'll meet you back at the table."

After Nathalie had reluctantly left her, disappearing to join her friend, Catharine finished her cider—and though she'd genuinely meant to ask for a still water, when the bartender set down another pint with a wink, she drained it again. And the one after it as well.

How many had she had? She couldn't remember. Her thoughts were stuck in a perpetual cycle of the disdainful way Fiona had said *infinitely boring* and the word *unrestrained* pulsing between her ears.

She was drunk. And tired. And incurably jealous—envious of things outside her control. She should have just slipped out of the pub and slept off what was promising to be a raging hangover back in her room. But when the bartender progressed from flirtatious banter to suggesting she join him at his for a nightcap once his shift was over, she politely declined and tottered her way back through the garden door.

Nathalie had returned to a chair at the end of their table, where two new faces had settled into the small group—the boy in the fuchsia blazer and a girl Catharine had never seen before. Catharine paused a moment, watching Nathalie. She was listening with diverted interest to Benedict waxing lyrical to his captive audience, and a spliff being passed between the chairs. It went from Maggie, to blazer boy, who then presented it to Fiona, who paused only for a moment, before giving a little *why-not* lift of her shoulders, and deeply inhaled. Nathalie laughed, and Catharine watched as she took the joint from the doctor's spindly fingers, setting the roach—now coated in Fiona's oxblood lipstick—to her lips.

It unmoored something in Catharine, the intimacy of the gesture, despite the voice of reason reminding her it had been shared around the table.

Unrestrained.

Was that what Nathalie wanted?

Catharine's thoughts were struggling to maintain a linear path. She felt very flushed—when had the mid-April evening grown quite so warm?—and the garden around her seemed to sway with the jangly rhythms of the Britpop guitar riffs humming in the background.

"Looks like you guys are having a good time?" She found herself suddenly standing next to Nathalie, uncertain when she'd crossed from the door. Nathalie, in the middle of a second puff, looked up, jerking the spliff from her mouth.

"Hey! I thought you'd gone home. I looked for you—"

"And miss all the fun?" She draped an arm around Nathalie's shoulders, sliding into her lap. "Tell me, why would I do that?" The world shifted, and Catharine couldn't tell if it was from Nathalie struggling to keep them both upright, or the cider-induced swimming in her head.

"Cate..." Nathalie's voice was quiet, her tone careful. "Get up."

"Then where would you have me sit?" She looked around the table, only vaguely aware all eyes were on her, until she settled on Fiona. The woman had shifted into the seat she'd previously occupied. If Catharine had been sober, she probably would have been forced to acknowledge that the move was done to make space for the new arrivals. But she was far from sober, and reasoning had washed away two...? three...? four ciders ago? Along with any sense of good judgment. She shrugged. "It appears my place has been taken."

Nathalie tried to push to her feet, but Catharine only planted herself more firmly and snatched the joint out of her fingers.

"This isn't you." Nathalie's voice was less than a whisper.

"But it's who you want me to be, right?" Catharine responded smartly.

"You are very drunk. *Lève-toi—tout de suite !*"

Catharine ignored the order to stand, tucking the spliff between her lips. She'd never even smoked a cigarette—let alone something like this.

The searing in her lungs hit her with surprise—it was nothing like the tranquil, halcyon calm everyone else seemed to experience when taking a drag. She couldn't control the coughing, her eyes instantly springing burning hot tears. For a moment, her only concern was breathing, until a radiating pain scorched her lower leg. She'd dropped the joint, she realized, and it had gotten caught in the folds of her skirt. It took no further prompting to get her to her feet, and the next thing she knew, she was in the vacated chair of Fuchsia Blazer, and the boy was on his knees, pressing a dampened napkin to her calf.

"Alright, there we are, love," he was assuring her, his delicate fingers administering to the burn. "Nothing a bit of Germolene and a good night's sleep won't fix." He smoothed the material of her skirt. "I wish I could say the same for this lovely wool crepe—though, I could see a snappy hem in its future—it would look stunning knee length."

Catharine struggled to focus enough to thank him, let alone even understand what he was saying. She felt hot. And queasy. And horrifically embarrassed. She had a cloudy recollection of sitting on Nathalie's lap. Of the stench of the spliff still clinging to her blouse.

It could only have been a few seconds since all of that had transpired... But then Catharine was accepting a glass of water from the boy's hand—when had he stopped holding the napkin to her burn?—and it occurred to her the two of them were alone at the table. Where had Fiona and Benedict gone? The other girl? Nathalie? Maggie?

The former was answered by a loud guffaw across the garden, where Benedict had moved on to entertaining another circle, and dragged Fiona along with him. But—the others?

She took a sip of the water, battling an instant wave of nausea.

"Where's Nat?"

"Gone to fetch the first-aid box. Thought you might need a plaster." He motioned at her singed skirt.

"I think I need to get to the loo." Catharine stood abruptly. She was terrified she was going to be sick.

The boy immediately had an arm around her waist, keeping her from tipping onto the hard flagstone flooring.

She remembered little of the trek to the toilets, aside from her gallant paladin—*I'm Marlon*, she vaguely recalled him saying— seeing her safely down the stairs and through the hall to the women's water closet. He offered to help her inside, but she reassured him she'd be fine, and slunk through the door, using the wall for balance.

There were only two cubicles, both with their doors closed. Catharine leaned against the sink, pressing her cheek to the cool surface of the hand dryer, trying to control her nausea.

"But is she like—you know...?" Catharine recognized Maggie's voice from the first toilet. There was a short stretch of silence, and Maggie continued. "Like one of *us*?"

"I already told you," came Nathalie's snapped response from the door opposite, "she's just drunk."

"Seemed like more than that to me. I mean, look at the way she clings to you. I'd say she fancies you, even if you don't see it—"

"She's just a fucking toff, alright? An old-money privileged brat, desperate to be someone she's not. No different than the rest of these Oxford types." The lid of a toilet slammed inside the cubicle. "Just another marionette who will marry one of those boatie boys, where they spend their summers on the French Riviera—her entire life revolving around entertaining her dolt-of-a-husband's insipid friends over tea and crumpets in their rose garden. In no way is she *like us, compris ?*"

A toilet flushed, and Catharine tried to convince her brain to command her feet to start moving.

Out. Away. Anywhere but here.

A fucking toff.

Maggie's donkey-bray laughter cut through the loud hum of the hand dryer Catharine accidentally bumped on.

"Alright, alright, I didn't mean to strike a nerve..." The latch rattled on the cubicle door, the rusted lever stuck in place.

Catharine didn't hear the rest of what was said. Her self-preservation had finally kicked in, and she was barreling into the hallway, just as Maggie got the faulty lock to slide open.

Marlon was waiting there, his gentle expression shifting to mounting concern when he saw her stumble toward the stairs.

"Cate?"

An old-money privileged brat.

"Are you all right?"

Desperate to be someone she's not.

Catharine fell in her rush up the first step, and gave in to accepting his arm.

In no way is she like us.

Maggie's shrill laughter sounded again from behind the closed door.

She leaned against Marlon. "Will you—will you just walk me home?"

Chapter Twenty

CATHARINE DIDN'T SHOW UP AT *Spires Cafe* the next morning. Nor did she go anywhere near *The Old Fire Station* for the matinee or evening performance of Nathalie's show. And same again for Sunday.

Instead, she holed up in her second-floor room in the Meadow Building, never leaving her staircase. She nursed her hangover—far easier to mend than her shattered heart—and poured her attention into studying the material that would be covered in Trinity Term. Material she'd already gone over. Twice.

Nathalie, apparently, didn't notice. Or at least, didn't care. It wasn't until Monday night, after Catharine had again found her morning coffee at a cafe as far away from Brasenose as she could get without a bike, that a note was left in her pidge.

C—
We need to talk.
Stop avoiding me.
N

Talk? Catharine crumpled the note and dropped it in the porters' rubbish bin. Nathalie'd already talked plenty. Until Friday night, Catharine just hadn't listened.

But she'd heard her then—loud and clear. *A toff. A marionette.*

A *fool*—not Nathalie's word, but one needn't be a playwright to read between the lines.

Tuesday evening, returning from a long, cold walk in the pouring rain—the April showers doing nothing to ablate the misery Catharine steeped in—she found another note, this time slipped beneath her door.

Cate,
   I need to see you.
   Please.

Still soaking wet, her jacket forgotten on the gray corded carpet of her entryway, Catharine marched the note down to the porter on duty in the lodge. She stood at the counter and explained that a student from Brasenose was harassing her, and waved the note in the air for reference.

The kindly old man knitted his wiry brows and jotted down Nathalie's name. He would handle it, he assured her.

After that, no further notes appeared. And every night, Catharine didn't know if she was relieved to find the sanctity of her demand for distance respected, or if she was even more livid at Nathalie for giving up without a fight.

By the time Friday rolled around—the week proving to be the longest of Catharine's life—she decided to drag herself down to Oxford Station and catch an afternoon train to Henley. As little as she wanted to go to the country, anything seemed better than wallowing around her room all weekend, replaying the endless rotation of questions that cycled through her mind:

Did Maggie see her leave the toilets? Had Marlon mentioned walking her home? Did Nathalie mean the things she'd said? And if she did, was she aware Catharine had overheard?

She pressed her forehead to the cool glass window, telling herself for the thousandth time none of the answers really mattered, and watched the spires of Oxford disappear.

WALKING UP THE WINDING DRIVE through the parklands—she'd skipped the route through the woods, unwilling to risk stumbling across some of her fondest memories beneath those canopied trees —she found herself disappointed to discover her mother wasn't in Henley.

"London," Mrs. Ainsley said that evening, serving her dinner in the Yellow Room. "Left two days ago. Didn't mention when she would return."

Catharine leaned into the comforting touch of the hand resting on her shoulder. How tempting it was to confide in her, this woman who'd known her all her life. Mrs. Ainsley wouldn't judge her, she felt almost certain of that. The stern household manager had always had a soft spot for Catharine. She'd been the one who taught her to cut out paper dolls and snuck her sweet treats from the pantry. Soothed nightmares, cooled fevers, read her the stories of Alice in Wonderland and Peter Pan, before tucking her into bed with a kiss in the winter. No tutor, no nanny, no governess—not even her own mother—had ever cared for her as Mrs. Ainsley had.

But Catharine didn't dare put her in that position. It wasn't right to burden her with secrets that could jeopardize her job.

So instead, she ate her dinner in solitude, and then tinkered on the Pleyel upright, wandering through the melancholic bars of *Nocturne in C-Sharp Minor*, until she could no longer stand the somber heartache drifting from her fingers. She snapped the fallboard closed and decided to call her mother.

The Belgravia house phone was answered on the second ring, but to Catharine's disappointment, the voice belonged to Mr. Fraser.

Which meant her father, too, was in the city.

She'd assumed he was in Amsterdam, where he'd been working to close a long-term berthing contract with the Amerikahaven terminal. A project slated to settle in May, which had given Catharine a false sense of security.

Her threadbare nerves unraveled another strand when he came on the line, ignoring her request to speak with her mother.

"Catharine. You're in Henley."

She'd have endured a one-on-one tutorial with Dr. Fiona Lough-lin—examining Lord Byron, or Wordsworth, even—if it would buy her the ability to rewind the clock six hours. Anything to prevent her from making the mistake of stepping outside the towering walls of Christ Church and forfeiting the excuse of 'education' that preserved the distance between her and her father.

"Yes." She stared at the chinoiserie wallpaper behind the piano, its hand-painted buttercup flowers and delicate birds disappearing into pastel swirls.

"Your timetable mustn't be too overloaded, then?"

Her timetable was hell—this final term of second year, the one every tutor warned would be the most daunting—but she'd hardly noticed the past week slip by, her mind anywhere but on her studies.

"It's manageable." Immediately, she knew she'd misspoken. She should have said it was so overwhelming, she'd needed the silence of the country to complete her reading. Anything other than allow him to think she had unaccounted time at her disposal.

"Good. Then you can join us tomorrow in London."

"I really need to—"

"I'm not interested in your excuses. You've flounced about for months now, doing as you please. Tomorrow, you'll present your-self at the townhouse. I'm hosting a luncheon, and I'm certain your mother would like to see you."

Catharine didn't argue. It was true, ever since Christmas, he'd asked little of her. He'd held up his end of the bargain, and she didn't want him reconsidering it now. She could tolerate one day in the city and be on her way back to Oxford by Sunday afternoon. Whatever it took to maintain the fragile ceasefire her mother had brokered between them.

"All right."

"Mr. Fraser will pick you up first thing in the morning."

CATHARINE WOULD RATHER HAVE SUFFERED luncheon in the stuffy grandeur of The Connaught, or the suffocating hauteur of Claridge's, or even the obscenely lavish bistro at The Dorchester, where opulence seemed to drip from the walls. Anywhere other than the six-story Georgian terrace, where her father's study window looked directly into the overstuffed library of the Sultan of Brunei's London townhouse.

But, she had learned the hard way, rarely did life ever cater to her preferences. So instead, at noon on Saturday, she stood beneath her father's Murano glass chandelier in the gold-leafed reception room, hiding behind a practiced smile, and watched her mother welcome and flatter the dozen guests trailing through the wide double doors.

Did she like these men who laughed too loud, drank too much, thought so highly of themselves? Catharine was certain she did not. But watching Emily Brooks sweep from arrival to arrival, her Ferragamo Vara heels clicking confidently across the parquet floor, she put on a masterclass of deception.

How good it is to see you, Lord Fairchild.

How well you're looking, Ambassador Beaumont.

Pleasure to meet you, Mr. Cleveland.

And so on and so forth.

Listening to her mother charm and placate these men she could dance intellectual circles around suddenly stirred something furious in Catharine. Something feral. Something clawing to get out. But something that kept silent, its wings clipped and talons tethered.

She couldn't stop thinking about what Nathalie had said.

Just another marionette who will marry one of those boatie boys… her entire life revolving around entertaining her dolt-of-a-husband's insipid friends over tea and crumpets in their rose garden.

It stung even more now, watching her mother play the part of the perfect housewife, her father the puppeteer, pulling every string.

A cold sweat trickled down her neck, dampening the delicate tulle lace beaded around the collar of her ivory dress. She had the irrational urge to climb to the top of the grand staircase and fling herself over the railing.

Would her father cancel the luncheon?

Would Nathalie regret what she had said?

She looked away from the marble balustrade, deciding both were unlikely.

Besides, she didn't have the courage for that anyway.

So she just kept nodding, smiling through her veneer, echoing her mother's *how do you do's* and *so kind of you to join us's* while tolerating winks, and smirks, and sweeping glances that never drifted above her chest.

After the final guest arrived—Sir Harold Aldridge, a veteran backbencher and her father's favored voice in Parliament—she followed her mum up the stairs, trying unsuccessfully to keep one step ahead of the MP, who fell into stride beside her, slipping his swollen-knuckled hand to the small of her back.

"And how is my favorite bluestocking faring, Catie? Still hard at work at Christ Church?"

The rasp of his brittle nails against the embroidered lace invoked a shudder she couldn't repress.

"Nippy in here, is it?" He wheezed a chuckle at the top of the staircase, steering her in the direction where he'd spotted her father. "Benjamin—I was just asking Catie about her studies. I can hardly fathom how she has any time for reading with all the boys who must be showering her with attention. Quite the young lady she's become." Again, he chuckled in that har-har way of his that jiggled all three of his chins.

"You're very kind, Sir *Harry*," Catharine replied, unable to stop herself. She knew Sir Harold loathed the diminutive of his name. *Handout Harry*, his colleagues in the Commons snickered in the hallways, a nod to his propensity to always have his palm up, his policies open to whoever wrote the largest checks.

Her father glared at her through his guise of civility, clapping the MP on the back. He knew damn well Catharine hadn't misspoken. He'd spent years drilling into her every particular, every idiosyncrasy, every preference of London's ruling class.

"Sir Harold—pleasure, always. Come, have a look at this Turner I just purchased at auction. A rare find, recently resurfaced. I think you'll appreciate the magnificent rendering of atmosphere—a schooner off the coast of Dover." He guided him toward his study, well aware of the man's love affair with maritime watercolor. Her father would have purchased the piece just for this occasion. "Couldn't resist," she could hear him continue, disappearing down the hall. "An absolute master in working so boldly with light."

An overwhelming stench of tawdry cologne turned Catharine's attention back to the drawing room. A man had circled near, fiddling with the label on a Cohiba cigar tucked in his breast pocket. He intended to look distracted, his proximity to her feigned as happenstance, but Catharine knew an unwelcome advance when she saw one.

"I don't suppose you've got a light?" He had a lazy, honeyed drawl that left no mistaking him for anything but American.

"I'm afraid I'm not in the habit of smoking, Mr. Cleveland."

His smile was as slow as his demeanor, and he leaned closer, clearly misconstruing her knowledge of his name as an indication he held her interest.

"Have we met before?"

"No, sir." She resisted the urge to step aside, despite her desire to get away from the overpowering scent of clove and bourbon. "My father makes a point of acquainting me with his guest list."

She'd read his name on the neatly typed manifest. *Carlton Cleveland, Council Chairman, Berkeley County, South Carolina.* In the notes, all it had said was: *Port of Charleston, terminal development.*

So this misfit American in his too-bright tie and overshined loafers—who was as incongruous here amongst these unprovincial, powerful titans of men as a burr in fine satin—was a patsy in her father's present ploy to edge *WorldCargo* deeper into the North American shipping network. It made sense that he would choose this oily, low-level, political upstart for his Southeast expansion aspirations. The smugness of his smile promised he thought too highly of himself, and the loudness of his gleaming Rolex suggested he was a man who could be purchased.

He was exactly the type of pawn her father preferred.

"Ah, your *father*." He elongated the word in his Deep South drawl, his eyes flicking in the direction the colonel had gone off with Harold Aldridge. "I see."

Catharine didn't know what he thought he saw, but she was certain his blinkered gaze could extend no further than the banknotes her father dangled above his nose.

Behind him, the gilded hand of a clock sitting on the rosewood side table struck half past one.

Two more hours. Three, at worst. And then she could board a train back to Henley. Or Oxford. Or the Shetland Islands, for all she cared. It didn't matter where she went, as long as it was far from here.

But wherever that was, it would still be without Nathalie.

She refocused on the room. On the role she'd been groomed to perform.

"How are you enjoying London, Mr. Cleveland?"

"Better now, I'll admit." His fingers were back tinkering on the cigar label. He gave her a conspiratorial smirk. "I thought I'd left all the pretty girls home in South Carolina. I'm pleased to see I've been proven wrong."

Catharine ignored the pathetically predictable pass. He wasn't the first of her father's guests to try to earn her favor with flattery, and he certainly wouldn't be the last. "Is it business or holiday that brings you to our humble island?"

"Well, I'm a man who's always enjoyed mixing work with pleasure—never seen much reason to separate the two." He leaned a little closer, lowering his voice. "If you know what I mean?"

The only thing in the room moving slower than the small hand on the clock was this man's mind. She considered politely excusing herself, but caught sight of Mr. Zakarian, the chairman of *Caspian Maritime Group*. A man who—when unaccompanied by his translator—liked to exploit the language barrier as an excuse to engage her with physical gestures, inevitably leading to his sweaty palms finding their way to her hips. The man was hovering on the threshold of the dining room, waiting for the opportunity to corner her alone.

The laughable arrogance of the ignorant American seemed the more tolerable of the two.

"I understand you are in politics, Mr. Cleveland?"

His fingers moved subconsciously from the cigar to the American Flag pinned on his opposite lapel, the smugness in his smile returning. "This time next year, you'll be addressing me as Representative Cleveland."

On second thought, Mr. Zakarian may have been the more sufferable alternative.

She forced a tight smile. "'*A man's worth is no greater than his ambitions.*'"

"Clever girl, pulling out the big guns. I imagine there's a line of men a mile long waiting to make you their Cleopatra."

It took Catharine a moment to register the reference, until she realized he'd misattributed the quote to Marcus Antonius—a far cry from Marcus Aurelius.

She let it go. She didn't imagine a man like him could tell the two apart.

He rocked back on his heels. "I won't be stopping there, of course. One term, maybe two. Then it's onto the Senate. After that," he shrugged, as if the answer was obvious, "the White House."

Her mind was back in Oxford, wondering if perhaps she should have allowed Nathalie to explain herself.

In front of her, the American shifted, expectant. "As in—President?" he continued.

She scolded herself for thinking Nathalie had any viable excuse for her to entertain.

"You know, of the United States? Similar to, say, your Prime Minister?"

Catharine dragged her attention back to the man in his poorly cut suit. "I'm familiar with the structure of the U.S political system, Mr. Cleveland." Over his shoulder, she saw her father had reentered the room. Harold Aldridge was no longer with him. He caught her eye, something behind his smoldering. He was furious.

All thoughts of Nathalie, of the inane self-flattery of the pretentious American, of the unbearable torpidity of the stubborn minute hand, evaporated. Her breath felt suddenly difficult to come by.

"I'm sorry—it was nice to meet you." She interrupted the South Carolina politician. At the moment, she couldn't even recall his name to excuse herself, but didn't care how rude her manner came across as she fled to the other side of the room. Her mother was there, nodding with feigned interest at something Lord Fairchild was saying. Catharine slipped deftly into the conversation, desperate to distance herself from the storm her father's rage was brewing.

Only once they were seated in the formal dining room, the three-course meal delivered in the classic silver service style demanded of the occasion, did Catharine risk another glance at the colonel. She was sure, by then, whatever had fanned his choler must have cooled. But despite Ambassador Beaumont's lively discourse about the upcoming Franco-British summit, she found her father's jaw clenched, and could see the veins in his hands. She knew him well enough to know he was not listening to a word the Frenchman said. His gaze, when it drifted to her end of the table, fell on her like lead.

Catharine couldn't focus. She dropped her salad fork and sipped water from the wrong glass, unable even to summon the embarrassment she ought to have felt when Mr. Zakarian, seated to her left, reclaimed the vessel with a wink.

The hours after the party had returned to the drawing room were torture. Catharine counted the departing guests one by one, knowing soon the safeguard of polite society would vanish, and she would be trapped behind the townhouse walls with nothing left to shield her. The minutes on the clock, so slow earlier, now slipped away like sand through her fingers.

Sir Harold was the first to go—she noted this only because he bade no farewell to her father—and then, with too little time in between, it was only the American, Mr. Cleveland, who lingered with his cigar, before he, too, finally departed.

Catharine attempted to contain the hum of her mounting anxiety by gathering discarded biscuit plates and half-sipped cups of coffee. Uncomfortable with the uncustomary assistance, Mrs. Clemmons, her father's housekeeper, stepped in to gently discourage her, but was interrupted by the colonel, who dismissed the woman with a flick of his hand.

A long minute ensued before the dull click of Mrs. Clemmons' sensible pumps vanished down the hall.

Pathetically, there was still a part of Catharine that hoped her mother would appear. That whatever she'd done wrong, Emily Brooks would be able to act as an intermediary and make her husband see reason. She was only downstairs, seeing Mr. Cleveland to the foyer.

But the logical side of Catharine knew the hope was nothing more than a chimera. She could count on one hand—with fingers left to spare—the number of times her mother had intervened on her behalf.

The silence from the hall promised that today she would not be adding another instance to her tally.

Across the room, Colonel Brooks did not move from where he was leaning against the wall.

"You must think yourself very clever, Catharine."

The statement was left as enough of a question to require an answer. She set down the stack of plates. "No, sir," she said, staring at the tea-sodden remnants of a *Langue de Chat*. "I do not."

"Don't you?" Her father's tone was conversational, laden with false pleasantry. "I would think a couple of years at Oxford—outshining your peers, earning a scholarship, all but guaranteed a First—might have instilled a sense of cerebral superiority."

"I am grateful for the education I have been afforded, which has allowed me to excel in my academic career."

She glanced up, and knew immediately it was the wrong answer. She could tell by the fine lines that shifted at the corners of his mouth—what should have been a smile, but on him was only a tightening of the lips. But in fairness, she knew there was no right answer. When he was in this mood, solving the *Riemann Hypothesis* would have been simpler than offering whatever solution he was after.

"Ah, yes. Your *academic* career. The one you've been provided in order to succeed in your *professional* career." He righted himself from the wall, moving with a languid, insouciant stride across the planked floor. "I wonder—with all your education, all your effortless accolades—if you have any real sense of what it takes to keep this empire operational? Is there any space left in that frivolity-filled mind to comprehend the sacrifices we must make—whether or not we wish to make them?"

This was not a question meant to be answered. She kept quiet, staring at the disintegrating biscuit, every nerve in her body aware how near he'd drawn.

To her relief, he passed by, circling the room again.

"Do you know how long I've had to suffer Harold Aldridge and his feeble-minded circle of fools to keep the impending EIA regulations from passing?"

Here they were getting to the heart of it. Her father had been lining Aldridge's pockets for years to sink a proposal calling for the environmental reassessment of cargo ships entering British waters. If the bill passed, overhauling the fleet to meet clean energy standards would cost *WorldCargo* millions. As a man of flexible convictions, the sausage-fingered backbencher had been more than amenable to stalling the emissions measure.

"A long time, sir."

"And is my pedant of a daughter aware that, as of last week, Aldridge withdrew his opposition?"

Catharine didn't dare look up. He had drawn closer again.

"No, sir."

"No?" His shadow darkened the plate her fingertips were resting on. "Then I imagine you also weren't aware that the entire purpose of today's luncheon was to court that old halfwit back into our favor?"

Catharine said nothing, acutely aware of where this was leading.

"Well?" He demanded, the shift from self-restraint to fury in his draconian posture instantaneous. It took everything in Catharine's willpower not to back away, fearing she'd incite him further.

"I did not know that, sir."

"Correct," he agreed. "You did not. And in your petty-minded ignorance, you felt compelled to *mock* the man whose vote could sway the trajectory of this industry's future. All because—in your academia-induced arrogance—you could not tolerate an imbecilic old buffoon calling you a monicker!"

Sir *Harry*. It was true. She *had* mocked him. But the transgression was so insignificant, so minor, the man had not even seemed to notice. Whatever Sir Harold's reasoning for turning tail on their agreement, Catharine knew it wasn't her doing. She knew her father knew that, too—but as always, in his outrage, she would be forced to play the role of whipping boy.

"You have become a vain, careless, self-centered girl who does not know her place! That is *not* who I have raised!"

"I meant no serious offense—"

"I do not care what you meant! It will not happen again!"

The blow she'd known was coming still caught her off guard, the force of his closed fist sending her sprawling to her knees. This was not the backhand from the day he'd demanded she quit rowing, or one of the open-palmed slaps delivered when she'd previously misspoken. Her teeth clattered as she hit the floor, and a bright burst of stars filled her vision, her left eye immediately watering, an involuntary tear streaming down her cheek.

She didn't get up. She didn't dare, afraid that if she did, he would knock her down again.

Towering above her, the soft leather of his oxfords showed triple on the polished herringbone flooring.

"If there is one thing you will learn in this world, Catharine, it is this: your pride, your hubris, your pathetic little ego—they all mean *nothing* when it comes to this family. You will smile, and nod, and thank these men—even should they treat you as less than the filth beneath their feet! Do I make myself clear?"

The claret-red patterns of the Persian runner spun and flickered in cadence with the throbbing at her temple. She closed her eyes, trying to drown out the echo, the crash of blood flooding between her ears.

She couldn't hear her own thoughts, let alone what he was saying. But she knew what he wanted, so she just nodded her head and assured him she understood, until she heard him walk away.

Chapter Twenty-One

Sunday morning, Catharine sat in the backseat of her mother's black Daimler as Mr. Wilkins, Emily's driver, returned them to Honour Stone.

They didn't speak on the hour-long drive. Catharine stared out the window, hidden behind dark sunglasses, and watched through blurred vision as the city fell away into the lush greens and pastels of the country in springtime.

Emily looked anywhere other than Catharine.

The silence continued when they ascended the stairs into the foyer, where Mrs. Mills, the housekeeper, couldn't quite stifle her gasp upon glimpsing Catharine's face. And it continued still, later that night, after they'd taken dinner in the Yellow Room, when Mrs. Ainsley brought a jar of arnica with their evening tea, leaving the homemade cream beside the milk and sugar—as if it were just another accompaniment to the tray.

It was only when Catharine stood to retire to her rooms that Emily at last broke the quiet that had befallen them.

"Catharine." Her hands worked the hem of the silk twill blouse she was wearing. "I don't—I don't know what to…"

What to what?

Catharine waited. *To say? To do?* Her mother didn't finish the sentence, and Catharine brushed her off.

It didn't matter. The time for that had passed.

It had passed ten years ago, when the Colonel made their eight-year-old decide which of her favorite kitchen maids to fire from the staff.

It had passed six years ago, when Emily Brooks did nothing while her husband berated their not-yet-teenage daughter for misunderstanding *comparative advantage* at Easter dinner in front of the visiting German Trade Minister and his wife.

It had passed last night, when she'd left a tea towel full of crushed ice in a crystal bowl in the hall in front of Catharine's London suite—and vanished down the corridor before Catharine had reached the door.

And all the thousands of major and minor offenses in between.

"Goodnight, Mum."

"Catharine, please—wait." Emily rose from her chair.

Catharine paused, her fingers resting on the brass lever handle. Again, a silence extended across the room.

"I could drive you to Oxford in the morning?" her mother finally said, bypassing whatever had been on the tip of her tongue. "So you don't have to take the train."

"Don't bother." Catharine clicked the handle open. "I won't be going tomorrow."

And she didn't.

Not Monday. Nor Tuesday, either. She couldn't bear the thought of seeing anyone she knew. Not with her eye swollen shut, the skin from cheek to brow the same color as the Mahonia berries still clinging to the shrubbery outside the chapel garden.

By Wednesday morning, the hue of aubergine had faded to a rust-tinged violet, the swelling decreasing to the point she could at least see shadows from the eye.

It could be covered, Emily quietly suggested over poached eggs and toast. *Of course, only if she wanted—if she was in a hurry to return to university.*

Which, she wasn't. Though she certainly didn't tell her why.

Just days earlier, she'd longed to confide in her mother, to share with her the hurt she felt. Maybe not the full extent of it—there was no one to whom she could confess what Nathalie truly meant to her—but her mother, she thought, might understand the falling out with a friend. The heartache it had wrought.

But that fleeting desire to open herself up, to allow her mother in, had been abandoned back in London. A mistake she wouldn't make again.

After breakfast, she spent the morning studying, working on her essays due at the end of the week. She wrote, rewrote, and rewrote again, her valuation of *Stakeholder Governance and Systemic Risk in Global Finance*—tearing up each draft and starting over whenever she caught her mind wandering.

How an evaluation of efficacy within a vested-interest corporation could make her think of the way Nathalie's pin-straight hair curled only at her left temple was something she couldn't comprehend.

At lunchtime, she closed her notebook, grabbed her sunglasses, and made her way down to the rear gardens. There, enclosed within the high stone walls, surrounded by the espaliered fruit trees and herbaceous border, she felt protected from the world. The gardeners had already tended to the area earlier in the morning, and none of the house staff was likely to make an afternoon intrusion.

She strolled along the raised vegetable beds and past the glasshouse, with its climbing vines and orchids, then wandered between the lily ponds and reflecting pool, before settling onto the iron bench facing the sundial. An hour passed, and then another, until the shadow on the gnomon indicated it was nearing four o'clock, and she was at risk of running late for tea.

Resigned to leave the peacefulness of the afternoon, Catharine slipped through the maze of wooden gates and started down the gravel path that led to the rear of the house. The day was bright and the weather balmy, which meant tea would be served on the terrace.

Her thoughts were far away—lost somewhere back in Oxford— which was why, until she reached the long, low steps rising out of the rose garden, she didn't notice her mother had company. She stopped, one foot on the first brick stair, her heartbeat skipping.

She would have known the sculpt of those shoulders, the curve of that waist, the precise angle of the elbow resting on a trousered knee—anywhere.

Nathalie sat with her back to the gardens, one slender leg thrown over the other, chatting casually with her mother.

"Oh, Catharine!"

Catharine was in the middle of an about-face, preparing to flee in the direction she had come, when Emily called her name. She considered ignoring her. She hadn't invited Nathalie here. She didn't want to see her. But the fledgling thought never took full flight before she abandoned it. She hadn't been raised with that kind of audacity—to so grievously disregard her mother.

She turned around, self-consciously readjusting the oversized sunglasses she'd lived in for the last four days. They covered the majority of her eye, but did nothing to disguise the bruising creeping down her cheek.

"What are you doing here?" Catharine remained at the bottom of the stairs.

"Catharine," Emily scolded, shooting her a frown. "Nathalie's been waiting all afternoon to see you. I've invited her to stay for tea."

"She can't." Catharine refused to look at Nathalie. "She has a Wednesday evening tutorial." It made her even angrier that she knew that—that she knew Nathalie's schedule as well as she knew her own.

"It was canceled." Nathalie leaned back, settling deeper into her chair. "In fact, I have no obligations until my lecture on *Revenge and Gender in Early Modern Tragedy* tomorrow afternoon."

That, Catharine knew, was a lie. Thursdays were the busiest mornings on Nathalie's timetable. But the falsity played straight into her mother's indelible instinct as hostess.

"Well, in that case," Emily insisted, brightening at the prospect of having someone in the house to buffer the discomfort between her and her daughter, "you must stay the night. It's hardly sensible to come all this way just to turn straight around. I'll have Mrs. Ainsley see to another place at dinner."

Leaving no time for dispute, Emily was on her feet, disappearing through the door.

"Before you take it out on her," Nathalie said as soon as the latch clicked closed, "I told her you were expecting me."

Catharine still hadn't left the bottom stair. She kept her face turned away from Nathalie on the pretense of gazing out over the garden.

"It doesn't matter. And I don't care what she says: you aren't staying here tonight."

Nathalie swiveled toward her. "I'm not leaving until we talk."

"Then you may as well bed down with the corpses in the chapel, because I have nothing to say to you."

"No?" Nathalie's demeanor remained infuriatingly calm. "Because I think it's the least you owe me—after nearly getting me sent down for harassment."

The terrace door swung open, and Emily reappeared, Mrs. Ainsley trailing with a tray of tea and finger sandwiches.

"Catharine—your manners, please." She gave a pointed look toward her empty chair. "I can't believe how warm it is," she continued, resuming her seat as the tea was served on the low stone table. "I imagine we're in for a hot summer."

Simmering at her mother's inane small talk, Catharine grudgingly climbed the stairs. She could feel Nathalie's eyes on her, feel her attention drawn to the bruising the cloudless sky refused to conceal. Sinking into her seat, she turned her face away, and to Nathalie's credit, as Emily blathered on about things that didn't matter, Nathalie managed not to stare.

ALL THROUGH TEA, EMILY CHATTED with Nathalie about Oxford. They talked about her recent show and how Nathalie enjoyed making her directorial debut.

Of course, then Emily wanted to know if directing was a path she might consider in the future.

Nathalie laughed and said it was unlikely—as it had recently been pointed out to her, she loved the attention too much to stray that far from the limelight.

At the recycled words, Catharine couldn't help but steal a glance in her direction, despite knowing it was exactly what Nathalie wanted. She didn't, however, return the smile cast her way, refusing to allow the Frenchwoman to think, under any circumstances, her presence was welcome. She had some audacity showing up here—entirely uninvited.

She kept quiet, offering only the barest one-syllable answers, no matter how her mother attempted to drag her into the dialogue, until eventually, the two women carried on without her.

By the time the sun dipped behind the red-brick chimneys towering above the turrets, Catharine's outrage at the intrusion had boiled over. She refused to sit there any longer, listening to chatter about Brasenose's feud with Lincoln College, or her mother's concern over how the late frost may have affected the delphiniums.

In the middle of Emily rambling on about a planned trip to the Côte d'Azur—of all the places her mother had to bring up, of course she'd mention the French Riviera—Catharine launched to her feet, nearly upsetting the table. The entire conversation felt like little more than a dark comedy, justifying everything Nathalie had said to Maggie.

"What are you going to go on about next? Tea and crumpets in the rose garden?" She was practically shouting, startling her mother, who had no way of understanding where the outburst had stemmed from.

"Catharine! I—"

But Catharine was already down the terrace steps, running along the gravel path that led to the gate behind the chapel. The warped old wood slammed shut on its rusted hinges as she tore across the acres of lawn stretching out in front of the manor.

She didn't know where she was going. The leather penny loafers she'd worn to stroll the gardens weren't suited for a race into the hills bordering the parkland, but she climbed the narrow deer track anyway, slipping and sliding in the mud from the early morning showers.

It wasn't until she'd reached the top of the hill, where the crest flattened out into a meadow ahead of the treeline, that she realized Nathalie was following her.

"Just leave me alone!" She hated the crack in her voice belying the tears that had sprouted somewhere between the garden path and her first stumble up the hillside. Her breath was coming in staggered, heaving gasps, as much from her spiraling emotions as the exertion of the run.

"Not until you talk to me!"

There were a hundred yards between her and the start of the ancient broadleaf woodlands, where Catharine knew she could lose Nathalie amongst the oak and beech and hornbeam. Just a short run into the coppiced understory. She could disappear, maybe lie down and cry until the moss and wild garlic swallowed her completely. Next spring, the bluebells would grow over her lifeless body.

Instead, she threw herself onto one of the primordial boulders that ornamented the ridge overlooking the valley, resigned to wait for Nathalie.

"There's nothing to talk about," she said once she heard footsteps approaching.

"The fact that you just made me chase you up a muddy mountainside wearing ballet flats says otherwise."

An unguarded piece of Catharine wanted to laugh—to roll her eyes at the foot Nathalie held up, the thin-soled slip-on covered in mud and leaf litter. But a different part of her, a newly bastioned part of her, erected its armor, demanding she cling to her outrage and not forget the ways Nathalie had hurt her.

"If you've come to apologize—"

"—I haven't," Nathalie waved her off, dropping onto the furthest edge of the boulder. She was still breathing hard, sweat glistening across her brow. "And I won't. Because I have nothing to apologize for."

The blatant rebuff was not what Catharine was expecting, and the blindside of it made the denial feel like an even more grievous injury. Tears that had begun to dry threatened once again.

"How can you honestly sit there and say that?" she demanded, turning sharply away to look down over the ridgeline. Several hundred feet below, Honour Stone spread out like a disease across the valley. "I heard what you said to Maggie—all of it!"

"I know." Nathalie pried her soaked shoes off her feet, dropping the mud-stained flats onto the rock to dry. "Marlon told me."

"If you can't imagine how hurtful that was, we truly don't have anything left to talk about—"

"Sit down, Cate!" Nathalie snapped, and the order was enough to pause Catharine from rising. "You were very drunk—and acting very stupid."

It wasn't something Catharine could deny, but it also wasn't something that gave Nathalie the license to say what she had said.

"Yes, I was! And I embarrassed you in front of your friends—I get it. But that doesn't excuse—"

"You think you embarrassed *me*? You think that's what this is about?" Nathalie's laugh was brittle, as jagged as the lightning-struck trunk of the yew tree lying broken in the grass. "You think I said what I said to Maggie because I was protecting *myself*?! I know you're not so thick as that!"

"Oh, you were protecting *me*, were you?" Catharine matched the incredulity of her tone. "A *fucking toff*—a *privileged brat*—"

"Yes! That's exactly what I was doing! And I'd say it all again! Do you have any idea how quickly Maggie would have run her mouth if she'd stepped out of those toilets with the knowledge that a prim and proper Oxford darling was *une broute-minou* ?"

Catharine flinched at the vulgar term, at the angry way Nathalie threw it.

"You didn't have to be so cruel—"

"And you didn't have to get so jealous! My God, Cate… I don't even know who you were that night!"

"Apparently an *old-money privileged brat, desperate to be someone she's not*!" Catharine flung the hateful accusation.

Nathalie drew a deep breath, closing her eyes, and Catharine could tell she was trying hard to temper her words. But the set of her jaw said the effort was a losing battle. She reopened her eyes, meeting Catharine's gaze, unblinking.

"Do you want me to be honest?"

The question yanked the knot tighter that had been forming in her chest. She managed a *go-ahead* gesture.

"We both know nothing I said was untrue. And that's why you're so angry—"

A strangled sound fell from Catharine's throat, half choke of fury, half laugh of disbelief. "Wh—! You can't be serious!"

"Then tell me where I'm wrong! Give me some reason to believe that any of this—" she motioned between them "—is real! That it's more than just a fleeting thing!"

The choke turned into a sound Catharine couldn't control. "You can't mean that!" she stammered, out of breath again—but this time, not from the exertion of the climb, but rather that it had been punched from her chest. As livid as she'd been, fragments of her had clung to the belief it was all a misunderstanding. That it was as Nathalie said—she'd been trying to protect her.

But—*we both know nothing I said was untrue*—the admission left a fresh wound Catharine didn't know how to defend.

"You're not the only one hurting here, Cate!" Nathalie's voice shook, laden with emotion, a fusion of rage brimming with sorrow. "Do you really believe this will go on forever? That when we leave Oxford, you'll not simply cast me aside to do whatever your father demands of you?"

"It's not—it's not like that," Catharine faltered, unable to fortify the words with certitude.

"And how is it not? Please—tell me where I'm wrong!"

There wasn't enough air to fill her lungs, let alone form an argument for an answer she didn't know.

"Are you going to run away with me to Paris? Become a temp secretary, or work the front desk at a youth hostel? Maybe do the books for some dingy little theatre company in the backstreets of Montmartre?" Visibly struggling to control her anger, Nathalie shoved to her feet, not waiting for an answer. "Or was it *my* dreams you wanted me to abandon? Perhaps you just assumed I'd be willing to live a quiet life in a flat you pay for in some hidden corner of London—while you jet off and marry one of your old-money boyfriends, carrying on in your privileged little world. Then what? You sneak away while he's playing polo and visit me like I'm some red-light district call girl? Was that the plan?"

Catharine fought the childish urge to cover her ears, settling instead for burying her face in her palms. The sunglasses that had previously felt like a safeguard dug into her cheekbones, fogging up with tears she could no longer stem.

"It's not like that!" she repeated, the words broken by a sob. "You know it isn't!"

The ensuing silence was ruptured only by the cry of a hawk high above, and then Nathalie's bare footsteps through the grass. Catharine kept her eyes closed tight, certain she was leaving, but was startled when warm fingers encircled her wrists.

"Then talk to me, Cate," Nathalie whispered, gently prying her hands from her face. "Because I don't know what to do." She slid to the damp soil, kneeling at Catharine's feet, intertwining their fingers. "I know you love me—but I also know I'll never be enough for you. And I don't know how this ends."

The hawk circled the ridge, joined by another, their piercing screams fading down the canyon. Catharine's thoughts once again drifted to the woods at the end of the meadow, to the pockets of dog rose and bramble, and the dark and shadowy places where she wanted to disappear.

She'd been raised her whole life to handle every type of situation—from drawing-room diplomacy to business negotiations. Taught when to laugh, to smile, to don an impassive face.

But this was not in her repertoire. She didn't know how to disguise her heartache. How to admit she didn't have the answers. She was terrified of saying the wrong thing and watching Nathalie walk away.

Forcing a deep inhale, she dragged her cheek across her shoulder. Still, the tears continued unchecked, dripping off her chin.

"I don't either." It was the only truth she could offer—the admission that she, too, didn't know how this would end. "But I can't bear the thought of losing you, even when it's unfair to ask you to stay."

She couldn't bring herself to look at Nathalie, too afraid of what she would see.

Again, the hilltop grew quiet. The hawks had flown, and even the wind ceased to ripple through the trees.

In the unforgiving light of midday, Nathalie reached to lift the sunglasses off her face. Catharine didn't have enough fight left to resist. When she heard Nathalie's sharp intake of breath, she closed her eyes, unwilling to witness her reaction to the exposure of her shame.

"Oh my God, Cate."

In the wake of the four breathless words, fingertips grazed her bruised skin, the compassion of the touch almost as unbearable as the exhalation of her name.

"I'm not going anywhere," Nathalie finally whispered when the silence had stretched too thin. She rose to sit beside her, slipping an arm around her shoulders and drawing her into her embrace. "Whatever comes, I promise you—" she brushed her lips across her tear-stained cheek "—you're not going to lose me."

Journal Excerpt, Nathalie Comtois
Brasenose College, Oxford

She's going to be the death of me, I swear.
She's Catherine to my Heathcliff. Tristan to my Isolde.
Eurydice to my Orpheus. Cleopatra to my Antony.
She makes Juliet seem tame.
I know I can't save her.
But I don't know how to walk away.

Chapter Twenty-Two

"I often find my daughter's flair for the dramatic tends toward exaggeration—but I will say, Cate, in this instance, she did not embellish the truth. You are as beautiful as she claimed. Perhaps even more so."

Catharine laughed, unprepared for the amity of the greeting. Nathalie's mother was older than she expected. Her complexion was darker than her daughter's, her brown eyes paler, her stature petite, but strong. There was a natural warmth to her, and when she leaned in to kiss Catharine's cheeks, she carried the faint scent of rosemary.

"You are very kind, Madame Comtois. I suspect Nathalie has painted me in a more flattering light than I deserve, but I thank you, nevertheless."

"I told you, Maman, did I not? Beautiful *and* humble."

"And so very formal," the Frenchwoman winked at her daughter, stepping aside to admit them into the house. "Please, Cate— call me Sabine. And make yourself at home. You are most welcome here."

Catharine managed a word of thanks before Nathalie impatiently tugged her further down the corridor, their bags bumping against the walls.

On the long train ride from Rome, where they had spent the first two weeks of summer, it had begun to worry Catharine that Nathalie might have misgivings about introducing her to her childhood home. She was aware her upbringing had been modest, her mother a working-class widow who, dawn 'til dusk during harvest season, labored in the vineyards. Their *échoppe*, Nathalie had explained—a style of nineteenth-century Bordeaux house built during the city's urban expansion—was small, unremarkable, and set amidst the neglected, yet culturally vibrant neighborhood of *Saint-Michel*.

"It can be a bit rough," Nathalie cautioned when they stepped off the train at *Gare Saint-Jean*. "Just keep your bags close."

The twenty-minute walk from the station had underscored the warning, and Catharine had been grateful, as they traversed the narrow streets with the haggling market vendors and rowdy children playing football in *Place Meynard*, that they'd arrived in daylight hours.

But if Nathalie found any discomfort in sharing this part of her life with Catharine, she hid it well. If anything, she seemed to unspool here, settling into the familiarity of her home the way one might slip into the comfort of a favorite jumper.

She tossed their bags beside the chest of drawers and flipped on a digital clock radio, tuning it to *NRJ*. The whimsical, syncopated rhythm of *Joe le taxi* buzzed through the cheap speaker plate.

"You want the wall or the outside edge?"

Catharine glanced around the shoebox room, surprised. "Am I sleeping in here?"

A flash of annoyance crossed over Nathalie. "I'm afraid the penthouse is booked for the weekend, Your Majesty, but you could always sleep in the garden with the earwigs and woodlice."

"No, it's—that's not what I meant. I just—your mum…?"

"Ah." A languid, wayward smile replaced her testiness as she realized Catharine's conundrum. "You mean because of *this*?" She tipped her head toward the single narrow bed. "Worried some-one's going to get the wrong idea about England's favorite puritan, virginal daughter?"

Catharine rolled her eyes at the playful jab, but couldn't stop herself from glancing toward the door. Nathalie's mother could surely hear their conversation.

"Caaate…" Nathalie scolded, shimmying her shoulders in time to the track of *The Rhythm of the Night* that had come onto the radio. "Let me assure you," she sashayed up to her, hooking her thumbs through her trouser belt loops, drawing their bodies together, "Your cover is already blown. My maman knows me well enough to know we aren't *just* friends." She bent to kiss her neck, and as much as Catharine wanted to lean into her, to relax into the comfort of her body after the last twenty hours on a train, the sound of Madame Comtois bustling around the kitchen forced her to pull away.

"Nat. Seriously."

"Relax," Nathalie's smile didn't falter, though her tone remained reproachful, "she doesn't even know your surname. And do you know how many *Catherines* there are in Britain? It's as if the English didn't have any other options between 1066 and yesterday."

"I know, but…" Again, her gaze was on the door, prompting Nathalie to stretch across the small space and tap it closed with the toe of her espadrilles.

"Better?"

"If we're trying to confirm her suspicions—certainly," Catharine retorted, but this time tipped back her head when Nathalie returned to brush her lips across her jaw. The upbeat hum of the music, the secludedness of the space, was suddenly exactly what she needed after their exhausting trip from Rome. "What a peaceful place," she mused, closing her eyes.

"When I was young, I hated that it had no windows. Every child raised in *une échoppe bordelaise* knows the curse of the *pièce noire*. But as I got older," her tone turned mischievous, the lips drifting to Catharine's earlobe twisting into a smile, "I discovered it was hardly a curse at all. You wouldn't believe the things I've gotten away with in this room."

"I imagine that's something I'd regret asking you to elaborate on."

"If you're lucky, I'll show you instead." Nathalie grazed a finger down her midriff, her lips trailing south, lingering there just long enough to draw a sigh from Catharine, before she abruptly straightened and stepped toward the door. "But only if you're lucky. And certainly not right now. What do you take me for—*une coquine*?" She stuck out her tongue, tugging on the porcelain knob, and disappeared into the hall.

After what Nathalie cheekily called *la grande tournée du Palais Comtois*—which included a whirlwind tour of the tiny kitchen, a nod toward her mother's bedroom, an advisory that the one-and-only bathroom had just enough hot water for a three-minute shower, and a breeze-through of the sitting room on their way to what turned out to be a lush and well-planted garden—the three women sat down to a simple lunch of cold meats and bread on the patio.

Sabine peppered her daughter with questions about their trip to Rome, wanting to know everything from what they'd eaten—*had they tried real carbonara?*—to if they'd tossed a coin in the Trevi Fountain.

Good, that means you'll return, you know she had said approvingly of the confirmation.

Catharine loved Sabine's genuine interest in what Nathalie had enjoyed most about the trip, and her delight in listening to her daughter describe a holiday she would likely never experience for herself. She could not fathom her own mother asking what had made her happiest over the fortnight. Or later, when Sabine and Nathalie stood hip-to-hip washing dishes in the kitchen, how the older Frenchwoman (unaware her voice carried through the garden window) questioned if they had kissed by the Tiber—*pity, you should have, everyone does, I've heard*—and if they'd held hands when they walked through the city—*I don't think I've ever seen you this smitten before.*

It was Sunday, which Nathalie explained was usually her mother's day off, but since the *effeuillage* had begun—she laughed at Catharine's look of confusion, clarifying that on the vineyards, *effeuillage* referred to the stripping of leaves, unlike in Paris, where it meant the stripping of clothes—Sabine, as *la contremaîtresse*—the forewoman—felt obligated to stop by and check on the workers.

"Would you two like to join me?" Sabine asked, tugging on her work boots by the door. "Unless, of course, you both have other plans?" She didn't have to look up from tying her laces for the innuendo to hit its mark, and Catharine flushed furiously while hurrying to slip into her loafers.

"We would love to!" she said, too brightly, and ignored Nathalie's smirk as they filed out the single door.

On the walk through the city, she tried to imagine a life in which her mother knew she loved a woman and simply didn't care. But as they passed a grey block of flats with laundry fluttering from rusted balcony railings, she chastised herself for the fantasy. Perhaps if her mother had married a more forgiving man, things would have been different. But as it stood—as a Brooks—the delusion was more fantastical than the graffitied bull with serpent legs painted across a weathered storefront that once read *Le Sillon*.

As they crossed into the commune of *Pessac*, Nathalie waved a careless hand toward a wrought-iron gate set in a stone wall. A modest sign—*Château Haut-Brion*—hung above the entrance.

"You wouldn't know it from here, but just through those gates sits Her Royal Wineness, the Queen of Bordeaux."

Sabine scoffed. "You give *Haut-Brion* too much credit. They may be a First Growth, but their vines have no soul."

"Maman is just jealous of their new high-tech vat room. Well, that and her disdain that the owners come from American ancestry."

Sabine shrugged. "It's true—American dollars have no business in the art of French wine."

"But the English do?" Nathalie prodded, winking over her shoulder at Catharine. Catharine knew, from Nathalie's stories of home, that it was a London financier who owned the vineyard where Sabine worked. The same man who funded Nathalie's tuition to Oxford.

"Monsieur Whitaker may be English, but at least he's wise enough to leave the vinification to those who know best."

"And I'm certain he knows he wouldn't survive a day without you, Maman." Nathalie snaked an arm around her mother's waist, giving her a playful squeeze. "You will appreciate this," she continued as they approached a wooden gate tucked between two neatly kept hedgerows. "Last summer, Cate came to Brasenose to celebrate *le 14 juillet*. And what did she pull out of the bottom of her sack? A bottle of *1961 Château Haut-Brion!* Just thrown in with the fruits and cheeses, crumbs stuck to its label!"

"No!" Sabine laughed, aghast, momentarily forgetting her rivalry with the competing vineyard and leaning past her daughter to cheerfully scold Catharine. "Cate! As if it were a *vin de table!?*"

"Go easy on her, Maman," Nathalie poked Catharine, "she is not an *œnophile.*"

"Tell me you didn't drink it!"

"We did!" Nathalie affirmed, leaving no time for Catharine to defend herself. "In *plastic* glasses! Sitting on the grease-stained sofa in the JCR—watching *Monty Python!*"

"*Oh, bon sang*! Every sommelier's worst nightmare."

Again, Catharine could feel the heat rise to her pale cheeks. She enjoyed the good-natured teasing, but dreaded where it was leading.

"Wherever did you come across a *'61 Haut-Brion?*"

"As you say, Maman," Nathalie interceded, "every girl is entitled to their secrets." She slipped her arm through Catharine's, shooting her a crooked smile.

Sabine raised one of her expressive eyebrows, giving the pair of them a look, but let the subject go. "*D'accord.*"

Catharine imagined the woman may have thought that meant she stole it, but offered no elaboration, deciding the assumption she was a miscreant was better than the truth.

They had stopped in front of the gate, which Sabine now jostled open. Behind the hedgerows, a long gravel drive led straight to a two-story stone house covered in wisteria. On either side, rows of vines stretched into the distance, covering acres of land. The vineyard was well-kept, but had an aura as if they had stepped back in time.

"Welcome to *Château Saint-Aurèle*," Sabine said with unmistakable pride. "You have tasted *Haut-Brion*—now I will introduce you to a true *vin bordelais*."

WHILE SABINE CHECKED THE PROGRESS of the *effeuillage*, Nathalie pulled Catharine onto one of the gravel walking paths separating the Malbec from the Cabernet Sauvignon. Because it was still early in the summer, she explained, the leaf-thinning would be focused on the east-facing vines of the Merlot.

"Which means—" she ran her hand along the older, thicker vines at the heart of the estate "—we are entirely alone."

"Is that how you used to seduce all the girls you've brought here?" Catharine stroked the velvety underside of a leaf. A small, tight cluster of green fruit dangled from the shoot, still yearning to ripen.

"*Used* to?" Nathalie tutted, catching Catharine's hand and pulling her further down the row. "Who's to say I've left those skills in the past?" She leaned down to pluck a sucker from a gnarled trunk. "But no, to answer your question, I prefer to reserve that for the barrel cellar."

"Pfft, alright, Don Juan."

Side-eyeing her, Nathalie smiled at her mock indignation. "Methinks I'm detecting a tone of envy."

"Oh, please."

"Two-foot-thick walls, low light, no windows…"

Catharine huffed. "Mildew, cobwebs, the smell of fermentation…"

Nathalie leaned over, brushing her lips against her ear. "Green is such a good color on you."

Encouraged by their isolation, Catharine turned her head, willing Nathalie to kiss her, but a sudden rustling in the low grass caught her attention, and the two of them jumped when a flurry of feathers exploded onto the path. An angry hen bolted between them, followed closely by a pursuing rooster, scattering gravel in their wake.

"I thought you said we were entirely alone," Catharine quipped, laughing.

Nathalie hiked a shoulder. "No chickens in the barrel cellar."

They continued along the row, Nathalie pointing out the features of individual vines, educating Catharine on how certain berries produced better wines. It was obvious some of Sabine's passion for the plants had rubbed off on her daughter.

"These pretty girls are the oldest in *Saint-Aurèle*," she said, stopping at the beginning of a new parcel where the trunks of the vines were distinctly thick, the arms wild and knotted, stretching toward the clouds. "My papa used to tease that they were the only ladies on the vineyard older than my maman."

"Rude!"

"No," Nathalie laughed. "It was the running joke between them. My maman was ten years older than my papa. She'd started at the vineyard as a teenager, brought on only for the harvest season, and eventually worked her way to what she is now—*la contremaîtresse*. She'd already been here twenty years when he was hired as the *chef de culture*—her supervisor. Needless to say, she was infuriated. Here was this much younger man with less experience suddenly giving her orders. It was hate at first sight. But—" Nathalie smiled to herself, twirling a delicate tendril around her finger, "—it turned out he knew his viticulture. He poured his entire heart into *Saint-Aurèle*, and, in the process, won my mother's. They were married just here," she gestured down the row, "amongst their favorite vines. She was forty. I was a surprise two years later." Allowing the tendril to slide through her fingers, Nathalie looked up with a rueful smile. "My maman likes to tell me that these old ladies, *les mémés*, she calls them—" she gave a playful swat to the nearest vine "—were witness to my conception."

Catharine laughed, but Nathalie's gaze remained fixed on the plant in front of her, her thoughts distant.

"Ironically, it was also in this parcel where he died. Just a stupid, senseless accident—a hydraulic failure on a straddle tractor he happened to be working on. My maman found him, pinned between the rows."

The leaves rustled, an evening breeze carrying the scent of impending rain through the vines. Gently, uncertain what else to do, Catharine reached for Nathalie's hand.

"I can't imagine how hard that must have been—for you and your mum."

"I was quite young—eight—so although, of course I missed him, I think my full understanding of the loss was incomplete. I missed things like the smell of his work clothes—soil and tobacco—or the way he'd come home late during harvest, exhausted, but never forget to sneak in my room and kiss my cheek."

She paused, releasing a soft sigh, before continuing. "But for my maman—it altered everything. It wasn't just the absence of his presence—the loss of her husband and father of her child—it was the destruction of her day-to-day life, her sense of self, her future dreams." She swallowed. "I know she still thinks about him every day. And me? I can't even remember how he said my name."

Exhaling sharply, she gave a little shake of her head, as if the memory was a slate she could wipe clean. "Sorry. I don't know what got into me. I've never really talked about it before."

Catharine squeezed her hand, raising it to her lips, and pressed a kiss to her palm. "Please don't apologize. I hope you know you can tell me anything."

"I wish you would do the same." Nathalie's look was mildly reproachful, but before Catharine could dwell on it, her expression shifted to mischievous insolence, and she knew the intimacy of the *tête-à-tête* had run its course.

"Come on, enough of that," Nathalie spun her away from the vines. "There's something I want to show you."

"It better be the barrel cellar," Catharine teased, allowing herself to get dragged down the row back in the direction they had come.

To Catharine's disappointment, Nathalie's mum intercepted them before they ever made it to the cellar.

"*Non, non, mes petites mam'zelles, pas si vite !*" she called from the château garden, where she was holding a clipboard. "I know exactly what you're up to. And the answer is *non*. Monsieur Whitaker will be here any minute. I won't have him stopping in to check the *ouillage* only to find you two—indisposed."

Catharine was certain her cheeks were going to spontaneously combust, but Nathalie just shrugged.

"He never checks for evaporation. Only you do that."

"Regardless," Sabine leaned against the low stone wall, "today, *le rendez-vous de Nathalie* is closed."

"Shouldn't you be off putting the fear of God into your team butchering the Petit Verdot?" Nathalie cast a playful retort, wandering across the courtyard. Leisurely, in a motion born of practice, she hoisted herself onto the wall and swiped a pencil from behind her mother's ear.

"If only the Verdot was the concern," responded Sabine, recovering the pencil and dropping it onto the clipboard she'd set on the moss-covered stone. "Gabriel noticed oil spots on a few plants in the north block. I'm going to have to stay late tonight to assist with the spraying. I'm sorry, *ma belle*."

"It's okay, Maman." Nathalie clicked her heels together, the grey dust of the vineyards billowing off her shoes. "When do you think you'll be home?"

Sabine sighed. "Well," she glanced at her paperwork, "with 133 vines per row, and 307 rows requiring treatment..." she started to jot down the numbers, "that's..."

"40,831 vines." Catharine supplied, without thinking.

Stunned, Sabine looked up, then back down at her figures, finishing the calculation. "Yes—40,831 vines to be treated." Her gaze returned to Catharine. "You can just carry that sort of number in your head?"

Immediately, Catharine regretted speaking. "Sorry, it's habit."

"I told you, Maman, Cate is brilliant. She's like a human calculator. You wouldn't believe how many languages she speaks."

Sabine ignored her daughter, still looking at Catharine. There was something in her gaze that made Catharine uncomfortable— as if she were seeing more than she should.

"Don't ever apologize for having the right answers, *ma chêrie*. Especially in this world dominated by men." The older woman reached across the wall, giving Catharine's arm a squeeze.

"Yes, madame. I'm sorry."

"And stop apologizing merely for existing. That's a bad habit for any young woman to get into—even if it's ingrained into your English brain."

"Yes, I'm sor—" Catharine caught herself, but not before Sabine laughed. Whatever tension had built, evaporated.

"Now," the woman rifled through her pockets, pulling out a crumpled hundred-franc note. "You girls go out tonight." She tucked the cash in Nathalie's palm. "Maybe to that little Portuguese grill you like?" Her attention drifted to her clipboard, before she paused, looking up again. "Oh, and Nathalie—I left a bottle of my special cuvée with Jean-Paul in the tasting room. Make sure you pair it with *mimolette*—and perhaps a bit of *saucisson sec*. I have some hanging in the window." She turned, starting across the garden, then glanced back over her shoulder. "And I mean it—you two stay out of that cellar!"

It was nearing dusk when they arrived back in *Saint-Michel*— Catharine carrying the unlabeled bottle from Sabine, and Nathalie lugging four others the flamboyant tasting room manager, Jean-Paul, had adamantly pressed upon them.

"Let's drink this down by the river," Nathalie suggested, after they'd stopped by the *échoppe* and dropped off the extra bottles.

She'd pulled a pair of dry sausages from the kitchen window and wrapped a wedge of cheese in a cloth. On the way out the door, Catharine saw her surreptitiously tuck the hundred-franc note under her mother's pepper mill—somewhere she wouldn't immediately find it.

Two blocks east, they passed under the arch of *Porte de Bourgogne* and darted through traffic on *Quai Richelieu* to arrive at the river. The streets were busy—nose to tail with cars and buses, pushbikes and scooters weaving in between—but the pavement running along the banks of the *Garonne* was deserted.

"Are you nervous?" Nathalie asked. Catharine could feel her watching her through her peripheral as she took in their surroundings: the crumbling wall of the quay, the graffiti covering the bollards, the long shadows cast by *Pont de Pierre*—the stone bridge stretching across the water. It was an atmosphere of neglect—a place that had been forgotten.

In truth, it was intimidating. The closest Catharine had ever come to that level of urban decay was watching from the tinted windows of her father's Rolls-Royce as Mr. Fraser drove them through the tattered streets of Hackney to the Docklands. There, she had viewed the barred windows and boarded doors from a kind of detached lens, unable to comprehend what life was like outside her protected bubble. Here, there was no diffusion filter to soften the focus of this unfamiliar world.

It *was* frightening.

And exhilarating.

"How could I be?" She redirected the question. "After all, I'm under the protection of my very own Casanova." She gave a pert look as Nathalie hopped onto the low wall separating the pavement from the riverbank. "Let me guess—we are on our way to another of the famous *rendez-vous de Nathalie*?"

"I knew you weren't going to let that go," Nathalie needled, taking Catharine's hand to help her over the wall.

"Not a chance," Catharine confirmed, the two of them momentarily silenced as they slipped and slid their way down the steep and weedy descent to the shoreline. Once the secure crunch of gravel sounded beneath the soles of her loafers, Catharine resumed her interrogation. "So—back to the tour of your indiscretions. How many girls have you brought to this fine location?"

The golden glow of the setting sun had shifted to the nautical blues of twilight, turning the murky surface of the *Garonne* into a Picasso of color. Nathalie stopped just shy of the first arch holding up the stone bridge, and leaned against the pier.

"You wouldn't like the answer," she said breezily, pulling a corkscrew from the sack of goods she'd dropped at her feet and uncorking the bottle.

"No? Try me."

"Well," said Nathalie, drawing out the pause for dramatic effect as Catharine stepped closer. Her face was lost in shadow, but still Catharine could hear the smile in her answer. "How high can you count?"

"Pretty high—if I use my fingers *and* toes." Catharine snatched the bottle from her hand and tipped it back, taking a long swallow. "Tell me about them."

"I don't think this is what my maman had in mind for her coveted cuvée," Nathalie scolded, recovering the wine only to follow Catharine's example. "You're a bad influence."

"And you're evading my question." Catharine stole another sip, feeling the headiness of the potent wine thread its heat through her.

"We'd be here all night."

"I'm in no hurry."

A lamppost along the bridge flickered on above them, revealing Nathalie's amused smile. "And what if you get jealous?"

Their mouths were less than an inch apart. Catharine could taste the richness of the red and black fruit on their shared breath, the earthy warmth of the tobacco leaf that lingered on the palate.

"Maybe I want you to make me jealous," she whispered, pressing her lips to Nathalie's ear as her fingers strayed to the top button of her high-waisted jeans. She liked this—the push and pull between them. The playfulness. The freedom. These past two weeks, her life had felt so far removed from her prison back in England.

A tremble shook Nathalie's sharp inhalation, and Catharine laughed, turning her cheek away when Nathalie leaned to kiss her.

"Uh-uh." She continued unfastening. "You're deflecting."

"You have a twisted side to you, Catharine Ann Brooks." Nathalie closed her eyes, leaning her head back against the grime-covered stone of the pier. "I like it."

Catharine deftly undid another button.

It was intoxicating—to be this person she wasn't. To stand there in the shadows, in the heart of a city she didn't know, and slip into the skin of a bold and daring affectation. Someone who knew what she wanted. Someone brash. Someone provocative. Someone with no fear of the future.

Was that how Nathalie felt on stage—free to live the lives of a thousand others?

"Well?" Catharine's fingers hovered, paused in their administrations.

"What do you want to know?"

"Tell me about the first one."

"Alright." Nathalie's eyes remained closed. "Her name was Valérie. She was the daughter of a fisherman from Lormont."

Tugging loose the final button, Catharine slid her hand inside the jeans, grazing her with her palm. "And?"

"She smelled like river mud, and her mouth tasted like aioli. Her fingers could untangle anything. We'd lie on the quay before sunrise and she'd talk about eels."

"Eels?"

"She said they were the only creatures on earth that never forget where they came from. They could travel thousands of miles in their lifetime, but would always die where they were born."

Catharine laughed. "Talk of the instinctual habits of anguilliform migration must have been a real turn-on."

"You'd be surprised how erotic marine biology can be when you're sixteen with someone's hand up your skirt." Nathalie shifted, dropping the bottle of wine to the sand and slipping an arm low around Catharine's hip, drawing their bodies together. "Or," her lips flickered at the corners, "maybe it *wasn't* Valérie. Maybe it was Manon—the girl who sat behind me in physics, writing dirty limericks about Joan of Arc that she'd slip into my backpack. After school, we'd meet in the churchyard and lie amongst the headstones, trying to out-sin one another."

Her breathing shallowed as Catharine slipped her fingers in her.

"But it could have been Élodie—the beekeeper's apprentice from the Pyrenees, who taught me how to harvest honeycomb, and could tie double knots in cherry stems with her toes."

"Her toes?" said Catharine, skeptical.

"You wouldn't believe what can be done with toes."

Nathalie's hand had drifted down, inside the waistband of Catharine's trousers, the other creeping up her blouse.

"I might be wrong—it may have been Anaïs."

"Anaïs?" Catharine fought the urge to press herself more firmly against Nathalie, aware she was losing the edge of her own game.

"Ten years older with a bright green mohawk. Her parents were acrobats from Montreal. She worked as a fire-eater at the traveling circus and could light a match off her spine. The last time we kissed, she told me my soul was shaped like a question mark, and then ran away with a boy who braided his armpits. Last I heard, she was in Marseille."

Despite her knees that threatened to buckle, Catharine laughed. "You're making this up."

"Am I?"

"Next, you'll tell me about the puppeteer from Strasbourg."

"How did you know about Béatrice?" Nathalie leaned away from the pier to kiss Catharine's neck. "She lived in a loft with her pet fox. Every puppet in her tiny, velvet theatre was named after one of her exes. When she undressed, she liked me to applaud her."

The low, rumbling engine of a flat-bottomed barge motoring beneath the bridge vibrated the stone of the arch, but Catharine paid it no mind. It was dark now, the street lamps above casting only a shallow halo of light that left them protected in shadow.

Determined to regain the upper hand, Catharine caught Nathalie's wrist, pulling it away from her, and firmly pressed her back against the wall.

"That's not how this works."

"I don't know," Nathalie baited, "seems to me it was working quite well."

Catharine paused her own endeavors long enough to force Nathalie into an indignant objection.

"Fine," she relented, her voice low, raspy. "You'll want to hear about Véronique, then—the taxidermist's niece who was convinced that in a past life, she was a lighthouse keeper." Her breath grew a little more ragged as Catharine increased her rhythm, leaning her body into her. "She was a shipwreck waiting to happen. At night, she'd call me her little mermaid and would only kiss me underwater." Nathalie turned her face, pressing her cheek against the century-old stone, even as she tried to maintain the flippancy of her tone. "Things ended when she told me she thought I'd look good mounted next to the swordfish on her uncle's wall."

"I can't imagine letting that one slip away," Catharine goaded, but the jest fell short as Nathalie tensed, tightening, aching for relief. This time, Catharine didn't withdraw, instead staying with her, Nathalie's hands grasping at her back, her shoulders—anything she could reach. And then a tremor ran through the length of her body, the ebb and flow that built and broke, before finally giving way to the weakness of release.

They stood for a long moment, Nathalie's erratic heartbeat slowly recovering against Catharine's chest as the brackish water of the river slapped the quay in the wake of the disappearing barge.

"Tell me something real," Catharine whispered, once the *Garonne* had stilled.

Nathalie's cheek, damp with humidity and perspiration, rested against her neck.

"Okay," she finally said, standing upright. "I'll tell you about the first girl I ever loved."

Catharine said nothing, suddenly uncertain if this was a story she wanted to hear.

"I met her when I was at my loneliest. I had been unhappy, and didn't even know it. Then I saw her. And I won't lie—like all the shallow schoolboys, it was her beauty that first caught my attention. She wasn't just *pretty*. She had the kind of beauty that would have sent Helen of Troy's thousand ships back across the sea. A girl so stunning, Perseus would have left Andromeda chained to her rock and chosen to marry her instead."

"Let me guess," Catharine interjected. "You killed her by waxing poetic?"

"Ah—there it finally is." Nathalie slid her hands inside Catharine's back pockets. "That jealousy you were craving."

"I'm hardly jealous of some schoolgirl crush that sent your head spinning."

Nathalie arched a brow. "You might be, once I tell you that behind that Aphrodite façade, she had the mind of Athena. Clever. Quick-witted. Wise beyond reason."

"Your perfect woman."

"Yes, but not without her flaws. There was something about her that felt a little dangerous—like loving her could hurt."

"Your Pandora, then."

"Hm." Nathalie considered the metaphor. "Perhaps." She reached for a clasp on Catharine's blouse, and laughed when Catharine twisted away from her. "This was *your* game, remember."

Chastened, Catharine turned back around. "So what happened to this girl with whom you were so wholly smitten? Cursed with unrequited love?"

"No, hardly. She loved me very much, I think. But even still, it scared me." Nathalie returned to toying with the silver fastener at her collar. "Because every time she kissed me, it felt like it might be the last."

Catharine closed her eyes, her heart quickening as she began to understand where this was leading. This time, when Nathalie's fingers slipped inside her shirt, she didn't pull away.

"What made you feel like that?" she asked, and almost flinched when Nathalie's lips brushed the exposed skin of her shoulder. "You said yourself, you know she loves—*loved*—" she corrected her tense, determined to stick with the protection of the story, "—you."

"You need to understand—" Nathalie's mouth drifted along her collarbone, "—this girl came from another world entirely. A world —I knew from the very beginning—that had no place for me."

Catharine swallowed. "Did you never consider she loved you for who you were, and didn't care about your differences?"

"On the contrary, it's one of the things I loved about her most. But—" Nathalie moved on to kiss her throat, to loosen the tie on her trousers, to ease her hand between her thighs, "—it didn't change our reality. It didn't lessen the fear of knowing, one day, she'd wake up and realize I wasn't the person she needed me to be."

"You're wrong." Catharine dropped the pretense, her breath hitching as Nathalie finally touched her, stoking a desire that felt nearly crippling. "You're exactly who I want. Exactly who I need." Her legs faltered, threatening to give out beneath her. She didn't understand how she could be so overcome with want, yet so close to weeping.

"Shhh, Cate," Nathalie soothed, holding her up, finding her mouth with hers. "*Ça va aller.*"

It's going to be okay.

Catharine kissed her back, wanting to believe her, and allowed Nathalie to turn her thoughts from past loves and future hurts, and everything in between.

Chapter Twenty-Three

On the final day of Michaelmas, Catharine sat through her last tutorial on Corporate Finance, listening to her tutor, Dr. Lydia Keene, pontificate on Modigliani and Miller's capital structure irrelevance theorem with only half an ear. She disagreed with the idealized theory and found little use for its application in the real world, but bobbed her head and offered a series of *ahs* and *that makes senses* at all the appropriate moments.

The only thing she cared about was reducing Lydia's habit of running over on their allotted hour together to the bare minimum. The sooner she got out of there, the better. She still had to put in a show of attending the Christ Church Christmas formal before dropping off her room key at the plodge.

And then, she'd be free—six weeks without lectures on books she'd already read, senseless advice from tutors who had no concept of her future, and carefully planned routes to avoid running across Edward or his mates on crew.

Just six weeks of Christmas break. Six weeks of Nathalie.

At 7 PM sharp, she sat in her academic gown in the Christ Church Great Hall, where the hammerbeam roof and honey-gold walls had been adorned with holly and ivy, and picked idly at her duck liver parfait.

All around her, students chattered about the holiday, comparing family traditions and tipping back red wine. A boy at her left elbow, one whose face she'd seen around the quad but name she didn't know, leaned over his plate of Norfolk turkey, introduced himself as Peter, and asked what her plans were over Christmas. His expression was kind, and Catharine surprised herself by giving an honest answer. Something that seemed to come rarer and rarer to her, of late.

"I'm going to the Scottish Highlands."

"Ah, a skier, are you?"

"Oh, no. Just a quiet place to study for Hilary."

So much for honesty. But she assured herself the mistruth was a necessity. Same as it had been when she told her mother she needed to attend a European economic integration conference in Hamburg, which unfortunately fell over the holiday. The truth that she and Nathalie simply wanted to disappear to the most remote corner of the earth (they'd settled for the UK), to cloak themselves in the snowy mantle of a tiny Scottish village, on what might be one of the last Christmases they spent together for the foreseeable future, was no one's business but her own.

"Sounds brilliant."

Catharine was about to ask him his own plans, anything to make the dinner hour tick by faster, but a second boy—this one familiar to her—interrupted their conversation.

"Up for a real chance there, Petey, my man. Laying it on thick in the hopes of lapping up Haverfield's sloppy seconds?"

The boy, Kurt Faber, was a theology student who'd taken to trailing Edward around like a damp spaniel the previous summer. A year behind her, he hadn't even been at Christ Church when she and Edward had been together.

"You really are only a single evolutionary rung up from pond life, Faber." Peter tipped back in his chair, leveling a look at the boy across the table. "This one time, I'll let it slide, knowing you must be reeling from the loss of your lord and master. But if you choose to open your mouth again, you'll be picking your teeth out of the Christmas pudding."

Kurt's lips parted, preparing a retort, but then he seemed to reconsider, ruminating over Peter's threat. He glanced down the length of the table, looking a little uneasy.

"You don't know, do you?" Peter's menacing tone turned entirely to one of pleasure. "Word hasn't even reached your little band of bootlickers."

"What are you talking about?" Kurt's voice grew smaller.

Catharine, too, was all ears.

"Your boy Haverfield's been sent down. Disciplinary committee voted on it this morning."

"You're lying!"

"You see him here anywhere, mate? Notice he's been scarce this last week, have you?"

The younger boy's Adam's apple pistoned as he took further stock of his surroundings.

It was true, Edward wasn't sitting with his usual sycophants. Catharine had noticed his absence as soon as she entered the hall, though she assumed he'd only gone home early. But it wasn't like him to miss a formal dinner.

"Sent down?" She stared at Peter. "Rusticated?"

His dark eyes shone with the glow of the banker's lamps sitting in the center of the table. "No. Permanent expulsion. Muppet's been paying for his papers. Anonymous whistleblower turned him in a few weeks ago. Apparently, the dean decided to make an example of him."

"He would have said something!" Kurt nearly shouted. Drawing a few surrounding pairs of eyes, he quieted. "He would have told me!"

"Sorry, chap." Peter's smile said he was anything but sorry. "If it makes you feel better, it appears he didn't tell anybody."

"You're certain this is true?" asked Catharine.

"Quite. My older brother is the Senior Censor's secretary. Wrote up the notice himself."

Across the table, Kurt flung back his chair, standing so quickly he upset a decanter of wine. His face had gone entirely ashen.

Aware of the stares from his peers, he sprinted toward the stairway.

Indifferent, Peter dropped his linen napkin over the burgundy spill, and hiked a casual shoulder at Catharine.

"Ruined his holiday."

"I think you might have." Catharine couldn't help but laugh, a vortex of emotions swirling through her.

Edward—*sent down*! The ultimate disgrace from a family of Oxbridge graduates.

She thought about what Anouk had told her the previous year—how he had been accused of assaulting another student. The girl had quit university, and Edward had been allowed to continue on as if nothing ever happened…

But plagiarism? Now there was a crime frowned upon by the patriarchy.

She stood, placing her napkin to the left of her plate. She couldn't bear to sit through the serving of the sherry trifle.

"It was a pleasure to meet you, Peter. I hope you have a lovely Christmas."

And then she was out the door and down the stairs two by two, off to find Nathalie.

A BLANKET OF WHITE STRETCHED across the horizon as far as the eye could see. In the distance, at the edge of the rolling Highlands, the boughs of Scots pine and silver birch hung low beneath the weight of the overnight snowfall.

Nathalie stood in the doorway of the stone cottage, wrapped in the quilt she'd stolen off their bed, and surveyed the acres of wilderness. "I thought you said it didn't snow here."

"Much," said Catharine, who'd woken hours earlier and watched the world turn white through the quaint sitting room window. "I said it doesn't snow *much*. Nothing like Chamonix. Or Verbier."

"It's practically a scene from *Dr. Zhivago* out here."

Catharine tossed the Russian edition of *Anna Karenina* she'd been leafing through onto the hand-carved rustic coffee table and unfolded herself from the sofa.

"Has anyone ever told you you have a flair for the dramatic?" she said, coming up behind Nathalie and wrapping her arms around her waist, resting her chin on her shoulder. The cold air was wafting in through the open door, diminishing the efforts of the wood-burning stove, but the view from the little porch was mesmerizing. With their hire car around the side of the house, there wasn't a single sign of civilization. Just the breathtaking rugged beauty of the Highlands.

"Do I?" Nathalie ribbed, turning to kiss her temple. "I don't think it's ever been mentioned."

Catharine breathed in the tranquility of the morning, the perfection of the past two weeks. Every day spent together in this wild, mystical place. It was Christmas Eve. Tomorrow, they would enjoy their last full day alone before being forced to return to England. The fabrication of the economic conference had bought her time, but she knew better than to push her luck too far. Her mother had given pretense of believing the excuse, but when Catharine had called to check in two days ago, Emily had issued a veiled warning.

"Your father will be home sometime before New Year's. I'm certain your educational obligations in Hamburg will have come to a conclusion?"

In other words: if she wanted to avoid undesired consequences, she'd make herself present at Honour Stone.

But they still had today, and all of tomorrow. She refused to think about the days beyond that.

"Let's walk to town."

"What?" Nathalie straightened. "In *this*?"

"It's little more than a dusting!"

"I'm sorry, but I'm afraid I left my skis at home."

"Not to worry," Catharine gave her an arch smile, tugging her backward by the handwoven quilt, "I saw snowshoes in the boot room."

Two hours later, after Nathalie had exhausted all of her stalling techniques—making breakfast, taking a shower, kissing Catharine so soundly on her way to get dressed that they'd ended up in a tangle of limbs on the floor of the narrow hall—the pair donned their coats and wellies and trekked the two miles to the village through the snow.

"I don't recall you whinging this much on our way through Wytham Woods," Catharine baited over her shoulder as they approached the only café on the quiet road that led through the center of town.

"To be fair, I had ulterior motives to get to the chapel."

"And now that you've had your way with me, I've what—fallen into irrelevance?"

A snowball whizzed past her head.

"Don't you dare!" Catharine shrieked, taking off laughing through the ankle-deep powder. She shouldered through the swinging door of the bakery with Nathalie right behind her, their soft clouds of breath disappearing in the warmth radiating from the deck oven.

"Good to see you back, lasses," greeted the shop assistant, whom they'd grown acquainted with over their multiple trips to town. About their age, always with a Walkman stuffed into the back pocket of his jeans, he smiled at Catharine before turning his adulating attention to Nathalie. There was no question he was enamored by the dark-haired beauty of the French girl. "Fair flurry on the go today, eh?"

"Oh, little more than a dusting." Nathalie shot Catharine an impish smile before leaning her elbows on the counter and toying with the tips of hair that fell, powdered with snowflakes, over her shoulders.

Resisting an eye roll, Catharine left Nathalie to her flirting and took a seat near the window. As the boy asked questions about

France she was certain he had no real interest in—all just a prelude to his actual motive: *would Nathalie care to join him for a 'wee dram' later that evening?*—Catharine watched a couple with two small children pile onto the pavement from a guest house across the street.

A little girl, no more than five, clapped her mittened hands with glee at the gentle snowfall. Behind her, a toddler bundled in a parka as thick as she was tall, squirmed to get down from her father's arms. The man laughed, dropping the tow-headed child at his feet, stealing a kiss on his wife's cheek.

"Butteries—fresh out of the oven," said Nathalie, appearing at the table, setting down a plate of what looked to be flat croissants.

Catharine looked away from the happy family, from the obvious love the father felt for his girls, and turned her attention to the Scottish pastries.

"How did your gallant admirer take your decline to join him for a *wee dram*?" asked Catharine, when the boy disappeared from behind the counter to retrieve something from the store room.

"You're assuming I declined?" Nathalie raised a brow, donning a smug smile as she sucked a gob of marmalade off her thumb. "Who's to say I didn't invite him back to ours?"

"His curtain haircut, for one thing," said Catharine dryly, spooning a dollop of jam on her plate. "The fact that he's listening to *Bananarama* on repeat, for another." She broke open the greasy roll, aware only too late that Nathalie had forgotten the napkins.

"Boyband hair and terrible choice in music doesn't seem like a dealbreaker," prodded Nathalie, enjoying Catharine's distress over the flakes of crust sticking to her fingers.

"Then there's also the obvious," continued Catharine, striving for nonchalance, despite dying inside as she raised her fingers to her mouth, licking off the crumbs with pointed deliberation.

"Which is?"

She managed to shrug coolly beneath Nathalie's shining gaze. "That I've never known you to have much interest in pastries with a filling." Even as she said it, her fingers still at her lips, she could feel her cheeks smoldering—but as Nathalie broke into a fit of coughing, choking from the bite she'd taken, Catharine chalked the spar up as a win.

"*Touché*," Nathalie conceded, once she was able to breathe again.

They finished breakfast and wished Craig—the disappointed shop assistant—a happy Christmas before heading back out into the cold.

The snow had started up anew, the brief morning sunlight retreating within the shield of dense winter clouds. As they left the village behind, heading for the single-track lane that led through the forest to their secluded cottage, they came upon the family Catharine had seen through the window. The two girls were playing in a snow drift that had built up on the edge of the road.

"Lovely day for it, isn't it?" greeted the father in a heavy Welsh accent as he added the finishing touches to a waist-high snowman. His wife, looking less enthused to be out in the weather, but still supplying a gathered sprig of holly to her husband for lack of a carrot for a nose, smiled as they approached.

"Don't mind him, he also enjoys a mad dip on New Year's Day," she said, rifling through her pockets to hand over a pair of acorns. "Bedwyr—for the eyes," she directed.

Nathalie, who could strike up a conversation with a lamppost, laughed. "We did the Loony Dook last year."

"Then you're just as of an unsound mind as he is." The woman's smile defused her crisp English lilt.

"Will you make snow fairies with us, Mami?" interrupted the older child, her long dark hair billowing from beneath a pink bobble hat. She was clutching the hand of the toddler, who was struggling to pull away.

"Oh." The woman looked slightly horrified—a reaction Catharine felt would have applied to her own mother—but Bedwyr, her husband, just laughed. "Yes, go on, Mami," he teased, clearly aware of her aversion. "I'll finish up ol' Frosty, here."

"I like making snow fairies, too." Nathalie cast the woman a sympathetic smile before kneeling to address the child. "Do you want to make one together?"

"I'm not supposed to talk to strangers," said the little girl adamantly.

"My name's Nathalie."

"You talk funny."

"I'm from France. This is my friend, Cate." She tipped her chin toward Catharine. "She's from England."

"So's my mam," supplied the child.

"Are you girls here on holiday, as well?" asked the mother.

"Yes." Catharine hadn't relished a conversation, but Nathalie seemed keen to linger with the children, so she offered a polite smile. "Up from Oxford."

"Ah, I was Cambridge, myself."

"You lot are meant to hate each other then, I think," said Bedwyr, readjusting the holly nose.

"My mum went to Cambridge," said Catharine. "Newnham."

"Trinity."

"She'd be jealous—they weren't accepting women at Trinity when she attended."

They chatted a bit of Oxbridge small talk as Nathalie flopped down in the soft powder, convincing her new pal to make a snow angel.

"Are you going to join us, Cate?" called Nathalie after a moment, sitting up, her dark hair glittering with ice crystals.

"Thank you, no."

"You English," winked Bedwyr, scooping up the toddler, who squealed with glee as he chucked her into the air. "C'mon then, Dillon," he hoisted her onto his shoulders, where she clung to his bright blonde hair. "Let's go scavenge a few more pinecones."

A short time later, when Nathalie was sufficiently soaked to the bone, and her newfound friend, Seren, had abandoned the castle they were building in order to comfort her little sister, who had face planted into the snow, the pair bid their goodbyes to the family and continued down the trail.

"Do you ever want kids?" Catharine asked as they reached the edge of the forest, the little stone cottage coming into view.

"Me?" Nathalie laughed, surprised. "God no. I'm too selfish."

"You're great with them."

"That's only because I can send them home." She glanced at Catharine. "Do you?"

"No." The word was abrupt, harsher than she meant it. But it was the truth. She couldn't imagine bringing a child into her world. Hers wasn't the land of snow angels and hot cocoa. Soggy mittens and fathers who swung their children through the air.

"For the record," said Nathalie, ever adept at reading her mind, "I think you'd make a wonderful mum. Because," she slipped an arm around her waist, "no matter who you pretend to be, I know you're not really as stuffy as Ol' Cambridge back there." She nodded in the direction of the village, but before Catharine could respond, Nathalie threw her weight against her, toppling them both into the fresh powder the wind had gathered at the foot of their porch.

"Nat!" she yelped, the shock of the bitter cold temporarily stunning her into inaction, but then, just as quickly, she was laughing, the two of them grappling at each other, flailing around the blanket of snow.

When they were thoroughly drenched—snow angels made, snow balls thrown, the round base of a snowman formed and abandoned—they dragged their stiff limbs up the steps to the front door, stripping off wet clothing in the threshold. Catharine's sides ached from laughing, her nose running, and fingers an uncanny shade of red in response to having lost her gloves at some point during the scuffle.

She had been skiing in Courchevel. Watched snow polo in St. Moritz. Ice-skated in Rockefeller. But never once had it been fun. Never had she felt the bite of fresh powder against her cheeks, or had snowflakes clinging to her eyelashes and hair. Not even as a child.

"I have something for you," said Nathalie, when they had drained all the hot water from the shower, pulled on flannel trousers, and buried themselves on the sofa under the quilt from their bed. Catharine lay with her cheek against Nathalie's chest, the scent of homemade hot chocolate drifting through the air.

"I thought we agreed to no gifts?"

"You wouldn't let me give you anything for your birthday—so, *tant pis*," Nathalie dismissed her, reaching for something behind them on the side table and pressing it into her hand.

It was a key—small, brass, insignificant.

"What is it?"

"A key."

"Why, thank you," Catharine tutted, "I can see that."

"To a flat. The one off Cowley Road."

Pushing herself onto an elbow, Catharine shifted so she could see her better. "Above the video shop?"

"Mm."

"Have you sublet it again?"

"Better—it's mine until summer."

"Until summer?" Catharine repeated. "You let it?"

"That's right. Your tutors must be impressed with your developing comprehension skills."

Catharine poked her in the ribs, but her thoughts were still fixated on the key. On what it meant.

The quiet studio.

Off the beaten path.

A private space.

Her last two terms of university—without Edward, without the curfew of a staircase, without the walls of Christ Church squeezing her into conformity.

"And it's just yours?"

"Well, I hoped it might be *ours*."

"No flatmates?"

"Just us. I mean, for appearances, you'll obviously have to keep your room in the Meadow Building—but," Nathalie looked oddly self-doubting, "I was hoping, in actuality, you might want to live with me?" She bit the inside of her cheek, a habit Catharine had observed when she was nervous. "I know it's not exactly the Ritz, but it was all I could—"

"Better than the Ritz!" Catharine stopped her, curling her fingers around the little key, the gift of freedom cold in the palm of her hand. "Better than anything!"

Nathalie exhaled, relieved.

"I have something for you, also."

"I thought we agreed to no gifts?" Nathalie returned, pointedly.

"It's—I think it might be silly." This time, it was Catharine's turn to grow uncertain. She'd spent months on the project, second-guessing herself all along the way. She wasn't romantic. She wasn't like Nathalie, who so often knew how to woo with words. She was too practical, too pragmatic to have that creative flair.

Still, she slid from their haven on the couch and retrieved a package she'd wrapped in brown paper, hidden amongst her clothes. She handed it over, a heavy pulse at her temple crescendo-ing as she worried she was going to look a fool.

Carefully, thoughtfully, Nathalie unfolded the paper to reveal a book. *Jane Eyre*, Catharine's favorite of the classics. But it was neither a first edition nor leather bound copy—just a hardback she had purchased from Blackwell's.

"I—" Catharine took a seat at the edge of the couch, anxious to explain. "I wrote things in it, um, marginalia," she stumbled, pulling it from Nathalie's hand. "Like I said, it's silly, and—"

Nathalie plucked it back, thumbing through the pages. Highlights lined the familiar passages—ones Catharine had chosen with care. In the margins, notes about how the words made her feel.

Silent, Nathalie read one annotated page after another, in no particular order.

Stopping at Chapter 27, she read from the printed text aloud. "*'I have for the first time found what I can truly love—I have found you.'*"

She scanned to Catharine's neat, even handwriting in the footnotes. "This is how I've felt since the first day I—"

"God, please don't read it out loud!" Catharine cut her off, flipping the cover closed.

"Shh," Nathalie scolded, opening the book again. Her fingers skimmed to another highlight.

"*'Wherever you are is my home—my only home—'*"

"Nat! Please!"

"What's wrong? This is the most beautiful thing anyone's ever done for me—"

"Will you just—will you read it some other time, when I'm not around?"

Nathalie laughed. "Why are you embarrassed?"

"Because I'm not good at this."

"On the contrary," Nathalie reached for her hand, pulling her down to her, "I think you're better at this than you think." But she let it go, sliding the book to the side table, along with the bronze key.

Hours later, after hot chocolate spiked with whisky, and drunken carols sung in French, after they'd eaten a cold dinner of bread and cheese, and made love on the creaking cottage bed, Catharine woke to find Nathalie propped up against the headboard, the copy of *Jane Eyre* in her lap. Her breathing was shallow, her eyelashes wet.

When, absently, she reached to run her fingers through Catharine's hair, Catharine pretended to be asleep.

Chapter Twenty-Four

From the top of the terrace, Catharine watched the two boys jostle and elbow each other on the garden grass, a football trapped between them. Nathalie, enjoying their laddish rivalry, sat perched on the frosted edge of the central water fountain, egging them on.

"You don't stand a chance against him, Geoff!" she hollered, her elbows plopped on her knees. "Getting beaten by a schoolboy—Malcolm, you're what, Year 7?"

"Year 8, miss," panted Malcolm, poking the ball through Geoff's splayed legs and running it down the lawn to an invisible goal. He was Mr. Fraser's youngest son, and like Geoff, a boy who had grown up on the periphery of Catharine's world.

"Year 8 or not, the scamp's a head taller," Geoff defended, slinging his arm around the younger boy's shoulders when he trotted back with the ball. "And a scrawny shit, to boot." He pulled Malcolm into a headlock, ruffling his hair. "Built like a damned gazelle."

"Maybe if you spent as much time rowing as you did raiding the fridge, you'd lose a couple stone," Malcolm taunted in return, lithely twisting free and jogging a few steps backward, out of arms reach.

"Typical sprog—get a whiff of attention from a pretty girl, and you suddenly think you're twice the lad you are." Geoff swiped for—and missed—the ball. "Swaggering around like a bloody tomcat on the prowl."

"As if you've not made it your entire life's mission to impress the colonel's daughter."

Geoff swiped and missed again, and Malcolm laughed, flashing him the Vs, before glancing up and realizing Catharine had returned to the terrace.

"Oh, sorry, Miss Brooks!" Malcolm winced, chastened at the sight of her.

"Is it really your entire life's mission to impress me?" Catharine teased Geoff, strolling down the stairs.

"I was just chatting rubbish, miss," Malcolm nobly cut in, coming to Geoff's aid.

"Are you saying he doesn't want to impress me?" Catharine trailed her fingertips along the chilled stone railing, hiding her smile behind a mask of disappointment. "You must think me unworthy of his attentions?"

"Oh, no," the boy, not yet a teen, stuttered, fussing with the cuffs of his coat. "It's not what I meant at all, Miss Brooks. I'm sure he finds you most worthy—"

"But you don't, Malcolm?"

"No, Miss Brooks! I mean, of course, yes, but—!"

"She's taking the piss out of you, ya knob!" Geoff whacked him on the side of the head, scooping up the ball. "You should see your face! You look like you're about to cack it!"

Malcolm, who'd inherited his father's pale Scottish features, had turned beet red from his neck to the tops of his ears.

"Ignore those two—they're bullies." Nathalie hopped down from the ledge of the fountain and tossed Malcolm a Lucozade bottle that looked suspiciously clear. "Have a sip of that—it'll make you feel better." She nicked a pack of Lammies from Geoff's back pocket and shook out a fag.

Catharine forced herself not to glance over her shoulder at the back door, to verify, for the hundredth time, that they weren't being observed. Her parents had left over an hour ago for a New Year's Eve party in London. Aside from the condensed holiday staff, they had the house to themselves. And even so? It was nothing unusual for Geoff to be there, waiting for his mother's shift to end so he could take her home. And Malcolm was staying with the Mills for the weekend.

"I wish you would relax, Cate," said Nathalie, blowing out a long cloud of smoke as the boys returned to their game. "You've hardly taken a breath since we got here."

It was true. For the past five days, since they'd arrived at Honour Stone, Catharine had felt nearly paralyzed. She could find nothing of the happiness, the carefree joy she'd found over the past few weeks in the Highlands. Her father had returned from Bangkok the same day they'd caught the train south to Henley, and his glowering presence had left her flinching at shadows. This last hour was the most she'd spoken to Nathalie since they got there, the closest she'd come to even touching her hand.

"I'm sorry."

"I don't want you to be sorry. I want you to be happy."

Catharine mustered a smile. "I'd be happier if I were alone with you." Her gaze trailed to where Geoff and Malcolm were once again battling over the ball.

"Oh, trust me," Nathalie blew out another slow, billowing cloud of smoke, her fingers surreptitiously grazing Catharine's thigh as she glided toward the fountain to put out the fag. "I have plans for tonight, and I assure you, they require us very much to be alone." She set the dog-end in the outstretched palm of the cupid rising from the water, before looking back at Catharine. "So as much as I enjoy listening to a pair of lads fawn over something they can't have, tonight you might consider being a gracious employer, and allow Mrs. Mills to go home early." She dropped her eyes suggestively to Catharine's mouth. "Just think—it would benefit you both."

With that, she swept her hair over her shoulder, snatched up Geoff's Lucozade bottle filled with vodka, and jogged across the lawn to join the boys in their fun.

THE SUN HADN'T QUITE DISAPPEARED behind the garden wall when the banging of the terrace door interrupted their horseplay.

It was a sound incongruous to the evening. Mrs. Ainsley never let a door slam like that, and a shard of ice had already rooted itself in Catharine's spine by the time she looked up to see a silhouette standing on the staircase above them.

It wasn't her father, but it was the next worst thing. It was Mr. Fraser. Mr. Fraser—who was supposed to be driving her mother and the colonel to London.

"Malcolm." The stoic Scotsman addressed his son, but his eyes remained on Catharine. The boy was unsteady on his feet, his cheeks ruddy with alcohol.

"Sir." He tried to take the stairs two by two, but tripped before he reached the terrace. He scrambled back to his feet, pleading with his father in a way Catharine knew all too well.

"I didn't—we didn't—"

"Wait for me in the foyer. I'll deal with you later."

Catharine knew the boy reeked of spirits, and Mr. Fraser would be no more forgiving than her own father.

"Mr. Fraser, this is my fault. I encouraged Malcolm to—"

"There was a downed power line on Burchetts Green." He cut her off as if she hadn't been speaking. "It was blocking access to the slip road. Your father opted to return to Henley, rather than sit in traffic. I was told to inform you your presence is requested in the dining room." He looked past her to Geoff. "Mr. Mills, I believe your mother is waiting for you."

"Sir, it was my—"

Catharine pinched him hard, stopping him mid-sentence. He would accept the responsibility for the alcohol, the cigarettes, the state of Mr. Fraser's twelve-year-old son, but then what of it? His shouldering the blame would only risk his job at the manufacturing plant, and put Mrs. Mills' position at Honour Stone in jeopardy. Catharine knew she was already in trouble. There was no reason for both of them to be on the receiving end of Colonel Brooks' anger.

"Happy New Year, Geoff," she attempted brightly, trying to pretend her whole evening hadn't been derailed. That she didn't know what was coming.

When Geoff had reluctantly climbed the stairs, glancing one final time at Catharine, Mr. Fraser turned on his heel and followed him into the house, leaving her alone with Nathalie.

"You don't need to come with me to dinner. Mrs. Ainsley can bring you—"

"Save your breath—I'm not leaving you alone with him," Nathalie snapped, brushing past her toward the terrace.

Ten minutes later, still in clothes that smelled of smoke, with grass stains on her knees from where she'd been tugged to the lawn—by whom and when, she could no longer even remember—Catharine stood in the threshold of the formal dining room, waiting for permission to enter.

The colonel sat in his usual chair at the head of the long mahogany table, and her mother perched on the edge of her seat, her fingers worrying her napkin.

"Catharine." Her father's eyes flicked behind her. "Miss Comtois. You may be seated."

Catharine could feel Nathalie's bottled rage, her resentment at the turn in the evening.

"Why, thank you," she ground between her teeth, passing Catharine on the way to the table, her tone unmistakably bitter.

Quickly, Catharine tried to rein in the atmosphere. "I'm sorry you had to miss your party," she said, taking her seat and looking toward her mother. "I know how much you enjoy the fireworks display at The Lanesborough."

As she knew it would be, the effort was pointless. The colonel leveled his glare on her from across the table.

"I understand you were found drinking and smoking in the rose garden." There was no rise in inflection at the end of his sentence to mistake it as a question.

"I—"

"She wasn't," Nathalie cut in before Catharine had any chance to stop her. "*I* was. Cate did not have a single sip, and I have never known her to touch a fag."

Clearly taken aback by Nathalie's bold intrusion, Benjamin Brooks turned steely eyes in her direction.

"If I were interested in your testimony, Miss Comtois, I would ask for it."

"No, instead you'd rather accuse someone who's done nothing."

"Nat," Catharine whispered, her pulse racing. She could not afford Nathalie's heroics in her defense. "Please, just…" *Just let it go*, she implored silently, aware of her father's scrutinizing gaze. Just let her handle it the way she knew how to handle it. Let him be right so that he could win. Whatever it took to get out of this as painlessly as possible.

"*Quelle connerie !*" Nathalie muttered under her breath, sliding back her chair.

The colonel stiffened. "*Qu'était-ce, Mademoiselle Comtois ?*" The set of his jaw promised he'd heard her correctly the first time.

She stood. "I'm sorry, I said: please excuse me, I am not very hungry."

"By all means." He did not rise as custom dictated. "Perhaps a lie-down will improve your disposition."

Catharine paused for a long time in the hall in front of Nathalie's door. The light was still on, spilling from the gap in the threshold, but there was no sound from within. It was dark out, but not late. Nathalie would almost certainly be awake.

But did she have the right to knock? That was the question. After the way things had unraveled in the dining room—after Nathalie had stepped in to defend her, and she'd repaid her with nothing but silence—would she even want to see her?

"I know you're standing there. I can see your feet beneath the door." The voice inside the room was flat, tempered.

With no real choice now, Catharine turned the old brass knob.

"I—" She opened the door only partway. "I just wanted to check on you."

"Here to see if my lie-down's improved my disposition?" Nathalie asked, resentful.

Catharine slipped into the room, gently pulling the door closed behind her. The pale celadon of the floral wallpaper flickered with the flame of a perfumed candle at Nathalie's bedside, the rambling roses and clematis seeming to twist on their vines. Beneath the scent of peony was the pungent smell of charred tobacco, the acrid tang of a cigarette Nathalie had no doubt smoked out the window. Her version of a *fuck you* to the colonel.

"I'm sorry I didn't stand up for you." Catharine crossed no further into the room.

Nathalie was leaning against the headboard, atop the covers, her journal propped on her lap. She didn't look up from the pages.

"I don't want you to stand up for me. I want you to stand up for yourself."

"You don't understand—"

"No, *you* do not understand, Cate." She dropped her pen into the gutter of the book and snapped it closed. "You're not a child anymore. You can't continue to allow him to control every second of your life. He doesn't own you, Catharine!"

"It's not as simple as you make it sound—!"

"Tell me—did he hit you tonight?"

Catharine thought about the bone china plate he'd shattered against the wall. The way her mother had tried to hide her flinch, lost behind her glossy stare. The threat he'd issued if she was ever caught alone with Geoff in the garden again—no matter that they'd not been alone.

But no, he had not hit her. Not this time.

"No."

"But he will."

Catharine found herself unable to lift her eyes from the patina glaze on the wide-plank floor. They'd never openly spoken about the escalation of his violence. The bruises and black eyes. It wasn't a conversation she wanted to broach. Especially not tonight.

"I don't know what you want me to do."

"I want you to have some courage, Catharine! For once, I want you to choose yourself!"

"What do you think I've been doing?" Catharine's eyes flashed up, emboldened by her anger. "Do you have any idea how much I've risked these past two years? What I risk every day to be with you?"

"Only when it's safe!" Nathalie flung her journal onto the bedside table, where it nearly upset the candle. "That's not bravery, Cate. It's convenience."

"That's not true!"

"Isn't it?" She laughed, the sound brimming with derision. "Then let me come to your room tonight."

"Nat…" Feeling every bit a hypocrite, Catharine lowered her voice, aware of the way sound carried through the tired walls. "I can't." She swallowed. "You know we can't. Not when he's here."

"And there you have it." Nathalie folded her knees to her chest.

"You're being unfair."

"And how is that? By wanting to spend New Year's Eve with my lover, instead of hiding across a hall?"

"Please," Catharine whispered, the word *lover* terrifying beneath this roof, said so casually out loud. "You know this isn't what I want, either—"

"I'm not asking you to own this, Cate. It's always been enough, keeping it between us. I just don't want you to shut me out tonight. He never comes to this part of the house. Have a little faith in me. Leave your door unlocked."

THE FIRE IN HER HEARTH had reduced to embers by the time Catharine heard the click of the latch, the nearly inaudible creak of hinges. It was past midnight. The muffled boom of fireworks had been going off around the countryside for over an hour.

She'd lain awake, staring at the shadows on her ceiling, silently beseeching Nathalie not to come—and praying, in equal measure, to hear her footsteps in the hall.

Now that she was here, with the uncertainty of the night behind them, Catharine found herself suspended between relief and fear.

She watched Nathalie's shadow move across the room, familiar with the darkness, familiar with which floorboards groaned. She'd been there plenty of times, after all. But she was right. The entirety of their relationship was built on conditions. Only when it was safe. Only when it was convenient. Only when her father was thousands of miles away. Only when the risk was low.

It was fair—Nathalie wanting more. Catharine understood her frustrations, her push to test the boundaries of this fragile flame they stoked. She didn't want a life dictated by restrictions. She hadn't been raised in that kind of world.

From where she lay, Catharine's gaze followed the silent silhouette to where it stopped in front of her wardrobe, the sound of the old walnut doors swinging open. She could hear the rustle of fabric, the purposeful pause as Nathalie searched, finally choosing something.

A dozen pounding heartbeats later, she crossed to the edge of the bed.

Catharine—partly from habit, partly from the restless need to do *something*—sat up and tugged her nightdress over her head. But before it had even settled on the floor, she was stilled by a firm hand on her shoulder, pressing her back against her pillow.

"Just wait." Nathalie's voice was no louder than the centuries-old hum the house always seemed to whisper.

In the low amber glow of the hearth, she could finally see what she was holding.

A pair of silk stockings.

"May I?" The question was genuine—Nathalie's fingers trailing down her arm, slowly, purposely looping the fabric around her wrist, revealing her intent.

It was something she'd teased about before—*why else would they make four-poster beds?*—but it wasn't a line they'd ever crossed.

Especially not here.

In this house.

This wasn't Bordeaux, the safety of that windowless room, an atmosphere steeped in protection. This wasn't the same as when Nathalie had rolled to the edge of that narrow single bed, pulled open the drawer of her bedside table, and in the dark, asked if Catharine would let her try something different.

She'd said yes then, without hesitation, without even knowing what it meant. She'd simply been certain, more than anything, that she trusted her. Wanted her in every way. Would allow her to make love to her however she asked.

And in Bordeaux, it had felt safe.

She could still feel the intensity of those first moments. The fullness of it. The discomfort fading into pleasure under Nathalie's steady, careful rhythm. The press of her body behind her, her mouth at her ear, asking if she was all right. The tender ache that had bloomed inside of her, lingering for days.

This seemed so much less. Just silk at her wrists. The surrender of something she was more than willing to give.

It should have been an easy answer.

But it wasn't the delicate fiber of the stockings that frightened her—it was the inescapable judgment built into the bones of this house.

A stillness fell over the room as Nathalie's fingers paused at the completion of her knot, awaiting her consent.

Catharine stared at the bind with its sheen of molten bronze glowing in the firelight. Another dozen heartbeats drummed against her ribs.

If her father had even the faintest suspicion… If anyone had seen Nathalie slip into her room…

He didn't, and they hadn't, she assured herself. It was late; the staff was in bed. And despite her father despising Nathalie for countless reasons—she was recalcitrant, a proletarian, an artist, a dreamer—none of them had anything to do with this.

But if he—

She cut the revolving chorus of static short, squeezing her eyes shut, desperate to ground herself in the present. She was so tired of living in fear, always suppressed by the shadow of *what if*.

Deliberately, resolutely, she raised her bound wrist above her head.

Nathalie held her gaze as she kissed her palm, and then fastened the stocking to the bedpost, before repeating the process.

A reserved part of her—the self-conscious whisper always lurking over her shoulder—wanted to shrink from Nathalie's gaze, from the unabashed way her eyes swept her body, unsheltered in the flicker of ember firelight. But there was an opposing side that found it strangely freeing, this relinquishment of control. Feeling the taut tug of silk, her arms stretched above her—a tactile reminder: she was no longer in a position to set the terms to which she was accustomed.

"I wish I could make you see yourself the way I do," said Nathalie, ever privy to her thoughts, aware of her vacillating emotions. She brushed her lips across Catharine's, and then bent, retrieving the tie from her discarded dressing gown.

It came as almost a relief when she draped the sash over Catharine's eyes, turning it into an improvised blindfold. The result—a vulnerable, yet liberating sensation.

A length of silence ensued, in which Catharine became reacquainted with the darkness. There, in the background, was the murmur of the house. The hiss and crackle of the hearth. The sound of Nathalie's bare feet moving along the floorboards.

She startled when, unexpectedly, a gentle kiss was placed on the arch of her foot, then the curve of her calf, the inside of her thigh, her opposite collarbone.

Unable to see her, to anticipate her movements, Catharine's body tensed, reflexively pulling at the bindings. She was unfamiliar with the powerlessness of the situation, the inability to respond with equal measure.

"Shhh," Nathalie's mouth was at her ear, her fingers tracing the ridges of her ribcage. "You're going to be very, very quiet." It wasn't a suggestion.

Catharine tried to steady herself with a shaky exhalation, listening to the familiar sound of Nathalie undressing.

The bed shifted. Again, she could feel the warmth of Nathalie's presence, her breath—sweet, smoky—at her lips, not quite touching. She tipped her head up, trying to kiss her.

"*Mais non, mon amour.* That's not how this works. I make the rules tonight." A hand trailed up her thigh, slipping between her legs only long enough to cut her breath short, before retreating.

The old wood of the antique frame creaked as Nathalie settled astride her, the fusion of their two bodies nearly searing. With an almost involuntary need, Catharine lifted her hips, seeking to wrap her legs around her, but was met with only an amused reproof, firm hands pressing her back onto the mattress.

"Oh, this is going to be hard for you," Nathalie whispered. "She, who likes to control everything." She was unmistakably smiling.

Catharine found it hard to breathe, hard to think, as—unhurried and without ever breaking contact between them—Nathalie eased her way up her body. Heat against her ribs. Her breast. Higher still, until thighs framed her face.

Knowing exactly what she wanted, Catharine raised her head, and couldn't help but laugh when she felt fingers anchor themselves in her hair, a sharp inhalation betraying the crack in Nathalie's composure.

"Slowly." Nathalie's voice was unsteady as she was forced to rise onto her knees in an effort to reestablish her command over the dynamic between them. "*Slowly,*" she repeated, brushing her thumb across Catharine's lips, tilting her chin up with a finger. "*Tu comprends ?*"

Catharine could only nod.

"*Bien*." With measured intent, Nathalie lowered herself again, guiding Catharine with nothing more than the rock of her hips, soft sighs and quivered breaths, taunting her with nearness, only to withdraw again.

"*Oui*—" the praise was little more than an exhalation "—*comme ça*."

It became maddening—the inability to reach for her, to hold her, to be left in a suspended state of aching anticipation.

In this one facet of her life, where she'd grown accustomed to control, she now had none.

And that, she imagined, was Nathalie's intention.

Somewhere in the house, an old pipe groaned. A shutter battered against a window. And regardless of the blindfold, she could feel the silent disapproval of her great-great-whatever's portrait glaring down at them from the wall—no doubt entirely appalled.

Catharine could no longer find it in herself to care.

She could think no further than the motion of Nathalie's hips, her full weight now against her. Nothing beyond the hand that had reached back, fingers beginning an excruciatingly unpredictable exploration: the slope of her shoulder, the curve of her breast, the sensitive groove between hip and thigh.

She twisted beneath her as the map grew bolder, more intimate, and could no longer stifle her muffled cry of frustration when Nathalie provocatively pulled away.

"*Non non, ma chérie*—" her voice just a whisper through the dark "—*pas encore*."

Not yet. Not yet. *Not yet.*

But Catharine could feel the growing desperation in the way Nathalie shifted, hear the ragged catch in her breath with each murmured direction, and knew she was losing the hold on her self-restraint.

When it finally seemed the rise and fall of it had become intolerable, the give and take to the point of breaking, Catharine suddenly found the sash tugged free, restoring her world into twilight.

"Cate—" Nathalie slipped a hand to the nape of her neck, the other still between them, "—*regarde-moi !*" It was her final breathless demand—their eyes catching, holding, Catharine straining at the ties—until Nathalie gave in at last, her head thrown back, body arching, and with a single broken gasp, she came undone, taking Catharine with her.

Lost in an untethered haze, Catharine gradually became aware of Nathalie's lips against her skin.

The silk had been unknotted, the stockings discarded to the floor.

"Does this hurt?" Nathalie quietly inquired, kissing the pale underside of her wrist where the binds had left a mark.

Catharine shook her head. She felt stripped, raw—but not from anything Nathalie had physically done.

Through the stillness, the house seemed to wake, the centuries-old creaks and groans whispering within the walls. A phantom stirring from its slumber.

"We could do it, you know," Catharine said, trying to silence the prison erected around her. "A life in Paris." She turned into Nathalie, seeking the comfort of her warmth. "Just you and me."

"We could." Nathalie folded her in her arms, her lips against her forehead, but the sigh that followed was deep and unmistakably laden with melancholy. "But I think we both know this is the closest I'll ever come to having you completely."

For a long time, Catharine said nothing. She lay in silence, listening to the wind against the shutters and the faint report of fireworks somewhere in the valley. The embers in the fire burnt out, taking the shadows with them.

"Maybe not all of me," she finally whispered, her cheek pressed to Nathalie's chest, consoled by the steady rhythm of her heartbeat. "But the only parts of me that matter are unreservedly yours."

Nathalie didn't reply.

Chapter Twenty-Five

"I AM NOT WHAT I seem," the woman on stage declared, her chin tilted defiantly into the footlights. A titter rippled through the audience. Even donned in breeches, a doublet, knee-high boots, and a dagger at her hip, there was no mistaking the femininity of her figure. The line was classic Shakespearean double entendre.

"She said it wrong," Nathalie hissed, leaning into Catharine in the dark theatre. "The line is: 'I am not what I *am*'—not 'I am not what I *seem*'!"

"Nat!" Catharine shushed her. The auditorium was small, a couple hundred seats at best. Sitting in the second row, they may as well have been up on stage with the actors.

But it wasn't really the distraction that Catharine was concerned about. It was a man at the railing of the tiny balcony. She had caught him staring at her throughout the interval.

First, when she and Nathalie ordered a glass of Glenmorangie at the bar, then again, when they returned from the loo. And just minutes ago, as the curtain rose on the third act, she glanced up to find his gaze on her once more. Boldly, he made no effort to turn away, even when their eyes met through the dark.

Diverting her attention back to the stage, she forced herself to wait until the end of the scene before taking another look in his direction. This time, to her relief, the stranger was absorbed in the action of the play, his eyes on the barrel-chested actor playing Sir Andrew. He clapped his hands on his knees and laughed along with the rest of the theatre-goers in appreciation of the bard's timeless humor.

Catharine relaxed. Twice more, when she glanced back, his focus was on the stage, and by the time she and Nathalie spilled out of the *Kenton Theatre* with the rest of the matinee crowd, she was no longer checking over her shoulder.

On the muggy walk to the river—it was uncomfortably hot, the last hurrah of summer—Nathalie pulled her hair into a scrunchie and picked apart the production. *Twelfth Night* was a favorite of hers, the dual part of Viola and Cesario a role she'd been aching to play as long as Catharine had known her.

"I hate that she played her like a clown—panhandling for laughs, flattening all Viola's wonderfully rich emotion. She's supposed to use her wit as a defense mechanism, not reduce her to a stand-up routine!"

"It's the *Henley Players*, Nat. Give them a break—they're an amateur theatre troop, not the Royal Shakespeare Company." Catharine snagged the Penguin biscuit Nathalie had pulled from her purse.

"Hey!"

"You have two more!" She tore it open before Nathalie could recover the chocolate bar.

"Then at least read the joke! What kind of monster are you?" Nathalie snatched the wrapper from her hand. "Why don't penguins like talking to strangers at parties?"

"They find it hard to break the ice."

"Well, stone me dead!" Nathalie laughed. "Look how far you've come, Cate Brooks—Doyenne of Penguin Puns."

They were along the river now, not far from where they'd sat drenched in the rain after escaping the regatta. The day Catharine had come to realize she was, without a doubt, falling in love with her best friend. The day she'd decided instead to go with Edward to Caldy.

Less than three years had passed, and yet, it seemed like a lifetime.

"I've had a sufficient teacher," she shrugged, catching Nathalie's eye out of her peripheral. The afternoon was unseasonably quiet, the docks mainly deserted. The further they got from town, the fewer people they came across along the Thames Path. It lightened Catharine's burden of secrecy—made her more reckless.

"*Sufficient*—!" Nathalie started, leaping to take the bait, but was silenced by half the chocolate bar Catharine shoved into her mouth.

"Quite. You've been an admirable educator."

"O'yah?" Nathalie's voice was garbled with chewing. "'N wh't ways?"

"Let's see—I've learned everything there is to know about packaged biscuits. I've finally come to understand the difference between a Carménère and a Petit Verdot. I've mastered the art of lying to my mother."

"Is that all?" solicited Nathalie, swallowing. Her gaze was coquettish beneath dark lashes. "I feel like you've learned a little more from me than that."

"Oh, I could probably think of another thing or two."

"Like?"

Catharine stopped along the trail. Half a dozen swans floated along the riverbank, hoping for handouts. A heron fished at the end of an empty jetty. Two Egyptian geese squabbled over a drifting bit of turf.

There was no one else in sight.

She reached to wipe away a streak of chocolate on Nathalie's lower lip. "Well," she said, low, seductive, tasting the chocolate on her fingertip, "there *are* a couple of lessons in particular."

"Such as?" Nathalie leaned closer, her fingers grazing Catharine's hip.

"How to procrastinate my responsibilities. How to recognize all the street names for hash. How to survive on pot noodles and terrible French films—"

"You're impossible!" Nathalie pushed away from her, laughing. "*'There's no more faith in thee than in a stewed prune!'*"

"How to apply a Shakespearean quote to every situation. Shall I go on?"

"The rate you're going, I think I'll pass." Nathalie kicked a bit of dirt up at her, sullying her shoes. "Speaking of Shakespeare—did you hear the way she butchered *'make me a willow cabin at your gate, And call upon my soul within the house—'*"

"How to have an entirely one-track mind…"

"Oh, please," Nathalie drawled. "The pot is calling the kettle black. Don't try to convince me you didn't tally the ticket price by number of seats sold to get a rough estimate of performance revenue as soon as we sat down. I know that's what you do every time we attend a show." Nathalie waved off whatever protest Catharine would have made—there was none, really—and continued down the trail. "But in all seriousness—I think I would make a very good Cesario." She slashed an imaginary dagger through the air. "Certainly better than *that* girl!" Still daydreaming the part, she extended a gallant hand toward Catharine.

Quickly scanning their surroundings, Catharine offered her fingertips for kissing.

"You might make a good Cesario," she conceded, twisting her hand so their fingers were intertwined, "but I think I prefer you as Viola."

"You don't say?" Nathalie's eyes danced, reflecting the Thames, her words warm, inviting. *"Tu es parfaite en Cate."*

The way she said it—the way she *meant* it when she said it—caught Catharine's breath, sending a tremble through her. She found she had to swallow away an unexpected tide of emotion.

These moments, these golden afternoons spent in laughter and sunshine, these ardent nights lost in fervor, in the promise of one another, were coming to a close. It was already September, and the two of them knew they were clinging to the last gasp of summer, trying to stave off its inevitable end.

They had concluded their studies at Oxford nearly three months earlier, sitting finals in June. Both had dragged their feet arranging their degree conferral—the formal ceremony which would make their graduation official—eventually settling on a date in October, as far out as their colleges would allow.

Catharine's twentieth birthday.

"Just think," Nathalie had razzed as they packed up the small flat off Cowley Road, "no matter what your father has up his sleeve, I'll finally get to spend the day with you. All it took was three years of mind-numbing studies, hundreds of hours droning on about *Beowulf* and *Doctor Faustus* and *The Canterbury Tales*, and an ungodly amount of time wearing a ridiculously archaic academic gown. Just for the honor to sit in the Sheldonian Theatre, listen to an old man recite a bunch of Latin, and receive a degree I'll never use. *But*—" she tossed Catharine a video they needed to return to the shop below, "—if it guarantees me the privilege to be with Catharine Ann Brooks on her birthday, it will have been worth every second of ink-stained fingers, overdue essays, and Chaucer-induced migraines."

Catharine had kissed her then, and by the time they got around to returning the video, the shop had already closed.

That had been when summer still lay in its entirety before them —a final season together, in a world Catharine knew would change, no matter how the cards of her life were dealt.

Now, however, with the degree ceremony less than three weeks away, the knowledge that Nathalie would soon be off for Paris slid through her like a knife, leaving her standing there on the bank of the Thames a little breathless.

They would see each other, they promised. Catharine would find an excuse to sneak away, fly to wherever she had shows. Nathalie would visit when Colonel Brooks was off in Melbourne, or Bangkok, or Tokyo.

But it would never be this again. It would never be the same.

Catharine couldn't bear to think about it for long.

"*You* are crazy," she said instead, deflecting Nathalie's acclamation that she was perfect as she was—something she was well aware could be no further from the truth.

"Only about you," Nathalie took her elbow, pulling her close as they continued along the water toward where Geoff would be waiting to row them across the river.

THE BLACKBERRY WINE WAS SWEET on Nathalie's breath, the corners of her mouth bearing the faint tint of the dark fruit. Catharine, already feeling the effects of the heady brew, leaned closer to her.

"Your lips are purple," she whispered, resting her forehead against Nathalie's.

"So is your tongue." Nathalie kissed her, tender, unhurried.

A mixtape filled with Catharine's favorite songs—Nathalie's gift to her after completing her finals—played in the background, the beat-up cassette player from their shared flat in Cowley incongruous with the refined sophistication of her room at Honour Stone.

"Should we go down and get another bottle?" Nathalie asked when they eventually drew apart.

Outside the window, the sky was dark. A full golden moon hovered above the woodlands, illuminating the verdant canopy of trees. It was late, but not so late that Mrs. Ainsley would be abed, the manor put to rest. Other nights, Catharine wouldn't have minded. She'd have joined Nathalie in looting the wine cellar, knowing the shrewd household manager would turn a blind eye.

But tonight—no matter how much she drank, no matter how long Nathalie kissed her, no matter what songs crooned through the crackly old speakers—she found herself uneasy.

It had started with the stranger in the theatre, his beady, watchful eyes, and then been heightened by Geoff's disclosure that her father had opened the manufacturing plant in Reading for the weekend.

She didn't know why it troubled her the way it had. A production deadline had probably been expedited, nothing more.

It was just—he'd always closed the factory during the *Turning Leaf Festival*, allowing the locals to celebrate the coming of autumn with their families. It was a long-standing tradition, and he was not a man to deviate from custom.

But the colonel *wasn't* in Reading. Geoff had confirmed that. He was in The Hague, where he'd been all summer long. On the phone the previous morning, her mother had casually mentioned that her father had no intention of returning to Henley for at least another fortnight. Emily's way, Catharine felt, of offering her peace while it was still to be had.

Regardless, she couldn't stand the thought of leaving the sanctuary of her room.

Reaching around Nathalie, she pulled the curtain to the window overlooking the courtyard closed.

"Let's just stay up here tonight," she said, and in an attempt to soften her erratic apprehension, brought Nathalie's hand to the belt of her wrap dress. "I'm certain we can find better things to do."

Nathalie was unfooled by her tight smile. "You've been anxious all day, Cate. What's bothering you?" Still, obligingly, she slipped the buckle loose as the haunting melody of *Ne me quitte pas* filled the room. A shiver pricked Catharine's skin—one she hoped could be mistaken for a reaction to the hands that drifted to her waist as her dress slid open.

"It's nothing." She brushed the concern aside. They had so few nights left together; she wasn't willing to ruin them with her perpetual cycle of unfounded foreboding. "Dance with me?" she asked instead, allowing the dress to fall to the floor. She brought her hands to the nape of Nathalie's neck, drawing their bodies together. She wanted to feel the steadfastness of her, the solace of her arms.

Nathalie pressed blue-tinged lips to her temple. "*Pour toujours.*"

The song was achingly slow, its three-four rhythm as sorrowful as its vocals. Catharine closed her eyes, willing the world to fall away, lost to everything outside the safety of the four stone walls.

They danced—little more than a gentle sway, Catharine's face pressed to the crook of Nathalie's neck—until the end of the track. Until silence filled the room. Until nothing else mattered beyond the brush of bare skin, the harmony of heartbeats, the taste of blackberry wine. And then they rewound the song and played it again. And again.

When Catharine woke, it was well after midnight, her limbs entwined with Nathalie's, the tangle of sheets carelessly kicked to the floor. Her heart was pounding, as if she'd been jolted from a nightmare.

She couldn't remember when they'd gone to bed. The night was recollected only in a series of flashbacks, the details a blur.

When they'd exhausted the mixtape, she knew Nathalie had eventually talked her into a second bottle of wine. Maybe a third. At some point, they'd drawn back the curtains and opened the window, laughing as they fed each other grapes while Nathalie smoked a cigarette with her legs dangling over the sill.

They'd made love on the cool hardwood floor—tenderly, torturously slow, the faint whir of the cassette player spinning in the background.

Now, her heart still hammering, Catharine held her breath, allowing the darkness to dissolve into shadow. The house was uncannily quiet, the silence broken only by the rhythmic cadence of Nathalie's soft inhalations and the gentle flutter of curtains. Carefully, she slipped from the bed and closed the window that had been left open. The moon was high, the flat-topped crown of the massive cedar of Lebanon casting an eerie silhouette across the lawn.

As she crawled back into bed, Nathalie stirred.

"Cate?" she questioned, groggy.

"I thought I heard something."

"You were dreaming." Without opening her eyes, Nathalie drew her into her arms.

"No, it woke me."

"The flutter of a butterfly's wings would wake you. You've been on edge all day." Nathalie kissed the corner of her mouth. "Now go back to sleep. We have a few more hours before dawn."

Catharine didn't know how to explain it: the way she knew something was wrong, the uneasiness that had taken hold.

"I saw a man at the theatre today. Watching us."

"He'd have to be blind not to. Every man watches you." Nathalie laid her cheek against her chest. "All other women fail to exist when you're in a room."

Catharine smiled despite herself, despite the gnawing anxiety that wouldn't let go. "I think you may be biased."

"*Non*," Nathalie murmured, "*t'es belle.*" Her head grew heavy, her breathing soft and even.

Catharine let her sleep.

Nathalie had grown comfortable in the absence of the colonel—in the peace that had come during these last few months alone. She could not wholly comprehend the fear Catharine lived in. And Catharine was all right with that. It was not a fear she should know.

For a long time, she lay awake, watching the spill of moonlight traverse the wood-planked floor, until she, too, drifted into a restless sleep, plagued with discomforting dreams.

THUNDER WOKE HER—AN ANGRY, chilling explosion that echoed through the walls.

Catharine's eyes flew open. She was surprised to find the room bathed in daylight—the ambient wash of late morning sun. The view from her window revealed a bright, cloudless sky. But again, a rumbling blast broke the quiet, and this time, Nathalie bolted up beside her, her large, dark eyes bewildered, her wave of rich mahogany hair falling in her face.

Catharine's heart seized. Then plummeted.

It wasn't thunder.

It was a hostile, demanding pounding coming from the hall.

"Open the bloody door, Catharine!"

The iron latch rattled, the solid oak shaking in its frame.

"Cate?"

The word was choked, the horror of understanding sweeping across Nathalie's face. She was looking for guidance. She needed Catharine to tell her what to do.

But there wasn't time. A key was scraping in the lock. Catharine felt faint. Lightheaded.

And then Colonel Brooks was barging across the threshold—stopping short in the center of her room.

Catharine couldn't look away from him. Couldn't move.

He was still in formal evening attire—black dinner jacket, barathea wool trousers, low-cut waistcoat, and crisp white dress shirt with its Marcella bib—but he was in a state she'd never seen before. A level of dishevelment she would have once found unfathomable in so meticulous a military man.

Cheeks stubbled. Collar open. Bowtie dangling from around his neck.

His eyes—brilliantly cerulean in the glow of morning light—were blazing. Almost wild.

Catharine shrank, immobilized with fear. Beside her, Nathalie wrenched the duvet from the floor, trying to cover them both.

"So the rumors are true." Her father's voice was low, dangerously measured. He stood, ramrod straight, and stared down at her with a disgust that burned straight through her core. "I'd thought it might be that boy—the foreman's son." His gaze flicked to Nathalie. "But I should have known better."

Go, Catharine wanted to tell Nathalie. *Please—now!* But she couldn't find her voice. Her command over her body felt severed, as if the architecture that held her together had come unpinned.

"*You—*" the word began as a whisper, crescendoing into a roar. "You are a disgrace!" He exploded. "An abomination!" Lunging toward the bed, he snatched up Nathalie's discarded blouse, flinging it in her face. "Get out of my house!"

"Father!"

Catharine was stunned by her use of the word. It was one she'd used so seldom before. But in her desperation, she was praying to appeal to any fragment of humanity that might live within him still.

"Please—!"

A blow from the back of his hand sent her crashing against the headboard.

"*Never* address me as such again!" He towered over her, his entire body alight with rage. "You are no daughter of mine!"

He drew back his arm, but before he could strike her a second time, Nathalie was flying at him.

"*Bâtard !*" she screamed, wild with fury. She was moving too fast, and Catharine was too dazed, to do anything to stop her.

She could only watch, horrified, as the colonel caught her wrists midair, and slammed her to the floor.

"Get up, slag! Get *out!*"

Sobbing, Catharine tumbled from the bed, falling to her knees at Nathalie's side. "Please," she begged, "let her go." She reached a shaking hand to help Nathalie with her shirt. "She hasn't done—" Her plea was cut short, her head snapping back as she was yanked to her feet by her hair.

"Put on your clothes," he hissed between clenched teeth, averting his eyes from her naked body. "We are leaving—*now!*" He shoved her toward her wardrobe.

Catharine stumbled, but kept her eyes fixed on Nathalie.

She needed her to know she couldn't stay, she couldn't try to save her. Whatever came next, she would have to face it alone.

She held her gaze, entreating.

On the floor, Nathalie hesitated. The seconds stretched into an eternity. And then, to Catharine's relief—and crippling heartbreak —she stood and ran out the door.

Chapter Twenty-Six

Birdsong filtered through the window. The melodic, flute-like tune of a blackbird, rich and mellow. A cheerful sound that didn't belong there.

Because it wasn't fair—for something to be so joyful, so carefree. For the day to be bright. For the city to be alive. The people on the streets vibrant with energy.

It should have been raining.

It should have been dark.

Anything to reflect Catharine's misery.

She pulled the duvet over her head. All she wanted was to go back to sleep.

She wasn't so impractical as to entertain the fantasy that she could turn back time and wake twenty-four hours earlier, finding herself next to Nathalie. That she could restart the day and alter history.

Nothing would change the reality that she was in London. That the morning before, she'd been dragged through the halls of Honour Stone like a common whore—half-dressed, barefoot, blood dripping from her chin—while the staff watched on, helpless to intervene.

It was only Mrs. Ainsley who cried out in protest, standing in the doorway of the grand foyer, begging the colonel to see reason.

"Sir, please—!"

But she was brusquely shut down by Mr. Fraser and pushed aside to let them pass.

Humiliated, Catharine hid behind her curtain of hair as she was hauled down the steps and shoved, unceremoniously, into the backseat of her father's idling Rolls-Royce. She hadn't had the courage to look out the window—back at Honour Stone, to whatever she was leaving behind. She already knew, whatever this was, whatever lay ahead—her life would never be the same.

So no, she wasn't so fanciful as to imagine that hiding beneath the covers would change anything. She just wanted the birdsong to disappear, and if she were lucky, maybe it would take her with it.

Of course, the world wasn't as merciful as that.

Before she'd even closed her eyes, a tentative knock came at her door—an interruption to the bustling sounds of the city. She assumed it would be her mother, and couldn't decide if her sudden presence came as an infuriation or relief.

She had been notably absent yesterday when Catharine arrived at the townhouse. As had she remained throughout the day, with Catharine confined to her suite. Eventually, Catharine decided she mustn't have been in residence.

And yet, that evening, she'd heard the muffled sounds of her familiar voice drifting up from the dining room. Pleading. Then capitulating.

However, whatever she'd surrendered—whatever she had forfeited on Catharine's behalf—she hadn't had the fortitude to come up and tell her herself.

It felt like the ultimate betrayal.

But as it turned out, the knock at her door wasn't her mother, after all. It was Mrs. Clemmons.

"Miss Brooks?" The woman's warbly voice called from the hall. She didn't wait for an answer. Catharine suspected she wasn't anticipating one. "Colonel Brooks requests your presence in the library. Promptly," she added, as if Catharine were unaware her father would accept anything less.

Catharine considered ignoring her. What was the worst that could happen? He'd come up and beat her again?

Probably.

It hardly seemed to matter if he did. He'd struck her so many times since leaving Honour Stone, another time or two weren't going to make a difference.

But what of Mrs. Clemmons? If Catharine failed to present herself, his wrath would fall on the old housekeeper. And Catharine didn't want that.

Murmuring her acknowledgment, she yanked off the duvet and swung her legs over the side of the bed. She'd spent so little time in London since leaving for Oxford, the room—palatial, grandly modern compared to her suite at Honour Stone—bore a strangeness to her now, like a space that had once belonged to someone else.

It was her *before* Nathalie room.

Because that was the only way she could measure her life anymore:

Before Nathalie. *During* Nathalie. *After* Nathalie.

Mechanically, she pulled on a cotton dress, the floral print feeling far too buoyant for the occasion, and stepped into a pair of suede house slippers. She glanced at her reflection in the wardrobe mirror. From the neck down, she was the *before* Catharine—poised and put together. From the neck up—her cheeks ruddy, her lips bruised, her eyes red-rimmed and bloodshot—*after*.

And all she wanted was *during*.

She turned away from the mirror.

The door to her father's library was ajar. She could hear his voice—the one he reserved for business—finishing up a phone call.

Two weeks. I will handle the logistics.

He fell silent, listening. Catharine could hear the impatient tapping of his pen against the leather cover of his desk calendar.

I understand. But in this case, time is of the essence.

A shorter silence ensued.

No, nothing like that. Her father was annoyed, his tone growing clipped. *I assure you, in that respect, there is no defilement in question.*

There was a long pause as the tapping quickened, his patience thinning. Then a curt laugh. Whatever was said, he hadn't found amusing.

Yes, well. It will benefit us both.

He said goodbye, and the call ended.

Catharine had no time to decode the conversation.

"Do not hover in the hall, Catharine," her father commanded from inside the library.

Numbly, she stepped from the shadows into the room, unable to force her feet further past the threshold.

The colonel didn't look up from his desk, the nib of his fountain pen scratching across his calendar.

"Tomorrow, you will contact your academic administrator to inform them you'll be conferring your degree in absentia."

A dull ache spread through Catharine's chest. She had anticipated this. She had known he would never allow her to return to Oxford, to sit in the Sheldonian, to celebrate her graduation with her peers. Not when he knew Nathalie would be there.

"What reason shall I give for the last-minute change?" she asked, grateful her voice didn't waver. She strove for insouciance. Fight indifference with indifference. Wasn't that what he had taught her? Prove to him, whatever more he did, he couldn't hurt her. She had nothing left to lose.

He didn't look up from the planner. "Because you will be moving to America—to get married."

The dull ache was suddenly a gorge—a chasm her heart had fallen into. The floor seemed to shift beneath her.

"I don't understand." Her mouth had grown so dry, she wasn't sure any words came out. They must have, because he at last looked up, his face unreadable.

"It's very simple, Catharine. Exactly what part of an adverbial clause of reason don't you comprehend? Perhaps you should have studied English instead of economics."

Catharine couldn't even grasp the implication of his belittlement.

"But—who?" was all she managed. "Edward?"

It was the only link in the anarchic chain of her thoughts that she could piece together. Nothing else made sense.

Her father laughed. "That boy—imbecile that he is—is leagues above you. We've already established that." He dropped his pen into its crystal holder, leaning back in his chair. "No. You belong with someone with a small mind, who won't outshine your own. Someone who will not meddle in the affairs of Brooks Corp. Someone who can be controlled." Crossing an ankle onto his knee, he drummed a tattoo against his calendar. "I've made arrangements with Carlton Cleveland—it's all been settled."

The name was only vaguely familiar. A man she'd met just once the previous April.

"The American?" The words were choked as she fought to take in air. "The Council Chairman?"

"Representative, now. South Carolina. I have to hand it to him— trifling intellect or not, the man is enterprising." He said this as if it mattered. As if Catharine cared about his status or ambitions. As if she could think of anything other than his lazy drawl and oily manner. His desperate combover and the stench of his economy cologne.

"No." It was the only thing she could think to whisper.

Her father uncrossed his long legs, unfolding to his feet.

"Do you know, Catharine, what tipped me off on your little affair?" His tone was calculated, his movements languid. The proverbial calm before the storm.

She didn't answer. He would tell her anyway.

"I was in Wassenaar. A dinner party. Haverfield was there. First I'd seen him since his boy got himself sent down. It must have touched a nerve, hearing Cornelis van Renssen congratulate me on your First. Because there suddenly was my old friend, up in his cups, choosing to boldly declare that while his son may have been expelled, at least he wasn't perverse." The colonel rapped his knuckles against the desk, underscoring the word.

Catharine flinched.

"Of course, this captured the attention of the table. *'What, Benjamin? You didn't know? My son has it on good authority that your daughter is a queer.'* Caught unaware as I was, it was still simple to neutralize the accusation. I merely pointed out that previously, Edward had claimed you'd bedded the entire men's *First Eight*. Which was it, then? Were you a deviant, or a whore? Or perhaps, I suggested, his boy just didn't know how to behave like a gentleman when turned down. That he was lacking any trace of honor— as evidenced by his expulsion. The table laughed, the charge dismissed on account of Haverfield's jealousy. But for me?" He'd crossed the room, coming to a stop in front of her. "The imputation unravelled a suspicion I had long begun to form. I'd thought at first it might be you and the Mills boy. I'd hoped for that, at least. But after what Haverfield said—I knew at once my instinct was right. It was you and your unnatural friend. So I came home."

He tinkered with the pull chain on a brass lamp stationed beside the door. He was so close to her, Catharine was certain he would be able to hear her galloping pulse.

"Have you any idea what you have risked for this family, Catharine? For the Brooks' name?" His glacial gaze turned to her, abandoning his fiddling with the lamp. "A *queer*, God damnit! He called you that in front of the whole bloody table!"

The intensity of his tone had heightened, but his volume didn't rise. What little remained of her self-preservation demanded she step back, away from him, into the hall. But she found her legs too unsteady to respond.

"So believe me when I tell you—it is fortunate a man like Cleveland doesn't have many questions, his blinkered perception confined to netting a wife well above his station. He will serve his purpose, Catharine. As you will serve yours."

"I can't," she whispered, despite herself. Despite her fear. What he was asking of her was unimaginable. Something impossible to give. "I won't—"

At once, his hands were on the neckline of her sundress, nearly lifting her off the floor. "Do not be so foolish as to imagine you have any further say on what you will and will not do!" He snarled, hurling her sideways into the wall. She hit the antique console table holding the lamp, the delicate rosewood collapsing as she fell. Something cracked. The stained glass of the lamp shade, or her arm, she couldn't tell.

"Two weeks from now, you will wake up in the morning to find yourself Mrs. Carlton Cleveland. And you will know—the only person you have to blame for that is yourself."

He stepped over her where she lay, unmoving, her knees drawn to her chest, and disappeared down the hall.

Chapter Twenty-Seven

A GENTLE TOUCH DREW CATHARINE from her torpor. She blinked, slowly reorienting herself in the yellow fluorescent light of the first-class cabin. Remembering where she was—where she was going.

An old woman sat beside her, her hand now on her arm. Catharine realized her cheeks were wet. She must have been crying.

"It's just turbulence, dear."

The woman gave her a reassuring pat, misinterpreting her tears.

Above them, the orange seatbelt sign burned a steady warning. The plane lurched, left, right, then dropped suddenly, causing an overhead bin to fall open. In the row behind them, a man shouted.

Catharine didn't tell the woman she'd prefer the plane to crash than land safely in Atlanta.

Instead, she thanked her for her kindness and pulled the drink menu from the back of the seat in front of her.

Johnnie Walker.

Jack Daniel's.

Chivas.

She turned it over, scanning the wine list.

"I recommend the *Mondavi Reserve*," said the woman, reading over her shoulder. "The winery is only a few miles from my ranch."

Catharine didn't want to chat. All she wanted was to be left to the misery of her solitude—to order a bottle of the *'85 Haut-Brion* featured amongst the reds and pretend she was lying on the bank of the *Garonne*. Anywhere but heading west over the Atlantic.

The plane pitched hard. Behind her, she could hear the passenger retrieving his motion-sickness bag. The elderly woman discreetly snugged up her lap belt.

Catharine dropped the menu into the seat pocket and leaned against the cool pane of the window. Outside, lightning flashed above the clouds. She wondered what it would be like—a drop into the ocean. Would sinking into the depths of blackness feel any different than she did right now?

She closed her eyes, trying to will herself back to Oxford. Back to the Cairngorms. Or to the previous summer, in Bordeaux. Even just so far as the afternoon at the theatre in Henley. But the furthest she got was a week ago—to the moment Nathalie found her way to the terrace house in Belgrave Square. The same day Colonel Brooks informed her she was to be married.

It was evening, and Catharine had been sitting with her parents at the dinner table. Supper had been served, but neither she nor her mother had touched their meal. They'd sat in silence as her father unrelentingly drilled into Catharine all the ways she was a disgrace. A failure. Unworthy of his family name.

Mr. Fraser had appeared in the doorway, apologizing for the interruption. He'd stepped to the colonel's side and whispered in his ear. Catharine could still feel the way her father's eyes had shifted to her, the utter fury that lingered there.

"Deal with it," he told the valet, who nodded curtly and disappeared.

Ten minutes later, Mr. Fraser was back in the threshold with a subtle shake of his head.

Colonel Brooks stood, his chair scraping across the polished marble.

"Get up, Catharine." He strode around the table. "You are going to have the pleasure of informing Miss Comtois of the good news about your impending nuptials."

For the hundredth time in the past twenty-four hours, Catharine felt like a rug had been jerked out from under her. That a pin had been driven through her lungs, expelling all the air.

She couldn't—she *wouldn't*—

Her father, sensing her hesitation, grabbed her elbow and hauled her to the foyer.

Nathalie stood on the landing. She was wearing the trousers and boatneck top she'd dragged on the previous morning, the silk scarf she'd worn to the theatre no doubt still lying on Catharine's bedroom floor.

"Cate!" Her voice broke when she saw her, her entire body wrenching with a cry of anguish as she rushed to where Catharine stood between the open double doors. "Oh, my God." Horrified, she reached to touch her face, skimming her fingertips over the bruising along her lips and brow. "You have to come with me. Cate!" she pleaded, her panic rising when Catharine didn't respond. Grabbing her hands, she tried to pull her down the stairs.

Catharine couldn't look at her. She could only stare vacantly across the street at the flag hanging above the Austrian embassy. At her feet, her father's shadow stretched along the limestone of the landing, making his presence in the foyer known.

"Cate—listen to me!" Nathalie released her hands when Catharine made no effort to move. "Look at you!" She seized her shoulders, shaking her—hard. "You *cannot* stay here! Come with me to Paris—we'll make it on our own!"

Catharine thought about Sabine. Thought about the way the Frenchwoman had hugged her goodbye the previous summer on the doorstep of her tiny *échoppe*. The way she had whispered in her ear that she was always welcome in Bordeaux.

And then Catharine thought about earlier in the morning, how her father had summoned Mr. Fraser to the library while she was still lying on the floor. How he'd instructed him to prepare a gift box for Mr. Cleveland. To sign Catharine's name.

"Be certain you include a bottle of *Château Saint-Aurèle's* finest merlot," he'd added, standing just feet from her in the hall.

She'd managed not to give him the satisfaction of looking up, but had understood the message all the same. The mention of *Château Saint-Aurèle* was not just saying he knew where Nathalie's mother worked. It was the reminder that nothing was outside his reach. Not Catharine. Not Nathalie. And certainly not Sabine.

Wherever she went, he would be there. And she knew, after years of watching him run Brooks Corp, that he could destroy a life with ease.

"I can't," she said firmly from the doorway, trying to break free of Nathalie's grasp.

She could feel her father behind her.

She could feel Nathalie's ascending desperation.

And she could feel the constricting confines of her invisible cage.

"Just—!" Her world was imploding. Crumbling. She couldn't breathe. "Just—stop, Nathalie!" she finally shouted, shoving her backward, yanking away. "I'm getting married!" The words sounded foreign on her tongue, as if they belonged to someone else. "I'm moving to the United States."

On the edge of the top step, Nathalie stared back at her, stricken. Catharine could see the threaded pulse at her temple and the tears welling behind her eyes.

"This isn't you, Cate," she whispered at last, stifling a sob. "You don't want this."

"We always knew how this would end." Her voice was dangerously steady, her gaze treacherously unwavering. "Don't make it harder than it has to be." She could hear her father in the way she said it, and something inside her splintered. "Now please," she rushed on, uncertain how long she could hold herself together before the fragility of her facade collapsed. "You need to leave."

She swallowed a wave of bile climbing up her throat. "And don't come back. It's what's best for us both."

"Cate!" Nathalie tried to catch her sleeve, but Catharine was already turning—desperate to conceal her tears—and retreating into the shadows of the house.

That was the last time she had seen her. The last she would ever see her, Catharine knew, as the plane jetted over the sea.

She pulled the window closed, and when the plane leveled out, ordered the Mondavi.

It was midday by the time she arrived at the ferry terminal.

London to Atlanta. Atlanta to Savannah. And then an hour drive to Hilton Head Island.

Labeling it a *ferry terminal* was a stretch. The marina was little more than a broken-down dockyard, littered with salt-crusted fishing vessels and a pontoon boat with a poorly printed banner offering sightseeing tours on the weekends.

When she'd boarded the plane at Heathrow, Mr. Fraser informed her that Representative Cleveland would not be present to collect her from the airport. She had assumed a car would be arranged. Instead, she'd dragged her suitcase through the single concourse and flagged a cab on the curb. The driver had laughed when she gave him the address on Daufuskie Island.

"Island's not reachable by land, hun," he said into his rearview mirror. "You'll have to catch a boat from Hilton Head."

He'd droned on across the causeway about *Tigers* and *Gamecocks* —words that meant nothing to her—and praised the Lord that hurricane season was nearly over.

Got off light this year.

Catharine remained silent, watching as the blistered hoardings and rusted chain-link fencing turned to shrimp shacks and bait shops, and then, eventually, nothing but pine forests and marshland for miles.

When they finally arrived at Hilton Head (*finest resort island in the Carolinas*, the driver boasted, pulling into the potholed car park at the marina), he pulled her carry-on from the boot and deposited it on a bench facing the water.

"'Fraid you missed the afternoon departure. Gonna have to wait 'til evening," he said, slapping a mosquito on his arm, leaving behind a bloody smear. "Welcome to the Lowcountry. Skeeters ain't nothin'. It's them no-see-ums you gotta look out for." He flashed a tobacco-stained grin and doffed an imaginary hat. "Enjoy your stay, but not too long. You'll catch island fever." And then he was gone.

Catharine sat on the bench in the hot Carolina sun, wondering what island fever was, resenting the sign swinging above the ticket kiosk—*Three Daily Departures: Morning, Noon, and Dusk. No Exceptions.*

Four hours later, a diesel-powered ferry boat fired up its engines. A handful of men wearing ball caps and polo shirts embroidered with *Haig Point* ambled down the gangway. None offered to help with her suitcase.

The trip across the Calibogue Sound was short, less than half an hour. The water was flat, and the sea air humid. When they docked on Daufuskie, a young man in a suit and tie loped down the splintered dock and collected her bag, carrying it to a waiting golf cart.

"Evening, ma'am," he said somewhat shyly, holding out his arm to assist her into the passenger seat. "I'm Jerome—Mr. Cleveland's valet. Welcome to Daufuskie."

He was her age, maybe younger—stiff and formal, but with a kind face.

He pointed out the Melrose Club as they left the landing, mentioning that Mr. Cleveland enjoyed golfing there on Sundays.

They passed the Historical Foundation and a weathered lighthouse, then turned onto a narrow dirt road that disappeared into the trees. Spanish moss hung from the broad limbs of live oaks, dangling into the understory like old, moth-eaten lace. The dense canopy blotted out the sun, deepening the surrounding sense of decay.

As they drove further into the center of the island, rusted bicycles and half-sunken boats began to appear wedged between the barbed trunks of palmettos and loblolly pines. Scattered wood-framed houses stood just off the road, all painted in similar shades of blue.

"You won't want to spend much time in this area, ma'am. Tension's been rising between the Gullahs and the folks from the mainland."

Catharine didn't ask who the Gullahs were. They were the least of her concerns.

Slowly, the landscape changed. The trees grew thinner, the air less stifling. Water appeared, glistening in the distance.

The Atlantic Ocean.

Somewhere beyond it sat England, more than 4000 miles away.

"Some of the most pristine beaches in the Carolinas, ma'am," said Jerome, his gaze following hers to the white sand shores. "And hardly ever a soul out to enjoy them. It's very peaceful," he added, perhaps sensing her growing feeling of isolation. "No ruckus from the tourists—even on holidays."

"And Mr. Cleveland—has he lived here long?" Catharine asked carefully. She was not certain what story he'd spun to his staff. Were they aware that they hardly knew each other? That this whole thing was arranged?

"All his life, ma'am. The manor's been in his family for centuries." Jerome did not appear to operate under the Brooks staff's code of discretion. Or perhaps he simply saw no harm in sharing the history of the Clevelands with the woman soon expected to share the name.

"When my father started with the family, they owned the majority of Bloody Point. Since the passing of Mr. Cleveland's father, however, much of the land has been sold. But don't worry, ma'am," he said, turning onto an unpaved road that ran along the coast. "I think you'll still find the grounds to be quite spacious."

Catharine did not tell him the entirety of the island could easily fit within the eastern parklands at Honour Stone.

She turned her gaze to the waves rolling onto the pale shoreline.

She could not ask the questions she wanted to ask—the things she most needed to know.

Was he amiable? Educated? Kind to the staff? Or were they careful not to misstep?

Did he drink too much? And if he did, did he become volatile?

How had he framed their sudden engagement? What version of her had he painted from across the globe?

Instead, burdened with propriety, she asked him about the weather—if it ever got truly cold.

And then they were pulling through a pair of open gates, the wrought iron oxidized with salt.

The tree-lined drive was graveled, littered with crabgrass and flanked by lawns that hadn't been mowed. They passed a pool. Tennis courts. A gazebo.

And there, at the end, stood a white, three-story plantation house, crumbling in various stages of disrepair.

Catharine did not doubt it had once been grand.

But now, the colonnade of Doric columns framing the imposing double veranda was stained orange, streaked with rust from the rain. Shutters hung loose and lopsided beside tall sash windows, ruining the symmetry of the façade. Rot had begun to eat away at the base of the French doors.

As the golf cart came to a full stop on the weathered cobblestone, an older man appeared at the top of the entry, bearing an uncanny resemblance to Jerome.

"Good evening, ma'am." He met her at the bottom of the steps. "I am Edwin—the butler. I trust my son saw you safely across the island."

Before she could respond, her name was called from the cavity of the foyer.

"Well, well—Miss Brooks." The man she'd met only once eighteen months earlier stood on the threshold, leaning against the door. "We meet again." He smiled smugly. "My most lovely betrothed."

His voice was slick. Oily. Laden with liquor. The same as she had recollected him from her father's drawing room in London. Only here, he somehow seemed worse. Even more revolting.

"Forgive me for being unable to collect you from the airport. The misfortune of arriving on my standing card night with the boys." He waved her up the eroding staircase. "But come, come. Welcome to Cleveland Manor. Let me show you around your new home."

FROM THE FOYER TO THE parlor, the kitchen to the library, the smell of brine and mildew followed them room to room.

Catharine tried not to stare at the molding cornice. The cracked archways. The rat droppings and cockroaches that littered the floorboards. She could feel Carlton's eyes on her, the unapologetic way he waited for her reaction.

"Not, perhaps, up to my fair lady's standards?" He baited, drawling out the words. At the top of the grand staircase, he stepped over the carcass of a mouse.

She knew better than to allow him to see her repulsion. To give the satisfaction of her disgust. Unlike the man who'd been desperate to win her favor back in London, he was no longer trying to woo her. Whatever her father had said—however he had sold her —this new version of the stranger knew she was not in a position to refuse.

"No, it—it has charm."

He laughed—a loud, braying sound that seemed to make the lights flicker in the hall. "Well, look at you—already the practiced politician's wife. Ha! Charm!" An amused whistle escaped through his teeth. "I've seen pay-by-the-hour motels with more charm than this old dump. With the election last year, I'd been spending all my time on the mainland, putting in a show of residence in Berkley County. So when things got tight, it made sense to let the house-keeping staff go. This money pit's been going to hell ever since. But don't you fret, darlin'—our wedding gift from your dear, generous daddy is going to see this place ship shape in no time."

He slid an arm around her waist, steering her down the hall. "I couldn't have my pretty little wife living in shambles, could I?"

Catharine said nothing. He'd dropped all pretense of formality, his hand sliding to her hip.

Lower.

She forced herself not to twist out of his grasp.

"Now here we are," he said, coming to a stop in front of a moisture-warped door. He kicked it open with the toe of his overshined shoe. "You can make yourself at home in here. Of course, there's no real sense unpacking. You'll be relocating to the master bedroom soon enough."

Panic must have registered on her face.

"Don't look so alarmed, m'dear. I meant *after* the wedding, of course. I'm a gentleman, after all."

"I'll be sharing your room?" She hated how small her voice felt here in this dank and dismal place—how his loud, brash presence seemed to suck what remained of the oxygen out of the thick, humid air.

"Do they not cover the terms of marriage in English boarding schools?" His smile grew wry, the stale smell of cigar smoke tangling with the bourbon on his breath. It was almost enough to overpower the stench of his cologne. "You do understand what husbands and wives do, don't you? Surely you've got some concept of the birds and the bees?"

"Yes," she managed, swallowing down the threat of sickness. It wasn't as if she hadn't known she'd be expected to share his bed— as if the horror of that inevitability hadn't consumed her.

But she'd also assumed life with him would be more along the lines of the one her parents led. A display of unity in public. A formal showcase of marriage. But behind closed doors? Separate rooms. Separate lives. She could not imagine a world in which she slept beside this man every night—forfeiting every corner of her privacy.

"Well, thank God for small favors." He shot her a wink. "Less of a learning curve. I mean, that is so long as you're not *too* familiar with the concept, if you catch my drift? I know how you college girls can be these days—all those cries for gender equality, refusing to keep your thighs closed."

The crudeness of his comment brought a rush of blood to her cheeks, which in turn, made him laugh. "I'm just yanking your chain, darlin'. I've been well assured you're a proper blushing bride."

Catharine felt her face grow warmer. The nausea returned.

"Now don't you go getting your panties in a twist. Knickers in a knot, I guess, in your case." He chuckled, amused with himself. "I know you British take your sense of decorum all too seriously. You're going to have to lighten up, sweetheart. Learn to let your hair down." He reached out, as if by example, and ran his fingers through a long blonde tress spilling over her shoulder.

Unable to stop herself, she swept her hair back behind her ear. "I'm sorry, Mr. Cleveland—but I am very tired. It's been a long day." She took a backward step into the room.

"But of course. I'll leave you to it." His smile was dim, lazy. How much of it was the alcohol, she couldn't tell. "We'll have plenty of time to get to know one another, I assure you." But instead of leaving, he leaned against the doorjamb, his hooded eyes bright beneath his heavy brow. "You know, I just can't help but wonder: what did someone like you, this shy, diffident girl, do to end up here?" He toed one of the bloated floorboards, peeling a strip of paint off the wall. "I mean, I'd like to believe you were just swept away by my irresistible charm, my fine southern graces— that you begged your daddy to call me up, just knowing the two of us, with our fine pedigrees, were destined to be together. But you see, child—I'm no fool." His smile remained, but his eyes darkened. "And nor do I believe your old man's interest in the Port of Charleston was so immense, it convinced him to give up his prized possession. I mean, look at you, pretty as a picture—he could have bargained you for a shot at the crown jewels." Shoving himself upright, he took a step toward her, bending his mouth close to her ear. "But I'll let you in on a little secret—I don't really give a damn what you've done. I'm just glad you got yourself scalded by whatever hot water you stepped into—because you, my dear, are the answer to my political prayers."

He straightened, dropping his hands to her hips, pulling her to him.

Afraid he was going to kiss her, she couldn't help but turn her head.

"You're going to have to work on your game face, darlin', if we're going to sell our whirlwind summer romance to all of my friends." He smiled, undoubtedly aware of her discomfort. "But that's all right," his lips brushed her cheek, "you're a smart girl. I'm sure you'll figure things out quickly." He kissed the corner of her mouth, laughing as she tensed, and then stepped away. "Sleep tight, darlin'. Don't let the bedbugs bite." And with that, he pulled the door closed behind him.

Shaking, Catharine dropped onto the sagging mattress, the reality of her new life sliding into focus. She gazed vacantly into the dimly lit room, hardly aware of the water-stained ceiling, the dilapidated chest of drawers, the musty duvet.

He knew, then, that she didn't want to be here—that everything about this was against her will. He knew, and he still didn't care.

Exhausted, lonely, scared, she dragged herself to her feet and went to the cracked window overlooking a weeded garden. A moth fluttered on the windowsill, bashing its body against the glass, desperate to get outside. She forced open the swollen frame and watched it fly into the night.

Staring into the darkness, tears collected behind her eyes. She blinked them back. It was no longer her right to cry. Whatever self-pity she might have once been afforded had been forfeited the moment she left Nathalie on those stairs and walked away.

Chapter Twenty-Eight

THEY WERE MARRIED ON A Tuesday—the day after Catharine's twentieth birthday.

In the unforgiving glare of the South Carolina sun, she'd stood on the withering lawn in the shadow of the desolate manor as two dozen strangers stared at her, swatting bugs in their folding chairs.

The pastor wore a plaid tie and loafers. He smiled too broadly and used words like *y'all*.

Somewhere between *"to have and to hold from this day forward"* and *"til death do us part,"* Catharine's mind wandered back to Oxford—wondering if, the day before, Nathalie had stood in the Sheldonian Theatre and had her degree conferred.

If she'd heard Catharine's name called *in absentia*.

If she hated her.

If Sabine was there.

If she hated her, too.

The evening had been stifling. Catharine's gown of Alençon lace —the dress her mother had once worn—stuck to her skin. When the pastor presented her with the golden band to place on Carlton's finger, her hand was shaking, and she dropped the ring in the grass. One of the guests laughed.

Then it was over.

She didn't remember *I do*. She couldn't have said if anyone clapped. All she could focus on was the sheen of sweat along the preacher's upper lip as he slapped Carlton on the shoulder, and in his heavy Southern drawl, said: *I now pronounce you man and wife.*

She could think no further than the repulsive feel of stubble on Carlton's chin when he leaned to kiss her—the repugnant smell of his bourbon breath.

At the reception, he steered her through a series of introductions, his hand firmly planted at the small of her back. Somehow, she managed to smile, to thank the guests for coming, to equally answer questions from the wives of his equally intolerable friends.

Yes, how fortunate was she to have found a man so driven.

Of course, it was love at first sight.

No, her parents had been unable to attend the ceremony, but they sent their best wishes and their blessing.

A reporter from the *Post and Courier* joked with Carlton about the 'shotgun' wedding and asked if perhaps he'd gotten himself in trouble with the colonel back in London?

"I mean, look at her," Carlton responded coolly, taking a heavy drag from his cigar. "Would you have been able to keep your hands to yourself?" He raised a suggestive brow, and the two men shared a laugh, neither concerned that she had overheard.

Catharine found herself fixated on the setting sun, aware of the time passing as it edged toward the horizon.

Beneath the cover of the veranda, shrimp and grits were spooned onto plastic plates by tuxedoed caterers, and a congress-man from Georgia made a toast.

"You're a lucky bastard, Cleveland." He swirled the melting ice in his Dixie cup. "If your life keeps going the way it is, we just might be suffering through *Hail to the Chief* every time you enter a room."

Glasses were raised to shouts of *hear, hear!* as the sinking globe of the sun touched the water. Catharine reached for a flute of champagne on a passing tray, but found her arm pressed down to her side by Carlton.

"The wife of the future president has got to be a law-abiding citizen," he chastised, unmistakably smirking. "Wouldn't want folks to think I support underage drinking."

The sun sank lower.

On the lawn, a string quartet struck up the opening notes to *Clair de lune*, and Catharine felt as if the wind had been knocked out of her. She stumbled when Carlton dragged her into their first dance, unable to shake the memory of ivory keys on an old upright… a whisper of French poetry… the promising glow of moonlight. As they slow danced, she stared unblinking at the last glimmer of sun vanishing beneath the Atlantic.

The scent of citronella filled the air.

"Everyone is watching," Carlton hissed against her cheek, pulling her tight against him in a show of being tender. "You better learn to fucking smile."

As the final strains of the melody faded from the cello, Catharine thought of Virginia Woolf—of how she'd filled her coat with stones and waded into the water.

She turned her attention to the sliver of moon rising out of the darkness, and for the first time in as long as she could remember, pled with any god who would listen to freeze it where it was, never allowing it to climb higher.

But inch by inch, it rose, as shot by shot, Carlton grew drunker.

And then, suddenly, she blinked to find the guests were gone. The band was packed. She was alone with him in the manor.

She'd promised herself she wouldn't cry. That it was beneath her. But she'd broken the promise as soon as he closed the door. As soon as he reached to touch her.

A promise broken day after day, night after night, those first months of marriage.

Until she learned, little by little, ways to wash him off her.

To clear her mind in the scalding stream of a shower.

To brush her teeth in the middle of the night so vigorously her gums bled.

To hang up her thoughts at the bedroom door, as if they were a coat she could slip on and off at leisure.

Until, at last, she could stare at her reflection in the mirror, and no longer recognize the person she saw there.

Because who she was, who she'd been—a girl who'd laughed beneath the boughs of a tree in Christ Church Meadow, a girl who'd felt the freedom of a winter breeze on Christmas morning in the Scottish Highlands, a girl who'd known the immense joy of being head-over-heels in love, of being loved so exquisitely in return—would not survive here. She had to leave that girl behind. Every single part of her.

And it was only then, by stepping into the role of a stranger, that she could dry her eyes—that she could begin to face the truth of her future.

To learn to find some semblance of peace in the art of pretending.

Pretending to sleep.

Pretending to laugh.

Pretending to enjoy the feel of his arm around her waist as he paraded her through the political circles of Charleston.

Pretending to be the dutiful wife—elegant, composed, compliant.

Chapter Twenty-Nine

A warm Mediterranean breeze swept over the rooftop terrace, fluttering the petals of fresh-cut freesia in their vase. Through the glass railing, the surface of the *Vieux-Port* was glassy, catching the first shimmer of city lights as Marseille leaned into twilight.

Catharine closed her eyes, savoring the quiet beauty of autumn on the southern coast of France. When was the last time she'd sat outside without the constant chorus of cicadas humming in her ear, or her linen trousers clinging to damp skin? When had she last looked to the horizon and not seen a palmetto or live oak drenched in Spanish moss?

More than two years. Three days shy of twenty-five months, to be exact.

Inhaling the scent of sun-warmed terracotta and sweet anise, she opened her eyes and listened politely as the server recommended a few apértifs. Then ordered a whisky, neat.

"I must confess—I've always had you down for a white wine kind of woman."

Startled by the intrusion, Catharine looked up to find the slender silhouette of a man gazing down at her. In the flickering glow of the candlelight, she recognized the cocksureness of his smile, his subtly accented English.

Emilio Herrera. The son of Álvaro Herrera—once Brooks Corp's friend and ally. The Barcelona shipping magnate Colonel Brooks had all but destroyed.

Catharine had heard rumor that the Herreras had clawed their way out from under their mountain of debt and back into the chess match of international logistics.

She wondered if Emilio—who'd always been friendly to her—knew the role she'd unintentionally played in capsizing his family business. If he did, he hid it well.

"What brings you to Marseille, Señor Herrera?"

"I imagine the same thing that brings you, Miss Brooks." He elevated one of his dramatic brows, gesturing toward the empty chair across the table.

How refreshing it was to hear her maiden name spoken by someone who didn't know this new version of her. Someone who knew her from before. Who knew nothing of her after.

She welcomed him to sit, twisting her wedding ring around her finger beneath the cover of the tablecloth. She could slip it off, tuck it into her purse—say nothing to correct him. Just enjoy a drink as Catharine Brooks again.

Instead, she said, "It's Mrs. Cleveland now, actually," and reached for her whisky.

"The worst news I've heard all week," he said, still smiling. "And believe me, it's been quite a week." He shook his head, good-natured. "Hearts will be broken across the globe when word gets out the most beautiful woman in Europe has given her heart to another. What a dire day for mankind."

Leaning back, he crossed his legs, regarding her through the same bright eyes she remembered from London—the day he'd kissed her hand and whispered *Brillas con luz propia, Catharine.*

A harmless gesture that had nearly toppled his father's empire.

Whatever had happened since, he hadn't let it change him. Absently, she wished she'd been able to cling to the same *joie de vivre.*

Uncertain she could rally a smile that would reach her eyes, she tipped back the remainder of her drink.

"So, the freight handling contract, then?" she said, steering the conversation in a safer direction.

"A futile bid—my father knows we'll never be able to compete with the likes of Brooks Corp. Regardless, he wanted me here all the same. I think secretly he hoped I'd run into your old man." He winked to show he was teasing, but still, Catharine dropped her eyes to the table.

"Emilio, what my father did—"

"—is not your fault, *hermosa*. So leave the past behind. I hope one day you and I might work together." He waved a sun-kissed hand. "But let's not talk business tonight. Tell me about you. It's been years now. Who is this lucky devil who's unwittingly turned every bachelor on the continent into an enemy?"

Catharine picked up the drinks menu she already knew by heart. What could she say about Carlton?

She could hardly tell him about the man who, when her father insisted she handle the account in Marseille, had become so enraged that she would miss a barbecue at the county fair during his reelection year, he'd thrown a Bible through the window. That as she swept glass from the Calacatta marble he'd imported to renovate his library floor, he'd perched on the edge of his bespoke Hermès sofa and berated her for being 'unsupportive.'

Never mind that it was *her* salary paying the bills. *Her* checkbook that funded his closet full of Brioni suits and the Bentley parked in the drive. *Her* work that fed his newly acquired rapacity for a lifestyle he liked to pretend was his by right.

She'd wanted to fling the dustpan at him, to remind him that the pittance he earned as a State Representative wouldn't pay for the Berluti oxfords on his feet.

Instead, she dumped the glass in the bin, left the Bible on the lawn, and told him if he had an issue with her business trip, he'd need to pick up the phone and call her father.

And a week later, she'd left South Carolina for the first time since she'd been married and flown to Marseille.

No, she couldn't tell Emilio any of that.

She dropped the menu on the table. "What are you drinking? Please don't tell me white wine."

Emilio's smile was artfully rakish. "I'll have what you're having."

They talked for three hours and through the better part of a bottle of *Macallan 25*. Emilio told her about his family's scrap out of the rubble, and how spite and two heart attacks had fueled his father's climb.

On the third round or so, the whisky dissolving her guard, he coaxed out the whitewashed story of her marriage—her move to the Carolinas.

"And you are not happy," he said, dropping his elbows on the table, his handsome face propped in his hands. "With your American politician."

There had been no inflection of a question, but Catharine treated it like one all the same.

"Do you know anyone who is happy all the time?" she said, mustering as much indifference as possible.

"Of course not. But any man who isn't devoting his life to making a woman as enchanting as you smile—is not a man at all."

She laughed. "You're a romanticist."

"Guilty." Emilio shrugged. "And you are a woman who should be loved by one."

Unable to look at him, Catharine picked up her glass, finding solace in the slow, mellow burn.

She wanted to be someone different. She wanted to be a Lorelei. A Jezebel. A femme fatale. The kind of woman who could boldly pick up the bottle of Macallan, brush her thumb across the handsome Spaniard's lips, and suggest they finish it in her room.

She'd been flirting with him, she knew. Enjoying the attention of a man who wanted her for *her*, not as some trophy on his wall.

And why should she feel bad for that? Carlton was anything but faithful. Not a month into their marriage, and he'd begun flaunting his revolving door of indiscretions, mistakenly thinking she would care. Too arrogant to realize she found it a relief—grateful for any woman who kept him from reaching for her even one fewer time.

But the problem was, she didn't want Emilio. Not like that, at least.

Yes, he was good-looking. And there was no question he was kind. He'd made her laugh, and somehow loathe herself a little less.

But no matter how she tried, she couldn't fan a fire that just wouldn't ignite.

Pouring them both another glass, she told herself it was simply because whatever part of her that could feel that way had been extinguished long ago.

She was frigid. Unfeeling. Carlton liked to remind her of it constantly.

You know, it's hardly surprising no man ever wanted you. You're like fucking a dead fish.

Or, more recently: *I swear, Catharine—my grandmother would have been a better lay.*

Then maybe he should try that, she'd countered—a suggestion which had earned her a slap across the face.

But still, there was a part of her that knew his accusations weren't true. She hadn't always been cold. Callous.

And late that night, after Emilio had walked her to her room and, with no expectations, kissed her cheek goodnight, she lay in bed—the world spinning in a whisky haze—and knew what she wanted. What she'd never stopped wanting all along.

Before she could change her mind, she dialed the concierge, and asked the woman a favor.

An hour later, shortly after 2 AM, the phone rang.

The same woman apologized for the delay, but was following up on her request.

Catharine listened with her eyes closed, taking in the siren's song of the Mediterranean Sea through her open windows.

"Très bien, merci." She breathed in the salt air, thinking of what Emilio had said—how she was a woman who should be loved.

She blinked back into focus. The concierge had asked her a question.

Did she want her to make the arrangement?

Oui. She didn't give herself time to think.

Bien sûr, madame. The woman assured her she'd have a flight booked to Paris by morning.

CATHARINE WAS NOT PREPARED FOR the intensity of her reaction, the nearly visceral response to first seeing her on stage.

She'd sat in the side loge of the *Théâtre du Châtelet*, her fingers worrying the crimson velvet of her seat, watching as the curtain rose, the warm stage light bringing the magnificence of the famous gold leaf proscenium into view.

And there, suddenly, was Nathalie.

Standing front and center, her back to the audience, the ring of a spotlight encircling her feet.

It would be impossible not to know her. Even in corset, bodice, teased wig of curls, the period dress of the seventeenth century. But Catharine knew the tilt of her head, the curve of her hip, the relaxed stillness of her fingers—how they hung at her sides, dormant, yet somehow still commanding attention.

She would know her here, in the heart of France, on Paris' grandest stage, just as she would know her in the darkness, in the cloistered lanes of Oxford, or on the bank of the Thames on a warm summer day.

A hush took over the theatre.

The audience rustled, anticipating, but Nathalie made them wait, every eye drawn to her even as she said nothing. In the dark, Catharine could hear the rasp of her own breath and realized her hands were shaking.

And then the beauty of the silence was broken as the actor playing Valère lumbered from the wings. *What, dear Élise! Can you regret having made me happy?*

Catharine hardly heard him, never taking her eyes off Nathalie.

When the concierge in Marseille had tracked her down playing the role of Élise in the Moliére comedy, Catharine had thought little of it. She'd read *L'Avare* as a child, and once seen its English translation—*The Miser*—at the Royal Court in London. But the play hadn't left a lasting impression.

Now, however, as the plot unfolded, she began to grow disconcerted.

Élise, the daughter of Harpagon, a man consumed by excessive greed, was being forced into marriage with a suitor twice her age. But passionate, rebellious, and already deeply in love with her father's steward, Valère, Élise refused.

I had rather kill myself than marry such a man, Nathalie hurled, down on her knees.

The show was meant to be satirical, with the outrageousness of Harpagon's appetite for avarice leaning into farce. The irony of a man who had all the money in the world, yet was shackled by self-inflicted misery. His willingness to cast aside his daughter's happiness in order to escape paying a dowry intended to draw laughs.

Throughout the auditorium, the theatre-goers tittered at the old miser's slapstick defense.

But Catharine did not.

Nor could she bring herself to see the humor when Harpagon chastised Élise, telling her he would rather see her dead than disobedient.

Perhaps it had been amusing four hundred years ago, when a woman's petition for independence could be seen as absurd. But today—as they neared the twenty-first century?

"You are free to take away my life, Father—but you will never take my heart." Élise's impassioned declaration reverberated through the proscenium arch.

Catharine had to look away.

How fitting it was—her, watching the headstrong Frenchwoman follow her dreams beneath the bright lights of Paris, while she sat in the shadows, confined to a purgatory of her own making.

She stared at the gilded etching on the railing, uncertain why she'd come here. Uncertain what she'd been expecting.

Two nights ago in Marseille, the detour to the French capital had felt almost a necessity. At least that's what she'd convinced herself on the short flight across the country.

She would attend the show and then wait for her at the stage door. If Nathalie was willing, maybe they would get a coffee, and Catharine would finally be able to tell her all the things she should have said two years ago—to beg for forgiveness for her many wrongdoings.

Never had she allowed herself the disillusion to believe it would change anything. At no point had she fantasized that it could be as it had been, that they could regain any of what was lost between them.

She had hoped, only, in seeing her, that she could find some semblance of peace. Of resolution.

But sitting there imprisoned in the comfort of her box seat, listening to Élise's fervent refusal to marry a man she did not love, Catharine could not quell the ache of her longing.

Maybe it was the familiar scent of dust and velvet, greasepaint and varnish that over the years had become synonymous with Nathalie, but she couldn't prevent her gaze from straying to the rafters, to stop her mind from wandering.

She closed her eyes.

The clock rewound, and at once, she was back in Oxford. Nathalie was a dozen feet above her, luring her up a rickety backstage ladder at the Playhouse.

A traveling production of *Macbeth* was being performed.

They had no business being there—Nathalie was neither company nor crew—but they were only weeks away from graduation, and a foolish sense of invincibility had overcome them. So when, during the interval, Nathalie had leaned over in her seat and whispered for Catharine to follow her, Catharine had not protested.

Nor had it been with little more than feigned objection that she climbed after her, toward the catwalk, trailing her silhouette into the dark.

At the top of the ladder, Nathalie caught her hand. Acquainted with every spotlight and fresnel, batten and fly system, she pulled her further along the maze of the lighting bridge.

Double, double, toil and trouble; Fire burn and cauldron bubble the witches chanted forty feet below.

And then Nathalie's mouth was on hers. She was kissing her. Kissing her so suddenly, Catharine had to steady herself against a follow spot platform. Kissing her so fervently, Catharine was out of breath.

Scale of dragon, tooth of wolf, Witches' mummy, maw and gulf...

Her lips were on her neck, her hands up her silk blouse.

Of the ravin'd salt-sea shark, Root of hemlock digg'd i' the dark...

Catharine resisted briefly. *The audience,* she cautioned. *The show...*

Nathalie pressed her back against the cold steel of the railing, her hands growing bold.

Slivered in the moon's eclipse, Nose of Turk and Tartar's lips...

Catharine forgot about the impropriety of it all. How, if they were caught, they could get sent down.

Or worse. So much worse.

And thereto a tiger's chaudron, For the ingredients of our cauldron...

The theatre, the lights, the auditorium with six hundred patrons visible through the slated walkway beneath them, failed to exist. There was only Nathalie. Her taste—red wine from the interval, lipstick and menthol. Her scent—jasmine and fresh soap. The feel of her—warm, addicting, forbidden.

Catharine's gasp was stifled by Nathalie's mouth.

Double, double, toil and trouble; Fire burn and cauldron bubble...

And then the world was spinning, the night swept up in the fervor that was only Nathalie Comtois.

By the pricking of my thumbs, Something wicked this way comes...

A man guffawed in the loge to her left, shattering the spell. Catharine opened her eyes and found herself back in Paris, the dream of Oxford nothing more than a distant memory.

On stage, Harpagon was begrudgingly permitting his children to follow their hearts and marry their lovers—just so long as it was at no expense to himself.

The Parisian audience was clapping, interspersed with cheers of *bravi* and *magnifique*. The cast was taking their bows center stage.

Catharine could hardly bring herself to look at Nathalie, who stood with her hands clasped between the actors who played Mariane and Valère.

She should go, she knew. She could be in line for the cloakroom before the curtain call ended. It was the wise decision. Her life was across the ocean now, thousands of miles away, amongst the marshland and reeds.

But instead, she found herself on *Rue Edouard Colonne*, waiting outside the stage door with a small gathering of patrons.

Standing at the back of the group, she anxiously twisted the programme.

It had been more than two years since she'd left Nathalie standing on the steps of her father's terrace home in London. Two years since she'd told her she could never see her again.

Two years that had changed her, dismantled her—forcing her to lose sight of who she was, of who she'd ever been.

She shifted, only vaguely aware of the light rain that had begun to fall.

Would Nathalie even want to see her? Would she be willing to hear what she had to say?

Without much time to dwell on the question, the stage door swung open, and there, the first actor to leave the theatre, stood Nathalie.

Dark hair tucked under a black fedora, silk scarf tied around her neck, she looked as vibrant as she ever had. Happy. Carefree.

Catharine watched as she smiled at the crowd, but instead of moving down the row of fans, signing programmes and receiving flowers, she hung back, waiting. A moment passed, and then the actress who played Mariane appeared, laughing as she slipped an arm around Nathalie's waist, whispering something in her ear.

The pair shared a smile that left Catharine reeling. A smile that said everything.

She knew the look, the closeness, the unquestionable expression of intimacy.

For an impossibly long second, Catharine stood frozen on the pavement, forgetting to breathe. Her heart, beating just moments earlier, clenched, splintering.

And then, allowing herself no time to think, she turned on her heel and fled into the curtain of rain—desperate to disappear before she came unglued at the seams.

Chapter Thirty

"You must just be tickled pink!"

Karen Calhoun, wife of U.S. Representative Samuel Calhoun, oohed and ahhed as Catharine led her on a dutiful tour of Carlton's new residence in D.C. The woman checked her reflection in the stainless steel of the double oven, then took a surveying sweep of the panel-front refrigerator and custom inset cabinetry.

"And oh my goodness—" she peeked her head around the corner "—I'd about sell my soul for this pantry!"

Covering her mouth with her fingertips, her eyes widened, as if she'd said something scandalous. "Of course, not literally."

"Of course," Catharine echoed, smiling politely.

She certainly couldn't tell the wife of the Georgia congressman how much she despised the gaudy marble floors, the two-tiered chandeliers, the imported textile drapery. Nor could she mention that she'd hardly gotten to know the house herself, having only learned about its purchase the previous week. It wasn't as if she could confide that the Tudor Revival mansion in the heart of Kalorama—one of the District's most prestigious neighborhoods— had been a far cry from the 'modest townhouse in Georgetown' Carlton told her he was considering.

"Lighten up, Catharine," he'd chastised, when she failed to fawn over the excessive estate. "I told you—it's all about appearances here on The Hill. I was lucky to scoop this place up before it went on the market. Herbert Hoover once lived on this street."

Catharine didn't point out that Herbert Hoover had been a president—and her husband nothing more than a newly elected freshman congressman, straight out of state politics.

"My word! Is this Waterford crystal?" Karen gestured toward a vase in the window above the sink, clucking appreciatively. "You see, when I was your age, I was still waitressing in Tallahassee." She shook her head, her gaze on the vase, reminiscing. "Sam's my second husband—first one was a bad egg." With a half-hearted laugh, she looked up at Catharine. "So believe me when I say: my hat is off to you, young lady—prettier'n a peach in June, and clever enough to snare a husband with ambition. The sky's the limit with a man like Carlton, I reckon." She checked that they were alone, then lowered her voice beneath the holiday music coming from the hallway. "He won't be a perennial seat-warmer like my Sam. I wouldn't be surprised if one day I was addressing you as First Lady."

Again, Catharine offered a demure smile.

Over the past three years of marriage, she'd grown accustomed to these simple, simpering women while navigating the political circles of South Carolina on Carlton's arm. Part of her had clung to the hope that, with his ascension to Washington, the minds of his constituents and their wives would broaden at the federal level.

That optimism, however, was quickly fading.

"So is this where the real party's at?"

A woman poked her head into the kitchen. Catharine recognized the short, dark hair and tanned complexion of Joanna Stratham.

Governor Joanna Stratham, she reminded herself, running through the mental checklist of attendee notes she'd memorized earlier in the day.

Centrist. Mid-forties. Graduated from Annapolis. Retired Navy JAG—rank of Captain—after 21 years of service. Made history two years earlier when she was elected the state of Maryland's first female governor.

A woman Carlton utterly despised for her sharp intellect, charisma, and political agility. But one with enough clout, he hadn't dared withhold an invitation to his inaugural New Year's Eve party.

"You know what they say about her," he'd grumbled after receiving her RSVP. "That flyboy husband of hers is nothing but a cover."

Catharine had ignored the insinuation.

"Oh, hello, Joanna," said Karen, serving a chilled smile. "Were you looking for the restroom?"

"Not sure I've ever found a toilet in a kitchen—but there's a first for everything, *Karen*." The governor smiled brightly, arching an eyebrow at Catharine. "Mrs. Cleveland." She acknowledged her with a nod. "Lovely place you've got here."

They'd met only once before, at a bipartisan women's leadership event Carlton insisted Catharine attend shortly after their marriage. Joanna had been Maryland's Attorney General at the time. In the limited conversation that had passed between them, Catharine remembered liking her immediately.

"I see this is where you hide the good stuff." Joanna gestured at the bottle of Macallan sitting on the counter. Without invitation, she plucked a glass from an upper cabinet and poured herself a finger. "Ladies?"

Mortified, Karen shook her head. "Excuse me—I should find my husband."

When she'd gone, Joanna shrugged at Catharine.

"Imagine being so boring that a glass of anything other than Chardonnay sends you sprinting for the smelling salts."

Catharine laughed, despite knowing she shouldn't.

She'd mastered her role as the perfect politician's wife, adept at the performance she'd been born to play.

She knew how to smile and nod at all the right moments, how to appear gracious and charming at all times. She remembered the details of everyone on the guest list—their children and hobbies, the first names of their wives. She ate what Carlton dictated she ate, dressed exactly as he desired: conservative, elegant, always refined. She knew when to speak, and when to fade into the background, certain to never upstage her husband, or question him in front of his colleagues.

But for some reason tonight, in the presence of this woman, she couldn't bring herself to don the facade.

"Ice?" Joanna asked, retrieving a second glass.

"Oh." Catharine considered the Macallan in Joanna's hand.

Carlton didn't like her drinking whisky—especially not when he had guests. It was uncivilized, unladylike, he'd rant—then down half a bottle of single malt himself.

"No. Thank you. No ice, that is," she corrected quickly, changing her mind. "I'll take it neat, please."

Joanna's smile was arch. "A woman after my own heart."

The governor was flirting with her; there was no question. But unlike the parade of Carlton's swaggering, ogling, handsy friends, Catharine found she enjoyed Joanna's attentions. They surfaced a feeling she'd learned to suppress—sweeping her back to another time, a different life.

"You must be looking forward to the new year," Joanna was saying, leaning against the counter, somehow managing to make the hideous marble look almost tasteful. "Some big changes on the horizon."

Catharine didn't know why she was disappointed. She shouldn't have been surprised that the Governor of Maryland would want to talk about Carlton. He was the rising star of his party, after all—or so the pack of jackals he surrounded himself with kept saying. Never mind that their enthusiasm always seemed to swell in proportion to the lining of their pockets, courtesy of her family's seemingly endless supply of contributions toward their campaigns.

"I am—we are, of course." Catharine tried to hide her sigh behind a slow sip of whisky. "It's been a long road to the Capitol, but Carlton is certainly ready to embrace the—"

"I meant *you*, actually." Joanna interrupted. "I read about *World-Cargo's* expansion into the *Port of Bandar Abbas*. The article mentioned you brokered the deal, gaining access to the *Strait of*

Hormuz. That's—" Joanna elevated her brow, blowing out a low whistle "—quite impressive."

"I think *brokered* might be a stretch. I simply proposed the deal through *WorldCargo's* Middle East regional director, and—"

"Don't sell yourself short," Joanna brusquely cut her off. "I spent a few years in *Tehran* on a liaison assignment before the revolution. Any woman capable of negotiating access to *Bandar Abbas* has more diplomatic finesse than every one of those silver-tongued committee kings in the Capitol frat house combined." She inclined her head toward the door, indicating the boisterous throng of good-old-boy politicians across the hall. "Finesse, *and—*" she tipped her glass forward, clinking it to Catharine's "—a whole lot of guts. I must say, from one rainmaker to another—nice work."

For a moment, Catharine was uncertain how to respond. She couldn't remember a time when someone had acknowledged the effort she put in—if at any point in her life, she'd ever been told well done.

A little flushed, she laughed, deflecting.

"I think you give me too much credit."

"I don't think I do. I pride myself on assessing people accurately. A woman doesn't survive long in this political circus without being able to read a room."

"And how would you assess me?" Catharine asked, stunning herself with the forwardness of the question. It was out of character for her to be so bold.

But there was something about this woman—the way she looked at her—that made Catharine feel like she was being seen for the first time in years. Seen in a world where everyone else gazed straight through her.

It wasn't a feeling she was ready to let go.

To her surprise, Joanna shed her bravado.

"I see a young woman who is highly educated. Exceedingly cultured. Ambitious in ways I don't think even she understands. But I also see a young woman who's been weighed down by expectations, whose sense of self-worth has been distorted by chasing other people's approval. A woman constantly surrounded by a crowd, yet who feels alone in the room." Joanna took a sip of her whisky, never taking her eyes off Catharine over the rim of her glass. "Am I far off?"

"I—" Catharine cleared her throat, having apparently lost the ability to swallow. "I don't…"

"*Catharine.*" The hostility in the two drawn-out syllables startled her, forcing her back a step from the governor, guilty of what, she wasn't even sure.

Carlton stood in the threshold, the ruddiness of his cheeks and dishevelment of his tie promising he'd already worked his way into the second half of a bottle.

"I've been wondering where you'd gotten off to." His Carolina drawl was more pronounced than normal. "It's almost midnight. Who was I supposed to kiss when they drop the ball?" As he stepped between her and Joanna, Catharine could smell the floral scent of cheap perfume. A smudge of lipstick stained his collar.

Whatever he'd been doing, he hadn't been doing it alone.

"Gov'nor." He tipped an imaginary hat toward Joanna, his smile tight. "You know I hate to interrupt you girls' tete-a-tete, but I'm afraid I need to steal my wife for a minute. That all right?"

Joanna neither stepped back nor shrank beneath his bellicose glare.

"I don't know, Mr. Cleveland—why don't you ask *her*?"

"Because I'm telling *you*." He hissed, the stench of rye on his breath as he caught Catharine's arm. His fingers dug into her elbow. "Ready to ring in the New Year, sweetheart?"

Desperate to avoid a scene, Catharine smiled apologetically at Joanna, unable to meet her eye, and led Carlton out of the kitchen toward the formal sitting room, where a raucous, drunken countdown echoed the broadcast in Times Square.

In the reflection of her vanity mirror, Catharine watched Carlton stumble into the room, as drunk as she'd ever seen him.

It was after three in the morning.

She'd hoped, as she tidied the house and saw the last guest to the door, that he would pass out in his study, where she'd left him opening a bottle of Michter's 25 and smoking Cuban cigars.

That had been nothing more than wishful thinking.

"Fuck it," he muttered, losing the battle with unknotting his tie, then tripped over the Turkish Oushak as he crossed to where she was standing. "I want that God damn rug gone by morning!"

Catharine unclasped an earring, saying nothing. She knew from experience he would remember none of what he said by the time he crawled from bed at midday.

He steadied himself against her shoulder, fumbling with the zipper of her dress, his entire body reeking of stale smoke and alcohol. And perfume that wasn't hers.

"Carlton." She stiffened. "I'm tired."

"Didn't seem too tired making nice with Joanna Stratham."

It was the third time he'd brought the woman up since interrupting their conversation in the kitchen.

Earlier, while watching the confetti fall across the television footage of New York City, he'd pressed himself against her back and whispered, "You think she likes watching?" And again, after Joanna had stopped to say goodnight, he'd waited until she was out of earshot, and then smirked at his legislative assistant, Pete Myers. "You know what they call her on The Hill?" he asked. The question was directed at Pete, but his eyes were on Catharine. "Governor Strap-On."

The two men shared a laugh while Catharine collected a crystal tumbler that had been knocked over on the arm of the Biedermeier sofa.

"She was your guest, Carlton," she said now, turning her face away as he leaned to kiss her neck. "I was being polite."

"Is that what you'd like to call it?" He tugged her zipper down.

When he finally staggered back across the room, trousers around his knees, he collapsed on her side of the bed, not bothering to undress.

Tonight, Catharine couldn't bring herself to pull off his shoes, unfasten his watch, leave a glass of water on the bedside table. She left him as he was and returned to stripping her face of the make-up he insisted she wear.

Slowly. Mechanically. Layer by layer.

In the morning, he would criticize her for being uncaring.

You know, most wives find joy in attending to their husbands.

Realizing she'd forgotten an earring, she unclipped it and dropped it onto the vanity, then paused with her fingers at the clasp of her pearl necklace. She stared at herself in the mirror, at the unfamiliar woman looking back at her.

A woman she no longer recognized.

Only, that wasn't quite true. She *did* recognize her—in the shape of her mother.

Not in feature. The two women looked nothing alike. They never had. But she saw herself in her now, in the way she had viewed her as a child. A woman whose eyes had grown dull. A woman who was distant, distracted.

In a fit of fury, she tore the choker from her neck—ironically, a wedding gift from her mother—and sent the pearls scattering across the floor.

By instinct, she glanced over her shoulder.

Carlton didn't stir.

The house, which had been overrun with people just an hour earlier, remained still.

She returned her attention to the mirror, a line she'd once read in *The Bell Jar* cycling through her thoughts.

The silence depressed me. It wasn't the silence of silence. It was my own silence.

She hadn't understood what Sylvia Plath meant at the time, but now, the quote struck an uncomfortable truth.

Picking up one of the fallen pearls, she thought of the stones in Virginia Woolf's coat pocket.

Then of what Joanna had said—being surrounded by people, but always alone.

Suddenly afraid of herself, afraid of who she'd become, she dropped the pearl and turned from the vanity, frantic to get away from the woman in the mirror, and quietly fled the room.

I DON'T KNOW IF YOU'LL ever read this. I don't even know if I'll send it—or even where I'd send it, if I sent it.

Catharine paused, the tip of her pen resting against the page.

It hadn't been her intention to write. She'd only picked up the journal to give herself something to hold, instead of reaching for the whisky. But once she'd set the pen to paper, it had been impossible to stem the flood of feelings. To stop the words from flowing.

There are things I need to say.

She sat in the dark conservatory, with only the glow of the moon through the walls of glass to illuminate the pages.

In the distance, an occasional firework burst with color across the sky.

Words I should have said all along. Apologies I owe you.

She wrote with no real purpose. No defined objective. Speaking only vaguely of her failings—too many to truly measure—and then more directly of her yearning for forgiveness, even when she knew it was unmerited.

I cannot pretend to know all the ways in which I hurt you. Yet I cannot also help but hope one day you will find it in your heart to show me grace I do not deserve.

The sky lightened overhead, the dawn waking to another year. Catharine looked away, refusing to acknowledge the inevitable arrival of the future—choosing instead to remain, for however long she could, in her memories of the past.

No matter how painful.

The pen continued its transgression across the empty lines.

I have learned to accept the possibility that you hate me. And I understand if you never wish to hear from me again.

Once more, she paused, watching the frost collect on the glass, its crystals reflecting the ambient light of morning. Somewhere outside, the melodic song of a cardinal broke the stillness.

Catharine begrudged the bird its cheerfulness, unprepared to relinquish the solace of the night.

I know you may not respond. I have sat here telling myself to prepare for silence. It is all I am entitled. I do not pretend to think otherwise.

Across the street, the lights lining the walled estates flickered off one by one, the neighborhood slowly waking. Embassies. Ambassadors. High-profile politicians.

The very essence of Carlton's dream.

It almost made Catharine miss the quiet of Daufuskie. The hum of the marshlands. The empty stretch of sandy beaches.

Almost. But not really.

Because no matter which hollow house she lived in—Honour Stone, the London terrace, the plantation manor, or this unfeeling estate in Kalorama—not one of them had ever felt welcoming.

She closed her eyes and took a breath. Then picked up the pen again.

I mean it when I say my intent was to write to you without agenda or expectation. But the truth is, while I have many sorrows over the choices I have made, and my regrets are plenty, my greatest regret is this: I miss you, Nathalie. And more than anything, I miss the dearest friend I have ever known.

Catharine stared at the pages she had written. Her neat, even cursive. Every *t* crossed. Every *i* dotted. No letter out of place, no word out of margin. Yet even so, there were subtle places where the ink was smudged—blurred by tears she hadn't even realized had fallen.

She should burn the book, she knew. Ascribe it to a cathartic exercise, then toss it in the fire.

But she couldn't bring herself to do it.

Instead, she tore the pages from the journal and found an envelope in the library. Uncertain where else to send it, she wrote down the address to the *échoppe* in Bordeaux—one she knew by heart—and slipped it into the bottom of the *outgoing* tray, where Carlton's secretary would collect it before he ever opened his eyes.

Then she resigned herself to climb the stairs, returning to the bedroom where she knelt dutifully on the floor and collected every dropped pearl. But this time, when she stood and looked in the mirror, a different quote came to mind.

It was Sylvia Plath again.

I took a deep breath and listened to the old brag of my heart: I am, I am, I am.

Chapter Thirty-One

Spring in South Carolina was the season Catharine had come to find most tolerable.

The air was cool. The afternoons often rainy. Whatever hellhole the bugs had crawled into for the winter, they'd yet to reemerge. It was the closest the weather ever came to resembling the climate back in England.

Some mornings, if the chorus of tree frogs was drowned out by the rustle of wind through the palmettos, Catharine could almost pretend she was waking up in Oxford. She could convince herself her day would begin with a cup of tea at *Spires*, waiting for Nathalie to trudge—ten minutes late, as usual—through the café door.

That fantasy, of course, was always short-lived, abolished abruptly by the abrasive cry of boat-tailed grackles or the labored hum of a shrimp trawler on its way back to the mainland.

It was then that she would open her eyes, dismayed to discover she was on the desolate island, waking up next to Carlton.

Or, if she were fortunate, it would be one of the mornings he was in D.C. And she, on the rare occasion of returning from a business trip or social obligation, would find herself alone on Daufuskie—tasked with preparing the manor for his weekend arrival, where he would entertain his Lowcountry friends, and play a little political tit-for-tat on the golf course.

This mid-March morning was one such instance.

It was a Thursday. She'd flown into Savannah late the night before, returning from a week of negotiating a *WorldCargo* contract at Port Newark.

It had become one of the few satisfactions of her life—these trips away on business.

Little by little, since moving to the States, she'd taken over the entire North and South American Brooks Corp operation, and despite her father's looming presence via phone call and email, she found she enjoyed the challenge. Not to mention the escape it offered from being nothing more than the wife of a politician.

Tomorrow, Carlton would take a private charter to Hilton Head, as had become his weekly routine since beginning his term as a U.S. congressman. Tuesday through Thursday, he stayed at the Kalorama estate just a few blocks from Capitol Hill. And then every Friday, it was back to Daufuskie. Unless she had out-of-town business, Catharine was always expected to join him.

This weekend, she was not looking forward to the campaign fundraiser he had planned at the manor. Just another night of listening to clowns in suits slap one another on the back and grease each other's palms, all the while plotting the downfall of their so-called allies between cocktails.

But that had become her status quo—the future as far as she could see it. And so, ceding to the inevitability that she needed to rise and get on with her day, she flung her legs over the edge of the bed and stood, staring over the tops of the towering red maples, to where the ocean lay glittering in the distance.

Edmund, one of the young groundskeepers Carlton had hired during the estate's renovation, was coming up the drive. Every morning, rain or shine, he brought the post on his walk from the ferry landing.

For the first weeks after she had written Nathalie, Catharine would meet him in the foyer, intercepting the mail. She knew better than to set her heart on finding an envelope with her name in familiar handwriting, postmarked *Par Avion—International*, but it didn't stop her pulse from quickening every time she sorted through the pile.

Nothing arrived, however, and as the months passed, she slowly came to terms with what she'd known all along: Nathalie had no wish to hear from her. Nathalie had moved on.

BY THE FOLLOWING AFTERNOON, WHATEVER pleasantry spring promised had vanished—as had any sense of tranquility, due to Carlton's arrival.

The fog had lifted, clearing the skies, and an early heat spell settled over the Carolinas. As the guests congregated across the lawn, the men sweating through their seersucker suits, sipping rum and Coke while their wives drained glasses of mimosas, Catharine drifted from one drab conversation to another.

Had she heard Senator Chisolm's son was expelled from Duke for smoking marijuana?

Was George W. truly emerging as a frontrunner?

How could the Senate possibly acquit Clinton after he'd disrespected the Oval Office?

None of the questions ever really awaited her answer.

Because, after all, what could a young Englishwoman possibly know about American politics?

She was asked instead about Kate Moss's fashion. Could she believe HBO had really aired a TV show called *Sex and the City*? Who had made this blackberry cobbler, and would she share the recipe?

How would her husband's guests respond, she wondered, if she queried them on the conflict in Kosovo? Or asked for their thoughts on Yeltsin's failing presidency? If she pulled out a map, could a single one of them locate the Kashmir border?

The sun set, and a recital of crickets began as Carlton pontificated his disgust over the shame Clinton had brought to the White House. He stood beneath the gazebo—his collar unbuttoned, empty glass of whisky in hand, and a smear of seafood sauce on his sleeve—and championed Bush's run on *family values*.

Coming from him, a stance that was truly laughable.

How these men—supposedly educated, historically monied—could toast to this buffoon's avowal to run for Senate in the next cycle, Catharine could hardly comprehend.

She stared at the red stain on his cuff. The strain of the buttons over his gut. The bourbon-induced blotchiness of his skin. She watched his gaze travel to the daughter of the caterer—watched the young woman—younger, even, than she was—smile back at him.

Slipping deeper into the shadows, her thoughts as dull and monotonous as the song of the katydids, she tried to imagine how she could be expected to wake tomorrow morning and do this all over again.

And again.

And again.

At midnight, Catharine found Carlton passed out in his study.

Congressman Lewis and his wife had drunk too much and missed the chartered ferry back to the mainland. She was on her way from seeing them settled in one of the guest rooms when she noticed the light still on in the hall. Peeking in from the threshold, she discovered her husband sprawled out, snoring on his sofa, and almost closed the door. But as she turned, a glint of metal caught her eye.

Careful to deaden her steps across the marble floor, she slipped into the room.

She hated it in there. It was his domain. His world of ego and self-indulgence. Simply breathing its stale air filled her with a sense of trespassing.

But the ornate letter opener lying atop the surface of his disorganized desk was familiar to her—even with it out of place, where it didn't belong.

The handle was a rowing blade, the steel hammered into the shape of an oar.

Catharine could still remember Geoff's exact expression as she unwrapped it on her eighteenth birthday, the pair of them sitting on the workshop floor.

"You're asking me to marry you with a letter opener?" she'd teased, then kissed his cheek.

The last time she'd seen it had been with the things she packed home from Oxford.

She picked it up, turning the gift over in her hand.

The colonel had fired Geoff and his father, Mrs. Mills, Mrs. Ainsley and the entirety of the staff at Honour Stone. Without notice, without settlement, or even an employment reference. All at the start of the holiday season.

Abruptly, she returned the blade to the desk, forcing her thoughts in a different direction. It wasn't a memory she could bear to relive again.

Sifting through the ash-strewn legal pads and unopened briefing folders, Catharine found the Jiffy bag the letter opener had arrived in. Her mother's orderly, precise script unmistakable on the outside of the package. Inside was still a note on monogrammed stationery.

Catharine,

I am sending a few things I thought you might appreciate.

I hope you are well.

Mum

The rest of the envelope was empty.

A tightening in her chest responded to the quickening of her heart. The date on the postage was from six weeks earlier.

Making certain Carlton was still asleep, Catharine began urgently sorting through the clutter. She found another letter, and another—both from her mother. And then, finally, with shaking fingers, came across what she was seeking.

A white envelope with red and blue dashes around its border. Her name on the front was smudged, a drink ring marring the handwriting.

The sensation of joy—longing—was only temporary, as she came to the horrifying realization it had already been opened.

A sinking terror washed over her. Whatever Nathalie had said—however she had responded—Carlton was privy to her secrets, to this last little piece of her she had kept carefully guarded.

He knew…

He *knew.*

On the sofa, he stirred, falling into a fit of coughing. Catharine paused, frozen, expecting him to wake. To see her there, discovering his deceit—and then going ballistic, accusing her of intruding. But he only groaned, the heel of his grass-stained loafer dragging against the leather upholstery, and returned to snoring.

Quietly, Catharine replaced the empty package from her mother, restoring the disarray of the desk to the way she had found it, and propped the letter opener on top of the stack of folders. With only the envelope from Nathalie in hand, she crept back to the hall, and then, forgetting herself, ran for the foyer.

It was written in French.

Leaning back against the splintered wood of the dock, Catharine's relief was so immense, she wasn't sure whether to laugh or sob.

French—a language of which Carlton didn't speak a word.

She stared into the cloudless sky and thanked the blanket of stars.

Nathalie *had* written to her. Less than a month after she'd sent the letter to Bordeaux, Nathalie had responded.

Despite the uncertainty of its contents, despite her acute awareness that it would undoubtedly contain things she did not want to hear, Catharine held the envelope to her lips, inhaling the comfort of Nathalie's presence. It was Nathalie's hand that had penned the address. Nathalie's breath that had sealed it.

Catharine unfolded the pages.

She'd run, still in the dress and heels she'd worn to the fundraiser, out the front door and down to the shoreline. It hadn't felt right, reading Nathalie's words in the oppressiveness of the manor. She needed the salt, the sea, the gentle sound of the water lapping against the pilings. She didn't care that it was after midnight. She didn't care that the staff would whisper amongst themselves that their mistress was behaving poorly.

She smoothed out the first page, and with a deep breath, started reading.

The letter was long, and true to Nathalie's nature, she did not temper the grief she'd experienced, or the anger she had felt, after first receiving Catharine's message. She acknowledged her hesitation to reply, and even admitted that she had considered sending the envelope back, *return to sender* written across the front in bitter red marker.

But line by line, the words lost their edge, and a familiar warmth slowly emerged.

Nathalie wrote of her adventures in the theatre. Paris. Milan. Even Moscow.

Would Catharine believe it, she asked, in her typical wry humor, that she'd finally landed the role of Phédre. Never mind that it had been in a back-alley theatre in Prague, and the director had never paid her.

It is harder than I thought it would be, Nathalie confessed. *The first year, there were nights I went without dinner. Even pâtes au beurre was off the menu.*

Catharine read on, smiling when Nathalie described the feeling of performing at the *Théâtre de l'Odéon—C'était comme être sur un petit nuage*—it was like being on cloud nine—and laughed aloud when she detailed a costume mishap that exposed her bare bum to the audience.

Personally, I think they got lucky.

And then Catharine came to the paragraph she'd been dreading. She set the letter down and, for a little while, sought counsel in the constellations.

It wasn't as though she'd ever deceived herself into believing Nathalie would sit around and wait for her. Had she not seen it the year before in Paris? Seen the way she'd laughed with her fellow actress—the way they'd smiled, secrets exchanged without ever speaking?

But still, finding it spelled out in ink, just another anecdote of her life, had sent Catharine spinning.

She took a moment and closed her eyes, listening to the steady cadence of her heart—*I am, I am, I am*—and then forced a long exhale.

When she resurfaced again, she picked up where she left off, and beneath the Carolina moonlight, read about the Spaniard Nathalie had fallen in love with, and the life they now shared.

Numb, unblinking, Catharine refused the palliative outlet of tears. She would be happy for her friend, she scolded herself. She would be glad she'd found someone to love her the way she deserved.

At the end of the letter, Nathalie wrote that she would be coming to New York City over the summer. She'd been invited to perform in the Public Theater's Shakespeare in the Park.

It's just a small role—Maria, in Twelfth Night.

And then, at last, came the question Catharine wasn't sure how to confront:

Would you want to come?

It was written so casually.

We could get a coffee after the show.

Catharine folded the letter and let it rest in her lap.

More than three and a half years had passed.

Did she want to see Nathalie?

The answer was simple.

Yes. More than anything in the world.

But was it good for her to see her?

That question felt more complex.

And yet—gazing out over the moonlit water, Catharine came to a slow realization.

For the first time in longer than she could remember, she found she could look at the ocean and not fantasize what it would be like to sink beneath its surface—to take her final breath. For the first time since arriving on this godforsaken island, she could go to sleep tonight and not pray, by some small measure of grace, she wouldn't wake to see the sunrise.

And that was answer enough.

Chapter Thirty-Two

A LITTLE GIRL SKIPPED ATOP the rim of the fountain, her arms outstretched, jumping and twirling as if she were performing a routine on a balance beam. With every step, the tightly coiled curls of her dark hair bounced, her laughter high-pitched and infectious. A few feet away, a man—smiling the same radiant smile—followed her with the lens of a camera.

Catharine watched the pair from where she stood at the railing of the Bethesda Terrace. Beneath her, Central Park was unfolding into a balmy July evening, the golden rays of sunset reflecting the honeysuckle growing alongside the water.

The air was thick with the scent of impending rain, but pleasant, nothing like the misery of summer in South Carolina.

But Catharine couldn't focus on something as simple as the weather.

She had grown too nervous.

Just across the lake, the matinee performance of *Twelfth Night* would already be over. Nathalie would have changed out of her costume and left the Delacorte Theater. She would be walking this way, here any minute.

Unless—she wasn't.

Unless she'd had the same misgivings Catharine had faced ever since stepping on the New York City-bound airplane.

Was it possible, even now, that she was standing in her dressing room, staring at her mirror, wondering how she could cancel on

Catharine? Had she already left a message back at her hotel—*I'm sorry, but something's come up. Maybe another time?*—the same as Catharine had considered doing for the past half hour?

Or would she just not show up at all, and leave Catharine waiting?

No. Catharine felt certain, no matter what her reservations, she wouldn't do that to her.

Ever since she had read that first letter months ago, sitting on the dock in Daufuskie, they had written back and forth, almost every week. At first, the topics remained light, the correspondence brief.

Nathalie shared anecdotes from her travels with different theatre companies. Catharine wrote about the new telematics changing the transportation industry.

Would you believe we've implemented real-time GPS tracking in every vessel in the North American fleet? was what she wrote, when she wanted to say *this morning I saw a butterfly whose wings reminded me of the color of your eyes first thing in the morning.* She told her about her success branching into Vancouver and Manzanillo, unable to translate *I miss the way you used to drive me insane by putting too much sugar in your tea.*

But as spring faded and their planned summertime meeting grew nearer, the letters got longer and more sincere. Nathalie shared her concerns over her mother's health and the disappointments in her career. Catharine wrote about her loneliness. Her days surrounded by people who never really saw her.

Occasionally, Nathalie spoke of the Spaniard. Catharine did not mention Carlton.

The last letter she received had come just days earlier, sent to the private post office box Catharine had quietly opened in the name of Brooks Corp.

In it, Nathalie described her first rehearsals in New York. Her repulsion over the passengers who ate on the subway. Her fascination with the Brooklyn art scene. Catharine had laughed, flipping through each page while dipping her toes in the water from her newfound sanctuary at the end of the little jetty.

Coming to the final paragraph, however, she hesitated. A sentence had been written and then scratched out, before starting again.

There is something I need to say—before we meet. Something I hope you'll understand.

Another sentence was struck through and rewritten, the handwriting growing indecisive and halting.

I look forward to seeing you. I want you to know that. If I'm honest, since I got your letter, I've thought of little else. But, Cate, I have to tell you—it also terrifies me. Because—

More words were scribbled over, the ink so heavy they were impossible to read. Catharine did not imagine she would have wanted to, even if she could.

Nathalie continued on the next line.

I can't—we can't—ever be what we were. I can't risk going through what we once did. Not now. Not ever. There was a smudge through the word.

Catharine's breath grew forced, shallow.

You see, Cate—I wouldn't survive you a second time.

A final sentence was started and abandoned, resuming on the last page. *Promise me—even if I'm the one whose resolve is slipping— promise me you'll never let us cross that bridge again?*

There was an ink stain on the paper, as if the tip of her pen had rested in one place a long time. And then, abruptly, in hastily scrawled letters: *But I'll never stop loving you. It's important to me that you know that.*

See you next week.

Bisous Bisous,

Nat

And that was it.

Catharine did not reread that letter the way she had the others, combing over every word. Nor did she fold and unfold it so often, the paper wore through at the creases.

She read it only once and then tucked it away.

Because she did understand. Even if it hurt, Nathalie was right. It was what was best. It was the way things had to be.

But still, in the days that had passed, she'd struggled to shake off her melancholy.

And now, leaning against the balustrade of the terrace, she couldn't help but worry that she'd made a mistake. That coming here would only open wounds that had never fully healed.

She scanned the footpath leading around the lake, wondering if she might yet have time to slip into the long shadows of the park.

At the fountain, the jubilant child had stumbled and scraped her knee. A hiccupping cry rising above the constant ripple of the water brought her father sprinting to her side.

As the first scattered drops of summer rain dampened the red brick of the esplanade, the man knelt and scooped her into his arms. Gentle fingers brushed dirt and grime from her pink *Power-puff Girls* t-shirt, and whatever he whispered against her spiraled curls made the child laugh, batting away his tender concerns. A moment later, she was up on her feet, begging for a piggyback ride.

Stunned by an unexpected flood of jealousy—the bitterness of a childhood shaped in desolation and despair—Catharine spun on her heel, resolved to leave, but was at once stopped short, a tailspin of emotion freezing her in place.

There, silhouetted in the setting sun, was Nathalie.

The two of them just steps apart.

Catharine reached an unsteady hand behind her, bracing against the balustrade as she tried to find her breath.

Part of her had hoped Nathalie would be unrecognizable—that the years that had passed would have changed her, transforming her into a person she no longer knew. It had felt safer that way, thinking of her as a stranger. Praying the story of their past would feel like the unfamiliar plot of a book she'd never read.

And in some ways, the woman standing in front of her, dark eyes unblinking as she met Catharine's gaze, was no more than the whisper of a person she'd once known with every particle of her soul.

She was older, no question a woman now, the blossoms of her cheeks given way to the slenderness of time. Her hair was short, swinging in a fashionable bob just below the curve of her jaw. The lipstick she wore was no longer the dusky rose of youth, but instead a deep blush, dark enough to detract attention from the subtle smile lines at the corners of her mouth.

Yet it was more than just the physical changes. There was a cautiousness to her that had never been there before—the hint of a barbed edge lying vigilant beneath the surface of her wary regard.

But then she smiled—and in the simple twitch of lips, all of the hurt, the years, the miles, and uncertainties ebbed into the past, and she was just Nathalie Comtois again, nineteen years old, brimming with cocksure confidence—the girl who'd once assured Catharine her only destiny was *Briller sur scène*—to shine on stage.

She took a step forward.

"Coucou, Cate."

The bustling world of the summer evening in New York City faded away, disappearing into the subtlety of the familiar French accent. The playfulness of the nickname. The warmth of her tone.

Catharine hated, suddenly, that she couldn't stop herself from remembering what that voice sounded like in moonlight... in a chapel in the middle of the woods... a theatre catwalk... the wildness of the Scottish Highlands... summer nights in Rome. Memories impossible to forget—yet too dangerous to recall.

She swallowed down the well of emotion, folding it away, and left it where it belonged. To another time, a different place. If she wanted this to work, it had to stay buried amongst the thousands of words and feelings she could never relay.

"Hello, Nat." Grateful for the stone banister behind her, she leaned against it, supporting her unstable legs. "You look well."

Nathalie dismissed the formality of her greeting with a mild look of reproach, before closing the space between them, and leaning in for *la bise.*

"I'd hoped you'd grown ugly," she only half laughed, stepping back from kissing her cheeks. "*Mais hélas*—you are more beautiful than I remembered. If that is even possible." She did not give Catharine time to flush, casually hopping onto the terrace railing, heedless of the significant drop on the other side. "Did you enjoy the show?"

Catharine stared out over the top of the fountain. "I'm sorry. I—didn't go."

"I know." Nathalie followed her gaze to where the lake was still shimmering in the last golden rays of light slipping behind the skyline. The rain, little more than a mist, rippled the surface of the water, reflecting the verdant hues of lush grass and weeping willows surrounding the shore. "The girl at the box office said you never picked up your ticket." She looked at Catharine. "I didn't really expect to find you here."

Catharine chose not to tell her she almost wasn't. That had Nathalie been just a few minutes later, she would already have been gone. That this—meeting here—was probably not a good idea, after all.

Instead, she settled on glib.

"You couldn't really expect me to sit through someone else playing Viola again. It would be insufferable—listening to you go on about all the ways you could have played her better."

The jest worked, and Nathalie laughed, easing the tension radiating between them.

"Usually, I'd agree with you—but in this case, the actress playing the lead is—" she kissed the tips of her fingers, before spreading them in the air, "*parfait*. And you know I don't say that lightly." Nathalie drew one leg onto the railing, leaning dangerously over the edge. "She was nominated for an Oscar last year—in *Elizabeth*. Have you seen it?"

"I don't get to the cinema much."

"Ah." Nathalie rested her chin on her knee. "Too many political soirees?"

And there it was, the dagger between them.

It was strangely liberating, having it out in the open—a blade they both could see. Catharine hadn't been certain if Nathalie would touch the subject, or if it would just hover above them, like *Madame Guillotine*.

A prideful part of her wanted to defend the accusation. To remind Nathalie she was busy with her own work, her life did not solely revolve around her husband.

But then, that had not been the purpose of the jab. And Catharine knew she owed Nathalie more than riddles and re-direction.

"Yes," she conceded, meeting Nathalie's eye, determined to face it squarely. "That is part of it. He's a congressman now, with his eye on the senate."

"So I've read." Nathalie flicked a loose bit of stone over the railing. "And you—" she held her gaze without blinking, "—hailed in the papers as the perfect politician's wife. Everything you were born to be, *n'est-ce pas?*"

An overwhelming rush of anger spiraled from Catharine's core. Did she really have the nerve to sit there, to taunt her, to insinuate that this was what she *wanted*? That she'd ever chosen this path. This prison. This so-called life she lived. Nathalie, who knew her better than anyone.

Nathalie, who had been there. Who knew what she went through…

For a fleeting second, she entertained the vision of shoving her off the railing. Of toppling them both to the ground. Then Nathalie could have her Shakespearean ending—the star-crossed lovers, the tragic story of their intertwined lives, finally complete.

Of course, that was nothing more than fantasy.

Instead, she turned to look out over the terrace and watched the father with the little girl swing the child onto his shoulders and disappear toward the footbridge by the lake.

"I should go," she started—

"—I'm sorry," said Nathalie.

They spoke over the top of one another, the words trailing off into the thick summer evening.

"I'm sorry," Nathalie repeated, more firmly, her leg drawn to her chest. The precarious way she was perched, Catharine worried she wouldn't need her help to plunge to her death. "That was cruel. I shouldn't have said it. I just…"

There was so much in that *just* that Catharine understood; she didn't need to explain. So much hurt between them. So much trust lost, she was uncertain it could ever be regained.

"You have every right to be cruel. And I know that." Catharine leaned over the railing, brushing aside her discomfort of heights to look into the arcade below, where a cellist was setting up his instrument between one of the Romanesque arches.

"Maybe. But I don't want to be. I didn't come here for that." In an easy, graceful motion, Nathalie swung her feet to the safety of the sandstone and stood, reaching a hand for her elbow. "I came because I miss you, Cate. I miss you in my life."

The rain was falling steadily now, enough to dampen the bare skin of Catharine's neckline, the thickening humidity curling the tips of her hair. She could feel the heaviness of her heart at the base of her throat, and the contradictory weightlessness that followed, a buoyancy seeping into her limbs, alleviating a fear she hadn't even realized had been harbored there.

Nathalie *didn't* hate her. She still cared. And she was willing to make room for her in her world—somewhere.

"I've missed you, too," she managed. Though how much, Nathalie would never know.

"Have you eaten?" Already, Nathalie was pulling her away from the railing, purposely leaving the gravity of the moment behind. "I'm starving. I think the last thing I ate was a hot dog from one of those street carts yesterday afternoon." She flashed Catharine a wry smile. "I was a little anxious—thinking you were going to watch my show."

"I'm sorry I didn't go."

"Don't be." Nathalie tucked her arm through hers as they start-ed down the slippery staircase toward one of the firefly-lit tow-paths. "We run for three more weeks." Ever so slightly, she nudged her shoulder. "It just means you'll have to come again."

THE CAFÉ WAS CROWDED, THE tables along the wall-to-ceiling case-ment windows filled with diners glad to be out of the rain.

Nathalie, however, appeared to be in no such hurry, strolling backward up the steps to the glass door, animatedly explaining how the little French café had recently been used for the location of a movie, which had brought it worldwide fame.

"I'm sure I already know the answer to this, but did you see *You've Got Mail*?"

Catharine stood on the landing, staring at her blankly.

"You know," Nathalie prompted, "Meg Ryan? Tom Hanks?"

"No. Sorry." Catharine tucked a strand of damp hair behind her ear, looking forward to drying off with a glass of scotch. "Are those actors?"

She was teasing—she wasn't so far out of touch with the enter-tainment industry to not recognize the names—but enjoyed Nathalie's exasperated cry of dismay enough to continue the charade. "Someone in your cast?"

"You're as exhausting as I remembered you to be. I thought I'd made that up in my head," Nathalie huffed, holding the door for Catharine to pass inside.

The restaurant was quaint. Very *Art Nouveau*, chic and bohemian, with a Parisian vibe. Red brick walls adorned with vintage posters. Heart-shaped chairs packed around small cafe tables. A wine menu that read like an almanac from Bordeaux. In one corner, a singer crooned an old French chanson, the lyrics unintelligible over the din of patrons.

It was exactly the kind of place Nathalie loved.

Brusquely, a waitress smelling of smoke and coffee grounds jotted down their order—a Macallan 18 for Catharine, a sickly sweet-sounding moscato for Nathalie—and then bustled off behind the bar.

"For as bougie as this place is, they make surprisingly excellent *gratin dauphinois*." Nathalie fanned the menu between her fingers. "Not as good as Maman's, of course, but for New York—I can't complain." She abandoned the laminated sheet on the table and moved absently to fussing with her hair.

Catharine realized she was nervous. Despite her air of bravado and predictable swagger, Nathalie was just as uncertain as she was when it came to navigating this delicate new territory they were treading.

Afraid to let the silence linger, Catharine surged ahead with the first thing that came to mind. "I like it," she blurted, gesturing at Nathalie's stylish bob, its curl lost to the rain. "It's a good cut on you."

"Do you?" Nathalie seemed genuinely pleased, sweeping the bangs from her eyes. "Majo hates it. She said it makes me look like a French Betty Boop."

"Majo?"

"María José. She goes by Majo for short."

"Oh. Of course."

María José. Nathalie's Spanish girlfriend.

Catharine busied her hands by picking up the menu, making a show of browsing the entrees. "Well, I'd say it's got a rather *Mia Wallace* feel to it, myself. Uma Thurman couldn't have worn it better."

Nathalie laughed. "Did the impervious Cate Brooks just make a pop culture reference? I thought that was above your set?" She thumbed a cigarette from a pack in her purse, rolling the filter between her fingers.

She didn't have to say what they were both thinking. How it had been together that they'd watched *Pulp Fiction* at the Phoenix Picturehouse the autumn of their final year at Oxford. How they'd sat side by side in the dark auditorium, sneaking toes up calves, hands along thighs, pretending to keep their focus on the Tarantino blockbuster. How Catharine had rolled her eyes at Nathalie calling the film a *masterpiece* and the bizzarity of the direction *genius.*

How she had secretly loved it.

How it had been the last time she'd been to the cinema.

"And Majo?" she redirected as casually as she could muster. "Is she a fan of art? Of theatre?"

Nathalie lit the cigarette and took a long drag. "She's a playwright. It's what she lives for." She flicked the fag against a ceramic ashtray, an outline of the Eiffel Tower disappearing beneath the ash. "Though," she shrugged, a hint of admission, "she may have been a better critic than a dramatist."

Catharine left the comment where it was.

The drinks arrived and the harried waitress took their order. The decadent buttered French dish for Nathalie. A mixed green salad for Catharine.

"Splurging tonight, I see." Nathalie wagged a challenging brow as the waitress scurried away. "Is that what life is like as an American politician's showpiece? House salad—no croutons, dressing on the side?"

She was teasing. But she wasn't.

Catharine took a sip of her scotch, bristling. Thinking of the way Carlton disliked her ordering dessert. How he'd glowered at her during the last state dinner when she'd reached for a bread roll, his own plate overflowing.

"I'm not terribly hungry," she deflected.

"Ah," said Nathalie, taking another drag of her cigarette, breathing it out with a sigh.

They carried on in stilted conversation, Nathalie revealing her plans after summer—she would return to Europe, maybe audition for an autumn production in Seville—and Catharine mentioning her recently formed partnership with Emilio Herrera down in the Port of Huelva.

"Well," said Nathalie, "the next time you're in Andalucía, we'll have to get together." She snubbed out the fag. "You can meet Majo."

Catharine ordered another scotch. And then a third. The waitress left Nathalie the bottle of moscato.

Slowly, sip by cautious sip, Catharine relaxed deeper into her seat. Nathalie quit fussing with her hair and fidgeting with her earrings. Laughter came more easily. And by the time Catharine picked through her salad, and nothing remained on Nathalie's plate aside from the glisten of melted butter, they'd fallen into a series of *do you remember* and *what about that one time* reminiscences.

Amidst an amusing recollection of the time Nathalie dodged a particularly ardent admirer—*I mean, really, he looked like Mr. Bean*—by hiding in the men's loo at her first college ball, a pair of school-age girls flung themselves into empty seats two tables over, laughing gaily over their dripping hair and soaked clothes. An ID was presented, which the same flustered waitress regarded dubiously before dropping off a cheap bottle of Zinfandel.

Catharine tried to carry on the conversation, but found her attention drawn back to the couple again and again, unable to take her eyes off the hands they intertwined across the table, the way they fed each other bites of cheesecake, their heads bent close together.

"Wanna take a picture, lady? It'll last longer!" barked the taller of the two girls when she discovered Catharine's stare. The other one giggled and flipped Catharine the finger. Flushed and embarrassed, Catharine snapped her focus back to Nathalie.

"You should see your face." Nathalie's smile was wicked, the deep browns of her mahogany eyes lit by the overhead chandelier. She nudged her with a toe under the table. "The audacity of teenagers these days, huh? Falling in love—unafraid to let the world know it."

"I just—" Catharine emptied her scotch and let the joke be on her.

Judgment loosened by alcohol, she set the glass down and said, "I went to see you once. At the *Théâtre du Châtelet*."

"In Paris?" This caught Nathalie off guard. "*L'Avare*?"

"Hm." Catharine acknowledged.

"You didn't tell me?"

"It—wasn't a good idea." Catharine left out that she'd waited at the stage door. That she'd seen her with that actress. It was a moot point now.

Involuntarily, her eyes flicked back to the teenage girls, where one was pressing her lips to the palm of the other.

"Come on," said Nathalie, following her gaze, "let's go and get dessert." She pushed away from the table.

"I thought you said this café was known for its *pâtisseries*?"

Nathalie shrugged, standing. "I know another place. Just across the park."

Catharine paid the bill and averted her eyes from the sniggering teenagers as she followed Nathalie out the door.

It was still drizzling, though less so now, and when she went to hail a cab, Nathalie stopped her.

"Your hair's already a mess. Let's walk!"

"Through Central Park after dark?"

"*Cate*." Nathalie drawled out the rebuke. "Where's your sense of adventure?" They were already halfway across Amsterdam Avenue. "You were never a coward before. Cairngorms? Christ Church Meadow?" She arched her brow. "Wytham Woods?"

They were both a little tipsy. More than, even.

Afraid to look at Nathalie as they stood on the corner waiting for the light, Catharine turned her attention to a television visible through the sticker-covered window of a sports bar. Footage of the previous day's Women's World Cup final against China flashed across the screen. One of the American players was shown pulling off her jersey after winning the match, twirling it above her head on live TV.

Nathalie exhaled an amused whistle of approval.

"If more women did that," she smirked, tugging on Catharine's hand as the light turned green, "I'd pay sport a whole lot more interest."

They worked their way past the neighborhood churches and townhouses, then darted across Central Park West, Catharine cursing Nathalie for dragging her through traffic on the slippery tarmac in heels.

"You're going to get us killed."

"Maybe that's my plan?" Nathalie slowed as they hit the walking path just short of the busier transverse. "*La femme tragique*—death by New York cab."

They were both a little breathless, slipping into the quiet of the park.

A man jogged past, his Walkman bumping against his hip, a golden retriever happily loping at his side. And then the path was empty, lit only by the lights of the city skyline.

"Are you sure it's safe, Nat—"

The inquiry was cut short. Unexpectedly—or expectedly, if Catharine was honest with herself—Nathalie stopped in the middle of the pavement and wheeled around. They'd been hand-in-hand, Nathalie pulling her along, but now they were face-to-face, with no space between them.

No space to think.

No space to breathe.

No space to temper foolish longings.

And then Nathalie was kissing her.

Kissing her in a way Catharine hadn't been kissed in years.

Kissing her in a way she wanted more than anything.

A way she could never steer her thoughts from as she drifted to sleep each night. A way she'd daydreamed over dinner, watching the two girls entangle their feet under the table, hands disappearing beneath the tablecloth, met with furtive smiles.

Kissing her in a way she shouldn't.

Kissing her in a way Catharine couldn't allow.

"Nat." Gently, but firmly, Catharine dropped her hands that had gone involuntarily to the nape of Nathalie's neck, and stepped backward, out of her embrace, disengaging herself. "We can't."

They were both breathing hard.

"Majo—" Catharine started.

"—she's not you." Nathalie was leaning forward again, her eyes squeezed shut. It was a plea. A whisper. Something almost pained. "No one is you—"

Catharine could still taste the grapey sweetness of the moscato, the hint of clove from Nathalie's cigarette. Her entire body was alive with the ways she wanted her, yearning in ways she'd nearly forgotten.

But despite how badly she desired to give in—or perhaps because of it—Catharine set a splayed hand decidedly against Nathalie's chest. "We *can't*," she repeated. And then, because there was nothing else to say, she continued, "I'm married, Nat." As if that mattered to her at all. As if that were the reason.

In the flickering light of the distant cityscape, she watched Nathalie's face—watched the emotions roll across it. Desperation. Hurt. And then, just as quickly, the shift to understanding, to reason, to acceptance. She watched Nathalie swallow. Watched her compose herself.

All the while struggling through her own racing heart, trying to keep from crumbling, from recanting her refusal. From leaning forward to find her mouth again.

But she had made a promise. One she was responsible for keeping for them both.

"I'm sorry," Nathalie finally said, turning her attention to fishing out a cigarette. "It's the wine. It's got me..."

Catharine could see that her hands were shaking. She dropped the first match.

Tentatively, needing to do something, Catharine took the matchbook from her hand, lit the flame, and held it steady between them.

Still trembling, Nathalie took a long draw and then exhaled a short, sharp laugh, tilting her face up to the starless sky. She took another deep breath before looking back at Catharine, offering her the cigarette.

"I don't smoke."

Nathalie's smile turned droll. "You think I don't know that?"

Chastened, Catharine took the fag and held it to her lips. She coughed without ever inhaling, and burned the tips of her fingers on a falling fleck of ash.

"Damn it."

Nathalie laughed. "You've always made such a terrible reprobate." She slipped her arm through Catharine's, leaning heavily against her for a moment, her cheek pressed to her shoulder. The world was still, the park silent. And then, with a suppressed sigh, she gathered herself and returned to pulling Catharine down the path. "This place," she said, shrugging off the electricity coursing between them as if it were a coat that could be shed, "it's a shithole, really. They're going to give you quite a once-over—wearing those heels, that dress. But let me assure you—they make the best banana pudding you'll ever have."

Catharine let her lead her through the dark, let her chat Manhattan's cupcake craze and the frustrations of her leaky sublet flat. She listened, laughed. Until the stiffness in their strides was gone. Until the smiles no longer felt forced. Until the accidental brush of a hip no longer drew a staggered breath. Until they left the danger of the solitude of the park.

Crossing onto 5th Avenue, Nathalie steered her into a back alley toward a neon sign that bragged *open late* above a donut shop door, the little parlor wedged between Chinese food takeout and a laundromat.

She ate her custard—Nathalie wasn't wrong, it was the best she'd ever had—and willed the meringue to help her forget the taste of moscato, the warm, sweet spice of a clove cigarette.

On the walk back to The Plaza Hotel, where Catharine was staying—*slumming it as always, I see*, Nathalie teased—Nathalie tarried at the corner of Central Park South and 5th. The light turned green but she didn't walk.

"Thank you," she said, quietly, allowing the sea of Sunday night pedestrians to part around them. She kept her eyes forward, not looking at Catharine.

Catharine didn't ask what for. She knew.

Nathalie went on anyway.

"For being who you are—and knowing me so well." She stared at the stains of chewing gum littering the pavement. "Better than I know myself."

Saying nothing, Catharine laid an understanding hand on her elbow. And then the *DON'T WALK* signal was flashing amber, and Nathalie was bolting across the street before it turned red, leaving Catharine to follow.

As they stepped into the towering shadow of the iconic hotel, Nathalie paused again.

"You could come see my show next weekend?" The suggestion was casual, though Catharine could tell she was trying to dampen the hopefulness from her tone.

"I can't." Catharine worried at the zipper of her purse. "Carlton —he has a—a fundraiser in D.C. I… we…"

"It's all right." Attempting to disguise her hurt, Nathalie turned her face away from the glow of the porte-cochère lights and the porters lingering near the street. "I get it—"

"But I could come the following weekend?" Catharine quickly interrupted. She caught Nathalie's brightening gaze and met it with the arching of a lofty brow. "After all, if the actress playing Viola is as good as you say she is—"

"Better, even. You will love her, I know it." Nathalie smiled. "Her name just happens to be Cate."

"Well," Catharine leaned forward, alleviated, finally, of the last strains of awkwardness that had persisted between them, and kissed Nathalie's cheeks. "Then how could I possibly miss it?" She made to go, then paused, looking over her shoulder. "But rumor has it the actress playing *Maria* is the one to keep your eye on." She smiled at Nathalie—not the first genuine smile of the evening, but the first one that felt unfaltering, the first one that felt complete. And as she turned away, slipping past the liveried doorman, she felt, after four long, nearly unbearable years, like she could finally breathe.

Chapter Thirty-Three

TWO WEEKS LATER, CATHARINE RETURNED to New York.

The Friday night in the city to watch Nathalie perform at the Delacorte turned into a long weekend. A single, clipped call to Carlton—*sorry, but the negotiations with Port Authority are dragging on.*

Followed by another, to attend the closing of Nathalie's show. And then, before summer was over, before Nathalie returned to Europe, a third.

It turned into chapped lips and salt-tinged skin on a ferry to Ellis Island. Whispered critique of the Kandinskys hanging at The Guggenheim. Laughter climbing all 354 steps to reach the Statue of Liberty's crown. A photo on a disposable camera—heads pressed together, the thick, briny wind racing up The Narrows whipping hair across their cheeks and eyes.

"You sure Majo's going to let you keep that one?" Catharine couldn't help but rib when Nathalie picked up the film from a 1-hour photo lab.

"Don't flatter yourself—I'll probably use it as a coaster," Nathalie returned, tucking the photo between the pages of the novel she was reading.

It turned into a tearful goodbye outside the international departures terminal at LaGuardia.

Postcards from Paris. Seville. Milan.

Late-night phone calls in empty hotel rooms. Letters surreptitiously opened while entertaining senators, governors, supreme court justices in Carlton's growing collection of homes.

Seasons changed.

Life went on.

Catharine listened sympathetically to Nathalie's heartache when Majo decided her 'energy' aligned better with a violinist from Moscow.

Nathalie flew into a string of expletives when Catharine confessed to paying off tabloids threatening to leak Carlton's affairs.

Y2K came and went without apocalyptic downfall.

The dot-com bubble burst. The NASDAQ fell.

Following the tragedy of *9/11*, the introduction of the Department of Homeland Security reshaped the entirety of the shipping industry. Catharine revised and adapted while many of Brooks Corp's rivals sank.

Somewhere in Alaska, a seaplane crashed into the Blying Sound, killing famed architect Alexander Grey and his wife, Martha.

Carlton won reelection to a second term in the House of Representatives. And then a third.

Across the globe, Nathalie went through what felt like an endless procession of lovers—from a prima ballerina to an Austrian opera diva, a Ralph Lauren model, and one of IBM's only female engineers. Over layover coffees and Sunday evening nightcaps, *tête-à-têtes* in Paris, and last-minute breakfasts when travel schedules allowed, Catharine listened patiently and counseled her through them all. It became an art, the way she learned to drown any hint of jealousy behind another finger of whisky and a practiced smile.

In the corporate world, the economic landscape was changing. With the evolution of technology, a new digital age emerged. Aware of his limitations, Colonel Brooks determined his empire would benefit from being led by a younger generation. So, without pomp or circumstance, or even so much as a phone call, the elder Brooks stepped aside and named Catharine CEO of WorldCargo.

Two years later, she found herself on the cover of *Fortune's* special edition, *30 Leaders Under 30.*

The headline: *Congressman's Wife Becomes Youngest Woman to Captain Billion Dollar Enterprise.*

"As if that imbecile has anything to do with it," Nathalie seethed, flinging the magazine into the bin on one of her first visits to Daufuskie. To that point, she'd met Carlton only twice, and likened him to an orangutan—then reconsidered, stating the comparison was an insult to apes everywhere.

"It's the twenty-first century, Cate," was her constant refrain—on the phone, in person, even in letters. "He doesn't own you."

She vehemently insisted Catharine learn to tell him no.

No, she couldn't drop everything and entertain his friends on a whim.

No, he couldn't buy another house, another car, another Rolex or golf club membership on her credit, her dime.

No, she didn't want to have sex with him.

It's not as easy as you make it sound, Catharine defended.

It would be, if you had a backbone, Nathalie would argue.

Then they'd give each other the cold shoulder for a few days, until one of them gave in and called the other.

And life would resume.

In a landslide victory, Carlton won a seat in the U.S. Senate. *The Washington Times* called him a meteoric talent—*the Son of the South.* The incumbent he had beaten called him a *Christian fraud* and *grandstanding scoundrel.*

Martha Stewart was sent to federal prison.

Vladimir Putin was reelected.

A catastrophic earthquake rocked the Indian Ocean, resulting in a Boxing Day Tsunami killing more than 225,000.

On his sixtieth birthday, true to his word, Colonel Brooks signed over forty-nine percent of Brooks Corp to Catharine, landing her on *Forbes'* list of *World's Billionaires.*

Nathalie begrudgingly humored her agent and spent months auditioning for the role of *Gabrielle* in an upcoming TV show called

Desperate Housewives. To the horror of her manager, when she was invited for a final screen test, she turned the callback down. She told him her heart belonged to the theatre, and she didn't want to lose sight of who she was as an artist. Subsequently, she was dropped by her agent and ended up spending the next two years performing in a non-Equity regional dinner theatre in Florida.

Catharine turned thirty.

Carlton was accused of sexual harassment by a junior aide. In a press conference, he recited *Proverbs 19:5: A false witness will not go unpunished, and whoever pours out lies will not go free.* He followed up the subtle threat by calling the young woman *unstable, disgruntled, and attention-seeking.*

The media took his side.

Back in Daufuskie, Catharine pointedly had her belongings moved from their shared bedroom to a different wing. When Carlton made the discovery, he shattered a Lalique crystal vase against a Boulle cabinet.

You think you can just do whatever the hell you please? he roared, half a bottle deep in a Macallan 19. *You are still my wife, God damnit!*

As if it were something she could ever forget.

However, despite his outrage, he also needed her to sign a check to pay off the outcome of his latest poor investment. An ill-timed necessity that forced him to concede.

"Good!" Nathalie praised her on the phone that night. "Now go and do the same thing in D.C."

Pope John Paul II died.

Saddam Hussein was executed.

Tony Blair resigned.

In a monumental election, Barack Obama became the first Black president of the United States. Catharine clung to a modicum of hope that the result might give Carlton an aneurysm. No such fortune was to be had.

Late one evening, Nathalie called. "Cate!" Her voice was percolating with excitement. "Have you seen the news? California legalized gay marriage!"

Times were changing. Society evolving. But Catharine felt like she was standing still.

Which was why, after negotiating a thirty-year lease on the Oakland International Container Terminal—the most lucrative contract of her career—she took a decisive step forward and purchased a waterfront home in San Francisco Bay, solely in her name.

Carlton was too busy attempting to evade an insider trading and ethics violation to care.

With three thousand miles between them, for the first time in her fourteen years of marriage, Catharine had something that was *hers*, and hers alone.

Away from the humidity and isolation of Daufuskie, free of the political circus in D.C., she swung open the door of her new bay front home and felt the quiet thrill of possibility.

"I should've known better when you said you 'bought a little place,'" Nathalie razzed as Catharine showed her from room to room.

She'd picked up the keys only that morning, leaving her suitcase in her regular suite at the Fairmont Hotel. If she wanted a change of clothes for the evening, she'd have to arrange to have it sent over by the concierge.

Running a finger along the glass railing, Nathalie followed her up the floating set of stairs.

"Kind of like how the 'quaint flat' you bought in London turned out to be a penthouse overlooking Tower Bridge. I think I've stayed in that one more than you have. Remind me: how many times have you actually been there?"

"This is different," Catharine disputed, continuing from the third floor toward the rooftop. "I want to make this a home. To have a life here."

"Hm." The sound was small, disbelieving. "And does your husband know that?"

"Nat, please." Catharine turned on the landing. "Don't be testy. I'm sorry I missed your show. You know if I could have been there, I would have."

It was no surprise she was still cross with her. The previous weekend, Catharine had been forced to cancel her plans to see her in a one-night-only run of *The Laramie Project* at the Geffen Playhouse in LA. It had been a fundraiser for *The Trevor Project*, a cause Nathalie had been immensely proud to support. But as per usual, Carlton had gotten in the way.

Had it been a work conflict or a travel dilemma—*any* other obligation—Nathalie would have been more forgiving.

But when it came to her husband, the subject forever remained a sore spot between them.

"Oh, it's fine," Nathalie waved a flippant hand, her tone suggesting it was anything but fine, "I'm sure dinner with the Governor of Alabama was riveting."

"Kentucky," Catharine corrected. "And no, if it makes you feel better, the entire night was dreadful. He's a seventy-something bald lecher who smells like decay and whose eyes never ventured from my décolletage. But that's neither here nor there. The point is: it wasn't something I could get out of, and I'm sorry I disappointed you."

"I—" Whatever Nathalie's response would have been was cut short as she stepped off the last stair and into the sunlight, the view of the Golden Gate glittering through the glass balcony. "*Waouh.*" Her eyes scanned the horizon.

Across the waterfront boulevard, the San Francisco Bay Trail paralleled the marina, the scattered masts of sailboats bobbing in the breeze. At the edge of the harbor, Saint Francis Yacht Club sat between the Golden Gate Promenade and the Marina District Lighthouse. Beyond that, the shimmering blue of the bay. And then there was Angel Island. Tiburon. Sausalito. The beauty of the northern California coast stretching out as far as one could see.

"It's—stunning," Nathalie conceded, strolling to the glass balustrade. She leaned over, watching joggers on the trail. Kids playing football. Dogs loping along the beach.

It was the location that had drawn Catharine to the coastal modern residence.

Yes, she had appreciated its contemporary architecture, its soaring ceilings and walls of glass that invited a wealth of natural light. The open-concept layout had been ideal. Everything about the house a contrast to the antiquated dreariness of Cleveland Manor.

But it was the view that had sold her. The promise of sunsets beneath the Golden Gate. Sunrises above Bay Bridge. The shadowy shape of Alcatraz rising silent out of midnight waters. The solacing sight of cargo ships rolling through the fog.

She clung to the hope that the Pacific would give her something the Atlantic had never offered.

"May I presume it receives your seal of approval, then?"

"It's beautiful." Nathalie pushed away from the balcony, turning back to Catharine with a tsk. "I never expected less. I only hope you mean what you said—about making a life here. That this won't end up just four more walls and another empty space." She leaned back against the glass. "Because, try as you might, you can't buy what you're looking for, Cate. All the money in the world won't bring you happiness."

"You think I don't know that?" Catharine snapped, unable to curb her defensiveness. "You think I—" She cut herself short, exhaling a long sigh, her attention drifting to the water.

Nathalie's concern wasn't unfounded.

It was just—for once, this place felt like it could be different. Standing at the railing overlooking the pewter sheen of the Pacific, it seemed as though some new chapter of her life was waiting to unfold.

But there was no way to say that without sounding ridiculous, and Nathalie was not in a mood to be convinced, as it was. So she kept the thought to herself.

"I know, Nat." She said instead, turning from the view. "I know."

On their way down from the rooftop, Catharine stopped in the sitting room, where a wall of windows led to another balcony, another sweeping panorama of the Bay.

"I realize it's a bit sparse on furnishings," she said, scanning the few pieces of furniture she'd negotiated from the previous owner —a Minotti settee resting beneath a charcoal and pencil Matisse, a Tompion grandfather clock ticking steadily beside the fireplace, a hand-carved cherry wood coffee table perched atop a Joseph Carini rug. On the balcony, a pair of rattan lounge chairs bade a silent invitation to sit and watch the sunset. Catharine gave a subtle nod in their direction. "But I thought perhaps you might stay the night? We could order in—play *Quatorze*. Or *Piquet*, even, if you'd rather?"

She wasn't sure why she was nervous to ask. Nathalie was almost always amenable to late-night card games. Take-out dinners, the leftovers eaten for breakfast. Over the past ten years, they'd spent many such nights together.

But tonight, it just mattered more to Catharine.

Not because it was her birthday—a day she'd deliberately dismissed for so long, she wasn't certain Nathalie even remembered—but because, for whatever the reason, she was feeling lonelier than usual. She craved Nathalie's amity. The warmth she would bring to this empty, unfamiliar space. She didn't want to spend the first night sitting on the balcony alone.

"I can't." Nathalie was still standing in the hallway. "Not tonight. I'm sorry."

"Oh." The word came out dull, disheartened, conveying more of her disappointment than she'd meant to let on. She hadn't expected her to say no.

"I'm having dinner with that artist I told you about. The one with the studio in SoMa."

"Ah." Catharine stared at the Matisse hanging on the wall. She decided she hated it. "Yes—the ceramist."

"Potter."

"Is there a difference?"

Nathalie's smile was honed. "You know there is." She remained in the threshold. "Will you be all right?" Her expression softened. "You seem low."

"Of course. Don't be silly." Catharine looked around, searching for something to do. There was nothing. "I've plenty to keep me busy."

Nathalie regarded her too long.

"You should go." Catharine brushed her off. "It's Friday night—traffic will be miserable."

"How long will you be on the West Coast?"

"I'm not sure—" she began, but was interrupted by the jarring ring of her mobile.

True as ever to his knack for trespassing across her life—no matter how many miles she put between them—it was Carlton.

She didn't have to answer to know what he wanted.

Tomorrow was their anniversary. Fourteen long, taxing years. He'd be calling to demand she return to D.C. He'd expect her to join him at one of the gaudy rooftop bars he liked to frequent. Parade her around like a show pony on display. Call the press, tip them off to the outing. Remind everyone of their idyllic marriage, the perfect couple—the South's favorite son, and his highborn English prize.

She sent the call to voicemail.

"I'm not sure."

Nathalie leaned against the wall, inadvertently bumping the digital display to ignite the fireplace, then turning it off again. "We could get breakfast tomorrow?"

"If you're awake for breakfast, I imagine the date with your ceramist didn't go as planned." Catharine busied herself toying with the remote that changed the tint of the windows overlooking the street. A press of a button and the view disappeared.

"It's just dinner."

"Mm." Catharine pressed the button again. The Golden Gate returned. "I know you better than that."

"Cate—"

Catharine's phone rang a second time, Carlton's name flashing on the screen.

"Christ." She double-clicked *end*. Immediately, he rang again. She dropped the remote onto the coffee table. "I've got to take this. Ring me tomorrow, then?"

Nathalie paused a long second, having something else to say, but Catharine, bitter with the evening, turned away.

"Hello, Carlton."

"*Catharine.*" His tone was scolding. "I've been trying to reach you."

By the time she hung up, it was dark, and Nathalie was gone.

A MUTED CREAK PULLED HER from her sleep.

Dazed and disoriented, Catharine opened her eyes, slowly adjusting to the shadows of the unfamiliar room. She gathered her bearings: the dove-gray walls. The clean lines and architectural minimalism. The Matisse.

Glancing at the time, she found it was earlier than she expected. Before dozing off, the bells of the longcase clock beside the fireplace had struck nine. Now, it was little more than a quarter after. It was just the darkness of the October evening, the chill seeping in from the bay that made it seem so late.

She blinked away the remaining lassitude of sleep and listened to the silence of the house.

Nothing was amiss. Whatever had woken her must have been part of a dream.

Her neck ached as she sat up on the settee. She'd drifted off in an uncomfortable position, too wrapped up in her emails to notice when the sun had set behind the bridge. She was cold. Tired. Stiff. In her discontent of the evening, she'd forgotten to have her luggage delivered from the hotel.

It hardly mattered. She'd caved to Carlton's demand—his insistence that she make a showing in D.C. for their anniversary. She would fly into Reagan early the following afternoon. Back to cocktail parties that dragged on for hours. Men in ill-fitting suits and their simpering wives. Small talk that threatened to drive her out of her mind.

I only hope you mean what you said—about making a life here.

Nathalie's presentiment hung in the stillness of the room.

That this won't end up just four more walls and another empty space.

Catharine stared at her stark surroundings, the transparent walls only an illusion of the freedom she was craving.

Because even made of glass, her reality remained—she was still imprisoned by walls.

Partitions. Barriers. Barricades. Palisades.

By any other name…

Call them what she might, it didn't reassemble the truth: these were just walls with a view. A view which meant nothing when there was no one to share it. No one to appreciate the brilliance of the bay. Three hundred sixty degrees of panoramic beauty, yet the story of her life stayed the same.

"You really should lock your doors, you know?"

Catharine's heart somersaulted, her surprise accentuated by a half-stifled scream.

Nathalie stood at the top of the stairway, backlit by the light in the hall. She was holding a bag, shrugging out of the leather jacket she'd been wearing.

"You've developed bad habits living on that God-forsaken island. I could have been anyone, strolling in here."

"Jesus, Nat!" Her heart was still hammering against her ribcage. "What are you doing?" She checked the clock again to see if she'd misread the hour. "You're supposed to be at dinner."

Nathalie gave a dismissive wave, kicking off her shoes. "I'm not really that much into pottery, to be honest. The artists aren't all they're cracked up to be." She glanced at Catharine, waiting to see if she'd caught the joke, and was rewarded with a roll of her eyes.

"Besides," she padded barefoot across the Carini carpet, "I had a craving for *gâteau au yaourt*—which, I must say, for a city full of immigrants, was not easy to find." She dropped two bags on the coffee table. One, a generic takeaway type that smelled like egg rolls. The other, a brown paper sack that read *La Boulange*.

Catharine stared a long moment at the latter.

Gâteau au yaourt. Nathalie's favorite birthday cake.

She'd not forgotten, then. Even if it wasn't a topic between them, even if, for more than a decade, Catharine had refused to acknowledge the day—Nathalie remembered.

And she was here, as she always was, when Catharine needed her most.

Even when it was least deserved.

Thank you, was what she wanted to say. What came out was: "I don't think I have any plates."

"Or napkins," said Nathalie, pulling a kitchen roll from the shopping bag. "Or utensils." Out came a pair of plastic forks. "Or drinks." She produced a pint of convenience store whiskey.

"I—don't suppose you might have a deck of cards in that Mary Poppins bag?"

"You invited me for a game of *Piquet* and don't even have cards?" Nathalie feigned exasperation. "What kind of hostess are you?"

"A terrible one."

"*Mais oui !*" Rummaging beneath the Chinese take-out containers, she dropped two packs of playing cards on the table. They were the souvenir ones sold at the tourist shops on every corner. *I Heart SF* on one box, the Hyde Street Cable Cars on the other.

"Fortunately—" Nathalie bumped her with her hip, forcing her to make room so she could take a seat beside her, "—I know you well. And still love you anyway." She snatched up one of the packs, shaking the cards onto the table. "Faults and all."

Surprised to find tears threatening to gather behind her eyes, Catharine distracted herself by beginning to sort the deck, eliminating all the numbers below seven, but Nathalie stopped her.

"Let's play *La Bataille Corse*. *Piquet* is too proper."

Catharine huffed. It was a children's game, similar to *Beggar My Neighbor*, only with the added chaotic element requiring players to slap the deck to win the pile. There was no strategy, no tactics—only luck and reflexes. She and Nathalie had often played it at Oxford, sipping whisky on the floor of Nathalie's Brasenose room, using it as an excuse to put their hands on each other.

It wasn't a game suited for the waterfront house with its million-dollar view, too tactile and abrasive on the artisan-crafted coffee table.

Which was what made the fun of it, the silliness of it, absolutely perfect. Even if she refused to admit it.

"You just know I play a better game of *Piquet* than you do," Catharine quipped, already beginning to deal for *La Bataille Corse*.

"Only because you cheat by counting the cards." Nathalie broke open the screw-top whiskey, taking a sip before passing it to Catharine. "At this, however, you don't stand a chance against me."

"Oh, please." Putting on a show of disdain, Catharine tossed Nathalie her hand, secretly delighted. "*Piquet, Quatorze, La Bataille Corse*—I can beat you at them all."

"In your dreams." Nathalie flipped the first card over.

Catharine laid down a king.

And somewhere, between bites of chicken fried rice and vegetable egg rolls, greasy fingertips and cheap whiskey sipped straight from the bottle, she found herself laughing more than she had in longer than she could remember. Laughing until her sides ached. Laughing while her palms stung from swatting at a King of Spades, a three of clubs, a Jack of Diamonds with an unexceptional photo of the Bay Bridge on its cover. Laughing until she forgot her loneliness. Her regrets. The things she would change, if ever given the chance to do life over.

Nathalie was the catalyst, of course, the axis who, since the day they'd met, had held her together.

Nathalie, whose effervescence filled the emptiness surrounding her. Nathalie, who lifted her melancholy with her sharp-witted humor. Nathalie, who brought a light-heartedness that made simply breathing feel easier.

Her friendship was invaluable. Having someone who knew her as well as she did, who truly understood her. Someone who could share a glance, a gesture, the infinitesimal hint of a smile, and know an entire language could pass between them without so much as a whisper.

The realization brought an unexpected sense of peace. A brighter outlook for the future.

It was after midnight by the time she conceded her loss, four rounds to two, and tossed her few remaining cards into Nathalie's growing pile.

"Fine, you win—but not because you weren't cheating." She was a little drunk—drunk enough not to care about the sweet and sour stain on her imported carpet—and perfectly, repletely happy.

"Was not." Nathalie put no real effort into the denial.

"You've been pilfering court cards."

"I'll only own to it if you can tell me which ones."

"King of Diamonds."

Nathalie humphed, kicking her feet up onto the coffee table. "Fine." From beneath her thigh, she flicked the king into the pile.

"Jack of Spades."

"Okay." The jack joined the others.

"Ace of Clubs."

"And?" Prompted Nathalie, waiting.

"Was there another?"

"You've gotten slow in your old age." Nathalie thumbed a fourth card from between the settee cushions. She held it up, the suit concealed from Catharine. "Most valuable card in the deck."

"Ace of Spades, then."

Nathalie sighed. "Oh, how I pity your poor, analytical soul." She used the corner of the card to flick a grain of fried rice onto the floor. "It's the Queen of Hearts. I don't care what your maths say—it trumps all others."

"Oh, honestly," Catharine scoffed, swiping the card. "That's only for the artists and fools."

To her surprise, Nathalie gave no sharp retort. Rather, she looked taken aback. Hurt, even.

"I know you don't actually believe that."

Her earnestness stilled Catharine. She stared at the card in her hand.

Nathalie was right. She didn't believe that. She still believed in love. But she'd come to accept that sometimes love changed. That what started as a flame—impassioned, all-consuming—could rekindle, transforming into something new. It could grow stable, collected, evolving into the steady glow of friendship, the smolder of mutual respect, an ember that no longer ignited an inferno of desire, but instead brought with it something calmer, more dependable. A simmer of affinity. A slow burn of gratitude. Neither better—just different.

That was the love she believed in.

Any longer, that was the only love she knew.

But how could she explain that to someone like Nathalie? Someone who wore their heart on their sleeve. Someone who could fall in love so freely.

So instead, she deflected, dismissing her sincerity. "As I said: artists and fools." She tossed the card onto the table, where it disappeared amidst the pile. "Now, onto more important matters—where is this *gâteau au yaourt*?"

Frustrated with Catharine's brevity, Nathalie didn't smile. "I'm serious, Cate."

"As am I. You promised me cake." Catharine swiped up the brown paper bag from *La Boulange*. Inside, she found the wrapped dessert, along with a newspaper—the *San Francisco Chronicle*—turned to the business section.

"I forgot to tell you—you made the paper," said Nathalie dryly, unmoving from her place on the settee. "Well, the wife of Carlton Cleveland did, at least."

Catharine scanned the caption at the top of the page.

Cleveland's Influence Extends West: Senator's Wife Locks in Oakland Port Lease.

She let it flutter to the floor.

Outside, the white light of Alcatraz flashed through the window, the only color to disrupt the blackness of the bay.

It was so utterly predictable—all of her hard work, reduced to a nameless mention, no more than an extension of her husband in a headline.

Nathalie gestured at the paper. "You do know you're more than this, right?" she said, forever reading her mind. Her sarcasm had dwindled, her expression growing solemn.

"More than what?" Catharine bristled, opposed to the direction the conversation had turned. "Poor journalism?"

"You know what I mean." Nathalie caught her arm before she could twist away. "You can't continue like this forever. You deserve more than *that*—" she flicked the paper with her foot. "More than *him*." She waved toward where her mobile lay face up on the table, seven missed calls from Carlton illuminating the screen. "This isn't who you are—!"

"God, just stop, will you?" Catharine jerked her arm free. "Quit pretending I'm someone different than I am. I'm never going to be who you want me to be." She turned away. It felt all too reminiscent of another day, another fight, more than half her life ago. Seventeen, young and foolish, on the bank of the Thames...

She stared out the window through the fog, where the beacon on the lighthouse continued to pulse its relentless warning.

How was it possible that so much time had passed, yet nothing had changed?

But then, that was hardly Nathalie's fault. Of all people, she was the last person to deserve her wrath. Not a single failure in her life had stemmed from Nathalie's doing.

She had only herself to blame.

"I'm sorry." Catharine exhaled a shaky breath, swallowing back the acerbity of her tone. "You're right." Her shoulders sank, the enjoyment of the evening dissipating. In less than twelve hours, she would be on a plane headed east. A whirlwind trip to star in Carlton's dog and pony show, and then back to Oakland early Monday.

She dropped her gaze to the pile of cards, the Queen of Hearts hidden underneath. Nathalie wasn't wrong. She couldn't go on like this indefinitely.

Risking a fleeting glance, she met Nathalie's eye, contrite. "I just —wouldn't even know where to begin."

Nathalie had no such reservations. "You can start by telling him you're not flying to D.C. in the morning. It's ridiculous, the bullshit he puts you through, knowing how much you've got going on."

"It's our anniversary—"

"He doesn't care about your damned anniversary, Cate! He just likes to watch you leap every time he snaps his fingers."

"Nat—" Catharine began, ready to dismiss her. "I can't—"

"Yes, you *can!*" Nathalie interrupted, snatching her mobile from the table. "For once, just listen to me: Call his office and leave a message. You have work here. Your own obligations. You can't continue to allow him to dictate your every breath."

Catharine wanted to laugh. If she didn't turn up in Kalorama tomorrow, Carlton would lose his mind.

But she didn't laugh.

Instead, she stared at the disparaging headline.

Senator's Wife Locks in Oakland Port Lease.

As if she didn't even have a name.

Following her train of thought, Nathalie set a gentle hand on her knee. "I know it's not easy, Cate, or as simple as I make it out to be. But you have to start somewhere." She held out the phone, an offering. "You owe this to yourself. Please—call him and tell him no. It may not change things overnight, but it's as good a place to start as any."

Haltingly, Catharine took the mobile, turning it over in her palm. She thought of what Carlton would say in the morning. The threats that would follow. How he would accuse her of being selfish, manipulative, out to "sink" his career.

But she also thought of all the ways she'd yielded to his every whim, sacrificed her own responsibilities to serve at his beck and call, bent to his will for years and years.

How he'd never once supported her. Respected her. Valued her.

How she knew he never would.

She dragged her finger across the screen, scrolling to C.

Maybe, at last, she was ready. Maybe here, in this new house, on this new coast, she could find a piece of herself again and begin to build a different life.

Glancing up, she caught Nathalie's steady gaze. She wondered briefly if she knew what she meant to her—if she had any idea that she was the reason she'd survived this last decade.

Predictably unfazed, Nathalie only gestured impatiently at the phone before sweeping up the wrinkled paper and turning it into an impromptu plate for their yogurt cake. "*Vas-y*, Cate."

Out on the bay, a cargo ship blared its horn, its mountainous silhouette gliding through the fog-covered shipping lane.

Catharine drew in a deep breath of sea-scented air, then tapped Carlton's name and listened to it ring.

Nathalie was right.

It was time.

Time to discover who she was as Catharine—and only Catharine. No longer reduced to the colonel's daughter. No longer just the senator's wife.

Journal Excerpt, Nathalie Comtois
Bordeaux, France

Something's up with Cate.
I'm not sure what, but she's been acting strange.
She filed for divorce from that neanderthal—finally!—yet she
won't say why, now, after 23 years.
I'll admit, part of me almost wonders if she's having an affair.
One could only hope. (God, if so, please let it be a woman)!
It would just be so unlike her…
Anyway, I'm determined to get to the bottom of it, so I've
decided to fly to California to surprise her for Christmas.
She may think she can keep a secret, but we both know
she's never been able to hide much from me for long.

Glossary

Backbencher — A Member of Parliament who is not part of the government or shadow cabinet; a rank-and-file MP.

Battels — Termly charges billed by an Oxford college (food, accommodation, etc.).

Bevvies — Drinks, typically alcoholic.

Bluestocking — An intelligent, studious woman; historically used patronisingly.

Bop — A "Big Organized (or Open) Party" college-based and often themed, held for Oxford students.

Bow Seat — The rower seated closest to the front (bow) of the boat; sets technical precision.

Brasenose — One of the colleges of the University of Oxford, known for its friendly ethos and central location.

Christ Church — One of the largest and most prestigious colleges of the University of Oxford.

Come up — To arrive at university at the start of term.

Coxswain (Cox) — The person who steers the boat and directs the rowers.

Degree conferral — The ceremony in which a university formally awards a degree.

DPhil — Oxford's term for a PhD (Doctor of Philosophy).

Échoppe bordelaise — A small 19th-century Bordeaux townhouse with a stone façade and long, narrow rooms.

Eights — Eight-oared rowing boats.

Fresher — A first-year university student.

Froggie — Mild slang for a French person (informal, teasing, rude connotation).

Go down — To leave university at the end of term (or permanently).

Gyp room — A small student kitchen or kitchenette in an Oxford college.

Hall — The college dining hall where meals are served.

Hilary Term — The spring term at Oxford (January–March).

Hoardings — Temporary wooden barriers or billboards around construction sites.

JCR (Junior Common Room) — The undergraduate student body of a college; also the physical common room.

Kickabout — A casual, informal football game.

Marquee — A large event tent used for outdoor gatherings.

Matriculate — To be formally admitted as a member of the university.

Michaelmas Term — The autumn term at Oxford (October–December).

Noughth Week (0th Week) — The week before term officially begins; used for arrivals and orientation.

Œnophile — A lover or connoisseur of wine.

On tenterhooks — To be anxiously waiting; in suspense.

"On the High" (on High Street) — A reference to Oxford's central High Street.

Pidge / Pigeonhole — A student's personal mail slot in the college lodge.

Pièce noire — The "black room" of a Bordeaux échoppe; a windowless, interior room.

Plodge (Porters' Lodge) — The staffed entrance of an Oxford college handling mail, security, and enquiries.

Rad Cam — Nickname for the Radcliffe Camera, an iconic Oxford library building.

Reading — An academic subject studied at university (e.g., "She is reading English at Oxford").

Red brick education — Attending one of the civic universities founded in the 19th–20th centuries (as opposed to Oxford or Cambridge).

Reader in English — A senior academic rank roughly equivalent to an associate professor.

Rusticated — Temporarily suspended from the university.

Sent down — Permanently expelled from university.

Single Sculls — A one-person rowing boat propelled with two oars.

Sitting collections — College exams sat under formal conditions, usually at the start of term, testing work from the previous term or vacation reading.

Staircase — A set of student rooms arranged around a shared stairwell; the basic residential unit in Oxford colleges.

Stalls — The downstairs seating area of a theatre, closest to the stage (orchestra seating in the States).

Stroke Seat — The rower who sits at the stern and sets the rhythm for the crew.

The Long Vac (Long Vacation) — Oxford's summer break (June–October).

The RSC — The Royal Shakespeare Company.

Tures — Narrow, twisting lanes or alleys, particularly associated with the Cotswolds town of Stow-on-the-Wold.

Trinity Term — Oxford's summer term (April–June).

Vac Res (Vacation Residence) — Permission for students to stay in college accommodation during university holidays.

Yobs — Rowdy, disruptive young men; hooligans.

ACKNOWLEDGMENTS

There are an endless number of people I need to thank, but none more so than my wife.

Donna, these books would simply never happen without you. You are the backbone to this little universe we have created. My inspiration. My muse. I love you impossibly much. And I will never be able to truly express how grateful I am for you.

To the incredible number of friends I have met through the world of Catharine Cleveland—Cate Brooks, in this case—how lucky am I?

Alaina, thank you for always being up for a literary chat, and freely sharing sound advice. Oh, and for keeping me up-to-date on the latest turkey and skunk shenanigans.

Erika—you're the first person I text when I need a straight and thoughtful answer. I value your opinion, but even more so, your friendship. Not to mention, your exquisite taste in film and theatre.

Sharon, thanks for slogging through my first draft! And letting me drag you miles and miles across New York City on the excuse of "research." And not snoring. A+ friendship.

Jess B—whenever I see your name pop up on my notifications, I know I'm in for a laugh (in the best way… just to be clear). You've championed these books since day one, and are essentially my one-woman marketing team—of which I am wildly grateful. I'm pretty sure you should own stock in Brooks Corp at this point. Thanks for our middle-of-the-night texts, sharing in my anxieties (takes one to know one), and eye-rolling equestrian nonsense.

Véro, you continue to come to my rescue and never laugh at me for my terrible French. Thank you for always saving me from massacring your language and preventing an untold number of faux pas.

Abby—thank you for continuing to bring these characters to life! Your talent is truly a gift.

Mahfuz, thank you for another beautiful cover and your attention to detail. Can't wait for the next one!

Alicia, Charlie, Jules, Jamie, Callie, Jody, Robbie, Mikall, Jade, Caz, Jess, Shawnee, Jesse (the list could go on and on)… the support you've shown me over this whole authoring journey never ceases to amaze me. Thank you, friends. From the bottom of my heart.

Mom—it means so much to me that you are always the first person who can't wait to read my latest work. And Dad—thank you for understanding how crazy I get the closer it gets to publishing day, and for being willing to watch your football games on silent. Love you both!

And lastly—Piper, Josey, Daisy, Brooklyn, MILF, and Ddraig—my little late-night walk champions and early morning snuggling companions—you make life chaotic and hilarious, and I wouldn't want it any other way.

XOXO,

Jen

COMING SOON BY JEN LYON

Duplicity: The Senator's Wife Book IV
Fade In, Fade Out: Sequel to The Unfinished Line
Curse of Queens Trilogy
Let Them Burn

OTHER BOOKS BY JEN LYON

The Senator's Wife: Book I
Caught Sleeping: The Senator's Wife Book II
Whistleblower: The Senator's Wife Book III
*The Unfinished Line**

**winner of the 2025 GCLS Ann Bannon Popular Choice Award—Gold*

ABOUT THE AUTHOR

Jen Lyon is an avid lover of sports, travel, theatre, and the ocean. When she isn't writing, Jen can be found sailing, browsing the shelves of her local bookstore, cheering ardently at an NWSL soccer match, or training horses at her Southern California horse ranch, where she lives with her wife, Donna, and their dogs and horses.

Follow Jen on IG @jenlyonauthor where she unapologetically spams her page with photos of her corgis, dachshund, horses and obscenely large Maine Coon cats.